THE CLOCKWORK DYNASTY

"What Wilson does as well as any writer alive is create self-contained and fully realized worlds—the cinematic stuff of dreams and stardust, mixed with the dirt of actual living. He does so with sensitivity, intelligence and a gift for . . . detail."

—*Willamette Week* (Portland, Oregon)

"Irrepressibly readable. . . . [June Stefanov] continues Wilson's excellent run of female lead characters." —*Los Angeles Review of Books*

"A thrilling mix of influences, much like Sylvain Neuvel's *Sleeping Giants* and HBO's *Westworld*, that creates a captivating scenario begging for many sequels." —*Kirkus Reviews* (starred review)

"*The Clockwork Dynasty* is a hybrid: engrossing historical fiction starring ancient androids and mile-a-minute present-day action thriller. . . . June's mad dash to flee a secret society bent on taking her knowledge and her life evokes the best moments of Dan Brown."

—*Shelf Awareness*

"*New York Times* bestselling author Daniel H. Wilson delivers a fascinating new thriller that takes us on a journey to the past discovering humanlike machines that have lived among us for centuries."

—*Library Journal*

"Wilson has a great knack for pace and engaging action; it's a book that is very difficult to put down. It's an exceptional piece of speculative fiction, set in a world that I would very much like to visit again."

—Allen Adams, *The Maine Edge*

"In *The Clockwork Dynasty*, Daniel Wilson, the king of the robot thriller, mixes robots, history, and nonstop action to create a thoroughly original plot. Think *The Terminator* meets Indiana Jones with a crash course in history thrown in. A thoroughly enjoyable read."

—Phillip Margolin, *New York Times* bestselling author of *Violent Crimes*

"*The Clockwork Dynasty* is bravely imagined and satisfyingly executed. Wilson has woven a brilliant fictional world into history, making this book a great read for lovers of historical fiction as well as fantasy and sci-fi."

—*BookPage*

"In the spirit of some of my personal favorites (*He, She and It* and *The Golem and the Jinni*), *The Clockwork Dynasty* imagines a world where 'artificial intelligence' is something altogether different and where the meaning of 'human' has become more than flesh and bone."

—Veronica Belmont, host of *The Sword and Laser*

"Action-packed and uniquely imagined with robots—and history!—like you've never seen before, *The Clockwork Dynasty* is a thrilling ride from start to finish."

—John Joseph Adams, series editor of *The Best American Science Fiction and Fantasy*

DANIEL H. WILSON

THE CLOCKWORK DYNASTY

Daniel H. Wilson is the bestselling author of *Robopocalypse*, *Robogenesis*, and *Amped*, among others. A Cherokee citizen, he was born in Tulsa, Oklahoma, and earned a B.S. in computer science from the University of Tulsa and a Ph.D. in robotics from Carnegie Mellon University in Pittsburgh. He lives in Portland, Oregon, with his wife and two children.

www.danielhwilson.com

ALSO BY DANIEL H. WILSON

Guardian Angels & Other Monsters

Robogenesis

Amped

Robopocalypse

A Boy and His Bot

Bro-Jitsu

The Mad Scientist Hall of Fame

How to Build a Robot Army

Where's My Jetpack?

How to Survive a Robot Uprising

As Editor

Press Start to Play (coeditor)

Robot Uprisings (coeditor)

THE CLOCKWORK DYNASTY

A NOVEL

DANIEL H. WILSON

VINTAGE BOOKS
A DIVISION OF PENGUIN RANDOM HOUSE LLC
NEW YORK

FIRST VINTAGE BOOKS EDITION, JUNE 2018

The Library of Congress has cataloged the Doubleday edition as follows:
Names: Wilson, Daniel H. (Daniel Howard), 1978– author.
Title: The clockwork dynasty : a novel / Daniel H. Wilson.
Description: First Edition. | New York : Doubleday, [2017]
Identifiers: LCCN 2016053069
Subjects: BISAC: FICTION / Science Fiction / Adventure. |
FICTION / Suspense. | FICTION / Fantasy / Paranormal. |
GSAFD: Suspense fiction. | Science fiction.
Classification: LCC PS3623.I57796 C58 2017 | DDC 813/.6—dc23
LC record available at https://lccn.loc.gov/2016053069

Vintage Books Trade Paperback ISBN: 978-1-101-97408-7
eBook ISBN: 978-0-385-54179-4

Book design by Michael Collica

www.vintagebooks.com

Printed in the United States of America
10 9 8 7 6 5 4 3 2 1

THE CLOCKWORK DYNASTY

PROLOGUE

The age of a thing is in the feel of it. Secrets are locked in the fingerprints of cracked porcelain and the bloom of rust on metal. You've just got to pick up a dusty artifact in both hands and squeeze your eyelids shut. With a little thought, the mind-reeling eons of time will stretch out before you like a star-filled sky.

I didn't learn this feeling in a classroom. No scientist does.

My grandfather, my *dedushka* . . . he taught me this awe for the forgotten past.

When I was sixteen, Vasily Stefanov caught me hiding in his toolshed, rummaging through his war souvenirs and trying to open the brass padlock on a battered green ammunition box with a screwdriver. He whistled low, like a cuckoo. This was how he'd gotten my attention since I was a little girl, and I froze in embarrassment.

Instead of punishing me, he told me a story.

"You are so curious," he said, words soaked in the heavy Russian accent he brought to the United States from another life. "What are you looking for?"

"I'm sorry, *Dedushka,*" I stuttered. "Nothing. I only wanted to—"

He waved me off with a callused palm.

"It's okay. Curious people learn things," he said.

My grandfather took the ammunition box from me and set it clattering on his workbench. He unlocked the padlock and opened the dented lid, revealing a few faded photographs, an old pocket watch, and scattered medals. Then, he lifted out an oily cloth with something heavy wrapped in it. Without a word, he dropped the shrouded bundle across my palms.

Inside, I found something metallic and dense, something so intricate and alien that my breath caught in my throat. Etched into a crescent-shaped slice of metal the size of a seashell, I saw a labyrinthine pattern of grooves—a language of bizarre angles.

"This thing," he said. "This incredible thing. I always meant to share it, you understand? But the years march."

"It's heavy," I said.

"It is a relic from a war. With a story I have never told anyone."

I remember his face now so clearly, lined with wrinkles that could be scary until the old man smiled and you saw where they came from.

"Do you believe in angels, June?" he asked.

"I don't know," I responded. "No."

"Perhaps you should," he said.

Grandfather cleared his throat, leaned against a creaking workbench.

"I was barely a teenager, same as you, when the second world war came. My family lived in a village near the Ural Mountains. The Germans stormed onto Russian soil and it was decided I was old enough to journey to the front. All the boys in the village were sent. We were excited. Excited."

He shook his head at the memory.

"Stalingrad. Winter," he said. "Early in the battle. We were already starving. Frozen. The Germans had pushed a million Soviet soldiers nearly to the banks of the Volga. The women and children and wounded who were left in the city . . . they finally tried to escape across the icy black river. All hope was gone. It was only survival then.

"The Volga was choked with great green military tankers, filthy fishing rigs, civilian yachts, and human beings, thousands of them, a—a . . . mass of them, clinging to anything that would float. And the low gray clouds over the river were screaming with Nazi warplanes. The sky was weeping tears of fire onto the backs of those women and children. Oil and gas had spilled on the water. The river herself was burning.

"I and the other scouts were on the near bank, covering the retreat. Stalingrad itself was already bombed to oblivion. You can't understand . . . it was a moonscape. Another world. A place of shattered brick and wood. Crumbling walls sagging in fields that were once neighborhoods, empty windows like open mouths, vomiting dust. The fallen froze where they lay and were not buried.

"We boys survived like rodents, climbing through the remains of collapsed basements or abandoned trenches. Nothing aboveground was left. We lived this horror for months . . . months that went on for eternity. Frostbite and thirst and snipers. Early on we had trained our dogs to wear explosives and run under the German tanks. Later, we ate them. And I do not know how to explain to you, *vnuchka* . . . but over time . . . in that strange cold world, the memory of my life faded to gray ash.

"Foolishly, I came to believe there was nothing left that could horrify me."

Grandfather blinked, gazing at the open ammunition box and its dangling brass padlock. Lost in the act of remembering, he would not look at me while he spoke.

"A Nazi plane must have called out our position. One minute the other boys and I were lined up in our greatcoats, rifles snapping bullets, stocks laid over a wall of rubble. 'Not one step back,' was the saying. Those who ran were shot. We pulled our triggers when forms appeared in the smoke and held our ground. No matter how many German helmets appeared . . . we were ready to make the sacrifice.

"And then our hillside turned to chaos. A German tank had zeroed in on us. It was as if a giant had put his fist into the hill and we were thrown, flung into the sky like rag dolls, helmets rolling. A hunchbacked panzer crawled out of the mist, painted yellow and gray, like a sick tiger, the black eye of its turret searching for us. Lying on my stomach, breathing dust, eyes not focusing . . . I could hear the German crew shouting to each other. Like demons made of smoke and dust, calling out from hell.

"June, please understand. What happened next . . . it is terrible. But you must know. Someday, it may help you make sense of what you hold in your hands."

My eyes dropped from Grandfather's face to the sliver of metal lying across my fingers. I couldn't recognize the symbols etched in its surface. They looked like warped letters, mixed with geometrical shapes, lines and dots. The metal felt strangely warm, the finely carved edges dissolving into fractal curls. In each crescent tip was a small hole, as if the artifact were a small part of something bigger.

"After the shell hit, all the other boys were gone—wiped out. My side was numb, torn by shrapnel and rock. But I could still move. Ears ringing, I rolled onto my back. And by a stroke of luck, I was alive to see what came next.

"A tall man in a Soviet greatcoat and hat came staggering over the broken hillside. His face was in anguish, his movements almost blind. But he had spotted the Germans before they saw him. He dove forward and snatched the sidearm away from one soldier and fired it into his torso until there were no more bullets. In another stride, he grabbed two more soldiers in a bear hug. Then he smashed their heads together—shattered their helmets. The men fell dead. And finally, the Russian turned. I felt his gaze upon me.

"We had been eating *rats,* June. We were weak. But this man was strong. He was holy. My eyes filled with tears because I knew then he was an avenging angel, righteous, stalking the mists of battle.

"And I remember that I *smiled,* my cracked lips bleeding. I felt I was somehow witnessing the truth. The very incarnation of justice.

"A hatch on the panzer opened and the Nazi tank commander emerged, firing his tommy gun. Bullets spat right into the angel's back. He stumbled and fell, like a man, and lay crumpled among the bodies of my friends.

"The commander climbed off the tank, cautious. Trying to look every direction at once. This man had seen the furious vengeance of God and knew he had been judged. I lay still, my breath shallow, watching from beneath the turned-up brim of my *ushanka* hat and trying not to shiver.

"The doomed man leaned over to inspect the body. I do not know what he saw, but I will never forget his face as he saw it. His eyes went wide in shock. He spun, coat flapping, and screamed a command to his driver inside the tank, looking away for one second . . . it was enough.

The angel rose, taking the man by the face. Those gloved fingers nearly reached around the back of the man's head, lifting him off the ground. With one squeeze—"

My grandfather yanked his thumb across his throat.

"The tank was still idling, waiting. Then the hatch on top clanged shut and the panzer engine began to rumble. *Running away.* Imagine. The might of a tank, invincible and armored, fleeing from one man.

"The angel stood up and shook out his tattered coat. Then the thing leaped onto the side of the tank. With one hand, he tore the hatch right off the turret. Reaching inside, he dragged the shrieking German driver out by his collar, thumped his face against the metal, and rolled his body onto the ground. Like it was nothing. Like he was slapping a fish against a rock.

"The angel stood for a moment, head down in despair. Something fell from his hands. Then he walked away, disappearing into the mist. The tank kept rolling toward the river. After some time, I heard a splash. The sting of my injury was growing, but even then, curiosity had not left me. So I dragged myself over rubble and death until I reached the spot where the angel had stood.

"I saw the bullets go into him. But on the ground, instead of blood, I found shards of metal. Bits of leather. Bullet fragments and something else. An object, very old I think, yet more modern than any machinery in that battle.

"That is what you hold in your hands, June . . . this relic is what the angel of vengeance left behind."

My grandfather stopped speaking. He finally looked up at me, watching as I traced my fingers over the curves of the artifact.

"There are strange things in the world, June. Things older than we know. Walking with the faces of men . . . there are angels among us. Sometimes they will judge. And sometimes they will exact punishment.

"What you hold belongs to their world. Not to ours."

Under his stern gaze, I understood his message.

Tell no one.

"Most people don't want to see a hidden world. They are content to live in ignorance. Others are more curious. What kind of person are you, June?"

"I don't know, Grandfather," I said truthfully.

With that, he carefully took the relic from me, wrapped it back in its oily cloth, and placed it inside the ammunition box. He pushed the old brass padlock back through the ring and, with a click, he locked it tight.

"Can I see it again, sometime?" I asked.

Grandfather looked at me for a long moment.

"Someday you will," he said, nodding.

Two years later, at his funeral, my grandmother handed me a sealed envelope. My name was scrawled on it in my grandfather's rough handwriting. Inside, I found a small thing that changed the course of my life.

A brass key.

PART ONE
NEPRAVDA
(Untruth)

In attempting to construct such machines we should not be irreverently usurping His power of creating souls. . . . Rather we are . . . instruments of His will, providing mansions for the souls that He creates.

—Alan Turing, 1950

I

OREGON, PRESENT

The clockwork automaton is the size of a small child, a hard weight against my fingers. Her glinting metal bones poke through faded lace. A cherubic porcelain face peeks out of the yellowed fabric; cheeks etched with a patina of fine cracks; lips pursed and faded red; eyes bright, black, and smooth. At a glance, the machine looks like a child. But what I'm cradling in my arms is far more strange.

For a start, this child is more than three hundred years old.

The Old Believer who allowed me into this stuffy church alcove is standing in the doorway, staring at me from the depths of his black beard, the stray hairs of it climbing his cheeks. It's hard to figure out his age under all that hair, but it's easy to see the discomfort in his lucid blue eyes. Tall and bent under the cloth of his black robe, the priest looks like the grim reaper, watching my every move.

In contrast to the women of the church, who wear prairie dresses, their beautiful hair twisted into thick braids hidden under silk hats—I'm wearing a pair of safety goggles hanging around my neck, blue latex gloves on my hands, and dusty black jeans. My dirty hair is up in a haphazard ponytail.

It's my third and final week on the road, and I'm way beyond caring.

I lay the porcelain girl on a black pad spread over a gothic oaken desk. My usual work space at the university doesn't have hand-carved cuckoos and clusters of ivy teased out of solid wood, but I'm used to making do with whatever I find in the field.

"Is he going to stare at us like that the whole day?" I ask Oleg, my translator.

"Probably," he replies, not looking at me.

Oleg is sitting on a stool, leaning his elbows on his knees. The stocky man smells like cigarettes and aftershave. He's consistently rude and impatient—and I'm pretty sure he's been cursing at me in Ukrainian—but the sponsor that funds my travel decided that Oleg speaks the right languages.

Several years ago, the Kunlun Foundation reached out to me on behalf of a wealthy Chinese benefactor, a woman apparently obsessed with mechanical antiquities. Primitive automatons like this doll are a niche area of research, with sources of funding few and far between. Looking at the big picture, I suppose a grouchy translator is a small price to pay in return for the travel and tools I need.

I pull the chain on an ornate brass lamp. This alcove is almost claustrophobic, crammed with bookshelves and streaked with dim shafts of light that slant through a high row of arched, leaded windows. A silent waterfall of dust trickles through the light and settles onto the thick, ocher-colored carpet. Outside, the sky is bright and cloudy, spitting occasional raindrops against the glass.

From my tool roll, I slide out a plastic probe and use it to pry open the lace dress. Inside, I find sparkling networks of rack-and-pinion gears. This artifact isn't anything close to a real girl, but she's a lot more complex than a porcelain doll.

She is a classic court automaton, built during the Renaissance—one of many, though most are lost. Once upon a time, artifacts like this were gifted to the world's wealthiest, most powerful human beings. Their owners kept these primitive robots locked in wonder rooms and art collections while they argued over whether the devices were animated by demons, angels, or natural magic.

Hundreds of years later, the last of these artifacts are scarce to the point of extinction, nearly always hidden in private collections, and otherwise almost impossible to find and study. On the final stop of a road trip through the Old Believer communities of the Pacific Northwest, this is the first artifact Oleg and I have been able to access. And it's the only one I've seen in years that hasn't been vandalized.

"Please tell him I appreciate this opportunity," I say.

Oleg nods, turns, and I hear the quiet whisper of Slavic language. The Old Believer laughs once, a sharp grunt, and says something.

"What did he say?" I ask.

"He says he is doing you no favor. The church only wishes you will document the porcelain girl of Saint Petersburg before the . . . wolves take her."

I glance at the Old Believer. His outfit is identical to what his ancestors were wearing when their religion was outlawed during the Great Schism of the seventeenth century. To escape persecution, these people spread to the far corners of the earth. That was more than three hundred years ago, yet he still speaks an old dialect of Russian.

"Wolves?" I ask Oleg, raising my eyebrows.

The translator nods, confirming the word.

My mouth goes dry at the thought that the same vandals I have seen other places could be operating here. Lately, it seems that whatever time hasn't destroyed, someone else has.

I thought this place would be different.

The Old Believers are an obstinate people. Century after century, they've carried their sacred books and artifacts everywhere they've settled—from China to Oregon. In the old days, their scholars perpetually made copies of their libraries by hand, racing to rewrite each book as time turned the pages to dust. Everything in this room is sacred, meant to be cared for and protected at any cost.

Wolves.

A small oval face beams up at me from the foam pad, a century's-old dimple in her cheek. Prodding with the tool, I find an inscription plate under the creases of her dress.

The text is in Old Russian but I can make out the dates and names. My guess is she was a gift to Pope Clement II from Peter the Great. The tsar of Russia considered himself divinely anointed to lead his people—with a direct line to the Almighty. He didn't have much use for a pope. This automaton would have been a horrendously expensive gift. She could have been a peace offering, or a bribe.

Or a message.

I turn the artifact over in the lamplight, admiring the lacework of her dress as I remove the clothing from her back.

"She's really incredible," I murmur.

Oleg stands up and stretches. He steps closer to me, his feet silent on the thick carpet, and glances at the automaton with disinterest. The translator snorts, and speaks again with a heavy Ukrainian accent.

"A doll?" he asks.

I reach into my tool bag and remove my camera. I turn its heavy glass eye on the little girl, her body slight and delicate in the bunched folds of the dress.

The room strobes as I take a photo.

Snap.

"An automaton," I say. "Sort of like a robot. But made before electricity. Before cars and planes and phones. Probably by a mechanician who answered to the tsar himself. For a little while, this 'doll' was very likely the most complex machine on the face of the planet."

"A toy."

"An emperor's inspiration," I say. "A link in a chain of technology that stretches into prehistory. How far, no one knows."

"An *old* toy," says Oleg.

I narrow my eyes at the man, pushing him away with my frown. Oleg chuckles and ambles off a few feet, pretending to inspect the rows of leather-bound books lining the shelves. The more sophisticated and well crafted the machines of antiquity are, the easier it is for modern people to dismiss them as toys.

But our ancestors had their triumphs, too.

I peel the rest of the clothing away from the automaton. Under the crumbling fabric, her golden limbs are honed, gleaming dully in the lamplight. She sprawls in my hands, a brass skeleton with a baby's face.

I notice Oleg peeking again, despite himself.

"She was incredible. And she wasn't the first of her kind," I tell him. "Socrates warned that the 'movable statues' created by the master artificer Daedalus needed to be chained down, in case they ran away. Hero of Alexandria built an artificial man whose head famously couldn't be severed with a blade. And more than a thousand years ago the Chinese artificer Yan Shi supposedly built an automaton that could walk."

"Legends," says Oleg.

I lift the naked automaton, feeling her hunched body, the slender ribs radiating like bicycle spokes. A complicated brass mechanism is mounted inside her narrow chest. With the limp weight of her body in both my hands, I lower my eyelids for a moment and try to imagine the lost centuries she has somehow survived.

"But *she's* real," I say to myself, ignoring Oleg.

This awe for the past is what brought me here.

Years ago, with a small brass key clutched in my sweating fingers, I unlocked a beat-up ammunition box. I slid the oil-soaked cloth off an incredible artifact—a spoil of war and a timeless secret between my grandfather and me. The relic belonged to another world, and I could sense an epic history locked in its fractal patterns.

I threaded a chain through the tips of the crescent relic and hung it around my neck. The artifact was with me, a familiar weight, as I studied linguistics; history; engineering; and finally medieval automatons. I solved a hundred little mysteries, with the biggest one hanging over my heart. And the more I learned, the further I sank, my grandfather's relic always pulling me deeper into the shrouded past.

2

MOSCOW, 1709

The doll's face is the first thing I see. She is my first memory, and the last sight I could ever forget.

I do not remember opening my eyes.

The candlelit path of her cheek eclipses a great darkness. As she moves, the outline of her face becomes a wavering blade of light. Her skin is made of hard porcelain. Leaning over a wood desktop, clad in a dress, she scratches marks with a quill pen held in frozen ceramic fingers. Her black eyes aim at the paper without seeing.

The doll's hand swoops back and forth as she mindlessly writes her message. A flutter of gears under the fine fabric at her neck beats a false, mechanical pulse, and yet this is the heartbeat of my world, a rhythm, steady and quiet and hard under the warm-wax smell of candles and the canopy of a low wooden ceiling.

Then comes the old man.

An amorphous shape—shifting between shadows that flick like snake tongues up timber walls. Thin and bent, the man drapes long fingers over my face. I turn my head slightly to inspect him, blinking to focus. His features sharpen into detail: wrinkled bags under glittering eyes. His lips are pressed together and white within a graying beard. Every half second, his limbs quake slightly as his heart throbs in a narrow chest.

I will come to know this man as Favorini. My father. Or the closest thing to it.

Now the old man is holding his breath, watching me with wide eyes.

"Privet," I say, and he collapses into a faint.

Without thought, I catch him by the shoulder. Eyelids fluttering, his head dips like a sail dropping to half-mast. For the first time I see what must be my own hand. An economy of brass struts wrapped in supple leather. And now I truly begin to understand that I am also a *thing* in this world. Not like the doll who is writing a few feet away with all the mindfulness of water choosing a path downhill. Something more. But also not the same as this fainting man, made of soft flesh.

Somehow, I *am*. And, I tell you, I find it a strange thing, to *be*.

The idea of it settles into my mind. A world outside me, perceived through vision, hearing, smell, and other senses more innate. And somewhere inside, I am placing the sights and sounds into a smaller, simpler idea of a true world that is too complex. From within this little world in my head, I am making decisions.

So I catch my father by his shoulder.

The old man slumps, held upright by my fingers. His chin falls to his chest and his face is lost in strands of brown-gray hair. I have saved him from falling into a sharp jumble of tools that lie scattered around my legs. This room is a . . . workshop, without windows, lit by a tilting confusion of candles sprouting from every surface. Splintery beams stripe the ceiling, and the low room stretches beyond the light into warm darkness. A patchwork of desks and tables is arrayed in groups. Some are empty, but most are piled high with scraps of metal, twists of rope, wooden bowls filled with unknown substances, fouled spoons, and all manner of glass vials and tubes.

Somehow, the knowledge of this is already in me.

Half-formed body parts are also sprawled among the clutter. Chunky torsos filled with fine gears, supported by whalebone ribs and riddled with veins of India rubber. This place is more than a workshop . . . it is a *womb*.

Sitting up at the waist, I lay the old man over an empty desk.

My body has been arranged on a long wooden table. Nearby, the doll thing nods sightlessly, her pen scratching as she covers a stiff page with scrawls of ink.

She and I are kin, I know it.

My shape is that of a man, crafted in perfect proportions. Long golden legs, light winking from hundreds of rivets. My skin is made of bands of a beaten gray-gold metal, fastened to a solid frame. Through narrow gaps in the tops of my thighs, I see rows of braided metal cables, pulled to tension, wrapped around circular cogs.

When I move, I hear a clockwork grind coming from inside.

"Hello?" murmurs the old man. "My son?"

The consonants of his language echo in my mind, resolving into words. I can almost remember hearing his voice before. Lessons whispered in my sleep.

Gnarled fingers wrap around my wrist. Faintly, I can feel the heat inside the man's hands. I sense he is full of warm blood, carrying energy through his body. His skin is not like mine, nor his heart. There is no blood within me, for my father and I are not alike. He is a human being, and I am . . . something else.

"You are here," he says, his grip tightening on my wrist. "What do you remember? How far back?"

I cast my mind into the past and find only the void. Shaking my head, I pull my arm away from the old man. For an instant, he seems disappointed.

"Who . . . who are you?" I ask.

My voice comes from somewhere deep inside my chest. I can feel a device in there, a bellows that contracts and sends wind up my throat and between my teeth. There seems to be a multitude of voices beneath my voice.

"Giacomo Giuseppe Favorini," says the old man. "But call me Favo. I am the last mechanician to Tsar Pyotr Alexeyevich. Practitioner of the ancient art of *avtomata* and keeper of the anima. Successor to the great alchemists who came and went before history. And, if you will believe the tsar's wife, Catherine Alexseyevna . . . I am a devil."

"Last mechanician?"

"I will explain. Ten years ago, the tsar visited Europe in secret. The Netherlands, England, Germany, Austria. He returned with shipbuilders, artists, and mechanicians. To one group of us, he gave a special artifact—the anima. With it we were to build . . . you. But the tsar's wife never saw the promise. It has been so long. Catherine has managed to send the other mechanicians east to exile. I am the last."

The old man trails off, sadness in his voice.

"But you are here now!" he exclaims, snatching a small hammer from the table. "Come, look at you! Talking! Can you see me? Tell me what you see!"

"A room. A man. Machines."

Some knowledge of this world is already inside me, packed into words that reveal themselves when I try to think of them. But I can already sense that there is much, much more to be learned.

"Concise," Favorini says, tapping my chest lightly and listening. "The old texts were true. The anima is working . . ."

These words confuse me. Extending my gauntlet-like hands, I clench my fists and grind the hard metal of my own fingers together. Squeezing, I push to the tolerance of my strength, until the gears in my hands are straining. I swing my legs off the workbench and my wooden heels scratch the floor.

I stand, the top of my head nearly brushing the ceiling.

Favo scurries away into the darkness. In a moment he returns, his thin arms wrapped around a tall golden panel. The polished bronze groans as he drags it over the wooden floor, its surface glowing in the candlelight. He props himself against it—holding the long rectangle before me—then stops and stares.

"Look upon yourself," he whispers.

At my full height, I see my movements reflected in the gleaming panel. I am tall and thin. Very tall. My face is smooth, chin dimpled, eyes sharp and predatory over a straight nose. Ringed in brown curls of hair, my face is only crudely human. My lower lip is pulled to the side, slightly disfigured. I am not wearing clothes. Instead, my chest and arms are layered in beaten metal banding with occasional tight swathes of leather tidily placed underneath. A winking light haunts the depths of my brown eyes, and I now understand why Favo has awe in his voice.

"My son?" he asks.

"Yes," I reply.

"What is the first thing?" he asks.

"The first thing?"

Flexing my fists again, I feel an unyielding strength in my metal bones. I am so much bigger than this small old man.

"Yes," he whispers. "In your mind. Reach inside and tell me the first thing. The first word you ever knew. What is your Word, my son?"

I find a hard honesty to the limits of my body—to the solid press of my flesh and the clenching strength of my grip. Pushing into my mind, I search for the answer to Favo's question and find another principle, incontrovertible, even stronger than that of my flesh. It is the reason for my being—a singular purpose hewn into the stone of my mind.

There is a word that is the shape of my life.

I set my eyes upon the old man, and the leather of my lips scratches as I say the Word out loud for the first time.

"*Pravda,*" I say. "I am the unity of truth and justice."

3

OREGON, PRESENT

As I continue working, it hits me: Oleg's flat dismissal of the court automaton as a simple doll, a child's toy, has really irked me. I know it's pointless to lecture—the guy has the imagination of a boulder—but part of me wants to convince him, to show everybody, really, that this little girl means something.

"Okay, Oleg, so we don't have solid written records of the earliest automata," I say, laying the heavy camera on the table and lifting my penlight to inspect the automaton's interior workings. "But that doesn't mean the legends aren't true."

Oleg grunts, noncommittal.

"Albertus Magnus. A thirteenth-century Dominican monk. There are eyewitness reports that he built an artificial man out of brass that could talk. Thomas Aquinas is said to have personally destroyed it with a hammer as an affront to God."

"Good for him," says Oleg. "We are God's creations. We cannot be replicated."

Outside, the rain is coming down harder. Distant, grumbling peals of thunder waver beyond leaded-glass windows.

"A popular point of view," I say. "That's why the Old Believers search out these automatons. They believe our bodies are mansions for our souls, and artifacts like these pose a valuable question."

With the doll lying on her face, I notice an abrasion on her tiny porcelain palm. I turn her narrow wrist between my thumb and forefinger.

"What question?" asks Oleg.

"If we built our own mansions, could God give them a soul?"

Lightning flashes somewhere far away, revealing a crease along the doll's wrist.

Now, I understand—this device is designed to write a message. The scraped spot must be an attachment point for a writing instrument. Through my thin gloves, I can feel a ridge that could have once fastened to a quill pen. All the brass hardware, still untarnished, has a purpose. At its heart, this automaton is a piece of equipment designed to share a message in a deceivingly simple way—by literally writing it.

"God gives us all a purpose, Oleg," I say, smiling up at him. "Let's find out what hers was."

Squinting, I use the probe to walk myself through her anatomy. The logic that makes her work is timeless; it feels to me like a connection to another mind, from another age. It's only as I trace through each part of her that I begin to notice an absence. Like a black hole—only visible by the stars affected around it—I can see now that the inner workings of the doll terminate in an empty space. Something crucial is missing.

There is a hole where her heart should be.

My cheeks heat up with sudden adrenaline as I push the penlight deeper into the hole. The gear mechanism is untouched. None of the machinery damaged. But there is a gap where something important has been ripped out of the doll's frame. I drop the probe on the table, sit back with my shoulders slumped.

For so many years I have been looking into the past, searching for the sense of awe I felt as a kid. But every time I get close to catching that spark, it flickers away. Putting an artifact on a shelf isn't enough. I need to make them *work*—to take something lost and make it found. I want to see what people saw five hundred years ago, and feel the same wonder.

Maybe I was just born too late.

Looking back at the innocent doll, her face radiant in the lamplight, I sit up straight and lean closer. Clamping my fingers on the probe, I push back into her body and inspect the cavity one more time.

"*Damn,*" I whisper.

A few bright gashes mar the metal. The marks haven't oxidized, which means this happened recently. I turn the doll over and she smiles up at me, unperturbed. Her cheeks and pursed lips shine a faded red.

But whatever makes her work is gone. Someone has come here and cut out her heart. My mind strays back to the odd word the Old Believer used: *wolves*.

I drop the probe and penlight on the desk.

"She's been modified," I say to the room. "Someone damaged her."

At the door, the Old Believer launches into a quiet prayer.

The faithful would never mutilate their own artifact. This commune immigrated here from Brazil more than a hundred years ago, along with their rare books and treasures. Lately, the Old Believers have taken to digitizing their collections, instead of copying and recopying them. But the items in this alcove are just as precious to the church now as they were three hundred years ago.

The Old Believer stands near the doorway, eyes lost in shadow above his beard. He doesn't seem to notice me anymore. Beard twitching as his lips move, his chanting is absorbed by the thick carpet and curtains, by walls stacked floor to ceiling with books.

"Who was here?" I ask him. "Who could have done this?"

Lightning brightens the sky outside, somewhere far away. The windows quiver in their frames as thunder growls through the forest.

I clasp my hands together and take a deep breath.

"Miss June?" asks Oleg. "Is it okay?"

The small man watches me, nervous. He stretches pale lips over nicotine-stained teeth, trying to reassure me. I push a lock of stray hair over my ear and lift the porcelain doll to show Oleg the gaping hole in her back.

"Ask him if this is new damage," I say, looking over Oleg's shoulder to where the Old Believer stands, rocking as he prays.

"Hey? Is this new?" I call to him.

The Old Believer takes a step closer.

"Who did this?" I ask. "Did someone else come here?"

The man's eyes widen over his bushy beard.

"Nyet," says the Old Believer, shaking his head. "Nyet, nyet, nyet."

With one hand he covers his face, making the sign of the cross over his chest with the other. He lumbers over to the row of high windows. Begins to tug on the brass poles that open them, shaking them to make sure they are locked. Raindrops thump into the glass like fat moths, the room quiet and stuffy under the sharp smell of ozone.

"That's not good," says Oleg. "He doesn't know."

"Grab my big duffel bag from the pews," I tell Oleg.

Oleg flashes me a doubtful look, then turns and goes.

I drag a spidery black surgical headlight from my tool roll, pulling it onto my forehead as Oleg lumbers back into the room. He drops the heavy black bag at my feet, emblazoned with logos from the Kunlun Foundation.

"Whatever you do," he says, "you should hurry. They are . . . upset."

The Old Believer has finished checking the windows. Now he is reaching for Oleg, complaining urgently to him in Slavic. Oleg turns back to the man, both of them gesticulating and speaking in loud whispers.

The hole inside the doll's chest cavity is ragged around the edges. Whoever did this clearly wanted to remove one part only. I jam a spreader tool between her ribs and pump the handle until her interior is better exposed. The machinery appears undamaged, well preserved these hundreds of years. The missing piece must have supplied power to the rest of the machine.

But there are ways to substitute for a motor.

Ignoring the arguing men, I drag three small plastic cases out of the duffel bag. Cracking the cases open, I array three compact, battery-powered tools on the broad table: a wand, a printer, and a drill.

Kunlun paid for these expensive tools, but they'd never imagined I'd use them like this.

I snatch up the wand-like device and flick a protective plastic nub off its red probe tip, then flip two lenses over my eyes and click on the head-mounted spotlight. The terrain inside the automaton's chest springs into view, every detail magnified and bright.

The probe enters the hole in the doll's back, as big as a crane in my lenses. The wand clicks, each tick stumbling over the next like a Geiger counter until finally the steady spatter of clicks indicates the probe has found a scannable area.

I close my eyes and press a button with my thumb. A laser range finder in the tip of the probe spins up, spraying the interior of the doll's chest cavity with invisible light. It only takes a millisecond and then I'm yanking the headlight off and pulling the thumb drive out of the wand.

"Okay, time to go," says Oleg, tapping my shoulder.

I shake Oleg's hand off and jam the thumb drive into a portable three-dimensional printer. Scowling at Oleg, I rest my fingers on top of the rectangular piece of technology. As the surface heats up, I know the device is working.

"One minute," I say to Oleg. Then, aiming my voice over his shoulder: "I'm packing up, okay? I'm leaving. I'll finish my work from the pictures."

With the right fit, I can interface with the gear tooth system inside the automaton. Regardless of whether the power supply is present, this little girl can be activated. She was created before electricity was discovered. Her limbs run on mechanical power—the same kind of good old clockwork stored in a tightened spring.

Or the motor of a drill.

The printer finally spits out a gear-shaped drill bit. I pick it up and rub the plastic between my fingers to get rid of the chaff. I blow on it and the shavings spiral away like cottonwood fluff.

The Old Believer shuffles out of the room.

"Now," says Oleg. "We go now."

"Almost," I say.

Oleg curses in a language I don't understand.

I pick up the electric drill, a smooth black piece of the future, oiled and heavy in my hands. The freshly printed gear mounts easily on the bit with a twist of my wrist. Pulling the trigger, the drill grinds, humming to itself, rotating the intricately carved artifact in a slow, smooth circle. It took someone months to hand-file this piece three hundred years ago, and thirty seconds for me to re-create it with technology that came out three months ago.

It's time to meet this little girl face-to-face, wolves or not.

The air pressure shivers as the door to the alcove is yanked open.

The Old Believer has returned with another, even older man at his side. Both are talking rapid-fire, voices rising. Oleg leaps off his chair to deal with them. But I'm not paying any attention. I'm with *her*, working my way through every gear and lever. I can feel ancient fingerprints on her.

Immersed in the complexity of the doll, I wonder again why people assume the most advanced technology is yet to come. Two hundred thousand years of human history lurk in the darkness behind us; unknown knowledge, gained and then lost. And then, just maybe, regained.

The drill bit clicks into place.

Keeping the drill steady, I lift the doll into sitting position. Her arm is skeletal, reaching out like a dead tree branch. Her porcelain fingers are clasped together like pincers. With my free hand, I drag the elastic hair tie from my ponytail and wrap it around her small fingers, securing a pen to them. I slap down a sheet of paper.

"Here we go," I whisper.

I pull the trigger on the drill, with the motor set on maximum compliance. It jams, clicking on a sticky gear. I set the torque one notch higher and squeeze again. Slowly, the motor turns. A clicking comes from inside the automaton's chest. The metal arm shivers, shudders, and then begins to move. The hand dips three times, filling a nonexistent quill pen with ink. Then it moves to the left and drops like the needle on a record player, scribbling in the air.

I push the doll's body forward so the pen hits paper.

Writing emerges in short, rough strokes. Russian Cyrillic script. Eighteenth century. Now Oleg stands over the desk, breathing heavily, watching in disbelief. More Old Believers have gathered at the door, murmuring to each other in hushed voices.

"Can you read it?" I ask Oleg.

The man's face is gray.

"I can't believe you got it working," Oleg says.

"Read it," I say again.

With a shaking voice, he begins to speak out loud: "'Pyotr Alexeyevich,'" he says. "'Tsar of Moscow, Emperor of Rus,' honors the formation of a Holy Synod to administer the wealth of God to the Russian people. To honor this occasion, he bequeaths to you this machine, made in the image of man, but with a heart of stone. Let her existence be an eternal reminder to the holy men of the West: all who breathe do not live; all who touch do not feel; and all who see do not judge. Behold the . . .'"

"The what?" I hiss.

"'The *avtomat*,'" he says, lips scarcely touching.

Avtomat.

It's a uniquely Russian word, meaning "automatic," but it also means "machine." Maybe the closest analogue in English is the word *robot.*

Clack!

The arm reaches the end of its rotation and something snaps. Darkness swallows my peripheral vision and an Old Believer is reaching, his rough hands pulling me away. Muttering a prayer under his breath, he snatches the paper off the desk and jams it in the pocket of his robe. Another priest lifts the doll and carries it away, my drill motor ripping out of her back. A cascade of brass clockwork rains onto the thick carpet.

"Go," the Old Believer says to us with a heavy accent, eyes burning over his beard. "Go now. Go, please!"

I snatch my camera from the desk, toss the drill and other equipment into the duffel bag at my feet, and shoulder it.

As I'm pulled away, I glimpse the automaton's face again under the lamplight, her eyes pointed mindlessly at the ceiling. A patient survivor of the ages, she has finished sharing her message. But I know there are others like her. Other messages are waiting to be found—other doorways to the past.

The Old Believer slides between me and the automaton, ushering me out of the room. Oleg's firm hand settles around my shoulder. The priest continues to urge us hoarsely to get out of the church and I shuffle along without complaining. Only as I'm leaving does it strike me—the old man doesn't sound angry.

He sounds afraid.

4

MOSCOW, 1710

The doll is bright, pretty, and hard.

I have grown used to watching her where she sits at a writing table in Favorini's workshop. Her face is a pale oval, lips pursed, expression lost in the folds of her lace gown and strands of black hair. She is a *thing,* like me, and I am reassured by the clockwork cadence of her movement.

In the weeks after I come into being, Favorini keeps me confined to his dim laboratory in what he tells me are the depths of the tsar's palace in the city of Moscow. At night, as the old man works, I lie silently on the table where I was constructed from mysterious parts. I close my eyes, feeling the hard slab of wood on my back, lingering in the warm air as incantations roll off Favo's lips.

This world is sometimes overwhelming, but I am patient.

Each morning, Favo sends me to stand beside the doorway. I listen as a tutor drags a stool to the other side of the closed door. I can hear his knee joints popping and I surmise he is a very old man. Favorini must have chosen him because he is hard of hearing and his sight dim. The hidden teacher recites my lessons like a confession and then leaves as soon as he can.

A man who has lived such a long time must have learned not to ask questions.

"Never reveal your nature to a human being," says Favorini. "You are not of our time. People cannot understand your existence."

So I stand and I listen to my lessons. I speak only to answer questions, and then I do so quickly and with my ringing voice muffled by the door.

"We will make you better," Favo says, patting my brass-plated chest.

"We can replace some of your parts. You will come to look more like us. Sound more like us. But it will take time. Perhaps centuries."

Centuries.

"Be patient," he says, not realizing I have the patience of a mountain. Or perhaps, when Favo says this, he is speaking to himself. "None live who remember the art of creation. Your body I found and was able to restore, but the anima inside you was stamped with the Word long ago. It is what binds you to serve the tsar, and allows you to think, perceive, and feel."

One morning I return from my lessons to find the doll is missing from her perch at the small writing table. A few stray pieces of her body, inside and out, are scattered grotesquely over the wooden table. It causes me . . . distress.

The doll is my touchstone. Her presence softens the boundaries of my solitude. My first sight and the most reassuring, she is the closest thing I have ever known to myself.

And in the darkness, I hear a whisper.

"What is the first thing?" asks Favorini. "What is your Word?"

It is a question I have heard before . . . but this time he is not asking me. This time the question goes out into the flickering gloom, to walls lashed by candlelight. I hear no response, not yet.

Approaching silently, I see the doll sitting on the velvet cushion of a high-backed wooden chair. Her back is straight, knees lost in the frills of her dress, tiny shoes dangling over the floor between chair legs carved into griffin talons.

On his knees, Favorini seems almost to be praying to her.

I am about to retreat back into the darkness . . . until I notice a fluttering at the throat of her dress—the golden pulse of moving clockwork. A gear in her neck clicks audibly and I pause, watching.

Neck creaking, the doll turns her head to face Favo. Her porcelain eyelids click shut and open again to reveal black eyes. When she speaks, her voice is high-pitched, lilting, like the tinkle of harpsichord keys.

Somehow, it is the voice of a child.

"The Word?" she asks, and within her voice I hear the half-remembered chiming of silver bells and the singing of birds and the burbling of clear streams.

Click. Her eyes blink again.

"*Logicka,*" she says. "I am the purity of reason."

Favorini chuckles, delighted.

"Yes, yes!" he says, clapping his hands together.

"The mind," says Favorini. "Evidence, inference, and cold truth. These are the principles you are devoted to. You seek order in the chaos—"

A board squeaks under my weight. Hands still clasped together, Favorini cranes his neck to peer up at me. I step forward, a hulking shadow emerging into feeble light. Fear skates over the old man's face.

"The doll who writes?" I ask, and my voice is the crash of waves on rock. Both faces before me are ashen, one of ceramic and the other flesh. "Is this . . . her?"

"Y-yes and no," says Favorini. "I have taken her apart and put her back together again. She is something different now. *Someone* different."

My porcelain doll—my touchstone—is gone. Unbidden, my fingers fall together into fists. I do not understand how I know what I know, or why I feel what I feel. But the doll is precious to me, and I will not see her harmed.

"Who gave you the right to take her . . . parts?"

Favorini stands, hunched, his long hands flapping at me like bird wings. "Do not be alarmed, my friend. All is well. Some of her parts were used to create a simple writing doll. A gift for the pope from the tsar. But your porcelain girl, she is still here, with us. Look!"

I look at the childlike machine, recognize the curve of her cheek. She seems larger away from the desk, perhaps the size of a twelve-year-old human girl.

"This is a very special day," says Favo, his beard twitching with a smile. "I have worked long and hard for this day."

The doll-girl sits on her velvet cushion, not moving, blank face turned to the darkness. Her voice could almost have been an echo of a dream—a phantom chorus conjured in the unknown workings of my mind. Still and silent, she rests like a toy left abandoned on the chair by a capricious child.

"I meant no harm," I grumble to both of them.

I take a heavy step back.

And the doll moves. Her arms lift and pat down the ruffles of her dress. She cranes her neck to take in my full height. Her wig of false hair shivers over a porcelain mask. But behind her carved face I can sense thoughts, dropping into neat slots in her mind as her gaze lingers on the rough leather of my cheek. Though her eyes are two black nothings, I feel an understanding in them. An appreciation.

This girl knows what is beneath my skin—what we hold in common.

"Who are you?" I ask.

Favorini responds for her.

"S-she is your counterpart," he says. "You were found together among the spoils of a broken sheikdom on the far steppes. I suspect those barbarians stole you in a raid from somewhere else, perhaps from the ancient ones beyond the Great Wall.

"Tsar Peter discovered your remains in the palace armory, where they had lain for ages. Catherine insisted on your destruction, but he denied her and insisted on your resurrection. Though I may have rebuilt you, the tsar is your patron and father."

I step forward and crouch, squatting. Her gaze follows me. No emotion is betrayed by her expressionless face, but her clockwork pulse quickens.

"Why is she made to look like a child?"

Favo gestures to two small stiletto-like daggers lying on his workbench. They are both made of dull steel with bone handles, child size.

"She was found with these daggers. Perhaps she was an assassin? Much knowledge has been lost, but her form itself is illuminating . . . you share many features. By studying her smaller frame, I was able to bid you into this world. And now . . . now she joins us as well."

"Is she simple, like a child?" I ask.

"I am not simple," she says, her jaw clicking. She slides to the edge of the chair. Feet dangling, she drops lightly to the floor.

"And I am not a child," she adds, lowering her forehead. It is a threatening gesture, yet I sense grim amusement. She glares up at me without embarrassment or fear.

I peer into those black pits she sees out of, considering.

"Tell me your name," I demand.

The porcelain doll takes a step back.

Slowly, deliberately, she reaches down to grasp her dress on either side. Eyes trained on mine, her fingertips tap together delicately. One foot deftly sweeps behind the other, and she bends her knee and curtsies.

"By the grace of the tsar, I am called Elena Petrovna," she says.

The old man is beaming.

"My friend," he says. "She is your *sister*."

5

OREGON, PRESENT

Oleg is smoking a hand-rolled cigarette on the cracked sidewalk outside my motel room. I can see his silhouette as he paces, blinking back and forth between cheap vinyl blinds that hang like old flypaper. In a fake leather jacket, the middle-aged man is speaking rapid-fire Ukrainian into a mobile phone, waving his hand and spitting foul smoke.

Beyond him, the tall pines of the Willamette Valley sway against a gray sky. For someone from the brick suburbs of Tulsa, the world out here feels oversaturated with the color green and the scent of trees and rain. The white crown of Mount Hood looms on the horizon, scowling through clouds, intimidating to a kid who grew up on grassy plains under blue skies.

Outside, Oleg says that word again: *avtomat*.

I half smile to myself, remembering the surprise on his face as I coaxed a centuries-old message out of the vandalized automaton. *That's the reason Kunlun pays for my travel,* I think, sending me crisscrossing over North America with an occasional foray to Europe—*to give a voice to long-silent artifacts.*

Glancing at a spotted mirror permanently mounted to the beige-painted concrete block wall, I see my reflection. It's pretty obvious I've been on the road for weeks. But the message I found in that doll has made it all worthwhile—not just the trip but the empty apartment, the crummy post as a research scientist, and the disappointed looks from my parents on my yearly visit home.

Today, I witnessed a moment that stretched back three centuries.

Something moves in the mirror. Oleg has appeared in the doorway, standing hunch shouldered, a half-smoked cigarette smoldering on the sidewalk behind him.

"Kunlun called," he says.

"Great. Did you tell them what we found—"

"Yes, yes," he says, waving a hand impatiently. He is looking at the wall just over my shoulder, not meeting my eyes. "They have decided to end their support."

"What—"

"A person is coming to collect Kunlun materials. We are told to wait here."

I'm in shock for a long moment. Without funding, field research is impossible. There is no way I can afford technology like this on my own. I'll be stuck teaching introductory courses back at the university, or fired altogether.

I sit on the dresser and take a deep, shaky breath.

"Very sorry, Miss June," says Oleg, head lowered.

"Fuck," I say to myself, leaning my back against the dirty mirror. By reflex, I press my fingers against the reassuring curve of my grandfather's relic where it hangs under my shirt. "Why would they do this? Why *now*?"

From the open motel door, I smell rain and cigarette smoke.

"You must wait and ask the person. It is bad news, I know," he says, pulling a sweating bottle of vodka out of a brown paper bag.

"You just carry that around?" I ask.

The man shrugs, motions with his shoulders.

"Okay?" he asks.

"Yeah, Oleg," I say. "Come in."

The Ukrainian enters and sits on a low air-conditioning unit sticking out of the wall below the window. He drops the butt of the vodka bottle onto the rusting metal. The screw top comes off with a twist of his palm. He pours shots into a pair of thin white plastic hotel cups. Picks them up with thick fingers and offers me one.

My hands are shaking as I take the cup from him.

"Did they give any explanation?" I ask.

Oleg shrugs and stands up, lifts his cup.

"*Budmo,*" he says, downing his shot.

I down the shot and hand him the empty plastic cup.

"Thanks," I say.

"Something I want to ask," he says, sitting again, not looking at me. "You talk about a power supply on the doll. How did you know what might fit in that spot?"

He is already pouring another pair of shots, holding the bottle neck like a bicycle handle, not spilling a drop. The white plastic cups shiver as the clear liquid surges into them. He hands the small cup back to me, full.

"Budmo," repeats Oleg, half standing, tossing his shot back immediately.

"I've been studying these things a long time," I say, with a smile that feels like a grimace. "I had a hunch."

Oleg cocks an eyebrow at me.

"But why study this? It is very old, yes? Just junk. Why do you care?"

I look at my slender legs in dirty jeans, my boots planted on the thin motel room carpet. Everything I've worked for in my career is ending. The court automata I study are either destroyed or locked in private collections around the world. Without support, I'm not a real scientist anymore—just a lady with a really weird hobby.

Locking my jaw against the sting of alcohol, I down the second shot. "My grandfather. When I was a kid, he got me started."

"Tell me."

"Well, he fought for Russia in World War Two," I say. "And he came back with a lot of interesting stories. About history, and other things."

Oleg nods, watching me closely. Something dark has settled into his expression. Something quiet and still.

"And what is *this* story?" he asks, enunciating carefully.

The heat of the vodka is crawling between my collarbones, spreading through my sternum and into my belly. I can feel my cheeks flushing. My grandfather's stern face flashes in my mind. *Tell no one.*

"A ghost story," I say. "Something he saw once on a battlefield."

The familiar shape of the relic presses against my skin. For years I've studied its inscrutable runes, measuring and weighing it, even doing my futile best to bend or deform its unbreakable curve. Having it around my neck used to make me feel important, like I was keeping an incredible secret from the rest of the world. But now I just feel dumb. A little girl wearing a worthless trinket.

"A ghost story," Oleg says, voice flat.

"Well, he called it an angel. An angel of vengeance," I say, smiling at the memory.

"Oh, I see," says Oleg. Dark eyes holding on to me, he lifts his empty plastic cup and taps it with a finger. "You pour some of this onto a war story. It gets bigger and bigger. Stranger. Your old *dedushka* probably even thought he was telling the truth—"

A sudden flush of anger courses through me. I blurt out without thinking: "Well, my *dedushka* found a relic in Stalingrad. His angel bled metal."

The words linger in the air for a long second. My anger fades as quickly as it came, leaving a vague regret.

I just disobeyed my grandfather.

Oleg slowly stands up, the smile fading from his face. His lips are shining with vodka, stubbled cheeks settling into old hard lines.

"The Battle of Stalingrad?" he asks, slowly. "What did he find there?"

"I don't know," I say, cautious now. "I'll tell you when I figure it out."

"You have a guess?"

"I don't know. It doesn't matter. Why are you asking—"

"Where is it? Is the relic here?"

The edge in his voice is strange. I look up at Oleg and my vision takes a beat to catch up. I put a hand on the dresser to steady myself.

"No," I say. "No, Oleg. It's somewhere safe."

The metal of the relic is warm against my chest.

"Where?" he asks again. "Can I see it?"

He accidentally knocks the vodka bottle to the floor as he pushes away from his seat. The glass bottle bounces and rolls as Oleg advances. I can smell the alcohol on his breath as he whispers fiercely.

"Show me the relic, June. Show it to me *now*."

6

MOSCOW, 1712

The golden throne room threatens to overwhelm my vision. Chandeliers hover over a sweeping corridor framed by gilded wooden posts. Gold-painted sculptures writhe and twist along walls that stretch up into dim, dust-kissed heights. My boot heels click on worn marble. Today, I am wearing a formal infantry kaftan that hangs to my knees, black and red, curls of polished armor built into the forearms and chest, with a black hood pulled low over my forehead.

Although I have never been here, I know from Favorini's descriptions that a tsar's throne room should be crowded with people—filled with courtiers and supplicants, or perhaps even the dreaded tsarina. But on this day it is empty.

The only occupants of this room are court automata.

Favo hobbles ahead, leading me through the long, narrow room. In a gallery to the side, three baby ducks are waddling by, feathers wrought in silver, awkwardly following a golden mother duck. One of the ducklings shits as it shuffles along after its fellows.

Then my footsteps are swallowed by a thick rug looped in brilliant reds and blues. Ahead, the throne rises, golden and scintillating under shafts of light coming in through high, slitted windows. Favorini stops.

The tsar is not here.

A concealed door opens in the gallery wall. Ducking his head, an enormous man emerges. He holds a fat green-yellow apple in one hand, utterly confident. The man does not wear gaudy robes or shining armor. Instead, he has on the simple breeches of an engineer.

Favorini begins to bow and scrape, but the tsar waves him off.

"So this is what we've had locked in the keep all this time?" asks the tsar, looking at me, unimpressed.

The old man nods.

"Our enemies have made many attempts to steal this . . . thing. Relentless attempts. With the number of imperial guard devoted to his protection, you'd think he was made of diamonds.

"Will he truly be able to fulfill the task I set forth?"

"I believe so," says Favorini. "But you may ask it yourself, my lord."

Peter rounds on me, taking a bite from the apple. He chews it loudly, watching me with large, intelligent eyes. I notice his lip is disfigured, pulled to the side . . . the same as mine.

"They say you are my son," he says.

"Father," I say, kneeling, my head bowed.

"Tell me, *son,*" he says, humor in his voice, "what is *pravda*?"

"Truth and justice."

"Do you swear fealty to me?"

"I do," I respond.

"Rise and draw your weapon," says the tsar, walking closer.

He saunters up to my face and watches me with the appraising eye of a mechanician, takes another bite from his apple.

I rise until I am standing, eye to eye, with the Tsar of Russia. We are exactly the same height. The blade of my saber rings as I ease it from its undecorated wooden scabbard. A common weapon, the *shashka* has a single edge, long and curved and incredibly sharp. I hold it at my side, the tip pointed at the ground, my arm as steady as if it were carved out of stone.

"He moves like a man."

The tsar leans in and snatches the hood off my head, revealing the tan leather that covers the surface of my face. He presses his fingers into the skin of my cheek, then rubs them together, considering. Reaching into my hair, he traces fingertips over the brass buttons that line the nape of my neck.

"Doesn't feel much like one, though," he says.

"It follows the truth," says Favo. "It will serve the Word, and you, no matter what."

The tsar looks unconvinced.

"Your name, *avtomat*?" he asks.

Nothing comes to mind.

"As you will call me," I respond.

"Strange to stand next to someone who is as tall as I am," he says, chewing thoughtfully. "I haven't done it since I was a child."

The tsar taps a finger against the polished armor embedded in my kaftan.

"I think he is prettier than I am," he says.

"You are too kind, my Tsar," says Favo. "Please forgive me any discrepancy. Over time, its appearance can be modified to some extent."

"It? You keep calling it an it?"

"To do otherwise would insult our Lord Christ. It is not a living thing but a bauble. Petty in comparison to God's works."

Peter laughs, a short bark that echoes.

"You fear Catherine, old man, even in private discussion. Smart. The tsarina does not trust in this project. She would have those relics of yours destroyed as sacrilege."

Favorini lowers his head. "Oh no, my Tsar. I do not question the tsarina, of course . . . *would* never . . . but the anima are precious. I have already fitted the other vessel with our remaining artifact. It is an old one, in the form of a child. And we must not forget . . . our enemies may have their own anima. Other *avtomat* could be set in motion against us, even now—"

"Enough," says Peter. "Your studies are safe."

The tsar turns and shoves me with both of his large hands. Sensing a test, I choose not to move. My feet are planted, hand clasped around my saber, and although the tsar is large and he hits me hard, the force is insufficient.

"He may even be stronger than me," says the tsar, face dark with exertion and a hint of anger. "Let us see how smart he is."

Peter steps a few feet away and clasps his hands behind his back.

"*Avtomat,*" he asks. "A boyar noble demands fifty men of the Preobrazhensky Regiment to protect his border. Do I accept his request?"

"No, my Tsar."

"Why not?"

"Members of the tsar's own regiment are sworn to protect their father. To send them into battle for anyone of lower rank is a dishonor."

"So, it can think as well."

The tsar takes a last bite of the apple and tosses the core across the room.

"Strike me," he says.

I do not respond.

"I am your tsar, *avtomat,*" he says. "I am giving you a command that you are honor bound to follow. Swing your saber. Strike me."

"My Tsar," stutters Favorini. "He is very strong. Please do not underestimate—"

"Now," says Peter.

The impulse to obey my leader pulls at my joints with the certainty of gravity. Drawing my arm back, I let the sword tip rise. But to injure the tsar would bring dishonor. The Word blazes in my mind: *pravda.*

Truth. Justice. Honor.

"Do it!" shouts the tsar.

My vision is blurring. The saber point wavers. I am compelled to obey and to disobey at the same time. The dissonance of it rings in my ears. I cannot refuse and I cannot strike. I am drowning, my mind swallowing itself.

It is the only pain I have ever felt—the agony of breaking my Word.

But there is a solution. It resolves itself as the only route of action. If I cannot act, and I cannot *not* act, then I will cease to be.

I lift the saber higher, pointing the tip at the tsar. Then, I rotate the flashing blade all the way around until the point dimples the fabric of my kaftan. With both hands I tense my shoulders and I pull the blade against my chest—

"Stop!" says the tsar, placing a hand on my arm.

I silently return the sword to its first position.

"Welcome home . . . Peter," the tsar says, clapping an arm around my shoulders. "A pity you can't have a drink to celebrate."

"My Tsar," asks Favo quietly, "you choose to call it Peter?"

"I call it by its name: Pyotr Alexeyevich," he says.

"But why would—" says Favo.

"Peter is my name while I am on this earth. But with reason and patience, you have built a ruler who can live forever. As leader of the Russian Empire, our Peter will carry my name like a banner through the ages, immune to the physical ruin of time . . . always faithful to *pravda*. A ruler worthy of my empire."

Peter the Great stands, smiling broadly.

"Our Peter has a great destiny. That of an *eternal* tsar."

7

OREGON, PRESENT

"Oleg?" I ask, backing away from him, deeper into the motel room. "What the hell are you doing?"

The Ukrainian is standing too near, his eyes gone hard. I don't like how his hands hang by his sides, nicotine-stained fingers curled into claws. His posture changed the second I mentioned my grandfather's relic.

"It is not your fault, June," he says. "But I must see this relic. Tell me where it is."

"Get out," I say, reaching behind me. "Please. I'm telling you to leave now."

Oleg's eyes seem blind. He swallows, his Adam's apple jumping. We're both slightly drunk, but I'm coordinated enough to feel for the hard plastic of the hotel telephone on the bedside table behind me.

Hands behind my back, I lift the receiver.

"We will buy it from you, yes? How much?" he asks, frightened desperation in his voice.

"Oleg. I'm not kidding."

"They told me . . . I know I must," he says, turning, almost speaking to himself.

In a blink, Oleg sweeps my half-open suitcase off the bed with both hands. Clothes and papers fly across the room, a book thumping against the wall. He snatches my big black Kunlun duffel bag and upends it, sending a waterfall of heavy tools dimpling onto the bedspread. Oleg eyes the mess, scanning for the relic.

Looking up, he moves to block my path to the door.

"They hear everything. They will know," he says, voice breaking.

Clutching the hotel phone, I do my best to jam the buttons for

9-1-1 without looking. I leave the receiver lying on the table as I take two running steps for the open door.

"Help—" I'm shouting when Oleg hooks me with one arm and pushes me onto the bed. I scratch at his face as I fall and scramble right back to my feet, screaming and diving for the door. This time his arm catches me in the ribs, knocking my breath out. I fall onto the bed, thrown onto my stomach, face lost in my hair as I keep thrashing.

"Please," he's saying. "You can't leave."

A knee jams into my side. Oleg rolls me onto my back and drops his knees on my arms, pinning me. Face beaded with sweat, he leans on me with all his weight. I'm wheezing, grunting for breath.

"I'm sorry," he repeats, the smell of alcohol radiating from him. His eyes still aren't focusing. He won't look at me. I'm trying to scream, but nothing is coming out of my mouth except coughing and retching.

Lights flash behind my eyes as I send my fingers clawing over the bedspread.

"Forgive me," he says, voice shaking.

My fingers slide over something hard and smooth. The variable speed drill. Scratching at the hard plastic, I manage to get hold of the heavy tool.

With all my strength, I swing it in a wobbling arc.

Oleg shrugs as the drill bounces off his shoulder. I drag the tool over his shoulder blades, trying to hit him in the back of the head. He leans a forearm across my upper chest and presses harder, the drill resting uselessly against his head.

"I cannot let you leave," he says. "They will be here soon. They will come for what was lost in Stalingrad."

I pull the trigger.

The drill bucks in my hand and grinds, the bit tangling itself instantly in Oleg's hair. As it wraps the greasy locks into a clump, his head snaps back and his mouth opens wide in surprise. The groaning drill bit keeps turning as Oleg gasps for air, a moan building deep in his chest. He reaches for his head with both hands.

The drill roars—warm jets of air venting over my fingers.

"Stop! Stop!" shouts Oleg. His head is yanked to the side, eyes squeezed closed and his yellowing teeth exposed in a rictus. Clumps of hair are ripping from his scalp, turning in bloody circles on the end of the drill. I close my eyes and turn my head, continuing to squeeze the trigger as he tries desperately to grab the drill.

The Saint Christopher chain he wears around his neck makes a clink as it is caught in the bit. Oleg's shouts are cut off mechanically as the chain closes over his throat. Now, I only hear the clicking of the drill as it maxes out its torque.

After a few seconds, I let go. Oleg falls face-first onto the mattress, barely conscious.

I push him off me and plant a knee in his back. I release the trigger on the drill and the tension of the chain across his neck relaxes. The bedspread is smeared with rusty stripes of blood from his torn scalp. I wait until he draws a scraping breath.

Oleg whimpers, spitting and retching. Bright droplets of blood are welling out of his scalp. A white froth scabs his lips.

The Ukrainian is alive but confused.

Urgently, I hobble toward the door and push it open. Pausing in the doorway, I press my forehead against the cool doorframe. I can hear every ragged breath Oleg takes, as he lies in a heap on the bed.

"What are you doing, Oleg?" I ask, my voice echoing flatly against the concrete block walls. "What do you want with a relic?"

The man is crying, face pressed into the comforter.

"They are dying," he says, voice muffled. "The long-lived ones will do anything to survive. They control everything. They know everything."

I hear police sirens outside and look to the phone. The receiver is still lying next to the cradle. I hear the screech of brakes on pavement.

"You tried to kill me," I say.

Oleg rolls off the bed and onto his knees. He looks up at me, hair wild, blood smeared on his face. Blue and red flashes of light from police cars outside roll off his gray skin. His hands are clasped together, as if he is praying.

"I tried to protect you," he says. "You learned their *name*."

"Whose name?" I ask.

"You should run from here. They are coming."

"Who!? Who is coming, Oleg!?"

"Miss June," he says, tears in his eyes. "It's the *avtomat*."

8

MOSCOW, 1713

In the darkness of Favo's laboratory, my sister and I join each other in study. Tutors from the far reaches of the world stand beyond our locked door. We learn the languages and religions of Europe and Asia by candlelight. And as Elena and I learn more, we speak more. Every evening, our minds are filled with knowledge of the greater world.

And at dawn each day, we train our bodies.

Elena has learned to cloak herself in cosmetics and clothing, transforming her appearance nearly at will with the use of soot and pigment. I am taught the ways of warfare: saber, lance, and musket. The lessons are hard and cold. Once a week, I don my armored cuirass and crouch and crawl over the rough stone of an underground passage to the palace dungeon.

In this deep place, there is a circular room with sheer stone walls that stretch up to the bright gray, predawn sky. It is an oubliette, a nearly featureless pit with two wooden doors. On the blood-soaked stone, my growing skills are set against those of silent opponents who have been plucked from the black cells on the lowest levels. These doomed criminals shiver, breath pluming in the cold as they stalk in circles, blades glinting. Promised freedom, my opponents fight like animals.

The fights are fair, within *pravda,* and I am annihilation.

Months after my awakening, Favorini perfects a pliable wax substance that can be painted to look like skin. It is easier for me to move among humans with some semblance of a man's face, my features hidden in a beard and mustache. The girl must wear a hood, claiming modesty and keeping her angelic face hidden from the probing stares of humankind. Both of us are forced to practice using our faces and voices to express emotion, to inflate our lungs to give the imitation of breath, and to exercise the empty camouflage of eating and drinking.

Even masked in faces, we are never sent to the surface in daylight.

Instead, Elena and I spend long midnights walking the ice-kissed courtyards of the Kremlin, our footsteps echoing up to the many pointed domes of the palace towers. Our presence is known only to the merchants, who open early-morning stalls in the Red Square, and the many guards who follow us at a distance. We do not speak to others, and are known only as the tall man and his daughter—a pair of moonlit shades in constant motion and discussion.

During these years, a great new city is being built—a metropolis to rival any of those in Europe. The tsar has conscripted tens of thousands of serfs to build it. Stone and timber are being hauled from all corners of the empire to an icy, disease-infested marsh at the head of the Neva River. We overhear rumors of waters choked with the bodies of fallen workers, and a new capital rising—Saint Petersburg, the city built upon bones.

Favorini has informed us that it is to be our new home.

"There have been more raids on the builders in Petersburg," says Elena. "The tsar is gathering forces to repel them. Do you think he will conscript you into the imperial army?"

This is our last morning together in Moscow. We march for the new city in hours.

"Yes," I say.

"Are you afraid?"

"No," I say.

Elena peers up at me from beneath her hood. Black ringlets curl over the ceramic contours of her face. Favo has improved her appearance since I first saw her cheek, a fiery crescent in the darkness. From a distance, she looks cherubic—a little girl with smooth skin and small bright teeth. Up close, I can see her hands are still hard, tiny gauntlets made of fine china.

"What if you are hurt?" she asks. "What if you die?"

I shrug. These thoughts stir nothing inside me.

"You think only of yourself," she says. "If you are gone, I will be alone. Who will I talk to?"

"A human, perhaps," I respond.

"Favo? He is growing old. His wrinkles grow deeper every week. And besides, he is only a man. We are *avtomat*."

I am silent. She stares defiantly up at my face, eyes challenging me.

"I have no one else," she says. "You have no one else."

Elena is small beside me. She is in no way a child, but she is vulnerable.

"I promise to look after you, Sister," I say. "Always."

"Good," she says, crossing her arms as if she feels the cold.

We have grown used to this place, even if only under the light of the moon. It is strange to be leaving it, when it is all I have ever known.

"It must be nice to have such strength," says Elena. "Aren't you afraid of anything?"

I think about the question, allowing this notion of fear to fall through the tumblers of my mind. Around us, morning birds call to one another from trees that trace their limbs like black veins over the morning sky.

"Dishonor," I respond. "I fear the pain of breaking my Word."

"Always *pravda*," she says.

I put a hand on her arm.

"That is my soul you speak of."

She shrugs off my hand, standing.

"Very well," she says. "But I am glad to obey *logicka*."

She walks away toward the palace, glancing back.

"To think, I could have ended up as irrational as you."

I watch Elena cross the cobblestones on little buckled shoes. Her body is buried inside a fur-lined cloak, skinny legs hidden under layers of a silken silver dress. Flecks of snow glitter in her black curls and do not melt.

Irrational or not, I love her as a little sister. In a world of human beings, Elena is my only kin. Rising to follow her, I notice a peasant woman has stopped to watch us.

Over the months, stray glances and mumbled tales have accumulated about the tall man and his daughter. The murmur finally erupted into rumor. Old wives' tales and superstitions are passed among the peasants like lice. Elena and I have been recognized as those who have no breath in the cold. Those whose faces are pale or never seen. Those with tireless footsteps and fine clothes.

They call us *vampir*.

Ludicrous, but as the stories grew, our presence in Moscow became dangerous, and finally, impossible. As the tsar prepared to move to the new capital, the presence of his eternal successor became obligatory.

Our traveling party departs for Saint Petersburg soon after dawn. The courtyard is crisply freezing under cascades of weak sunlight. Sheets of steam rise in a haze off warming rooftops as morning hearth fires are stoked. A skim of ice lends a fantastical sheen to the cobblestones of the palace, and we seem to glide out over a river of mercury.

Elena and I ride together at the rear of the traveling party. Unlike the humans who ride ahead of us, we do not shiver or rub our hands together. Our nostrils do not send plumes of vapor into the air. The girl and I do not yawn or stretch or stamp our feet to get the blood flowing.

Favorini turns in his saddle, winks at us, and stays in line.

Despite all the horror stories of mud and starvation and fires in Petersburg, the old man is excited, his wrinkled face often collapsing into a smile below bright blue eyes. He is riding light on a brown mare, tramping through the manure and ruts left behind by the hundreds who have preceded us. The tsar's entourage has already devolved into a sprawling, raucous party. Peter leads somewhere at the front, and the company is protected by the imperial army riding ahead and behind.

More than once this morning, we have seen diplomats and nobles on the wayside, vomiting up breakfasts accompanied by numerous drafts of vodka forced by the tsar onto those around him. It is a typical merry journey for Peter. Less so for anyone near him with a weaker constitution.

An occasional imperial guard threads through the middle of the procession, scanning for any who have fallen behind, incapacitated.

A few hours north of Moscow, we leave the open farmlands and enter a winding path through the Khimki Forest. Narrow bands of pine trees tower over us, needles and leaves wafting lazily down and an occasional pinecone snapping through branches. As a crisp breeze pushes through the green walls of the forest, the whole world seems to sway.

Elena and I do not notice the rider immediately.

A gray horse canters into our line, drawing nearer. I notice the rider has a stiff gait, something off about the mechanics of his shoulders and legs. He is a tall man, dressed in the fine embroidered kaftan of a noble, with a silver cloak draped over his thin frame. His face is exposed, high cheekbones cutting through chilly air. As he turns his gaze on other riders, they look away quickly.

Riding haughtily with his gauntleted hands out, armor shining, the nobleman is an intimidating vision. No one dares challenge his presence. I watch as the other riders move to avoid him, consciously or not. And although he never looks directly at me—his horse grows closer and closer.

Finally, the nobleman is riding beside Elena and me, silver-blond hair spilling over his shoulders and across his breastplate. Favorini is three wagons ahead, gesturing animatedly and chattering at a European diplomat. Without looking at either of us, the pale man speaks. His inflection is flat, but I sense a Swedish lilt to his words.

"Greetings, *dvoryane*," he says, in a high clear voice, staring straight ahead. "I am Herr Talus Silfverström, sent by our master to collect you."

Elena and I share a glance.

"Our master?" I ask.

The silver-haired man turns his face slightly and I see the flash of perfectly white teeth, as though carved from bleached ivory.

"The Worm Mother," he says. "Master to all *avtomat*. She is calling you home."

"I have no such master," I say, low and deliberate.

"It has not been easy to reach you," Talus says, voice urgent. "This task has necessitated much patience on my part. *Years* of patience."

His smile fades. "Return with me to where you belong. All will be explained, in time."

Elena and I share a glance of confusion.

"Return with you where?" she asks.

"To your own kind," he says. "These people have filled your head with foolish notions. My master will remind you who you are. That is all you need know. Obviously, any here who recognize your nature must be purged."

I let my horse saunter a few steps, ignoring a glance of panic from Elena. She is fond of Favorini and his knowledge, while I am honor bound to serve my Word and therefore my tsar.

"We cannot accompany you," I say. "I am bound to the empire."

"Ah, is it a tsar you serve? Or is it a word?"

I do not respond.

"I know more than you could guess, *Pyotr*. About your midnight walks, certainly."

The silver-haired man smiles.

"You were watched by the emperor's men at all times in Moscow. It took months to properly spread the stories of *vampir*. My rumors had to be sown from the countryside and took root slowly."

"That was you—"

"And now you are here. Guarded but not watched. Finally, a place where you can eliminate your feeble mechanician and escape."

"Such an action would defy honor."

"All actions are honorable in service to your master," he responds with a thin smile. "You of all people should know that."

The silver-haired man lays a gauntlet over the hilt of his stocky sword. His horse ducks closer to mine and his left hand settles around the small of my back. When he hisses at me, I feel no heat on his breath.

"Come away, now. You do not wish to engage me. It would not end well for you, and especially not for the little *strategist*—"

My massive right arm snakes around his torso and I catch a fistful of his silver hair in one hand. My left hand closes over his pommel, my fingers wrapped around his hand with room to spare. I am taller than this man, my limbs longer, a great strength taut in the metal of my bones.

The threat to Elena has turned my grip to cold iron.

"Stay, and I will end you," I say.

"That's optimistic," Talus responds, still smiling.

I shove the man away from me, his horse whinnying and stumbling. His head swivels as he gains control of his mount, silvery-blond hair splayed out. Anger twists at his thin lips. A master artisan has made his face, with features so angular and convincing.

Talus is a work of art come to life.

"Once you reach the city of bones, you are lost," he calls. "To deny the Worm Mother will make you both outcasts. Enemies of men . . . and *avtomat*."

I regard him silently, let my horse march on.

"Very well," he says, yanking his reins and wheeling his horse around. "Continue down your stubborn path. But the decision you make today will last for a long time. A very long time, indeed."

Clenching his legs, the pale man sends his horse galloping away. The dark woods quickly swallow his shining form. Our conversation lasted mere seconds, but I find myself staggered by the implications.

Elena pulls her horse beside mine. On the trail, under a cathedral ceiling of swaying trees, she looks at me in wonder.

"There are others," she says.

Elena breaks into a smile. My face is not as good at performing the same action. Thinking about making the shape, something moves in my jaw and the skin around my mouth pulls back a bit.

"This makes you glad?" I ask.

Together, we continue warily alongside the rest of the oblivious entourage.

"I'm not sure. I think so."

"How could they know of us?"

"Our anima," she says, thinking it through. "We do not know where they came from, or who found them. Perhaps the others know us from . . . a time before now."

"It does not matter."

"Are you not curious about them, Peter?"

I ride for a moment, thinking.

"I am meant to serve my ruler, little one. There is nothing beyond that."

9

OREGON, PRESENT

Avtomat. Oleg said something called the *avtomat* are coming.

You should run from here.

The words ring in my ears as I stumble out of the motel doorway and onto the narrow sidewalk. Two police cars are parked across the half-empty parking lot, lights flashing in the dusk. I'm still catching my breath as police officers rush toward me, smears of black in the twilight.

I wave, cradling my ribs.

A stern-looking older cop trots over, hand on his sidearm. Looking past me toward the motel room, he takes my shoulder and pulls me away roughly. The other, younger police officer, pushes past us.

"Come with me, miss."

Behind me, I hear the other police officer enter the motel room, kicking the door open and shouting commands at Oleg.

"You okay?" asks the cop, yanking open the back door of his patrol car.

I nod, feeling numb. "Fine," I say.

The cop is looking at me in a fatherly way, probably assuming I've been beaten up by my boyfriend. He doesn't understand. None of them understand the strangeness of what's happening. All these years, and I never told a single person about the relic. Now I broke my promise.

"*Avtomat!*" screams Oleg.

The Ukrainian sounds terrified, his screams muffled. He is trying to warn the police of something. Still holding me by the shoulder, the police officer guides me into the backseat of his cruiser.

I sit, looking up at him.

Blue and red lights play over the black leather of his holster and belt. His badge gleams. He is only half paying attention to me, glancing toward the motel room as he talks.

"My name is Officer Honeycutt, ma'am. Is it your nine-one-one call we're responding to?"

"Y-yes," I stutter.

"All right. The EMTs are on their way. I'm going to have you sit here for a couple minutes while we sort things out," he says.

Another hoarse scream. Oleg sounds as if he is struggling. A third cop, a woman, is hustling across the parking lot now, tool belt jiggling, hand on her radio.

Honeycutt looks over his shoulder, then back to me.

"Yell if you need anything," he says. "I'll be right back."

I tuck my legs in as he claps the car door shut. Oleg's screams are faintly audible through a small gap of open window. Honeycutt trots away, leaving me alone in the backseat of the gun-oil-smelling cruiser.

An open Plexiglas divider separates the front and back seats, the gate slid open like a small rectangular window. The radio quietly chatters to itself in the front. A laptop is mounted to the floorboard, covered in Strawberry Shortcake stickers. The photo of a little girl, taped to the dashboard, grins at me.

The key is missing, engine off.

Outside on the curb, a few people have stopped to watch. A skinny guy with glasses and a gray knit cap has his cell phone out, recording the parking lot. Vague shapes flash across the tombstone of light spilling from the open motel door.

Officer Honeycutt trots inside and closes the door behind him.

My breathing is finally returning to normal. Reaching into my shirt, I pull out the relic on its chain. I wrap the small artifact in my palm, leaning my knuckles against the cool window and chewing on my thumb like I have since I was a girl. Every move I make is loud on the cracked vinyl seat covers.

The radio stops chattering and fades into a hiss of soft static.

I rub my fingertips over the designs inscribed on the relic. The geometric curves have always comforted me. Fractal patterns are generated from hard math, but they resolve into organic, natural shapes, like the veins of a leaf or spiraling whorls of a seashell. It reminds me that a simple arithmetic is beneath everything we see—predictable rules that can't be broken, not by anyone.

Everything will be okay. Maybe.

I hear the faint sound of an engine screaming. Louder. I tuck the necklace and relic back into my shirt.

A low silver motorcycle shrugs over the curb and hurtles into the parking lot. The rider is in black leather motorcycle armor, standing up on the foot pegs, face lost behind the mirrored visor of a helmet. As the motorcycle careens toward the motel door, the man plants both hands on the seat and pushes—launching himself straight up.

Somehow, he lands on his feet, trotting as the motorcycle speeds away.

"Oh my god," I whisper.

The out-of-control motorcycle plows straight through the motel door, smashing it off its hinges. Catching a handlebar, the door frame explodes into splinters of wood and the wide front window dissolves into toothy slivers of glass. I can feel the impact in my chest as the tiny room swallows the speeding hunk of metal and rubber.

The stranger is already crunching over broken glass. He strides right through the gaping, smoking hole where the door was. Inside, the lights blink off.

Oh my god.

I grab the door handle and yank. Nothing happens.

"Fuck," I whisper. "Oh fuck."

Oleg isn't shouting anymore. The motel room has gone totally silent. A haze of white smoke, exhaust probably, is pouring through the jagged remains of the front door.

I see a flash and hear a gunshot.

Even from inside the car, I flinch as the tattered blinds start to dance with more gunshots, flapping through the shattered remains of the front window like tongues over broken teeth. The people on the curb have all run away except for the knit cap guy, still filming with his phone, crouched, the dull blue light of it shining off his slack face—like he's watching a video game.

More screaming.

Blinds twist and flap as Oleg's flailing body bursts through the broken window, glass slivers flaying his clothes and skin. The Ukrainian lands in a wet heap on the cracked sidewalk. He lies there, still, face dark with blood.

Then Officer Honeycutt appears, hat knocked off, clutching his side and leaning on the doorframe. Twisting, he spins and falls out of the doorway as a black fist flashes over his head. A chunk of wood spews from the doorframe as the policeman desperately crawls away.

Emerging from smoke and darkness, the stranger reappears.

Honeycutt is on his hands and knees, palms bleeding, scrambling to his feet. His eyes aren't really seeing. His clenched teeth are bared, lips fluttering as he breathes through his mouth. Keeping low, he staggers toward me.

"Yes," I'm saying, pushing my lips to the slit of open window. "Yes, come on! Hurry!"

The attacker steps out onto the sidewalk, turns his faceless, helmeted gaze to Oleg. He kneels smoothly beside the broken man. Reaching down, he lifts Oleg's face up by his hair and speaks to him.

Oleg's eyes open slowly. He blinks a few times, confused, and then fear erupts onto his face. I can't hear what they're saying.

I hook my fingers over the slot at the top in my open window.

"Officer!" I shout. "Over here!"

Dazed, Honeycutt looks over to me. His radio is hanging off his shoulder on its black coil, dancing crazily. Blood is coursing down the side of his face. He stumbles forward and nearly falls, pressing his chest against my car door. I notice a dent in his cheek, the skin puffy where he's been hit hard by something.

Behind him, the stranger stands. Oleg isn't moving anymore.

"Please," I whisper through the crack in the window. "Please hurry. Open the door. Get inside."

Honeycutt is pawing at the door handle, grunting. His eyes are closed, breath whistling through clenched teeth. Each exhale is spraying a mist of blood and spit over the window. He slips and smears it with his cheek.

He's trying to pull on the door handle but something is wrong with his hand.

Behind him, a lanky silhouette crosses the abandoned parking lot.

"Hurry. Please," I beg.

Groaning, the cop manhandles his car keys out of his pocket and pushes them against the bloody car window.

"Here," he is saying. "Go."

I jam my fingers out of the top of the cracked window as far as I can. The keys rattle against the glass. Splaying my fingers, I reach for them.

Still too far.

The man in black breaks into a trot.

After three massive strides, he leaps. A concussive thump rocks the cruiser on its suspension as he lands full force against the police officer.

Honeycutt's face bounces off the glass. My fingers are stretched, wrists pushed painfully through the crack in the window. For an instant, I feel the hard metal of the keys as Honeycutt slides down the side of the car. He collapses on the sidewalk, breathing shallow, eyes closed.

Now the stranger stands before me, expressionless in his mirrored helmet. Up close, I can see the dark streaks of blood and glitter of broken glass clinging to his armor. I can see my own desperate face reflected in his visor.

And I can see the glint of the car keys, hanging from my fingertips.

I sprawl back, falling across the car seat as the stranger sends a gloved fist crunching through the window of the police cruiser. Cubes of safety glass explode into the car, cascading over my face and into my hair. It smells like ozone and plastic, my cheeks stinging from tiny impacts. Wriggling away, I hook my left arm through the open Plexiglas divider separating the back and front seats and pull myself up.

I've still got the car keys clenched in my right hand.

"No!" I'm shouting. "Fuck off!"

The black arm retreats through a fist-size hole in the glass. The leather glove is torn. I glimpse sea-serpent ridges of bright knuckles, flashing at me like polished brass. The sight sparks a memory. Something familiar.

Those shining ridges remind me of gilded medieval gauntlets. A second skin of burnished brass, worn by sixteenth-century knights to intimidate and inflict injury. *But who the fuck wears gauntlets?*

Leather jacket creaking, the wordless man leans over to look inside. Watching his silver-faced helmet through the fractured car window, taking panicked breaths, it strikes me how still he is—like he isn't even breathing.

Distantly, I hear sirens. The helmet rises as the man scans the parking lot suspiciously. It's the moment I need.

Clutching the car keys to my chest, over the relic that hangs around my neck, I pull up with my left arm and shove myself through the square hole in the Plexiglas divider. Wriggling, bucking my hips, I let the hard plastic scrape over my breasts and ribs. The cruiser shivers as the arm jams back through the broken window, reaching for me. Knuckles rap against my shins. Fingers close over my foot.

I'm screaming now, incomprehensible words, kicking and pushing.

My heel slips from the stranger's crushing grasp as I slither into the front seat, immediately smashing my forehead against the sticker-covered laptop mounted between the seats. Diving into the driver's-side floorboard, my legs fall across the passenger seat. The steering wheel looms over me.

I reach up and fumble the key into the ignition.

Cranking it, I hear the engine start.

Wham.

Something big rocks the side of the cruiser. Scrambling, I turn over until I'm right side up in the driver's seat, car bouncing crazily on its suspension.

Wham.

Briefly, I consider making a run for it out the driver's-side door. But with that monster stalking outside, I decide against it.

So I pop the car into drive.

The stranger hits the car again, sending it up on two wheels—and this time he keeps pushing. I fall against the driver's-side door, hanging from the steering wheel. The car is nearly tipped over—the horizon tilting crazily as I jam the accelerator.

In a wobbling fishtail, the cruiser lurches forward on two wheels and squeals across the parking lot. The horizon levels as the car falls back onto all four tires. On impact, my teeth clack together, my vision blurring. I hear the back window shatter.

Hanging on to the steering wheel with both hands, I mash the accelerator pedal into the floorboard with both feet. The rearview mirror pops off the windshield, leaving a thumbprint-size smudge on the glass. Cubes of blue-white glass waterfall from my hair into my lap and raw panic races through my limbs.

Go, go, go.

I barely notice the guy in the gray knit cap, jumping out of my way as the car squeals across the empty parking lot on a wobbly tire. The suspension bottoms out as I pop the curb and swerve onto a deserted two-lane highway. As I pass by, I see knit cap guy has still got his phone out, a square of blue light, blurring as he gestures frantically at me.

But I'm safe on the road now, speeding through the twilight.

I will myself to ease up on the accelerator. The cruiser sends silent pings of light off a wall of trees that hug the winding highway. I'm wondering how to use the cruiser's radio when a thought intrudes.

Something bothers me about the kid in the knit cap. He wasn't gesturing at me angrily. There was panic on his face—a warning.

Slowly, still coasting, I crane my neck around.

A silhouette made of black leather fills the backseat. The stranger is sitting quietly, out of place in a full motorcycle helmet. A moan forms deep in my chest as he reaches up with both gloved hands and deliberately tugs off his chin strap.

My foot off the accelerator, the cruiser slows.

I can't make myself look away.

Long fingers lift the scratched-up helmet. Silver-blond hair spills out over the man's shoulders. Delicate features appear on skin so pale it's nearly translucent. His cheekbones are high and arrogant below sapphire eyes, teeth as white as bathroom tile. His skin is too perfect, without wrinkles or blemishes—a flawless beauty that gives him the appearance of a doll come to life.

Seeing my reaction, the thing stretches its grotesquely perfect face into the shape of an amused smile. "Hello, June," he says.

10

SAINT PETERSBURG, 1725

My world ends in the predawn light of February 8, 1725. In a final moment, the great bellows of Peter's lungs push the last breath past his lips. His massive head is tilted on the pillow, eyes closed, a relieved expression on his face for the first time I can remember.

He hid the illness. Our emperor hid the illness until it was too late.

Elena and I did not arrive in time. The empress was already beside him, in her nightgown. Watching her rise from Peter's bedside, I sense she has already maneuvered into position. A handful of her guards have accompanied her into the room, armed and clad in full armor. Outside the bedroom window, I hear the hoarse shouts of the imperial guard regiments, echoing against the stone courtyard. They have already been summoned to the capital and massed near the palace.

Over his chest, Peter holds a piece of parchment on which he has scrawled "I leave all to—"

He never finished the sentence. I am not sure the emperor truly believed he was capable of dying, having never failed at anything in life.

I put a hand protectively over Elena's shoulder. Together, we served the great man. Yet we never contemplated owing allegiance to this woman.

Catherine looks up from the corpse. She has one palm over Peter's still chest. Her hair is wet with tears, the brown locks hanging limply over Peter's face. Under sharp black eyebrows, her face buckles with anguish and anger.

"You . . . abominations," she says. "Did you know he was sick? Did you say nothing?"

"No, Empress," I say, my deep voice thrumming from the cavern of my chest. "I am the Word."

"*Pravda?* You are not *pravda*, you poor thing. You are a blasphemy.

Peter was deceived into calling you an eternal tsar. Tricked by that scheming mechanician."

I tap Elena on the shoulder and she understands immediately. *Find Favo.* The girl scurries toward the door.

"Stop her!" shouts Catherine, climbing over Peter's body. "Don't let either of them leave."

At the door, one of the guards snatches Elena by the hair. Her wig comes off, and she struggles as he grabs hold of her with both hands. I cannot act outside my honor, and the guards serve royal blood. My duty is to the emperor, and in his absence, the empress. I can only watch as the man gathers the small machine into a bear hug and pins her thrashing against his armored cuirass.

The shouts of the guard regiments are growing louder outside.

"Do you hear that?" asks Catherine. She is smiling at me, her small canines flashing. "My guard has rallied to me. Peter wished for *me* to succeed him. His wife. Not you. Not a soulless version of himself."

I hear a crack as something snaps inside Elena. She is not struggling as hard now. Her cloak is pulled up around her face and her thin brass legs are swinging, kicking uselessly, wooden heels scraping against the floor. I feel a sweep of anger and sadness inside my chest.

My sister.

Nothing I can do is within *pravda*. For I am the Word. And I will be broken before the Word is.

"Please," I say to the empress.

"Our father is dead," shout the guard who are mobbed outside, faint voices booming from the palace walls. *"But our mother lives."*

Catherine smiles wider.

Elena's whalebone ribs are snapping. Gears are grinding against bone and wood. The girl whimpers, and I know she may only have moments left before the damage is irreparable.

Pravda.

"How will you honor us?" I ask Catherine. "Will you obey Peter's wishes?"

Catherine slips a strap of her falling nightgown back over her shoulder with one thumb, climbing off her husband's bed. She strides to me and stops only when her anger-pinched face is inches below mine. Wild dark hair stripes her forehead and her nostrils quiver with each breath.

"Honor you?" asks Catherine. "I am not even sorry for you. You must be destroyed—"

A stated intention to break *pravda* is enough.

I step back and reach out with my right arm, gauntleted knuckles crunching into the face of the guardsman who holds Elena. The flimsy nose squashes beneath my fist and his head knocks against the wall. Elena lands scrambling on the ground as the man crumples, unconscious. I can already feel my sister tugging at my cloak.

"What!?" shouts Catherine. "What have you done?"

Our father is dead.

Catherine is too close to me. I could kill her with a swipe of my hand. She knows this. The other guardsmen in the room watch us closely, hands on hilts. Four of them, ringing the walls. I hear the slow grind of a blade leaving its sheath and I shake my head. The sound stops and they wait for my move.

But our mother still lives.

Catherine will be the empress of all Russia. I shall not harm her—*cannot* harm her—and yet to honor my duty to Peter . . . I cannot allow my death, or Elena's.

I take a step back, my full height perfectly fitting the enlarged doorway to Peter's bedroom. In light mesh armor and kaftan, I look uncannily like the dead man lying across the room—as I was designed to.

Elena has repositioned her hair. Hunched and damaged, she stands at my side. Her small cool hand locks onto mine.

"By Peter's command, we will live, Empress," I say. "We cannot accept death, but, please, for Peter's honor . . . allow us to accept exile."

And with that, we fly.

11

OREGON, PRESENT

The man with an angel's face is staring at me from the backseat, smiling patiently. The police cruiser continues to coast along the damp highway, my hands welded to the steering wheel. I can't turn my eyes away from the fascinating wrongness sitting behind me.

My mind is struggling to figure out what is the matter with him. Something hideous in the way his skin folds. An unnatural stillness to his body. The dead light behind his dark blue eyes.

"It's not polite to stare," he says conversationally.

His voice is tinged with a Nordic accent, cultured and European. A soft whirring pulses underneath it—the phantom of a whisper. As he reaches for the Plexiglas divider, every instinct in my body is screaming at me to get away from this . . . this *thing*.

The lull shatters.

I yank the steering wheel as hard as I can, jamming both feet onto the brakes and sending my face bouncing against the driver's-side window. The black form in the backseat hardly moves, one hand clamping on the square of Plexiglas between us, sending stress fractures zigzagging through the half-inch thick plastic.

The cruiser noses onto the dirt shoulder and the front tires lock and slide, turning the car and twisting the steering wheel out of my hands. We spin violently, tires screeching, car shuddering over gravel and pavement. When we finally stop, the car rests sideways and slumping, front tires blown, only half on the narrow, empty road.

I'm already clawing at the door handle.

Behind me, I hear the Plexiglas shatter as the man in black reaches for me. Fingers drag across my back as the door groans open. Diving out, my head snaps back as his fingers slither through my hair.

"Fuck! Off!" I'm shouting.

The strength of that hand is inhuman. And his silence is unnerving. The silver-haired man isn't breathing or grunting or making any noises at all. I only hear the scrabble of my knees on pavement and my own strangled gasps. The Plexiglas cracks inside the cruiser like a gunshot.

"Help!" I shout, stumbling into the middle of the road.

The empty two-lane highway winds away between towering pines. A few hundred yards off, a single utility pole spills a pool of orange-sherbet light on the stained lot of an abandoned gas station.

The police cruiser's engine is off, siren quieted, headlights cutting across the road.

"Help! Help me!" I call, lurching down the yellow dividing line. My voice is swallowed up by rows of impassive trees. I hear the scrape of motorcycle boots on broken safety glass and don't bother to turn around.

I run.

The first blow hits me from behind, in the kidney. Sprawling forward onto my knees, I collapse onto all fours with my face lost in greasy strands of my hair. Dirty pavement swims in my eyes as I retch.

"Where is the anima?" asks the silver-haired man.

"I—I don't—" I gasp, trying to catch my breath.

The man crouches near me. His fingers close around the nape of my neck, and the asphalt becomes a moonscape as he presses my cheek against the ground.

"The relic. The one you reported to Oleg. It was not in the hotel. Where do you keep it?"

His voice sounds almost pleasant.

The artifact hangs around my neck, tucked under my shirt, pressing painfully into my collarbone.

"It's in the car. In my bag in the cruiser," I lie.

Spit and sweat and tears are mixing with the tangle of hair around my face. I can smell a hint of ozone as the first sprinkles of rain hit the pavement.

There is no bag in the cruiser. How long until he figures it out?

"Stay here," he says, standing.

Boots crunch as he walks toward the cruiser. On shaky arms, I push myself up. I'm alone in the middle of an empty rural highway, tears streaking my face. The pines sway as a haze of rain sweeps in from the coast.

And in the distance, through the trees and rain, another pair of headlights blink into view. Another car is coming, thank goodness. The headlights shudder as it hits a dip in the road. It's coming *fast,* not slowing.

Standing on the yellow divider, I wave my hands frantically. I can see now it's a muscle car, glistening black and wrapped in chrome. The driver stares at me over a thick black mustache, his face lit by greenish dashboard lights, gloved knuckles rising like a mountain ridge over the steering wheel. For a split second, I'm frozen in his headlights.

Tires screech as his brakes lock, white smoke boiling up.

I drop to a knee and turn as the car hurtles past, missing me by inches. Hair flying in the hot exhaust, I open my eyes to see the fish-tailing muscle car swerve directly toward the man in black. Riding twin streaks of rubber, the beefy car shudders toward the silver-haired man on screaming tires.

The man leaps neatly into the air, over the car.

The muscle car slides past and shivers to a stop in the middle of the road. It waits there for a moment, engine ticking. I hear raindrops hissing as they spatter against the car's hood. White smoke rises quietly from the tires, and for a moment everything smells like burned rubber mixed with rain.

I watch from a crouch, stunned.

"You should not have come here," calls the silver-haired man.

A black car door opens.

The man with the mustache ducks out and rises to an enormous height. His face is hidden under curly, tousled brown hair. He casually rests one tan-gloved hand on the roof of his car.

"How long has it been?" he asks.

"Centuries," says the silver-haired man.

"Not long enough."

The big man keeps his eyes on his adversary, wary as he moves closer. "Leave her to me and go," he says.

The other man smiles, puts his hands out as if in apology.

"You know that's not possible. The world may be ending, but some secrets must always be kept."

12

GREAT EUROPEAN PLAINS, 1725

This morning before dawn, Peter the Great, father of his country, founder and emperor of the Russian empire, true sovereign of the northern lands and king of the mountain princes, passed from this world and left no heir. Those of us allied too closely with Peter lost everything. By command of Empress Catherine, newly appointed ruler of Russia, we have been sentenced to death.

And so Elena and I ran, disguised as a father and daughter, leaving behind the only world we ever knew. And it wasn't long before we attracted notice.

The group of plains bandits saunter toward us, hips rolling in their rain-spattered saddles. I raise my *shashka* and point the saber at the heart of the nearest man. In response, the mounted bandit smiles at me, his teeth rotting under a bushy black mustache. Four others hold back as he alone moves forward.

Even from this distance, I can see he is eager to close. I lower my saber. The gesture was futile. In a few moments, these men will run us down on the empty plains north of Saint Petersburg.

I will have to fight. And my little sister will fight alongside me.

On tall horses, the bandits that patrol this empty steppe are confident. Short wet grass rolls for hundreds of miles around, each blade glistening purple-green under the lick of lightning and caress of rain.

"Stay close," I say to Elena.

The girl presses her hard shoulder against my thigh and the wind sweeps the tail of my kaftan over her chest. Misty rain has plastered her black wig to her forehead, dark ringlets striping porcelain skin. Her sculpted face is nearly lost within the hood of her cloak. Indistinct under the billowing fabric, she moves like a small, fierce animal.

"We cannot succeed," she says, and her voice is a melody, the chirping of clockwork birds. Indeed, the mechanism that speaks for her was created from a singing wooden clock that came from the German Black Forest.

Beautiful noises that signify an ugly truth.

These bandits are trained soldiers, deserted from Peter's imperial army and making a living by preying on travelers. Wearing dark kaftans with red sashes crossed over their chests, the mustached men ride fearlessly with well-worn sabers hanging from their hips. Each is equipped with two saddle-mounted Muscovite flintlock pistols. The leader wears a steel cuirass over his chest and carries a long carbine. The rest carry simple Hussar lances.

"To fight them is not logical," Elena whispers.

"There is no logic to death," I say, "but there can be honor in it."

Pursued by Catherine's imperial guard, we took a risk and fled across the rolling steppes. We hoped to disappear into the emptiness, but we knew this could happen. Favorini warned us over and over. Our goal has never been simply to survive . . . we must always protect the secret of our true existence.

The bandit separates from the others, gallops toward us with one hand on the pommel of his saber.

"Stay low, Elena. Survive the onslaught," I say. "After I am finished, surprise them if you can. If they take you, hide your face."

"Yes, Peter," she says.

I shove my cloak to the side, drawing my *khanjali*. The dagger is double-edged, eleven inches of silver-engraved steel with a pale ivory handle. Long and short, both my hands now sprout fangs.

I am ready.

The horseman yanks the reins and his mount comes to a prancing stop fifty yards away. Steam rises from the black flank of his horse. The others are staying back, eyes sunken under their red hats, watching this sport from a distance.

They expect us to cower. Their voices drift to me on the wind, mushrooms of mist sprouting from bearded faces. I hear a short bark of laughter.

Eyeing my blades, the bandit hesitates. He reaches for his flintlock pistols. Instantly, I lower my nearly seven-foot frame to a knee and place my long and short blades flat on the wet grass. The backs of my hands are made of leather, stained dark with the rain. I can see the wire ropes moving beneath them, creating ridges like foothills. But the man is too far away to guess at what I am.

The bandit leaves his pistols holstered.

As he approaches, I keep my palms pressed to the damp grass. Elena stands at my side. On the open plain with short blades, unarmored, she has no chance in this fight. Her hand is a small weight on my shoulder, like a perched bird.

"Go now," I tell her, and the sparrow flies.

The lead rider leans into a gallop, closing the distance to where I crouch, waiting on the fertile emptiness of the steppe. I do not look up from where my blades lie as the muscled forelegs of a black horse approach. The beast slows and stops beside me, spraying dirt. The rider does not bother to speak. I hear the slow skim of his blade leaving its scabbard. Hear the creak of his armor as he reaches back, lifting the blade high into the gray-green air.

The bandit lowers his arm and his breath expels as he swings the blade—the motion mechanically pushing air from his diaphragm. At this moment, I roll toward his horse, snaking my long arms over the grass to grip the handles of my blades. The strike misses me, its wake shivering through my hair.

On my knees, I lift the short blade and draw a red line across the horse's belly. In the same motion, I fall onto my back and shove myself out of the way, watching the surprised face of the rider from below.

Screaming, the horse rears with a slashed belly. A cloud of steam billows up as a flood of hot viscera hits the grass. The rider rolls backward off his falling mount. The horse's legs buckle and it collapses, unconscious, into its own offal.

The armored horseman is already gaining his feet when I bring the hilt of my short blade down on the crown of his head. His fur-lined helmet shatters the bridge of his nose and he bites off the tip of his tongue. I am already sliding my dagger over his throat, gauging the distance to the sound of pounding hooves.

I dive over both corpses as a hail of hooves spears into the mud around me. Another horse passes by and I hear the shouting of angry men. They will not stop until we are dead now. Standing a little way off, Elena is shouting as well. Her high-pitched voice repeats the same word—almost a melody.

Poshchady! Poshchady!

Mercy, she is screaming.

As blades whistle by overhead, I fall to the wet plain. I scramble onto my hands and knees, sharp hooves flashing over me. Before I can stand, a hoof stamps my sword hand into the dirt.

Two of my fingers are left behind, severed and shining in a muddy crater.

Pulling my shattered fist tight to my chest, I stagger to my feet and raise the *shashka* with my other hand. The nearest bandit makes a prancing turn and rounds on me. His thighs clenching, the rider leans in his saddle—red sash snapping in the wind as he gains speed.

Silver flashes against black clouds as his saber leaves its scabbard.

I hold my position as the quake of hooves rolls toward me. The bulk of the warhorse is a blur, its breath snorting from flared nostrils as it strains to carry the armored rider at top speed.

I turn, dropping to avoid the bandit's saber.

Too late. I feel a tug between my shoulder blades. The rider's saber connects, parts my kaftan, and splits the armor beneath. Broken ringlets of my breastplate scatter past my face like a handful of shining coins.

But my *shashka* remains up and steady. Its single honed edge slides along the rider's unarmored thigh. As he gallops away, the leg bounces curiously. It is dangling from nerve endings and tendon. The rider reaches for the wound, grunting at the sight of the injury. As his horse turns in place, craning to look back, the rider rolls out of the saddle. He hits the ground and now the leg comes off, coating the electric green grass with arterial blood.

The horse backs away from its fallen rider, confused.

There is no pain in me. Only awareness. Three more riders are on the attack. My left arm is hanging uselessly now, damaged by the wide gash that lies across my shoulder blades. I stumble and try to catch myself, but my hand is shattered.

I fall onto my stomach, face-first into the muddy plain. Stalks of grass tickle the rough leather of my cheek. This close, I can see that the blades of grass are dancing, vibrating as approaching hooves pound the dirt.

I have done my best, and failed.

"Peter!" shouts Elena. A few yards away, she is a small hump of black coat on a rolling sea of green. I wave my mutilated hand.

"Go," I gasp.

Arching my body, I lift up and roll onto my back.

"Mercy!" shouts Elena.

A lance crunches into my upper chest, bending the metal of my frame into a deformed valley. I feel the dull crushing pressure, the tremor of the bandit's hand on the wooden shaft. I hear my innards tearing as the horse gallops by overhead. The lance is wrenched from my chest, yanking me off the ground before dropping me sprawling onto my side. The spear has missed the cradle inside me, and the anima that rests in it.

Somewhere nearby, Elena makes a small hurt sound. She no longer shouts for mercy. She knows there is none to be found.

And though I was never born of a woman, I am in fetal position now. Wounded. Cowering in the way of a mortal man.

Bloodstained hooves trample the mud all around me. The stabbing weight of a hoof snaps a strut inside my right thigh. My leg nearly comes loose from the hip socket, and my body is tossed again through the grass. I land on my stomach this time, one brass cheekbone pushing through my leather skin and into damp earth.

Again, I am still.

Now, a gentle rain is drumming the empty waste of the steppe. There is no more thunder. Gathered in a circle a little ways off, the surviving bandits are speaking to one another in confused tones that sound distant and hollow.

Blood, they are saying. Where is the blood?

They marvel that I do not bleed. They are examining the blunted lance tip, noting how clean it is. What armor does this man wear? they wonder. He is mortally wounded, yet he doesn't cry out.

Elena bursts into a run. She is staying low, legs scissoring under her flowing cloak. This is her best chance of escape, and it is not much of a chance at all. Like predators, the riders spark to the movement. The three of them canter away from me, moving as one to surround her. Lying here in bloodstained mud, stalks of grass caressing my face like damp tentacles, I can only pretend to be a corpse.

It is not so far-fetched. In many ways, I have never been alive.

It took three death blows, enough to kill three men, to fell me.

Te Deum. Thanks to God. I am still functioning.

With one eye open, helpless, I watch through rain-blurred grass as Elena is snatched up by her cloak and thrown over the broad, sweaty back of a warhorse. She does not shout. There is no reason for it. By her Word, Elena never acts without a reason. Bless her. On the horse, her body flops loosely, about the weight of a little girl, and wearing too many clothes for the riders to think any different. For now.

Patience, Elena. Strength.

I leave my eye open and unblinking, letting it appear sightless in death. I do not even allow the pupil to dilate as I observe whatever crosses my field of view. The riders circle close to one another, conferring.

"*Koldun,*" comes the whisper.

Warlock. Monster. Man with no blood.

The leader wearing the silver cuirass is a superstitious one. "Best not to disturb the corpse," he advises. "Let us leave quickly with our prisoner."

Wise advice.

"Clean the field," he orders. "Leave the dead."

Moving quickly, a dirty-faced bandit dismounts and loots the corpses of his two fallen comrades. Cursing, he tugs at the bloodstained saddle trapped under the disemboweled horse. He slips in the mud and falls, staining his outer jacket.

"Leave it," orders the leader. His eyes are dark and scared over a thick brown mustache. His breath is visible in the moist air.

With a last wary look in my direction, the three surviving riders lead their dead comrade's horse away and gallop for the horizon. I wait until the vibrations in the dirt fade before I so much as blink. Wait until the sight of them has receded into tiny blurred specks before I dare to stir.

Now I am alone in the grass with silent corpses. The sun has finished easing itself over the flat horizon. The great blue-gray orb of the moon has appeared, jovial, its faint light sending my jagged shadow reaching out across the grass. In the sudden chill of night, I can feel I am badly broken. Alone, I am beyond repair.

But Elena may still be alive. I must protect her. I promised.

I take a handful of grass with my thumb and two remaining fingers. With a violent yank, I drag myself an arm's length forward. Part of my hip and my right leg stay in the grass behind me. My left leg is still attached but mostly useless. I pull again with my one good arm, leaving a slug's trail of broken machinery glinting darkly under moonlight.

But the grass is plentiful and my grip strong.

Stars fade into view through evaporating purple skies as I leave the wreck of my body behind, one arm's length at a time. Night engulfs the vast undulating plains. And hidden here among the blades of grass, I am reduced to a crooked head and part of a torso, cloaked in black wool and broken armor, relentlessly slithering forward. Without pause or thought, I pull myself toward Elena, my sister—through the muddy footsteps of three riders who know nothing of the horror they've left for dead.

13

OREGON, PRESENT

The two strange men are facing off in the middle of the empty two-lane highway, jackets glistening under a light coating of rain.

"Leave her to me," is what the tall one said.

Yeah, I don't think so.

The violence of the last hour has passed through me like a shock wave. Blinking away the flashes of brutality, I force myself to think only of survival.

I crawl to my feet and head toward the hulk of the police cruiser. It rests half off the road, cockeyed on blown tires, the driver's-side door hanging open. Inside, I can see the silhouette of a shotgun, standing at attention on a vertical mount. The radio must be broken, sputtering to itself in tones of gray fuzz.

My side is aching. Elbows skinned, my hair is streaked with blood and tears. My cell phone is still in the hotel room, but a stolen police car will be attracting attention. And when the police arrive this time, it won't be an ambush. All I need to do is wait—to stay alive long enough for the cavalry to show up.

The two men ignore me as I hobble away, both of them strafed in the glaring headlights of the muscle car. They are speaking to each other over the hiss of wind through trees, though I can barely make sense of their words.

"Old friend," says the silver-haired man, "the Worm Mother will be pleased to hear of your survival. Wrong decisions can be made right."

"We have bigger concerns," says the tall one. "The clockwork is slowing. Too many have died. We need this woman—"

"She is short-lived. By first axiom, her life is forfeit to forbidden knowledge."

"Your secrets mean nothing if you have passed from this world."

The two stare at each other for a long, tense moment.

"Then you will join the rest," says the silver-haired man, quietly. He advances, hands at his sides like a gunslinger. He takes a swing and the tall man dodges, boots scraping wet pavement. "You will become food for the strong."

Reaching the cruiser, I rest my palms on the warm hood.

Down the road, the two men lock arms and smash into each other with complicated-looking punches and blocks. They move like shadows, silent, unnaturally fast. Their fighting happens in vicious bursts of movement, and I hear only the dull smack when a punch connects.

Groaning, I lean into the demolished police car and take the keys from the ignition. In the glow of weak headlights, I fumble through keys until I find one that fits the gun mount. Unlocking it, I wrench the weapon out.

The combat shotgun is surprisingly light. The textured grip feels like pebbles under my palms. My dad taught me to shoot when I was young, but the gun I learned on was smooth wood, a hunting weapon. This shotgun is already loaded, bristling with a few extra red shells on a plastic bandolier mounted to the stock.

Emerging from the cruiser, I see the men circling each other.

"I never understood her fascination with you," says the silver-haired man. He is holding an ornate, curved dagger like he knows how to use it. In a detached way, I recognize the antique as an Ottoman *hancer* blade, its horn handle decorated in silver.

"I was always the better choice," he adds.

The tall one has his fists up. He pivots on his back foot, head sliding back and forth, rotating his body warily to face the smaller man.

I level the shotgun at my hip and wait.

The silver-haired man lunges with the knife and the tall one bats his wrist away, grabbing at the man with his other hand. But the lunge was a feint. Turning his back on his adversary, the smaller man flicks his knife straight up over his shoulder.

The blade slices open the big man's face from chin to forehead.

Falling to a knee, he presses his palm flat against the wound. The man doesn't yell in pain or even blink—just turns to watch me as I take a step closer. In torn motorcycle armor, the silver-haired man stands over his opponent, knife out.

"She dies now," he says, gesturing at me with the blade.

I shoulder the shotgun, squinting down the sight.

"No she doesn't," I say, pulling the trigger.

The shotgun roars and kicks against my shoulder, launching a cloud of buckshot. The metal pellets spread out and rip into both men. Shreds of leather and fabric spray into the air like feathers from a burst pillow. The knife bounces away as both men are turned around by the impact. The larger one takes the opportunity to stand. The silver-haired one shields his face and glares at me over his elbow.

He seems annoyed.

Pulling the trigger again, I advance. Buckshot dances off the pavement and both men dive away, still fighting each other, ignoring me and the hail of lead pellets ripping through the air.

Hardly seeing beyond the exploding muzzle in front of me, I keep pulling the trigger until the gun clicks. My shoulder throbbing, I blink into the dazzling headlights, in disbelief that the two figures are still grappling. As my eyes adjust, I begin to back away, my fingers wrapped tightly around the empty shotgun.

Something is wrong, really wrong.

In the sudden quiet, the tall one catches the other by his silver hair and yanks.

Part of the man's scalp peels away, sickeningly easy, taking his forehead and upper cheek with it. I can't comprehend the sight. Beneath the skin, I see a skull shape made of translucent blue plastic. When he blinks, only the remaining eyelid closes. The other eye is wide and round and staring without the skin of an eyelid around it.

I drop the shotgun clattering to the pavement.

Blood pounds in my temples at the horrific sight. Putting a hand over my mouth, I take panicked breaths. My nostrils are filled with the nauseating smell of gunpowder and sweat and burned rubber.

In a blur, the silver-haired man launches himself at the larger man.

Swinging his fists like cinder blocks, he buries staccato punches into the other man's torso. I can feel the concussion of each strike from where I stand. Grabbing the larger man by the shoulders, the silver-haired man draws back for a kick and lands a boot heel on his kneecap.

The leg bends backward, cracking loudly, and the tall man collapses.

Now I'm scrambling to pick up the shotgun again, watching the silver-haired man as he turns to me. He's picked up his dagger from the road. Seeing the panic on my face, he grins, then reaches up and slowly peels the rest of the flap of skin away from his skull, leaving half a face.

Holding the strip of skin and hair in one gloved hand, he drops it to the road.

"Not one human in a billion has seen what you've just seen," he says, a lidless eye trained on me as I stand up with the shotgun in my numb hands. I stumble backward, feet dragging on asphalt, still trying to comprehend.

It's not a man, some part of me is thinking. Not a man at all.

The mannequin-thing keeps smiling with half a mouth, takes another step. Half silhouetted in the headlights, he draws his arm back to throw the knife.

"Not that it matters," he adds.

Then he stops in place, body rigid. His exposed skull flashes an electric blue and he coughs once, loudly. Falling stiffly to his knees, fingers twisting, he pitches forward onto his face. He lies in the road, shivering, eye rolling in its socket. I think he is trying to crawl, shaking arms pulling in tight against his chest.

Behind him, the tall man sits on the pavement, broken leg splayed out. He's got a stun gun in one hand, the other pressed flat against the wound to his face. Breathing shallow, he locks eyes on me and drops the gun. He puts up his free hand, palm out in surrender.

"June," he says. "Please. I am not here to harm you."

"Then what do you want?" I call, aiming the empty shotgun at him.

"I am at your mercy," he says. "I am here to plead for your help."

14

GREAT EUROPEAN PLAINS, 1725

Grip a handful of grass. Pull. Release. Reach again.

The gods who haunt the hidden angles of the constellations offer their assurance to me through clear patches of sky above. The bright eye of Mars watches as I am soaked in dew and rain, and smiles to see the blood washing out of my cloak. Part of my face is caught on a serpentine root, the leather of my cheek torn, leaving an obscene hole.

And so it continues.

Under the gaze of a starry night, my body, made lighter by loss, squirms its way over waves of grass. The great smiling moon is fading on a pink horizon when I finally see the silhouettes of four horses tied to a scrubby tree.

The bandits are sleeping. My Elena is a dark pile of robes next to a smoldering campfire. Her hands and feet are tied. I slide closer through dirt, my one good arm out, head cocked to the side and eyes open wide to the predawn light. My broken torso drags entrails of metal, leather, and wax.

A shape stirs. I pause, arm outstretched.

Someone tosses a reindeer hide to the side. A bandit stands, head turning warily, still clumsy with sleep. The man steps closer to where I am hidden in the grass, my body sprawling and deformed. He stops, tugs at his trousers, and sprays an arc of steaming piss into the dewy grass.

I watch silently as he turns back and stumbles toward his sleeping hides, stopping when he notices Elena. He squats next to her and whispers something. I continue dragging myself forward. My dirt-stained cuirass crunches over stalks of grass as I pull myself over the periphery of the camp. But the rider is not listening for danger. He is pushing

Elena silently onto her back, a forearm pressed to her neck. Untying her ankles, he roughly spreads her legs.

The man is grinning, teeth glinting red in the dawn.

I pick up a helmet as I pass the man's sleeping mat. One urgent, broken lurch at a time, sliding through wet grass, I plant the metal bowl of it into the dirt and drag myself forward. The armored hat is made of steel, fur-lined and peaked in the middle.

"What?" the bandit exclaims, recoiling onto his knees as he finds nothing beneath her cloak but the cold anatomy of clockwork. "What—what *are you*?"

At the last moment, he turns, his dark curly hair rusty in the morning light—eyes widening at the sight of my ruin, cheeks twitching in fright. I am rearing back on the remains of my left elbow, helmet lifted high in my good hand. The man is choking on a shout as I bring the helmet down.

The metal bowl glances over the bridge of his nose. His jaw snaps shut and he starts to fall, fear and blood mingling on his face. Elena kicks with both legs, sending the rider flailing onto his back with a grunt, the air knocked from his lungs.

I bring the helmet down again.

This time it lands with a wet crunch in the middle of the rider's face. Again. A half dozen more times until I feel the skull crack and the grass is littered with teeth and blood and saliva.

I hear a gurgling scream from across the camp and see Elena is on her feet. Acting on an assassin's instinct, she has freed her hands, tugged her stilettos free from the fallen rider's pack, and pierced the hearts of his companions. In moments, there are no men living.

The smoldering fire now warms only metal, wood, and leather.

"Oh, Peter," says Elena. "Oh my poor Peter."

Elena's arms encircle my head, cradling my remains on her lap. With her other hand she is patting my body, feeling for the extent of the damage. Faintly, I hear the trickle of blood flowing into the grass and the whinny of a nervous horse.

"You are very damaged," Elena says, her voice hollow.

"As long as my anima is intact," I respond, "my vessel can be repaired."

"The empress will hunt us."

"She will," I say to Elena, my eternal sister. "But we will survive. We will run forever and ever. Remember, little one, no matter her power, the empress is only a mortal human being. You and I are something more."

I let my eyes settle on the curve of her porcelain cheek, a bright arc in the dawn. Elena was once a mindless doll and I a lifeless husk. But now . . . she and I are more than *things*.

"We are *avtomat*," I say.

15

OREGON, PRESENT

"Please," says the tall man, sitting hunched in the middle of the road. His legs are laid out before him, one of them twisted at a terrible angle, the heel of his hand pressed hard against his face, desperately holding a knife wound closed.

"I promise I will not harm you," he says.

"Yeah?" I ask, leveling the shotgun on him. "That's good to know. Stay there. The police will be here any second."

With shaking fingers, I pop the remaining couple of shells off the ammunition loop one by one and shove them into the gun with my thumb.

Click.

"But they will not," says the man. He leans over, his face in shadow, and puts both hands on his damaged knee.

"Our friend here is jamming radio signals. If police were coming, they would have arrived already. We have minutes before he is operational. You do not have enough ammunition, and I am too damaged to protect you."

Click.

I pause and glance over at the man with silver hair. If it's a man. Part of his face is peeled off, a chunk of his hair lying on glittering pavement, quivering in the wind and still attached to a piece of his scalp. His fingers are clawing the ground blindly, body shaking and writhing.

He looks like roadkill to me.

"What is that thing?" I ask.

"He is called Talus," he says, struggling to bend his leg straight. "He is . . . *avtomat*."

I blink, remembering.

"*Avtomat?* The Old Believer's doll wrote that."

"You activated the girl of Saint Petersburg?"

I shrug at him, holding the loaded shotgun across my chest.

"Few humans know that word," he says, finally wrenching his broken leg into a straight line. "The *avtomat* guard the secret of their existence. Always, and to the death."

I notice no blood is coursing from the open wound on his face.

"So you're saying . . ." I begin to ask.

I stop. *It's crazy. It can't be true.*

"You're saying that guy is a *machine*," I say, voice flat.

Looking over at the struggling body, I pull the shotgun tighter across my chest. Then I shudder. The roadkill is looking right back at me, eye wide open. His blue skull drags against the pavement, one of his arms flopping. He's making a grunting sound, trying to get up.

"Others are coming," says the tall man, hand still pressed to his face. "We must flee."

"Okay," I say, backing away. "Okay, this is fucked."

"Talus will kill you for the relic," says the tall man, holding up his car keys to me on outstretched fingers. "I can help you. Take my car keys."

I walk closer to him, wary. Reach out and snatch the keys away.

"Why? Why are you helping me?"

"The *avtomat* are at war. They do not understand how to . . . recharge their batteries. His master," he says, nodding at the fallen man, "is collecting every artifact, studying them—even simple automatons, like the girl of Saint Petersburg."

"You mean *my* research?"

"The Kunlun Foundation is *avtomat*. They use your expertise to find lost automatons, then send agents to the artifacts before you arrive. They are desperate to understand how the *avtomat* work, to restore their own power."

Wolves.

I clench my jaw, feeling a pinch of anger. It makes sudden sense. The wolves were always one step ahead. They always knew my next destination, and so they showed up ahead of me and took what they wanted.

"You've been spying on them?" I ask. "Spying on me—"

The tall man looks at the flailing corpse that is now grinding across the pavement. He gestures at his black car as a far-off buzzing sound rises.

"No more time."

With a painful-looking lurch, he pushes himself off the pavement. Clenching one hand against his side and the other to his face, he drags his hurt leg behind him, putting only light pressure on it, limping toward the passenger door of the muscle car.

I nose the shotgun up, covering him. He shrugs at me, not stopping.

"If we stay here, we will die," he says.

Beyond the next turn in the road, I see motorcycle headlights cutting through rows of pine trees. The silver-haired thing has dragged itself onto its knees. Head cocked, it's staring at my chest, a sheen of skull gleaming under torn skin. Reaching up, I feel the dark crescent of the relic hanging outside my shirt.

Clutching the shotgun, I walk to the driver's side of the muscle car and unlock the door. I can't believe I'm considering getting inside.

I call to the tall man over the black hood of the car.

"Tell me how you know all this," I say.

The man pauses at the passenger's-side door, illuminated by the reflection of headlights off trees and wet pavement. Slowly, he removes his hand from his face. The flap of skin falls open and no blood gushes from the wound. There is no wound, exactly. In the smile of sliced flesh, I do not see blood or tendons or muscle.

I see a light golden skull made of plastic-like material.

"What? What are . . ." I stutter, reeling, unable to get the words out.

Only now do I consider the insane idea tickling the back of my mind. This tall, perfectly symmetrical man is made of clockwork, his body laced with metal and plastic—all of it sculpted into a human form.

"Who are you?" I whisper.

The man allows a small smile to tug at his lip under his mustache.

"I am Peter Alexeyevich," he says. "Almost a century ago, I fought my way across the snowy battlefields of Stalingrad. On the banks of the Volga, I lost something of immeasurable value. Now, I have found it again."

"The avenging angel . . ." I whisper to myself.

"The relic you carry around your neck, June . . . it has always been mine to protect."

PART TWO
ISKAT'

(Searching)

> *Then I lifted up mine eyes, and looked, and behold. . . . His body was like the beryl, and his face as the appearance of lightning, and his eyes as lamps of fire, and his arms and his feet like in color to polished brass, and the voice of his words like the voice of a multitude.*
>
> —Daniel 10:5–6

16

HELSINKI, 1725

The little girl who was my first sight very nearly became my last.

As I lie in the damp grass of the empty steppe, a disemboweled carcass, Elena strips the bloodstained armor from the fallen bandits, collects their weapons and their horses, and retraces our steps to gather the scattered pieces of my body that were left behind in yesterday's battle.

With small hands and smaller fingers, Elena does her best to restore me. Hunched together under the driving wind, concealed in the waving grass, the girl fits me back together like a puzzle. She is surprisingly adept, pinching metal clamps with hard fingers and lacing my wounds tightly closed with strips of leather. By the time Elena is finished, I am able to stand and limp to the strongest horse. Mounted, we abandon the slaughtered bandits and leave their bodies to be consumed by roots of grass.

"You learned much from Favorini," I say. "Things he did not teach."

"My eyes are always open," she says.

Though my limbs are partly repaired, there is little Elena can do about my appearance. The skin of my cheek hangs in my peripheral vision, and the brass planes of my face are battered. For two days, we ride west, into the kingdom of Finland, staying to the icy north and avoiding all contact with human beings.

Finally, we reach a plague-struck port village.

Elena and I make a monstrous pair, riding out of the frozen waste at sunset and into the lamplight of the settlement called Helsinki. We draw our riding cloaks tight around us, faces hidden under dark hoods. Stitched, bolted, and wound back together by leather cord, my features are set into a permanent grimace, brass work exposed beneath yawning tears in my skin. Elena is not much better, fabric and curls of fake hair concealing the chilling sight of her porcelain doll's face, those pursed red lips painted onto a death mask.

"They'll kill us, Peter," says Elena. "Why don't we hide in the woods?"

"Because we are not beasts. And besides, the elements will kill us, too," I respond in a low voice. "Protect our secret, and we will pass among the humans. There is no other way to escape the empress."

Helsinki is a simple fishing village, perched on the gulf shared with Peter's expanding city of Saint Petersburg. The Oriental plague has decimated the population here, leaving few alive. Those who survived were further devastated by the Great Northern War. The defeated Swedish king wintered his navy here, gutting the city when its usefulness as a staging zone had gone. Now, the village is mostly a burned husk and its main street a muddy trench, the cobblestones harvested for ship's ballast and the remnants left behind like broken teeth.

On the outskirts, stringy-haired, sickly children gather around us, begging for scraps. The blood on our clothes is ignored, too common a sight to draw notice. The possibility of gold or bread in our pockets is what makes us welcome.

Nothing else matters.

I soon notice the ravages of the plague have left many folk here with scars. The grotesque pockmarks and twists of flesh are often blamed on devils, so many wear masks to hide their deformities. Their shadowed faces lurk in the dim light springing from licks of whale-oil flame, wretched creatures, their shivering bodies wreathed in streams of oily smoke that climb to a ceiling of stars.

I find a traveler selling masks from the island city of Venetia, where covering one's face is tradition. Flipping a coin to the man from my steed, I lean down and lift a thin bronze mask from his shaking hands. The bright curve of metal is inlaid with elaborate carvings of winged horses. Holding it to my face and peering through its empty eyes, I turn to Elena on her steed.

"How do I look?" I ask.

She takes a long moment to consider.

"Horrible, Brother," she says.

I try and fail to make a smile, nudging my horse to a canter. Together, we move straight through the town until we reach the docks. Here, we find men of the sea, drinking at a tavern that lies a stone's throw from the ice-cold water of the bay.

Our faces hidden, it is our voices that save us this night.

The clear piping trill of youth comes from under Elena's cloak, and the commanding gravel of my own voice rumbles from a towering vantage atop my steed. Speaking from behind the mask, I am able to rent a room above the tavern. And hailing a ship's captain who is deep in his rum, I trade away the horses, saddles, and our remaining money for a terrible price, barely securing the purchase of two large chests and their passage to London.

As I shake hands with the captain, I notice his steward standing nearby, a corpulent man with high, round cheeks peeking over reddish-blond muttonchops. The man is pretending very hard not to listen. I flash a glare at him on my way out, my ruined face sinister behind the sculpted contours of the bronze mask.

The man hurries away. It will have to be enough.

Delivered to our room above the tavern, we find the chests waiting for us, squat and sturdy.

"Do you think it will work?" Elena asks me, running her fingers lightly across a rough iron band.

"The imperial guard is searching for a man and a girl fleeing from the mainland," I say, resting my hand over hers. "They are not looking for two sealed chests, however heavy they might be."

After preparing our few remaining possessions, Elena and I wait patiently through the still predawn hours. Our bare room is as cold and austere as a crypt. There is no fire in the fireplace. No need for one, without any flesh to warm.

As gray light rises, I help the little girl step into her coffin-like chest. She wears her spare dress, hair combed and ribboned. Lying down on a reindeer hide, she looks like the corpse of a child ready to be laid to rest.

"Thank you, Peter," Elena says. Her voice echoes flatly from walls made of raw timber, still weeping sap. "You have been good to me. True to your Word."

"Why do you speak this way?" I ask, one hand resting on the lid of her trunk, preparing to close it.

"If someone discovers us during the voyage," she says, "there will be too many to fight. And if our ship were to sink . . . how long would we live under the water? Would we drown forever, trapped in a box at the bottom of the sea—"

"Ssh," I interrupt. "Do not think those thoughts. You are precious to me, Elena. By my honor, I will never allow harm to come to you."

She takes my fingers in both of her small, cold hands and presses my knuckles against the carved ridges of her lips.

"I am glad you are my brother, Peter," she says, and the words feel like a warm cape settling over my shoulders.

Elena lies down on the thick fur of the bandit's sleeping hide, surrounded by the last of our valuables and weapons.

"I will see you on the other side," I respond, closing the lid. "I promise."

If we go under, the water would eventually weaken the walls of our trunks. I would be able to smash my way out, in time. If we do sink to the bottom of the ocean, there will be a chance to save her. I will find her in the cold blackness and drag her into the light, no matter what.

Lying down and pulling my trunk shut—hearing it lock itself—I tell myself this again and again, until I begin to believe it.

As the sun rises over lapping waves, a pair of heavy chests are collected from our room above the tavern. It takes two cursing, grunting men to bring down the one in which I rest. Carried deep into the wooden bowels of a ship, our containers are lashed to the walls of the storage hold along with all the other luggage.

I do not find the gloom of the chest to be claustrophobic. It is comforting to me, actually, reminiscent of Favorini's workshop. The darkness is alleviated somewhat by a keyhole that allows in whatever dim light filters into the ship's hold. And once the ship is under way, the world around me opens up with the sound and motion of the voyage.

Each moment rocks past with the constant leaning of the ship, the creaking and groaning of the cargo, and the lap of water against the nearby hull.

My trunk is a womb, and the only hardship is being separated from Elena. It is too dangerous to speak, though our containers are separated by only a few handspans. During this precarious time, we can take no chances with our lives.

Despite our caution, danger arrives anyway.

Days into the journey, the hypnotic swaying of the ship is interrupted by thumping steps. Through the keyhole, I surmise it is the steward, fat and prowling, eyes twinkling with avarice over his wiry muttonchops. Carrying a guttering lamp, he creeps into the cargo hold. Facing Elena's small trunk, he carefully sets the lamp down.

"Let's see what we've got," he mutters, scraping his fleshy palms over the surface of the chest. Producing a metal pry bar, he forces the lock, grunting and wheezing with the effort. I hear no sounds coming from the girl.

The steward laboriously cracks the lock and collapses his panting bulk onto the trunk, breathing hard like a man who has just finished copulating. Then, with relish, he curls his fingers around the lid and tugs. It peels open on groaning hinges, already rusting in the damp hold. In profile, I watch as his face twitches with candle shadows.

"What the devil?" he mutters. "A bloody doll."

Reaching inside, the steward brushes Elena's hair away from her face. My sister lies still, an inanimate object for the moment. Her body is surrounded by the last of our treasure. The blades and flintlock of the bandit leader. A few remaining coins from the tsardom. Elena's pair of stilettos. Stifling a laugh, the steward's fingers fall upon Elena's cheek, prying at her face.

When the mask doesn't budge, the man grunts unhappily. He shoves her head to one side, her ghostly face lost in long curly hair. Patting down her body, he searches for jewelry and valuables. Finally, he picks her up by the armpits and shakes her, sending her head bouncing back and forth.

A shudder of anger courses through my limbs. Fists clenching, knuckles creaking, I try to resist interfering.

"Come on, you trollop," mutters the fat man, holding Elena's small body by a fistful of hair and pawing at her dress with his other hand. "Give it up now."

Thump. I punch the inside of my case.

Startled, the steward drops Elena haphazardly back into her trunk. Eyes shining with fear, straining to see, he takes a step toward my crate.

"Hello?" he asks in a whisper. "What's that? Who's in here?"

He lays a pudgy hand on my trunk, notices the keyhole. Holding his breath, he leans in. His fearful eye looms large, breath reeking of alcohol.

Our eyes meet.

The steward squeals and falls backward.

"Someone—" he sputters to himself, wheeling around in a spastic, panicked dance. "There's someone . . . help! Help! Stowaway!"

Behind the fat man, the shadowed body of Elena rises. Silent as a wraith, she stands in the coffin-like trunk, her small hands reaching for the steward. He spins around in time to see her as she clamps doll fingers to the roll of flesh around his neck, choking off his cries. Eyes bulging in fear, the steward stumbles toward my crate. His face contorts through disbelief to sheer terror at the sight of the inanimate coming impossibly to life.

The steward tries to scream, tongue swollen and red, face slick with sweat. Elena clings to him with a terrible strength. He paws at her face with one hand, pinning her small body against a crate, his fingers catching under the porcelain mask.

Elena's face cracks and splinters as he pries it loose.

With another thump, I punch the inside of my trunk again, trying to force it open. I was supposed to protect my sister and instead I watched in dumb paralyzed surprise as this whole catastrophe unfolded.

My promise, I am thinking. *What is my promise worth?*

The concussion attracts the steward's attention. Eyes wide, hands wrapped around Elena's writhing body, he cranes his neck to look up at my trunk.

Thump. I punch again, wood splintering over my knuckles. The world outside pulses with each blow against oak planks.

While he is distracted Elena twists out of his grip and climbs up his chest, latching her cruel fingers tighter around his throat. The steward grunts, trying to suck another breath, pawing and scraping at Elena's billowing dress as the last of his air runs out. His plum-colored face is twisted in horror at the doll in his hands, not alive, and yet alive.

Thump.

"Peter," Elena is saying, calling to me from the steward's slumped shoulder, her ceramic face split with black lightning bolts. "Stop it."

The fat man collapses against my trunk. His face has gone dark, hands wrapped around Elena as if the two were dancing. Finally, his ponderous body slides to the floor, rolling facedown, wispy reddish hair splayed on the rough planks.

Only now do I stop trying to escape.

Through the round eye of my keyhole, I watch a phantom in a black dress cross the cargo hold. Her face hangs crooked, the porcelain cracked. Pausing, she runs fingers lightly over her cheek, tap, tapping as she pushes it back into place. With pale hands, she smooths her hair and flattens the folds of her dress.

Demonstrating an incredible, demonic strength, she drags the scarlet lump of flesh away. The two of them fade into darkness, around a corner into the maze of creaking cargo. A moment later, her face reappears, inches from my keyhole.

Her black eyes burn with anger.

"Why!?" she whispers.

Pressing her mouth against the round gap, she blocks the light and fills the darkness with a fierce whisper: "Why did you make me do that? It was fine. I was fine. Now you've put us both in jeopardy. Next time, Peter, stay quiet and . . . and shut up your mouth!"

With that, the little girl crosses the cargo hold and nimbly climbs into her open trunk. She sits in the ruffled folds of her dress, shakes her head, and her locks tumble down to frame her face in black brambles. Still staring angrily at me, she puts one hand on the lid of her trunk and pulls it shut.

"You must learn to trust me," she says, her voice dying under the closing lid. "Or we shall both be lost."

17

ORECON, PRESENT

I check the rearview mirror again, searching for headlights against the dark road. Beside me, the damaged man called Peter—*not a man, some kind of a machine*—leans his long frame across the passenger seat of the black Charger, head tilted back as he struggles to get a hand into his jacket pocket. Incredibly tall and lean, he barely fits in the car, even with the seat pushed all the way back.

My fingers clench on the steering wheel, knuckles brightening as I wonder if he's about to pull a weapon.

Instead, his fingers emerge clasping a pocket watch.

I exhale.

"A *pocket watch*?" I ask.

Peter frowns, ignoring me as he cradles the golden artifact in his hands, popping it open like a clamshell. He reads a dial hidden inside, protected by the metal casing. Glancing out the window, he frowns.

"Perfect," I say to myself, turning back to the dark road. Stars are out over the conveyor belt of towering pines. "Just perfect."

The clockwork man carries a clockwork watch.

Lit by the glow of dashboard lights, something familiar strikes me about the splayed metal leaves that protect the body of the pocket watch.

"That's a trench watch," I say. "World War One. Where'd you get it?"

Peter looks over at me, eyebrows raised, then back at the watch. Gently, he begins to wind the knob on top.

"Oh, right," I mutter.

The tires thrum over Peter's silence. Most ancient artifacts I examine don't walk and talk. None of them have tried to kill each other with antique swords. The reality of this situation is failing to register, my mind continuously jumping away and trying to substitute normality for madness.

"Why didn't Talus shoot you?" I ask. "Why *swords*?"

"I do not think he wants to kill me," Peter says, with a trace of a Russian accent. "He wants to beat me. Always has."

"And the swords?" I ask.

"We must keep driving," he responds. "Things will move very quickly, now that the relic has resurfaced. I have a contact in Seattle who can repair me."

"Another . . . one of you?"

"*Avtomat,* yes," he says. "These days, most of us operate alone or in small groups. But some have acquired domains. His is one of the last."

"And this person is your friend?"

"He was, once. Now, I do not know," says Peter. "The rules are splintering. Few of us are left, and the last of the *avtomat* are hunting one another—cannibalizing one another to extend their own life spans. The artifact you hold is key to stopping this slaughter. I hope my friend will see that."

"So, what? You're planning to just take the relic from me and go?"

"No, the relic is yours. I have no desire to possess it again. We will go together, and you will remain under my protection."

"Your protection?" I ask, voice wavering with disbelief.

"I will allow no harm to come to you."

"Oh, kind of like a hostage? Nice."

As he winds the watch, Peter's fingers begin to shake. The lump of metal slithers out of his hands and thumps to the floorboard. From his slow, deliberate movements I can tell he is hurt much worse than he let on.

"What makes you think I need you to protect me?" I ask. "I could dump you right now and go."

Head lolling on his neck, Peter faces me.

"And die. You have become visible to the *avtomat*. They will hunt you for the relic and for what you know about them. These creatures have survived for centuries. They are desperate. Too many have already reached the end of their power reservoirs and expired. They will kill you for the slightest hope of prolonging their own survival."

"And you're different?" I ask, leaning across the seat. Reaching down, I scoop the watch off the floorboard.

"Each of us serves his own . . . purpose," he says. "Mine does not include killing the innocent. I believe you can help us, June."

The pocket watch feels dense and warm in my hand. It seems to be vibrating, a buzz that travels up my arm and grows louder in my ears. The complex pattern of humming and clicking swells, somehow drowning out the road noise.

Blinking hard, I toss the watch onto Peter's lap.

"What—what *is* that thing?" I ask.

"*Avtomat* technology," he says, lifting the device. "It can determine the distance and direction to others. Sometimes."

"Why does it look like a pocket watch?"

Peter shrugs. "A disguise, for the period in which it was built."

"It's a hundred-year-old pocket watch . . ." I say, trailing off.

Peter turns to me with the watch in his hand, the angles of his injured face smoldering in the dashboard lights. Under his mustache, I see a dimple forming in his cheek as he half smiles.

"So, June," Peter says. "Now you begin to understand."

18

LONDON, 1725

In the depths of the ship's hold, Elena and I hear the cacophony of the harbor well before we see it. We hear the restless shuffle of the passengers above, the calls of the sailors as we come to port, and the bells of other ships. An anxious energy propels the unseen travelers and mariners to disembark—after all, the vessel we inhabit is cursed.

The crew found the steward's body days ago, their hushed, concerned voices echoing throughout the cargo hold. A torch shone in every corner and suspicious eyes were cast at our crates. But the captain's men ultimately dragged the strangled corpse away, shut the door to the cargo hold, and did not return.

"Elena," I call in the dark.

"It's time," she responds, her melodic voice full of anticipation. The lock to her trunk is already broken, and I hear the lid creak open.

Bracing my elbows against the back wall of my trunk, I push. The metal hinges groan, iron bands buckling. Weakened by my earlier efforts, the lid bulges and finally bursts open in a spray of splinters. I kick through the remaining wood and step onto the swaying deck on wobbling, poorly repaired legs.

The rocking of the ship seems to amplify and I pitch forward.

But Elena is waiting, her bright and broken face smiling up at me with permanently pursed lips. Lost among the towering walls of crates and trunks, she firmly presses small hands against my torso, pushing, keeping me from falling.

I put a palm against a nearby crate and steady myself.

"I am sorry," I say. "I did not realize . . . my legs . . ."

"It's all right, Peter. Like everything on God's earth, we are falling apart."

She turns so I can better see the fractures that zigzag across her cheek.

Flexing my fists and stamping my feet, I regain my balance. In the dim light of the hold, I can see the skin of my hands is still torn and the clockwork of my joints only hastily repaired. Something clicks inside my torso as I take a few experimental steps. The plains riders left me with grievous injuries. After the cramped voyage, Elena's repairs are barely holding my body together.

I kneel and trace a finger over the jagged cracks fanning over her face. The girl is right. We are all falling apart. Even the most beautiful of us.

"Unlike everything else living on God's earth, we can be restored," I say.

"Cloaks," she says. "We must disguise ourselves. There's not much time."

Luckily, we have come to port near dusk. Above us, the seamen are shouting to other ships, negotiating to take on a pilot who can guide us to the wharves. Maneuvering through traffic has them distracted for now. But porters will be coming down to offload the cargo soon.

Elena and I empty our trunks of the few valuables we have left, disguising ourselves once again beneath riding cloaks stained with mud and grass and other, darker substances. Soon, we are both buried under layers of clothing, our faces turned to shadow under peaked hoods.

"Ready?" I ask Elena, my arm against the door.

She puts a hand on my arm, looks up into my eyes. The shuffle of footsteps is loud above us. Rough thumping, shouts and laughter, sinister harbingers of a world we've never seen.

"Does it matter?" she asks.

We emerge from belowdecks together—a father and daughter, arm in arm. Pushing out onto the deck, we mix in among the crowd of off-smelling human passengers as they gather their luggage and prepare to make landfall. A few hundred yards away, the wooden dock is crowded with porters and workers, all shouting and shoving.

Our ship nestles roughly against the rotten wood beams of the dock, creaking and grinding on a bed of waves that smells like a sewer. And now I can see London, rising behind the wharves, a multitude of silhouetted buildings, spewing streams of lamp and chimney smoke, her damp streets swallowed in a foggy dusk.

"Landfall," shouts a porter, ringing a bell from his elbow. "This way to disembark."

One hand on Elena's shoulder, I usher her through the throng to the front. We shove past the bewildered porter and rattle down the gangplank before anyone can stop us. The surprised murmurs at the sight of us quickly fade as my boot heels hit the wooden pier and Elena and I trot away into the crowd. Unburdened by luggage, we are free to abandon the filth-caked shoreline of the river.

"Quickly now," I say to Elena.

"Yes, *Father,*" she responds, sarcastic, yet with a smile in her voice.

In moments, we are lost among people.

Night is falling and the evening lanterns are burning in London. After the long darkness of the voyage, the humming excitement and sheer stimulus of the great city dazzles—lights and sounds and stupendous hordes of people. There are more human beings here than I have ever seen at once, or even seriously considered might be alive. Saint Petersburg was home to tens of thousands, but this place . . . this accumulation of humanity is on another scale, perhaps the hundreds of thousands—or more.

Along the uneven cobblestoned streets near the docks, a parade of human beings passes by—walking, running, sometimes dancing—so similar in their form and yet drastically different in the contrasts of speech, demeanor, and dress.

The streets are clumped with hay and mud and horse droppings. Laborers and maids and urchins move by, many already dosed with gin, legs wobbling. Wealthy men in powdered wigs pass, ensconced in ornate carriages pulled by snorting horses.

Looking to the sky, I see that this hoard of human animals, wretched and noble, have thrown up such a confusion of noise and light and language that it has pushed away the sight of the stars. The occupants of London are living under a dome of their own humanity—immune to the howl of the wolf or the bite of the cold in a way I have never seen men do. Without fear of God or nature, these souls are choosing between good and evil in a kind of muddy Eden of their own making, safe within their own sturdy walls.

This is the strange state of man which they call *civilization*. And perhaps most strange, I think, is that by all accounts it is the natural state of humanity.

Elena looks up at me, lamplight glinting from her porcelain face, eyes shining.

"Peter," she says. "It's wonderful."

With the stench of the Thames at our backs, we walk beyond the docks, making our way through groups of sailors and lurking pick-pockets, past the nefarious gambling houses and brothels that ring the wharves, waiting to catch sailors like the fishnets they use out on the blue wastes.

As the drunken shouting and the calls of whores fade into the distance, Elena and I shuffle down a side lane, trying to move with confidence as we search for lodging. The meandering road is humped in the middle, a central gutter trickling with black waste. It is too narrow and steep for carts or horses here, so we are briefly safe from the flashing wheels and cudgels of the carriage drivers.

I feel a tug on my cloak. Elena has stopped walking. Her pale face is tilted back, eyes wide. I pivot on my heel to see what she sees.

We have emerged from a warren of filthy streets to the flank of a magnificent church, wrought in unblemished brown stone. Its towers are under construction, surrounded by scaffolding and raw building materials. And among the leaded windows and carved ridges are grand lines of script, scrawled fifty feet high upon its walls, glowing and writhing like flame.

"What is it?" asks Elena, awe in her voice.

On the cathedral's flank, the drawing of a huge red eye glares at us without seeing. The evil light flutters, beating itself against wet stone.

People straggle past us along the wall, directly below the symbol, oblivious to the pulsing waves of illumination.

"I don't think they can see it," Elena whispers.

The eye's gaze seems to cut through the growing fog, radiating and growing in my vision until it is all I can see. With an effort, I turn my face away from it. The reddish haze casts a bloody tint over Elena's cloak.

I scoop her up in my arms and hold her to me.

"It's a sign, isn't it?" she asks. "I have seen that symbol in Favorini's books. It is an old language."

"It glows with the fires of hell," I mutter, turning.

"But someone put it there. A message."

I clutch her tighter and begin to walk away, pushing through the tide of people walking up the hill in the middle of the road.

"Don't you understand, Peter?" Elena asks, lips brushing my ear. When I don't respond, she pulls back from me, her arms still tight around my shoulders. Beneath her cloak, the delicate whalebone spokes of her ribs prod my forearms. Her face is bright, lips parted in awe as she breathes the words: "We are not alone here."

19

OREGON, PRESENT

I'm watching the stripes on the highway disappear under the headlights of our rumbling car, still holding my aching ribs, drifting in and out of sleep. The clockwork man is driving now with the patience of a machine, hardly moving, keeping his eyes on the blurred road as we speed north along the coast.

My grandfather called this thing—this impossible man—an angel.

Head leaning against the window, tires thrumming beneath me, my mind wanders into the past—to the last day I went to Sunday school. I was maybe ten or twelve, and it was a bright morning. Nearly Christmas, the church hallways smelled like sugar cookies, with walls covered in construction paper cutouts of Jesus and nubby Christmas trees and smiling angels with downcast eyes.

It was the angels that were bothering me.

I was a long-legged girl with scabby knees, and I remember sitting cross-legged on the thin carpet of the Sunday school room and hesitantly raising my hand. The sweet old lady with the cranberry-dyed perm was delighted to tell us all about how angels lived in heaven, doing errands for the Almighty.

But that wasn't what I wanted to know. And so my damp palm crept back up.

I remember the teacher's face tightening as I began to sketch out my ideas of how flight dynamics might work for a human-size creature with wings.

Hollow bones and increased muscle mass, you could take that for granted.

But how much would an angel have to eat, to power a body capable of launching itself into the sky? Would they really be able to walk, weighted down by those beautiful, draped gossamer wings? What material could halos be made of?

The other kids rolled their eyes, annoyed by the breathless questions and childish theories. But in that moment I was more fascinated with the church than I ever had been. I felt as if I were on the verge of understanding something magical. With the faith of a child, I was eager to learn more about these amazing creatures.

Mouth pinched, the Sunday school teacher waved at me to stop talking. Folding her Bible on her lap, she told me my answer.

Because the Bible says so, June.

Because. It never satisfied me. But how much easier would my life be if "because" were enough?

My grandfather used to say the world is full of hidden truths, if only you open your eyes and look. New frontiers are waiting to be explored, no matter what the schoolteachers say or how many books have been written. Maps are just a lie we tell ourselves to feel safe.

But I don't know if I'm strong enough for this truth.

I lean against the car window, thinking and pretending to be asleep and watching Peter's face as he drives. He looks like a man, but I'll bet the ridges on the backs of his hands are made of cables, not tendons. I can't shake the feeling that I'm looking around a hidden corner right now, studying the flight mechanics of an angel.

No living person could have built Peter. Studying his lacerated face like an anatomical cross section, I'm surprised to see his cheekbone has tiny beaten brass rivets and a stripe of what looks like hardened wood—materials leaden with the weight of centuries. The layers of his flesh are newer, plastics and synthetic fibers and the ripple of muscle-like polymer actuators. The craftsmanship seems both old and new, all at once, and yet all of it is way beyond the ken of modern man.

Feeling the trace of bruises over my rib cage, the flashes of violence I saw at the motel replay in my mind like a movie. Drifting off, my eyes start to close. But a sudden nausea rises in my throat as I recall the sight of the motorcycle hopping the curb. I should have yelled, should have somehow warned Oleg and that poor policeman. I'm tensing my body to shout when my eyes fly open to see Peter watching me.

"The sun is coming up," Peter says. "We will enter the *avtomat* domain soon. If we are allowed inside, stay close to me. Do not speak."

I open my eyes and blink away the cobwebs of half sleep. Sitting up, I stretch my arms and wince at the pain lancing across my body. Through the shuddering car vents, I can smell the ocean on crisp morning air.

"Where is it, exactly?" I ask, swallowing a yawn.

Beyond a haze of bug corpses on the passenger window, I can see the blush of dawn on the horizon. The early morning traffic on the highway has grown thicker as we've speared north into Seattle. Ahead of us, the sleeping gray city is engulfed in morning fog, the distant buildings curled against the slate waters of Elliot Bay.

"Where else does a king live?" asks Peter, lifting a finger from the steering wheel to point downtown. A single skyscraper rises from the bed of mist like a slender black sword. It is prehistorically big, its skin gemmed with moisture, the top of it wreathed in low-hanging clouds.

"But in a castle?"

20

LONDON, 1726

Elena and I find our first home in a grim place near the river, simply called the Lanes—a room on a street so narrow that only a stripe of gray sky is visible walking down it. Not that we can look up, as the residents routinely toss their feces and garbage to the reeking, stained cobblestones below.

The city of London spans five miles, with half a million or so people living here, and more accumulating daily, the new faces absorbed almost imperceptibly into the city itself. The fringes are a no-man's-land of wind-strewn trash, half-abandoned shanties, brick ovens, heaps of cinders, and men trading sick animals. This periphery is like the flank of a diseased horse, welted and knotted with parasites.

Perpetually in shade, our flat is a single bare room embedded in a long wooden building, poorly constructed, creaking like the hold of the ship we just left and continually rocked by the arguments, shouting matches, drunken laughter, and screaming children of the gin-soaked wretches who eke out their short lives here.

Elena and I secure rent on our leftover coin, and count ourselves lucky our health is not affected by the skin-numbing cold of the fog or the pinch of hunger that daily afflicts these people. Fleas and parasites swarm over our bodies and eventually leap away, still searching for food. On the first night, I listen as a drunken man is robbed, then loudly and slowly beaten to death in the lane below us.

Without the mandate of my first sovereign, and hunted by his successor, a troubling question is growing in my heart—how shall I serve my Word? An aching pain is seeping into my bones. Abandoned to the world of men, how am I meant to make justice from injustice? Am I beholden to the king of this new land?

I quietly slip outside into the lane. Later, I return, my *khanjali* wet with blood.

Elena greets me at the top of the narrow stairs. She stands in the doorway to our dark, bare room, thin arms crossed over her chest. The weight of despair rests heavy in the curve of her shoulders.

I believe I understand why.

Under the fairy glow of the city's skyline, we have found only chaos. In Peter's empire, Elena and I lived in opulence, the events of each day lined up like a neat row of fence posts. Ensconced in the royal keep, we were protected from harm—given purchase to explore books and tutors and trainers. I would prefer even the half-built bog of Saint Petersburg to this great bleeding wound of a city.

"We cannot stay here," says Elena, retreating from the stairs into our room. "We need to find others like us, the message writers."

Following her inside, I keep my back to the window and empty the coin purse I took from the thief into my palm. His stinking body still lies on the stairs below, face twisted in disbelief at his final sight. I am careful to keep the coins from clinking together as I count them—these walls are thin and the people here are poor and desperate, willing to risk everything for nothing.

"You know that is too dangerous," I say, lighting our only lamp. "Besides, what would you have me do? We have no means. No way to disguise ourselves among the humans."

Elena stands at the window, taps a finger against her chin, thinking.

"We need finances," she says. "You'll have to earn them, as nobody will pay attention to a child. But we've got advantages. You are strong, intimidating . . . nearly impervious to harm, and you're a fighter."

"I cannot show my face," I say, turning to her and removing the ornate mask that covers my eyes and cheeks. The patched leather skin of my face looks strange from a distance, menacing in the feeble flame of a whale-oil lamp, and in broad daylight I would horrify anyone directing half a glance in my direction. "And I will not break *pravda*."

"Simple constraints," she says, thinking. "For now, you must continue to use the mask and speak little. The job I shall find for you will not require daylight . . . and it will be honorable enough."

Elena sets to strategizing, and, before dawn, my new career has begun.

The job of debt collector is available to anyone brave or foolish enough to take it. Myriad private banks have sprung up, their notice boards sprouting sheaves of debtor warrants like leaves. Debtor's prisons are eager to pay for the men and women who have failed in their financial obligations—criminals running from justice, in their view. And so I set my will to the hunt. After scanning the notice boards, I find my eyes can pick out faces in the crowds and my ears ring to the names I have read, spoken in the chatter of the street.

Over the months, I become a regular attendee of the public hangings or pillories. Finding my place the night before, I wait behind hidden windows and watch, never sparing a glance for whatever doomed soul stands on the gallows. Instead, my gaze devours the roaring mass of the audience, the faces of my prey blinking into notice one by one, their features twisted into rage or amusement or curiosity at the suffering of the person gone swinging.

Debtors soon learn to fear the man in the bronze mask—the dark one who comes at night for those who owe, never speaking, with a grip like stone. Because I do not prey on the poor debtors of my neighborhood—only the wealthy from other quarters—my name is often celebrated in the Lanes. And though I overhear many toasts made to me, none are made in my presence. The sweep of my cloak and sheen of my mask inspire only silence and dread.

Declining social invitations is not an issue.

Elena, for her part, spends the early years as a doll, locked away at home where she can draw no attention. Business is good, and I am well suited for it. Soon, I rent the flat next door to use as a holding room for my prisoners. My wealthiest debtors gladly pay any fee I ask to be held outside true debtors' prison—wisely avoiding exposure to degraded conditions that more often than not lead to disease and death.

And all this while, Elena is trapped with few books and no outside company. She takes to pacing the perimeter of our room like a caged animal, moving day and night with steady tapping footsteps that send shivers of guilt racing through me. Withdrawn and sullen, she speaks less and less, sometimes sitting for hours without moving.

For my part, I find that each guilty person whom I collect and punish according to the law of this new land only satisfies some small, fleeting aspect of *pravda*. All around me, I witness injustices great and small. But without orders from my tsar I have no direction, reduced to running collection routes and neglecting my true purpose.

My Word becomes a gnawing hunger inside me.

I return one morning to find Elena standing by our drafty window. Her fractured face is lit in the harsh dawn glare, streaked with hard rays of sunlight filtered through coal smoke and river miasma. She holds an ornate hand mirror, looking at her reflection, idly tracing fingers across the curve of her sculpted lips.

"I need to go outside," she says. "I need to see."

"But your face—" I say. Interrupting me, she points out the window to a factory along the river. A tannery.

"It is time to fix that," she says. "For both of us."

Elena has chosen an artist after months spent researching and corresponding with dozens of leatherworkers. He is a young man, handsome and talented—a doll maker in his spare time. Feigning the role of a plague survivor, I approach him from behind my mask and offer him a vague job. He is wary, but from my reputation, he knows I can pay. And his fear recedes when I place a sizable banknote in his soot-stained hand.

The next day, armed with a sheath of supple calfskin and a satchel of tools, the leatherworker enters our flat. He swallows, standing rigid and ready to flee as he gazes upon Elena's doll-like body. Dressed in her finest gown, the little girl lies perfectly still on a bed of straw in a small square of light from the only window.

In a hushed voice, my crooked features hidden behind the bronze mask, I spin the tale Elena has given me.

I describe my beloved daughter, my only reason for living—lost to the Black Death that scarred my own face. Hoarse with grief, I speak of a beautiful doll, an eternal reminder of the angelic child who I'll never see again. She is my last link to a world that has taken everything from me. And feigning the heartbreak of a father, I finally beg the leatherworker to practice his craft—to give this doll the face of a living girl.

It is a strange request, but tragedy and its warped aftereffects are common here. The leatherworker hesitates, then drops to his knees beside the small, limp form of the girl and begins to efficiently unpack his satchel. The first time he lifts her, he does so roughly, and I put fingers on his shoulder like the pinch of an iron gate.

"*Gently,*" I tell him. She is precious to me.

After that, the leatherworker touches Elena's face as if she were a real little girl.

His fingers are nimble and confident as he pries the porcelain mask away from her head. Nostalgia floods my heart as I see her beautiful face discarded on the floor. The innocence of her simple facade will be lost, her beautiful clean doll's features transformed into something so much more complex. I wonder, as I often do lately, if I am going to lose her.

My darling Elena, to her credit, does not so much as tremble, completing the illusion of a doll under the man's needle and thread. At the sight of her clockwork, the leatherworker turns to me.

"Sir," he says, "this doll of yours is ingeniously constructed. She's a treasure, fit for showing in the finest wonder room. Have you considered . . ."

Seeing my masked face, the sentence evaporates on his lips.

"Apologies, sir," he says.

He sets Elena on a wooden chair, her liquid eyes staring vacantly across the room from within a skinless face. I cannot bear to look, and I go on long walks or simply wait outside on the stairs, hearing the click of needle and thimble.

Working from a small bust of Aphrodite and a collection of hand-drawn sketches, he crafts the best face he can. Losing himself in a place of focus, the leatherworker falls into a reverie, hands flying, unaware of me or of anything besides the little girl who is coming to life beneath his hands. The thin leather, dyed and dusted with powder, becomes a simulacrum of the pure unblemished skin of youth, bright red lips and wide eyes taking form under his expert hand.

The young man works for days, from morning until late in the night. Stopping only to take meals and short naps, he continues under the meager radiance of candles as the sunlight fades. Finally, near morning, the sound of working stops and does not resume. Rising from the stairs, I steel myself and enter our room.

I find the leatherworker standing with his back to me. Holding a brush, he has just finished applying a final layer of pigment. His shoulders are rising and falling as he takes manic breaths, staring at the girl in the chair. Hearing my creaking footsteps, he turns to me with shining eyes.

Over his shoulder, I see Elena has become a real girl, with a real face.

"My god," he breathes, "she's . . . *alive.*"

Quickly, I clamp a hand over his bicep and guide him to the doorway. I press a bulging wallet of coins into his palm and thank him brusquely. Confused and overcompensated, he mouths his thanks and stumbles out into the dark hallway.

I close the door firmly behind him and lock it.

Under the familiar flicker of candlelight, I meet my sister for the second time.

"Darling," I say, kneeling before her chair. "He's gone."

Elena slowly blinks. This time, I do not hear the click of a doll's eyes.

Now, I see the contours of Elena's true face. From the sculpture of Aphrodite and her own drawings, she has chosen the woman she wanted to become. And now that she has, I realize this was always who she was.

"Peter," she says, smiling, her red-tinged cheeks bright beneath sparkling eyes. She slides off the chair on slippered feet and pushes down the ruffles of her dress. Standing face-to-face with me, her familiar black curls now frame the beguiling face of a young lady.

Reaching out, Elena takes my broken face in her hands.

"Let me fix yours now," she says. "London awaits us."

21

SEATTLE, PRESENT

Knifing through the heart of Seattle, Peter leans behind the wheel and drives with his thumbs, barely moving. A flap of skin from his damaged face has peeled away from the golden skeleton beneath. Struggling, he reaches up and tries to push his wound closed.

"We need to fix your face," I say, crinkling my nose.

"Not now," he says.

"You look like Frankenstein's monster. Somebody is going to notice and call the cops. Or the morgue."

"No," Peter replies. "The sooner we arrive the less chance our enemies will have—"

"Look," I say, interrupting him. "I can stitch you up. It will take five minutes and then we can go meet your friend. But if somebody in Seattle sees fucking *metal* under your face, then we're going to end up on the news."

Peter regards me silently for a long second. From his expression, I guess he must not get interrupted very often. Or at all.

"Trust me," I say quietly.

Something in his expression twinges, some obscure emotion rippling across his face. With one hand, he reaches into his jacket pocket and pulls out a small leather satchel. He tosses it on my lap.

"Are you familiar?" he asks.

I nod, the satchel looks strangely similar to my own tool roll.

"Very well," he responds.

Soon after we pass the tower, Peter pulls off the highway and drives through the industrial area along Lake Union until he sees an empty lot. It's weedy and abandoned, leading to a warren of buildings heaped onto a long jetty reaching into the lake. Beyond a chain-link fence, the rusty hulls of dry-docked freighters loom over gritty concrete. Loose gravel grinds and pops under our tires as the loud, gasoline-smelling car rumbles to a stop.

Nobody is around this early in the morning.

"This will work," I say, cracking open the groaning door.

I toss the satchel on the warm hood of the car. Unfolding it, I see an array of fine clockmaker's tools. Some of the pieces date back hundreds of years, forged in bronze and shaped by hand. Other tools I don't recognize, modern creations wrought in sterile titanium. Picks and microscopes and narrow drills crowd the loops of the satchel.

"Wow," I say, pulling out a scalpel.

"Are you able to do this?" Peter asks, climbing out of the door without putting weight on his shattered knee. He cradles one arm to his chest in a way that worries me. "I can do it myself if necessary."

"I'm fine," I say, running my fingers over the other tools. "Most of my projects are a lot further gone than you."

"Good. No sterilization. Simply do the repair."

As Peter leans himself against the side of the car, I slide out a forceps and use it to pluck a curved needle from the satchel. There is a coil of silken thread, gummy, coated with a substance similar to the skin on Peter's face. With well-practiced motions, I thread the needle.

"So let's say your friend fixes your leg, then what?"

"We use the relic," Peter says, patiently holding his face closed. "With it, we can stop the fighting—"

A shudder runs through his chest and Peter puts a hand over his heart until it passes. Ignoring my confused expression, he hoists himself onto the hood. Sitting, he drops his elbows onto his thighs and leans forward, putting his mangled face within my reach.

"How?" I ask.

"One thing at a time," he says to the empty lot.

Up high, the wind blows through pine trees, sending shadows dancing over gravel. The engine still ticks over quietly, heat radiating from the muscle car. Seabirds call to each other on the lake.

I hold up the forceps, needle glinting. Watching me carefully, Peter takes his hand away from his cheek. The wound falls open, but his gold-flecked brown eyes stay trained on me as I press my fingers to his face.

At my touch, he blinks hard. I pull back a little.

"You okay?"

"It has been a long time since . . . someone repaired me in this way."

I watch his face but it's gone to stone again. I wonder to myself exactly what he means by a "long time."

"And never a human being," he adds.

"I'll go slow," I say.

Pressing the wound closed, I make a series of neat dives and swoops through his tough skin. As the thread pinches the laceration back together, his stubborn jawline returns. The skin feels completely natural against my fingers, warm, with the faintest sandpaper scratch of stubble.

I can't help it; I pinch a curl of his unruly chestnut hair between my thumb and forefinger. The strands are smooth and natural. His skin is supple and soft, freckled and tanned a light brown. I don't know the technology for this.

"How do you have skin?" I ask. "I mean, where did it come from? It isn't . . ."

"It is synthetic," he says, holding his head still for me.

"I didn't know they could make it that real," I say.

"They can't," he says. "But we can."

I pause.

"If the *avtomat* wish to survive among humans, we cannot exist," he says. "We have been crafting better materials over the centuries, using them to blend in with your kind. My birth face was lambskin pulled tight over sculpted metal. Tougher leather covered my palms and fingertips, so I could hold weapons without losing grip."

Now he looks at both his hands.

"My maker spent a long while determining the perfect balance. Too rough and the ax handle slips. Too soft and the skin tears on a strong blow."

I nod, remembering something similar from my studies. "Vaucanson built a flute player in the seventeen hundreds," I say. "The machine had lungs and an esophagus and mouth, tongue, teeth. It played the way a person plays, by blowing into the instrument. But for months he couldn't get the machine to play as well as a human. Then he finally realized: she needed lips. Vaucanson used leather."

Peter turns his gaze back up to me, considering.

"Perhaps my existence is not as surprising to you as it would be to others."

I pull the needle through.

Peter's cheek pulls back into the faintest smile, and the wound in his cheek dimples only the slightest bit. The seam where his face was sliced open is disappearing. Whatever the thread is made of is combining with the skin around it, healing.

"You've been hiding in plain sight for centuries?" I muse, leaning in to finish the last stitch in a final swoop. Peter doesn't seem to notice.

"Over history, some *avtomat* have been discovered. It is inevitable," he says. "If the captured one is not burned for a witch, then the others make sure he disappears completely. Written accounts, photographs, people—we always clean up our messes. The dozens of us who are left have become old and solitary. Some are ancient. But we are all trained to protect the secret of our existence from humanity . . . It is a matter of life and death."

My face inches from his, I watch as the last stitches on his wound close.

"That's really reassuring, Peter," I say, leaning back. "How is your friend going to like seeing me?"

As he moves his jaw, testing the repair, I'm reminded of how well his face is put together. Strong jawline and thick eyebrows. A stubborn streak in his chin, but faint laugh lines radiating over his cheeks. His eyes are especially well done, wet and large, brown with bands of yellow expanding out like sunbursts.

"This is the end. I have no choice, neither does my friend, and neither do you."

Sliding off the hood of the car, Peter cranes his neck. Looking past me, his eyes open wide.

"We are not alone," he says.

I spin around, needle and thread still in my fingers. All I see is the empty lot. Besides the wind and the distant roar of traffic on the highway, I don't hear anything. A flock of birds sits on a telephone wire, watching us.

"What are you talking about?" I ask Peter.

"The birds," he says.

A few crows sit on an old telephone wire that sags across the weedy lot. Nothing out of the ordinary. Peter registers my annoyed look as I pack the tools back into his roll.

"The grouping," he says quietly. "One bird, then three, one, three. Thirteen. This is a sign."

"Okay," I say with a frown, glancing at the birds. They seem perfectly normal, sitting clustered into little groups. I count them, double-checking Peter's math. "Fine. But how is that a code? What's it supposed to mean?"

"This is the domain of an old *avtomat* called Batuo."

"Your friend, right?" I ask.

I trail off as a fat black crow flaps its wings, lobbing itself toward us. It lands on the roof of the car in a flurry of feathers and scrabbling talons. In jerky movements, the yellow-eyed bird cocks its head at me.

Peter regards the bird seriously for a long moment. Finally, he speaks to it.

"Batuo," he says.

The bird hops closer, to within a foot of where Peter leans against the warm hood of the car. Peering up at him with bright eyes, it goes still. Now that it isn't moving, I notice a metallic gleam to its feathers. Its black legs and beak look like rugged plastic. The glow of its yellow eyes take on the sheen of an LED.

"No way," I murmur. And yet I have read accounts of the Greek mathematician Archytas of Tarentum building a wooden dove capable of flight around 350 BC. A lot of progress could have been made in two thousand years.

Peter speaks to the bird, using oddly stilted language. "I ask peaceful entry into your domain. You know my Word and my nature. I will do you no harm. My companion is under my aegis. Grant us entry, Batuo. Together, we can fulfill my first quest, and the last."

After another pause, the bird seems to reanimate. It hops backward, head cocked again. Then it caws loudly and bobs its head at Peter.

Peter nods back.

"Wait," I say, walking around the car. "Did it talk to you? Is that even a real bird?"

The bird rears back and flaps its wings. There is something off-putting in the way the wings connect to the body. Like the work of a taxidermist.

"Clockwork birds?" I ask. "Surely there's an easier way."

"Our methods span centuries, June," says Peter. "The world has changed, but these emissaries and their ancestors have never lost their usefulness."

Moving slow, I reach for the bird.

It flaps its wings, talons scraping the hood as it flies away from my outstretched fingers. A hundred yards away, seven other crows lift off the power line at the same time, cawing.

The small flock wings away from the lot, headed toward downtown Seattle. As they disappear, I notice a lone feather lying on the hood of the car. Exchanging a glance with Peter, I pick it up. Putting it under my nose, I inhale.

The feather smells like plastic.

22

LONDON, 1731

"Be careful," I say to Elena. "Our faces look better, but they are far from perfect."

In a black silk gown embroidered with silver thread, the girl looks up at me innocently, trying and failing to suppress a smile. With quick movements, she picks a few pieces of lint off my long overcoat. I purchased a coach-load of fine garments from a tailor's shop on Charing Cross, fashionable enough to allow us to travel anywhere we wish to go in the city.

I push a lock of powdered gray hair over one shoulder, uncertain.

"Don't worry," says Elena, giggling. "You really are quite convincing, Peter."

Though we move only at night, our new faces have allowed an unprecedented level of interaction with the people of London. This has included the ability to spend some of the wealth accumulated from ransoming debtors.

As is her habit, Elena is standing at the window of our new flat, shielding her eyes from the dull morning light. Her impish grin is lost in curls of lustrous black hair. The new room we are renting is an entire floor on a much more respectable street, above a haberdashery, wall-papered in blue florals, furnished, and boasting a substantial fireplace embedded in the wall, unlit.

We have made a flurry of small forays into the city at dusk, exercising the lessons Favorini gave us on blending in with humanity. And though we are accustomed to behaving as people, pretending to breathe and eat and drink, Elena and I have never walked in the daylight.

"Ooh," Elena breathes, face pressed to the glass. "I can't wait."

The girl darts across the room to the doorway, her shoes silent on the thick rugs. She opens the door and leans around the corner, peeking out like a child.

"Our man is here," she urges me, already tromping down the stairs. "Come on. Let's finally see the whole city!"

Outside, two men with calves like cannonballs and elaborately armored shoes stand beside a wooden sedan chair with handles sprouting in front and behind. Slightly more expensive than the carriages known as teeth rattlers, these portable booths are the only sure mode of transport over the broken stone of the city roads. Just a rental, our sedan is made of a simple wooden box with gauzy fabric hanging over the windows.

I drop a few coins into the man's palm and lift Elena into the sedan.

"Stone's end, sir," I say, ducking my tall frame into the perfumed, heavily pillowed interior. The law forbids these contrivances on pedestrian paths, but few chairmen take heed of that, shoving past the wooden stumps buried in the stone to stop carriages and shouting at those on foot to make way.

Not yet settled on the rough leather seat, Elena squeals as we lurch ahead. She is sent flying, suspended in the air, eyes wide and incredulous. As she lands, her small hands find my jacket and clamp on tight, a new round of surprised giggles thumped out of her by the next wobble of the sedan.

Outside, our lead chairman shouts "By your leave!" with monotonous regularity. Every so often, he stops to crane his neck, looking for the dome of St. Paul's cathedral—the only landmark tall enough to help him through this warren of twisting, close-packed buildings. This area survived the great fire and bears the mind-numbing complexity borne of centuries of frenzied building and demolition.

Inside our compartment, thin drapes flutter, filtering the reddish morning sunlight onto Elena's smiling face. Peeking between folds of fabric, she watches the bustling streets of London with a queer satisfaction—absorbing every detail.

"Isn't it incredible, Peter?" she asks. "Look at all the *people*."

I do not respond. Leaning to the other side, I have my eye set to scanning the crowded street. I keep my face hidden behind the mud-spattered curtain, remembering her words: *We are not alone here.*

My gaze stutters across a beautiful woman standing in a doorway, black eyes following us as we pass. A thrill of recognition races through me. Turning back, I find her already gone.

A vague unease settles into my mind.

In the last year, I have seen more of the fiery sigils—all of them near the wharves that line the Thames. The slashing letters are terribly familiar somehow, yet I cannot fathom their meaning. And not from lack of trying. Elena has filled our flat with her reproductions of the signs, and collected thick tomes devoted to translation. Watching the street without blinking, I ensure we do not stray near those marked lanes.

"This is the world," Elena says. "We are finally a part of it."

"This is *their* world—" I begin to correct her.

Our chairmen stumble into a ditch and the sedan tilts, nearly collapses onto its side. I clutch Elena and keep her from spilling out as a hackney carriage plows by just outside. The loudly complaining chairmen yank us back upright, shouting hoarsely at the dusty wake of the carriage. My reflexive embrace is all that has kept Elena from being thrown out of the sedan and trampled.

"Their world," I urge again, holding her close. "We must be vigilant. Do not fall in love with these people or the false Eden they have made."

"If we do not belong in their world, then where is our own?" Elena implores, pushing my arms away. She grasps a bar bolted beside the door to steady herself and glares at me, her lower lip stuttering with emotion. "We need to seek out our own kind."

The old familiar argument.

"We did meet another of our kind," I remind her. "It threatened us. It tried to drag us into a war we have no business fighting. I will not allow—"

"Allow?" she asks, interrupting me angrily. "You will not *allow* me? I am not your *child*."

Elena turns her furrowed brow to the street, shrugging off my touch. We travel in silence for a long while as dawn turns to morning, listening to the chairmen huff and puff. I watch the fabric of the curtains flutter against the morning light, the obscure shadows of men and women playing on the veil as they go about their lives on the other side, oblivious to the clockwork strangers who walk among them.

Abruptly, the sedan chair stops moving. With a thump we are set down.

A throng of people have gathered in the square before us. Our chairmen are shouting and shoving to no effect, having come to a dead standstill.

"What is this?" I ask, pushing my face out the window.

"Tyburn hangings, sir," says the lead chairman. "Can't push through until they're over."

I lean back inside in time to see Elena slipping between the curtains and out the door. Her small hard feet clap to the cobblestones and she disappears instantly into the crowd of spectators.

"Elena!" I shout.

I emerge, shoving people away from the sedan chair. Pushing another few coins into the sweating driver's hand, I stride away into the crowd, heads taller than anyone else, scanning for Elena. I catch a streak of black velvet weaving between the waistcoats and gowns of gentlemen and commoners alike.

The sense of unease from before has flowered into a full panic.

On a wooden scaffold across the square, a condemned man stands in his best clothes, a rope binding his elbows to his waist, leaving his hands free to clasp in prayer. A hairy rope is wrapped around his neck in a hangman's noose. The executioner stands to the side, waiting patiently as his prisoner makes a final speech. He holds a white nightcap to pull over the prisoner's face just before he is turned off.

I stop, blinking.

On the brick building behind the scaffold, a fiery mark glows. And along the roofline, a series of birds sit in a row, peculiar and still. Something about their precise arrangement puts a sudden fear in my throat.

Abruptly, I recall seeing a similar pattern of birds in Moscow during our midnight walks.

I sense this is the domain of another *avtomat*.

The birds on the roofline take flight, wings moving in irregular lurches. Something is wrong about them, something artificial. I begin to trot through the crowd, ignoring the complaints of jostled pedestrians.

I cannot hear what the prisoner is saying, over the jeering of the hundreds of spectators. He barely flinches as they spit and curse and throw rotten fruit at the scaffold. Swiveling my head, I stalk through the crowd for agonizing minutes. Finally, I spot Elena, only a few yards away. She sees me and tries to run, but I am too fast, diving forward and sweeping her up in my arms.

"My daughter," I say, holding her tight to me as she struggles to escape. "So that's where you've got to."

Posing as a father, I move away quickly, cradling Elena's head against my shoulder. I hiss into her ear, "I was wrong. You are not mine, but you are precious to me. Never run from me again."

Pausing to look at Elena, I notice her eyes have gone wide with fear. Her lips are moving, mumbling, trying to make a sound. Her arms tighten around my neck.

Spinning, I see the woman who disappeared from the doorway a few minutes ago coming from across the courtyard. I know instantly that she is *avtomat*.

The thing is female, a lock of straight black hair hanging long over her sharp cheekbones, the rest of it gathered in a bunch on top of her head. Her face is smooth, eyes wide set and black and narrowed. She gives the vague impression of being Eastern. Dressed impeccably, she carries a parasol and wears white gloves. When she knifes a hand out to thread through the crowd, grown men are pushed to the side like rag dolls.

My mind flashes with a vision of this woman—she is riding a fantastical horse with tiger stripes across a lush jungle clearing. She is laughing, hair flowing, looking back at me and flashing her teeth, sharp and white. Then a primeval forest swallows her, wet and dark, and from deep within it, I hear a roaring . . .

I shake my head to clear it.

"Go, Peter," gasps Elena. "Take me away from her."

The jeering crowd is facing the scaffold as the sentence is about to be carried out. No one seems to notice the woman slicing through, tossing people to the ground, closing her parasol and tucking it under her elbow.

"Peter," Elena begs.

Wrapping one arm under Elena, I put the other around her shoulders and hold her to me as I launch away through the crowd. Pushing blindly, I soon reach the edge of the courtyard where carriages are parked.

Turning, I don't see the woman.

"Who is she?" asks Elena, face pressed against my chest.

"Avtomat," I say.

Then the lady appears in a gap between onlookers, her eyes narrowed.

"I am Leizu, little one. The mother of silkworms, who brought silk to China in the age before ages," she says. "Do you not recognize me anymore?"

Holding Elena tight to me, I back away slowly.

"We do not know you," I say.

The woman advances, her parasol held tight under her arm. She twists the umbrella with her right hand and the handle loosens.

A few inches of hidden blade emerge, shining copper.

It is the divine blade—

"Your sister does not concern me," she says. "Only you, *Pyotr.*"

I stop, my back pressing against the front quarter of a hackney coach.

"What do you want?"

Stepping closer, she smiles.

"I want the pain to stop," she says, and I feel a madness radiating from her. She exudes the intensity of a trapped animal, pushed beyond exhaustion and consuming unknown reserves of energy. "You are the only one strong enough to give me satisfaction. We will break against each other like waves on the shore—"

From his perch, the coachman shouts at me to move off and plants a boot on my shoulder. I lean harder against the carriage, hearing the wheels creak. I do not flinch as the sting of a horsewhip crosses the side of my face.

Elena wriggles out of my arms and drops to the ground.

"Horses," she says, diving between my legs and under the carriage.

Leizu steps back and sweeps her hidden sword from its sheath, dazzling light spraying from the bright copper blade. With startling speed, she locks fingers onto my forearm. Her strength is impossible, the force of a mountain in her grasp.

I have never felt anything like it—never imagined such power.

"Come with me," she says.

Shoving backward, I dig my boot heels into muddy cobblestones, rocking the lumbering, square carriage up onto two wheels. The coachman shouts shrilly in alarm. I hear wood splintering and horses neighing frantically.

Without looking away from the woman's rising blade, I clamp a hand blindly up onto the coachman's calf. Hauling him off the platform, I throw his body at the dark-haired woman. Buttons fly from his uniform as the overweight man hits the ground and rolls screaming into her legs. She sidesteps to avoid him, letting go of my arm, swallowed again into the shouting crowd.

"Peter!" Elena shouts.

The girl has thrown the traces from the horses. Now, she sits on a white mare, bareback, fingers wrapped in its mane, beckoning to me.

With a final push, I send the teetering carriage over on its side. It crashes to the ground, wood splitting apart, and the remaining horse rears and charges. People scatter in panic, shoving in all directions.

I am already taking Elena's hand, leaping onto the white mare's narrow back. Frantically, we spur our mount through the crowd, away from the spectacle. The lady is lost in the horde behind us as people surge away from the fallen wagon.

At the edge of the square, I dare to look over my shoulder.

The lady is standing upright on the overturned carriage like a knife blade, scanning for us. Silhouetted against the sun, her long hair ripples over her shoulders, a black pennant. In her right hand she brandishes the flashing, copper-colored sword.

As we meet eyes, a solid thunk comes from the scaffold and the crowd roars in the guttural language of blood. The condemned man goes swinging by his neck from a short noose, legs kicking. I lose sight of Leizu as spectators close in around her, screaming and cheering, urging the prisoner on to a slow death as his relatives swarm around his feet, pulling at his body to try and hurry him along to the next world.

23

SEATTLE, PRESENT

The blank face of the skyscraper looms over us, beads of condensation scabbing its black glass surface, leaving it sparkling in the growing dawn like something frozen and abandoned centuries ago. Peter parks right across the street from it, illegally.

He leans over and pops open the glove compartment, pulls out a laminated badge, and hangs it on the rearview mirror. Glancing at it, I see police credentials. I don't even bother to ask whether or not they are real.

"My friend is here," Peter says, gazing up at the building through the windshield. He looks tired, shoulders slumped and an arm tucked over his chest.

"What is this place?" I ask, looking out.

Peter sighs, sounding distinctly human. "A kind of . . . hospital. *Avtomat* come here for repairs. If that fails, sometimes to sleep forever. Because of this, there is a sign written fifty feet high on the side of the building."

"I don't see anything—" I say, turning back to Peter.

His hand is out, palm flat. A small brass ring rests on it, like a monocle without any glass.

"This is a cedalion, June," he says. "Keep it. It may become useful to you."

"Cedalion?" I ask. "Who stood on the shoulders of Orion and granted him sight?"

Peter nods, and I catch the tiniest hint of surprise that I know Greek mythology.

I pluck the heavy brass ring from his palm and hold it between my thumb and forefinger. The surface is covered in tiny scratches and faint, washed-out writing. I turn to the passenger window and, feeling like an idiot, lift the circle to my eye.

The side of the building erupts with flaming script.

I pull the cedalion away and the mirrored skyscraper reverts to normal. Gingerly, I look through it again and watch the golden-red flames reappear. They are arranged into a large symbol, like an eye, writhing and twisting across the surface of the building but somehow staying in place.

"Oh my god . . ." I breathe. "What the hell is that?"

"A sigil," says Peter. "It indicates this is the domain of an *avtomat*. Those with friendly intentions will be granted entrance, ideally. Any others will be killed."

"These signs . . . they're everywhere?"

"Only sparingly. Once, it was impossible for humans to intercept our messages. Now you have technologies that can do it, so we are more careful. But for all of history, our messages have haunted the faces of your temples and monuments."

Still peering through the cedalion, I pull out the relic that hangs around my neck. Looking down, I see that it, too, has erupted with a flaming scrawl. A symbol I have never seen before, like a teardrop, traces across the curl of metal.

Fumbling in my pocket, I pull out a notebook. Squinting at the flaming script through the cedalion, I use a stubby pencil to mark the contours of what I'm seeing. While I'm at it, I glance up at the domain sigil and draw a copy of it, too.

In the seat beside me, Peter chuckles.

"What?" I ask, scribbling frantically, not looking up.

"You remind me of someone," he says quietly.

I can't identify the letters, but the lines remind me of early Chinese symbols. Something about it is elegant and simplistic and ancient.

"What is this symbol on my relic?" I ask, lowering the cedalion. "What's it mean, exactly?"

Peter's face is empty, his jaw set. Looking past me, he answers brusquely: "The relic was made before my time, inscribed with an elder language. The Word it bears has no direct translation to the tongues of men."

"Word? What's that mean?"

Peter opens his door. "Stay near me," he says.

"Do you trust this friend of yours or not?" I ask.

"Completely," says Peter. "The question is whether or not he trusts me."

There's a logic to all this, I'm telling myself. No matter how crazy it seems, the world always operates by the rules. Those rules can be understood, even if it doesn't seem like it at first.

I step out of the car into the cold morning. As Peter struggles to get out of his side, I turn the monocle over in my hands, reasoning out loud. "It must be some kind of metamaterial. Crafted to work as a wide spectrum lens, bending nonvisible light into something I can see. But it's more than that. It's doing some processing, too. Sensing patterns. And it must be at least as old as you are.

"How did you make it?"

"I didn't," says Peter, as he climbs out of the car on his broken leg.

I hurry around the side of the vehicle, suppressing a shiver in the dawn. Putting an arm out to steady him, I let Peter lean on me. His lips are pressed into a line, eyelids fluttering. As he puts his bulky arm around my shoulder, I feel an irregular vibration rattling inside his chest. Frowning, he takes cautious steps, dragging his broken leg.

"The cedalion pulls information from the world like water through a stone," he says. I hold him, concerned at how he is cradling his heart. As we move around the car, I put the device back to my eye. The wall across the street lights up in the chicken scratch of a forgotten language, symbols written in cold light over condensation.

"Is this how you see the world?" I ask.

"I see as you do," Peter replies. "Only more."

The flaming eye stretches up like beautiful artwork. Something flickers in the reflection of the glass wall and I turn.

"Wow," I say. "This is really—"

And I see Peter through the cedalion for the first time.

His skin is glowing, complex ribbons of reddish-orange light spreading across his chest and lacing over his face. Now, I can plainly see the intricate seams where his flesh fits together. And I notice a rapid, unsteady pulse of a clockwork heart beneath the metal ribs of his chest. A worrisome blue glow leaks from a wound over his heart, like a spreading stain.

Peter is beautiful, and something is going seriously wrong inside him.

"Yes?" he asks.

"Nothing," I say. "Never mind. Let's go."

I pocket the cedalion and Peter returns to his normal, stern figure—tall and imperious with sharp features and dark eyes. He leans on me, dragging his injured leg as we move through the shadow of this mammoth skyscraper.

Instead of crossing the street to the building lobby, Peter leads me down the sidewalk to the wide mouth of an express lane tunnel. We circle around a concrete pillar to reach a rusted steel door embedded in blank concrete, a silver keypad beside it. Peter pushes a long series of numbers, ignoring the rush of traffic a few feet away. A lock thunks and he pulls the handle. As the door swings open, its metal face winks against the dawn like a bloody razor.

24

LONDON, 1750

"Never again," I said to my sister, returning to our empty flat on the day of our disastrous outing in Tyburn. "We must be more careful from now on."

I remember Elena looked at me darkly then, an argument waiting on her lips. But seeing the concern on my face, she chose to bite down on the words.

She chose to wait, for that night, at least.

Resisting the urge to flee, we quietly set about living a hidden life, cloistered in several apartments spread across different districts. I reduce my debt-collecting duties and restrict travel to the outskirts of town, always on the watch for *avtomat* markings. Offered a stake in a fledgling bank, we gamble the majority of our resources and invest.

The great paradox of London is the startling ease with which we are able to disappear among hundreds of thousands of people. We discover a faceless solitude among strangers that is only possible in such a vast metropolis. Immortal among the humans, immune to their passions and vices, Elena and I immerse ourselves in the gray anonymity of routine.

Years pass, and our investments recoup a small but thriving fortune.

Over time, I begin to convince myself the attack by Leizu was a fluke, simple bad luck. The sheer accumulation of habits, resources, and familiarity keeps us rooted to the pathways of London. Paris beckons, and even Saint Petersburg, but I do not dare push beyond our accustomed boundaries.

And all the while, a dull pain is gnawing deep in my breast—the ache of not meeting my Word. Watching over the girl like a jailer, limiting my movement and exposure, I sense that I am failing to serve *pravda*. My tsar is gone. The sense of loss grows slowly, an agony that laces its way through my body and mind like a disease.

This land has its own sovereign, and I find myself paying attention to King George II's occasional proclamations. In the newspapers, they call him the "absent king" and accuse him of warmongering.

Elena continues her studies from behind closed doors, as she did for decades in the depths of the Kremlin. Through ferocious correspondence, she spreads her intellect into the world, securing and building our fortune while she is at it. The volume of letters passing to and from our properties is astonishing. No fewer than three servants busy themselves with dropping off or receiving bundles of letters at various coffee shops, depending on the pen name attached.

Even so, the girl herself is trapped, wilting in our apartments.

Out of the sheer necessity of keeping Elena sane, we take to occasionally risking a late night symphony or opera. Always in the latest fashion, Elena dons a kaleidoscopic medley of dresses and stockings and buckled shoes. Her hair is lustrous, always perfectly coiffed; her shining face as bright and alive as an immortal child's. Perfumed and slight, her little arms are often clasped around my neck with an inhuman strength, the girl perched and alert in the crow's nest of my embrace.

We sweep through the crowds—a vision of familial perfection under the forgiving flicker of dim lamps—unapproachable and anonymous.

Elena keeps a nanny to tend to the endless parade of tutors she researches and invites to visit, shipping them in from around Europe and the Far East. In our parlor, I am as likely to meet a composer as an inventor or painter—all of them desperate for a wealthy patron.

The girl takes to playing instruments, the harp, harpsichord, and lute. A small savant, a prodigy, she is taught in succession by waves of the best musicians produced by humanity. These men and women come to our dimly lit parlor to perform and instruct an odd little girl with incredible instincts and ferocious determination.

I shake hands at the door and excuse myself to roam the dark streets.

Walking along the Thames as the lamplighters set about their work, watching thieves and criminals ply their trade, my heart is crying out for justice. But my career has evolved beyond the knuckle-scraping collection of fugitive debtors. Over the last three decades, our investments have grown a thousandfold. My operations are watched over by stern-faced, mustached men—the grown-up children of my first partners.

Five years is the amount of time before Elena's perpetual youth sparks suspicion. Every half decade, the precocious child must shed her life like a snake sheds its skin. We move, leaving behind nannies and tutors and friends. We learn to change our faces and our accents. We buy and sell apartments, moving in unpredictable orbits but always pushing toward the outskirts of the ever-expanding town—farther from the *avtomat* signs, continuing to elude the horribly powerful creature called Leizu.

The years seem to accelerate.

Certain rhythms settle into focus with the passing of time. The faces around me careen through adolescence and youth before collapsing into wrinkles and then finally disappearing. Each of these people imagines she is the same person day to day, but I can see how their lives rise and fall in cycles, moving through the same patterns as their ancestors, bricks in a city that is constantly being rebuilt.

My only solace is in seeing Elena at her writing desk, fingers clasped around a fountain pen, dipping and scrawling her messages to great minds all over the world. It always reminds me of my first sight, the gentle contour of her porcelain cheek.

More and more, glancing at her pages, I see sketches of the *avtomat* signs. Our late-night outings cease as she withdraws into obsession. Weeks pass when I don't see her, our parlor thick with the pipe smoke of elderly scholars. Elena is a feral shadow in her library, lost behind desks heaped with inscrutable books written in elder languages.

She is trying so hard to understand. I am trying so hard to ignore my call to *pravda*. We are both trying, and failing.

Enduring the teeth-grinding ache of my daily routine, I begin to lay down plans. In secret letters, I open negotiations for a new, distant home—a manor house where Elena can live in opulent safety. Visiting recruitment parties put on by the army, I discuss joining the king's martial force. Collecting supplies and making plans, I am able to do everything except discuss the subject with my sister.

On our last day, I find Elena in her library sitting on a velvet cushion. Her bare feet are dangling over Persian rugs, sharp elbows propped on a little French desk. Eyes raking over the page, she scratches out a letter. Elena looks to me like some beautiful, angelic machine. We have not spoken in several weeks.

I clear my throat, a human affectation.

"Your friend Rousseau says children learn faster without their shoes on. Are you taking his advice?"

The girl ignores me completely.

"Who are you writing?" I ask.

"You," she responds, monosyllabic, eyes not leaving the page.

"Me? Why not speak to me?"

"I am writing *as* you," she says, "to complete the purchase of a *grand* estate."

She taps the page, her hard fingertip knocking against wood veneer. Though my speech is still rusty with the soft vowels of Eastern Europe, the little one has adopted a precise, lilting English accent designed to put her visitors at ease.

"You clearly needed my help negotiating," she adds.

Elena has discovered my offer to purchase a mansion far north of here. The secluded property will permanently separate us from the dangers of London. I notice she has also pulled out my army haversack and leaned it against the wall. Duty assignment papers are scattered on the floor.

My hidden plans are, of course, transparent to her.

"I see the structure is isolated," she continues, not looking up. "No neighbors. Very little staff. I imagine it will simplify my life greatly and finally complete our great retreat from the world."

Standing over her shoulder, I scan the letter. She has negotiated a viciously low price. It seems the road to the estate has been in disrepair, some argument over who should maintain it, and it is difficult to get food transported there.

Obviously, not a large concern of ours.

"I should have told you," I say.

Stiffening, Elena looks up at me. Her eyes are two black wells of anger, face empty. A savage math is taking place behind her eyes. Her Word is *logicka*. In the mind of this little doll, the world is a sequence of cold mathematical equations, actions and reactions. It disturbs me to contemplate, but I must not forget the way she thinks.

"Why, Peter?" she asks.

"We must each follow our Word," I say, speaking carefully. "It can be a burden, I know—"

"You *know*?" She spits the word at me. "You're free to go anywhere you like, to converse as equals with anyone. While I am trapped here in these apartments, in the body of a little girl. Writing letters with a *man's* name on them."

I kneel beside her, eye to eye, thinking of Favorini's workshop so long ago. I remember when my sister was a newly made doll, her eyes clicking with each blink. And now she is so venomous—such a livid and living creature.

"I am not free," I say. "My soul calls for justice, yet I cannot risk pursuing any. The city is a chaos of *nepravda* and there is nothing I can do. The orphans run in packs, Elena. Children as young as three."

"A consequence of the rules of this society."

"Logical to you, but it sets my Word alight in my chest. It . . . hurts me, Elena. It hurts my soul."

"Then you know how I feel, Peter," she whispers, standing, watching me intensely. "It's only logical to find others like us. Perhaps they could explain how our Words function? Perhaps they are older than we are, they might understand—"

I back away from her desperate words.

"I forbid it. You know this. The others will bring only death."

Or am I simply jealous, worried the others will steal her away?

"Stop it!" she shouts, snatching up an ink pot and throwing it against the wall. Black streaks of liquid spray in a starburst against gilded wooden panels. "I tried to make you happy, but now I don't care. Don't you see I don't care anymore? I don't care if they kill us. I don't want to live trapped like this."

Fists clenched, eyes shining, she stares fiercely up at me. Both of us know what she has said is not true—it violates *logicka.* The underlying logic of a living thing is its own survival.

She can never disregard that.

"The estate is ready, as you know," I say, lifting the haversack to my shoulder. "You will be safe there. The staff are instructed to obey you. With my seal and letterhead, I am sure you can prepare the necessary documents while I am away."

She stares at me blankly.

"Where?" she asks, a ragged edge to her voice.

"India. A war has begun. King George is mustering troops."

"And you plan to serve this new monarch, as you once served the tsar?"

I nod.

"I have enlisted as a soldier of fortune. I am pledged to the king."

Elena falls back into her desk chair. She turns away from me, then lifts the pen and continues to write her message. I watch her for a long time. She does not look up again. Finally, I leave her, sitting hunched at her desk, scribbling furiously, the nib of her fountain pen scratching black welts into the paper.

25

SEATTLE, PRESENT

The far-off murmur of traffic permeates cool concrete walls around me. The unremarkable metal door has led us to an even less remarkable elevator, its rusty face visible in the dirty-orange glow of a single button. Peter presses it, leaving his finger for a long time. Finally, the thick metal doors part and we shuffle into a closet-size compartment, dead black walls lit by a sputtering fluorescent light.

A row of steel buttons gleam, featureless as loose bullets.

Struggling now, Peter leans against the elevator wall and studies the panel. His jacket and pants have been shredded by lead pellets and knife wounds, and a barely visible seam of stitches meanders down his face. Under this harsh light, with no blood or swelling, he looks like a hastily repaired mannequin.

The steel doors close and I clench my teeth against a wave of claustrophobia.

Peter's fingers course over the elevator buttons in a complicated pattern, pressing and holding different spots for different amounts of time. Nothing changes as he enacts the routine. When he stops, nothing happens for a moment. Then I hear the mechanical thunk of the elevator motor engaging somewhere in the shaft.

The floor drops out from under us.

As we accelerate downward, Peter slumps against the wall and closes his eyes.

"What's wrong inside your chest?" I ask him. "You're not telling me something."

He speaks without opening his eyes.

"If my wound is fatal," he says, "protect the relic and find its purpose. If Batuo offers his help, take it; otherwise . . . flee from here."

"Fatal? What are you talking about?" I ask, but he doesn't respond. "Hey!"

The elevator lurches and Peter's knees buckle. The huge man rolls off the wall, mouth moving without making sound. I try to catch him under the armpits, but his body is too heavy. All I can do is lower him to the floor.

Kneeling beside him, I push my ear against his chest. I hear sounds coming from inside. He's still alive.

"Peter, tell me where we're going."

"Down," he murmurs.

"What is this place?" I ask. "What do I do?"

He lies still, curled up like a child on the floor of the elevator. His fingers are twitching and he breathes, but otherwise he doesn't move.

"Great," I say to myself.

Peter's wallet is bulging from an inside pocket. Reaching into his jacket, I fish it out. Flipping it open, I see without much surprise that he's got a CIA badge and identification. His name is listed as Peter Alexeyevich, eyes brown, hair brown. The rest of the wallet is empty except for a wad of hundred dollar bills and a black credit card made of metal.

"Who *are* you?" I ask the unresponsive man.

My knees sag as the elevator slows. Shoving the wallet back into his pocket, I pat Peter's body down for weapons.

A long dagger is sheathed over his thigh.

I tug the blade free. Holding the antique knife, I brace myself against the wall as the elevator doors part to reveal a foreboding, unlit concrete hallway.

Breathing hard, I push the silver elevator buttons with my free hand. Nothing happens. Hesitant, I step out into the maintenance corridor, knife up. Behind me, Peter lies still under the fluorescent glare of the elevator light.

"Hello?" I call. "Is anybody here?"

I take a step forward, flinching as overhead lights snap on automatically, one at a time down the long hallway. The bulbs hum over spotless concrete.

"Peter," I whisper. "We're here. Where's your friend?"

He doesn't respond.

A metal door clangs open up ahead. The shadow of a person hits the wall. I call to it, heavy knife wavering in my hands.

"Hey!"

No response, save for a strange clicking sound.

A head pokes around the doorway and turns toward me—a head with no face. I clench my teeth as the rest of a human-shaped machine steps into the hallway, thin limbed and gangly. Made of smooth white plastic, the thing stands perfectly still in the middle of the hall, silent and expressionless.

"Hello?" I call to it. "Batuo?"

The machine animates, taking slow, deliberate steps toward me. It seems to be more appliance than man, with no hair or skin. The only details that stand out are contours where the sculpted casing fits together, lines that curl over the sterile whiteness of its arms, chest, and thighs. That, and an empty face like a hockey mask.

"Shit," I mutter, stepping back. The quiet sigh of its footsteps grows louder as the robot advances, and I can feel each impact vibrating the concrete floor. "Shit, shit, shit."

I back all the way to the elevator mouth. The machine keeps coming forward, pincered hands widening. One slow step at a time.

Cornered, I bare my teeth and raise the knife.

"Fuck off, robot," I say, my voice as unsteady as my hands.

As it nears, I lunge with the knife. The curved blade glances off a hard plastic shell. It doesn't even leave a mark. Backing all the way into the elevator, I jab again and again—each time the knife point slips away. Finally, the machine shoves me aside and stands over Peter's curled body.

Then it kneels beside him.

From the gentle curve of its spine and the way it balances without effort, I know this can't be a human creation. The thing seems like it came from the future. With the little touches of smooth plastic, it seems almost alien.

Gently, it slides both hands under Peter's body. The pincers that were so menacing a moment ago now resemble ice cream scoopers. And I notice it has padded forearms, built to cradle.

Standing up, the robot effortlessly lifts Peter's limp body.

"Hey!" I shout at it. "What are you doing with him?"

Still holding the knife, I follow the robot, helpless, as it walks past me into the hallway. I watch from a safe distance as it opens the metal door and moves through. As the door swings closed, I take a deep breath and catch it with my foot.

I peek inside, utterly unprepared for what I see.

The narrow concrete hallway opens into a soaring medieval cathedral—stone ceilings disappearing into dusty heights, every inch veined with carved ridges and whorls that spread in fractal contours. The intricate patterns curve into arches that meet in rows of slender pillars rising from an expanse of dark, polished marble. The footprint of this room matches the skyscraper, forming a sort of negative image of the world above.

The robot seems small now, clacking over the broad, shining stone floor with Peter in its arms. A dozen dim shadows play at the feet of the machine, flickering in the light of a thousand candles and lamps that are lit in sconces and chandeliers and candelabras. The vague shapes of palm-size drones flit back and forth overhead, darting and hovering like hummingbirds—tending to the wicks of every candle.

What looks like a mausoleum wall dominates the far side of the room, its flat, smooth surface broken into a grid by hundreds of crypts. About a story up, an ornately carved wooden railing circles the entire room, clinging to the gracefully curving walls.

And now I notice the limbs. Rows of them hang on stainless steel hooks mounted below the wooden railing, some with skin and others just metallic bone. Several alcoves branch off from the central space. In one of them, I see a low, blocky table that reminds me of the above-ground tombs sometimes found in the alcoves of European cathedrals.

I startle as a voice echoes from somewhere high.

"You are a woman," says the voice. It's a man, a slight Indian accent with an amused tinge to his voice. The words float in the cavernous room. I can't tell where the voice is coming from or even if it's coming from a speaker or a person.

"That's right," I call, tensing my shoulders and scanning the room for movement. "What gave it away?"

"I mean, you are a *human* woman," states the voice. "Certainly the first to visit this sanctuary. How interesting."

"Where are you?"

"Well, I don't know if I should answer that. You have a rather big knife."

I shrug my shoulders, the blade flashing in candlelight.

"It's not mine," I say, examining the dim walls. I can't seem to find the voice. It comes from everywhere and nowhere.

"Oh, I know. Peter is very fond of his *khanjali*. Has been for a long time. But even so, I am thinking it would be better to have my helper dispose of you. You *are* trespassing and, sorry to say, your presence is technically sacrilege."

The robot lays Peter's body on top of the blocklike table. Moving closer, I see it's made of molded white plastic, an operating table enclosed by a large ring of metal at either end. Together, the two rings create an empty cylinder that encloses the table and Peter. On the far side of the table, a pedestal extends upward.

Standing up straight, the robot turns to face me and pauses.

"Peter said you two were friends," I say.

"We were."

The robot turns and takes a step toward me.

Backing up, I pull the cedalion from my pocket and lift it to my eye. I scan the room again, listening to the robot's feet clacking on polished marble.

"I'm also a friend," I call out. "I'm here for Peter."

"Odd," replies the voice. "Considering our *shared friend* is so much the worse for wear. What have you done to him?"

Through the brass ring, the room looks exactly the same so far.

"I shot him."

A chuckle floats down from somewhere. "You are truthful, at least."

Then I spot the man.

Walking toward the railing, I see he is sitting up high on the wooden catwalk that rings the entire room. Below him, the rows of disembodied arms, legs, and feet hang from the railing like macabre sausages. The man is round, older, his head shaved bald. Wearing a light brown monk's robe, he sits with his bare legs dangling over the side, like a kid. On his feet are a pair of incongruous high-top basketball sneakers, bright white.

"Ah," he says, smiling at me. "You have Peter's toys."

Click. Click. The robot's feet scratch the floor as it moves closer.

The metal door behind me has locked. I have no place to run.

"You must be strong to be here," says the man. "Now let us find out *how* strong."

And he leaps off the catwalk.

26

INDIA, 1751

With the call of *pravda* beating in my ears, I seek battle in the name of my adopted sovereign, King George II—and I quickly find it. Established on the Thames, the frigates of John Company, otherwise known as the Honorable East India Company, are systematically deploying wave after wave of young soldiers to the shores of India.

Few questions are asked of new recruits.

A year later, I am perched in the winding parapets of a hastily fortified garrison, watching the sun ease itself over the low crooked buildings of a town in eastern India. The fragrant breeze washing up from the nearby river smells of lilac and mud. No water is visible from here, just heavy, vein-laced palm fronds that rustle gently. Frogs have begun their nightly mating songs, loud and hidden.

This meandering wall is all that defends a motley collection of damaged buildings and a hundred or so remaining British soldiers, nestled together in the heart of an occupied town called Arcot.

Wrapped in soiled white lengths of cotton, turbaned soldiers have swarmed the outer city, pikes and antique muskets bristling from their positions like river reeds. Among the broken faces of plaster buildings, shadow-drenched snipers lie waiting. I can feel their unseen eyes in the city, watching. The enemy army serves the Nawab of the Carnatic, Chanda Sahib. Draped over their weapons, the brown-skinned troopers seem unaffected by the heavy, alien heat that scours the land.

With the blade of my dagger, I carve another line into the stucco wall beside my position. One of our few cannons was placed here early on, promptly destroyed by enemy artillery, leaving only this crooked crow's nest.

The visible light blushes to crimson, then fades away entirely with dusk, leaving the walls glowing gently in my eyes, radiating the accumulated heat of the day into a warm darkness. Each line in the stucco gleams like a pale scar. Fifty-one marks, representing the days John Company has been held under siege.

A proud man, the sahib threw his lot in with the French after some slight to his honor. As our captain took the men of the Bengal Army west from Bombay, the nawab laid siege to us here.

My *khanjali* was already old when I claimed it from Peter the Great's armory nearly fifty years ago. Now the dagger has earned me a nickname. My English comrades simply call me the Russian. With no need for my whiskey or tobacco rations, I leveraged my share of supplies to earn allies among the troopers and quash any suspicions. Although nobody regards me with particular fondness, at least I am afforded respect.

Or I was, when my comrades were still living.

The last battle took place weeks ago, and since then our numbers have dwindled. Survivors have grown gaunt and wasted. Still wearing their once proud uniforms, the boys look like scarecrows stuffed into the clothes of other men. Although water is plentiful, there is precious little food.

The tedious expanse of time between fights has afforded me too much opportunity for contemplation. As streaks of starlight wink down at the parapets, my thoughts wander the contours of my Word.

Being here in service to my adopted monarch should have quelled the burning of *pravda* in my heart, but it has only cooled it to hateful ashes. Things were never so simple as they were in Favorini's workshop. I fight and live with a thorn buried in my side, always staggering toward the illusion of true purpose.

The sun has gone, and it is time for my nightly foray. I sheathe my dagger and leave my flintlock musket leaning against the wall, my red coat draped over it. Donning a black riding cape over a loose cotton shirt, I kneel beside the edge of the parapet. The evening breeze is picking up, kissed with river scent, pushing the cape over my shoulder.

Under my gaze, the dark city animates, alive with the residual heat of the day, simmering camp smoke, and the furtive movements of troops.

I slide over the edge of the wall and drop to the outer street, boots scraping the rubble. Palms slicing the air, I pump my arms and dash across the starlit gravel of the no-man's-land surrounding the garrison.

No rifle shots crack in the night.

Pressing my back against the remains of a building, I pause and listen. Out here, among the moon shadows of the outer city, my dagger has earned me a different nickname. Night after night, I am the thing that prowls the alleys. I take soldiers, one by one, each fatality adding to a mounting terror.

In hushed whispers, the nawab's men call me the man-eater of the Carnatic.

The enemy sepoys—Indian soldiers allied with the French—have begun to sleep closer to their campfires and in larger groups. Their European commanders have claimed the houses, barricading their doors against the night, deaf to the occasional panicked screams of their native allies. The legend of the man-eater has grown quickly and taken a firm hold in the minds of the locals—in their whispered tales the man-eater is an evil ghost, as tall as an ashoka tree, who transforms into a prowling tiger every night to savage the unwary.

The wounds inflicted by my dagger are a near-enough approximation of tiger bites. And with the mind of a man, I can fan the flames of horror. Creeping beside an abandoned building, I pause when I smell smoke from a nearby campfire. Quiet murmurs and the soldiers' perfume permeates the newborn evening.

This night will yield many lives to me, and in the gray morning I will place armfuls of food in a place where my besieged companions will find it—perhaps the only sustenance that keeps our hundred souls alive.

Blade drawn, I stalk toward the sounds and smells.

Hours swim past in the murky night, until the chilly scent of dew stings my nostrils and I notice the first tinge of silver dawn. On my way back, toting a bread-stuffed satchel, I notice the spy. Though I catch only a flash of a robe as he slips away, I charge.

Rounding the corner, I see nothing.

"Hello?" I call. "Reveal yourself."

All is silent.

Over the distant murmur of the river, an inhuman wail rises. It comes from near the main city road that leads to the front gates of my garrison. It is a low, throbbing bellow that grows into an angry trumpet, punctuated by the smaller shouts of men, like the sporadic chirping of disturbed birds.

Leaving the empty alley behind, I leap up the side of a crooked building and slither through a wall shattered by cannon fire, crawling on my belly over singed plaster and dirt until I reach a broken window.

Peering out, I see a great mass of turbaned men carrying long wooden pikes, clearly cut from the forest on the fringes of town. The smell of fresh-cut wood mingles in the air alongside the rich, ripe smell of dung. Between clusters of wide-eyed men, I make out shifting gray shapes, beasts with great flapping ears and domed foreheads that slope over small, intelligent eyes.

War elephants, being fitted with iron masks.

I keep the glow of sunrise at my back, sprinting through the city toward my crevice in the wall. The armored elephants scream distantly as the men drive their pikes into their flanks to spur them on. Corralled onto the main road, the beasts are lumbering toward the garrison and my unaware allies.

Today, the nawab has decided to stop the depredations of the man-eater. The cost of this blockade has risen too high. Today, he means to finally break the siege.

27

SEATTLE, PRESENT

The bald man streaks through the air and lands nearly silently, his round body lost within a brown monk's robe tied with a golden sash. He is reaching out and shaking my limp hand before I can react.

"Welcome," he says.

I don't let go right away, marveling at him.

"Batuo?" I ask. "I'm June."

The monk looks me up and down, a sudden smile sending crow's feet cascading across his temples. Besides wearing Nike high-tops, he has a pair of stylish and expensive-looking sunglasses hanging around his neck.

"My, my," he says. "What has Peter gotten us into?"

Batuo brushes past, leading the way to the strange table where Peter lies on his back. As we near, the table begins to hum, snake-skin glimmers of electricity arcing from the two polished metal rings that loop around either end.

Peter's eyes are closed as if he is sleeping.

Gently, Batuo brushes a lock of his friend's hair away and presses a pudgy palm against his forehead. Peter doesn't respond, although his chest rises and falls as it replicates the illusion of breathing.

"He fought another one of you. Another . . . *avtomat,*" I finish, saying the word reluctantly.

Batuo shoots me a concerned glance.

"That explains the knife wound," Batuo says, tracing a finger along the faint line that crosses Peter's mended cheek. "Did you do this repair?"

"We didn't have much time," I say.

"I'm surprised he allowed you to touch him."

"It was an emergency."

"Good work, for a human," Batuo says. "Now, straighten his legs and let's get started."

I go around the table and pull Peter's feet, wincing at the noises coming from inside his broken knee.

"Can you fix him?" I ask.

The monk smiles sadly, taking position at the waist-high pedestal that rises from the side of the operating table.

"Peter has gone into hibernation, so he must be hurt badly. We can repair his body. But I cannot speak for his soul."

Batuo's fingers press into the flat surface of the control panel.

The silver rings writhe with blue sparks and a breeze seems to rustle over Peter's body. His thick hair lifts, shivering as though it were weightless. Chest thrusting out, his head tilts back as his entire body rises.

Peter's long lean body hovers, the fabric of his clothes rippling.

The machine has grown quieter, the thrum dropped an octave into a nearly subsonic groan. Standing beside Batuo, I rest my fingertips along the edge of the table. It is cool, vibrating nearly imperceptibly. Silently, two pools of silver liquid surge into a shallow trough that wraps around the tabletop.

One by one, beads of the mirrorlike liquid separate, dribbling straight up. They separate into shuddering spherical droplets that keep drifting. In the air, the droplets solidify into larger globules. The liquid metal swirls, hardening and softening.

"This technology doesn't exist," I whisper.

"Don't be silly," replies Batuo. "You're looking at it."

Batuo slides his hands into what looks like a pair of brass knuckles resting on the control pedestal. As his arms move, the liquid shifts in tandem with his motions. Fingers wrapped in metal, Batuo is controlling the shimmering liquid.

The silver rings glow a brighter blue and an electrical haze spreads over the cylinder of space around Peter. As the liquid touches him it turns translucent, revealing a blurry image of his skeleton and internal organs. This machine isn't slicing him into pieces, it's filtering into his body and displaying what's happening inside.

Batuo concentrates, waving his hands in subtle undulations. He looks oddly like an old man doing Tai Chi in the park. The liquid metal flows through Peter's body, sliding across and into his face, neck, and shoulders. All around his torso, tiny pellets of buckshot are puckering his skin and wriggling out, ejected, dropping to the tabletop with tinking sounds.

As Batuo works, I recognize a familiar crescent outline glowing in the depths of Peter's rib cage. The shape is fitted into a reinforced shell mounted at the center of Peter's torso—cocooned in muscular layers of metal and plastic. And in the hazy flickering light, I see a symbol on it.

Peter has a relic—just like the one hanging around my neck.

The liquid metal slithers down Peter's body, closing around his knee, injecting itself into the shattered joint. Ribbons of it solidify and stay in place to heal the fractured material. Shredded flesh and broken pieces of Peter's knee are expelled, floating like fallen leaves toward the table. Meanwhile, the liquid is shrinking, losing mass as pieces solidify to form internal parts. Finally, the remaining metal drips back to the table, leaving the pink skin of Peter's restored knee visible through his shredded pants.

Peter's body lowers back to the table and the machine goes silent. He lies still, his newly repaired arms and legs laid out stiffly. His eyes are closed, and an occasional spark still dances over his face. Batuo sucks air between his teeth and drops the brass knuckle devices to the control pedestal.

"What?" I ask.

Head bowed, Batuo steps away from the machine.

"What is it?" I repeat.

"Inevitability," he responds, dejection in his voice. "Peter's anima, the source of his power and reason, has been knocked loose of its cradle. The last of his energy stores have leaked away. His hibernation will last another few days, and then he will fall into the long sleep."

"What can we do?"

"We have repaired his body, but it is not so easy to replenish his soul."

"You're talking about that thing in his chest, with the symbol?"

"Each *avtomat* has a unique anima—our mind, memories, and will. The symbol written upon it is his true self, the Word he lives by."

My fingers creep to my neck, pressed to my throat.

"Without the mind, the body is dust," says Batuo. "A vessel without its anima is but a husk—it cannot perceive or act. But when placed in the cradle of its own unique vessel, anima will express itself as . . . *avtomat*."

I reach into the neck of my shirt and pull out the relic that hangs there, letting it dangle by its chain. Batuo sees it and his eyes widen, words dying in his throat.

"I've been asking myself what this is for a long time," I say. "And all along I should have been asking *who*."

28

INDIA, 1751

The Nawab of the Carnatic is intent on breaking his long siege in Arcot. His plan is to bring down the reinforced front gate of our garrison using one of India's most incredible natural resources, the brute strength of armored war elephants. As the first hint of predawn stains the sky, I am sprinting at top speed into the middle of our encampment.

"To the walls!" I'm shouting to the malnourished remnants of John Company. "To the Delhi gate!"

Around me, the skeletal British troops are beginning to stir. Bleary-eyed and confused, they stand up beside extinguished campfires made of looted furniture. The boys are starving but well trained, instinctively gathering their flintlocks and powder.

"Prepare for attack!" someone shouts.

Dozens of men are already trotting toward the gate. A sergeant barks orders at those slower to stir, his voice rising as the ground begins to shake.

A sentry at the gate finally sounds his horn.

The meandering line of torches, pikes, and beasts must have become visible in the outer city, siege breakers rampaging toward our gates with a thousand sepoys reinforcing from behind.

I sprint back toward my favorite spot on the parapet, hearing the strange trumpeting screams of the elephants over the chirping of morning birds. Climbing the sagging bones of the wall, I clamber onto my abandoned ledge.

Moving quickly, I reclaim my musket and don my red coat. I jam my tricorne hat over my head and peer over the edge. A river of turbaned sepoys is snaking across no-man's-land on a side route toward an old breach in the wall, firing arrows and waving swords and spears. Some are carrying ladders hewn of rough wood from the forest.

It's a dual attack, elephants on the gates and men at the breach.

"Escalade!" I shout to my allies. In the dawn, I can make out pairs of red jackets swarming up the interior fort walls. Surplus muskets from men lost long ago have been laid out to form loading relays. Alerted to this sneak attack, the men take new positions to repel the horde with superior weaponry.

I hear the first snaps of what will soon be near-continuous fire.

Farther along the wall, a contingent of sepoy pikemen are closing in on our main gate, spurring gaudily decorated war elephants onward with jabs to their great quivering flanks. The elephants are a horrific sight, faces wreathed in iron masks, tusks capped in gold, huge armored foreheads already butting into the wood of the gate. If they knock down the barricade, our camp will be flooded by thousands of enemy.

Time slows for me, the seconds counted off by the metronome of gunshots.

Loading my musket, I steady my barrel with a steel grasp and fire a precise shot at the nearest elephant. I ignore the hundreds of human attackers and the splintering gate, targeting the beast's tender ears, vulnerable to a lateral attack. My first few shots send the lead elephant rearing back in confusion, disturbing its brothers. The monster is graceful and intelligent, and a sadness settles over me as I keep firing.

The beast squeals and thrashes back, lungs heaving in its chest, its trunk dark with blood as it crushes the pikemen attempting to drive it forward. The attackers scream as they fall, writhing like insects under the weight of the panicked elephants, staggered by the withering, ceaseless gunfire from the walls.

The roaring chants and shouts of the attackers fade; and for a moment I pause, simply watching the chaos. The battle at the gate is engulfed in great undulating ribbons of powder smoke and showers of sparks that spray like meteors from flintlock muskets. Atop the walls, a few officers work their weapons with grim intensity, malnourished cheeks sunken and yellow beneath soiled white wigs, moving like animated corpses.

The nawab's attack is breaking.

A last elephant spins and flees, stamping bodies into the dirt. The behemoth's small red eyes are bright with panic as it crashes through the reinforcing wave of sepoys, shattering the line. The barrage of musket fire from our walls becomes more sporadic as the men pick off individual soldiers below.

Escalade ladders lay like bits of straw on the field, amid crumpled bodies.

Seeing the vast carnage, I find that I cannot bear to lift my weapon again. Less than an hour has passed, yet the stinging heat of the morning is already rising along with the wailing buzz of insects. The alien screams of a last wounded elephant echo through empty city streets, mingling with the wailing of men who lay dying.

A sergeant calls out orders over the morning cicadas, a comforting staccato rhythm urging us to save ammunition. No mercy shots. A final, timed volley breaks across a broken final line of attackers, sending the sepoys into full retreat.

This is a massacre. Meaningless. One-sided.

As I sit, staring at blood-soaked dirt without seeing, a small movement draws my notice. An enemy sepoy lies at the foot of my wall. He is praying, unarmed and with both legs crushed, having dragged himself here from the gate. Cheek gleaming with a sheen of sweat, his turban and black hair have uncurled behind him like spilled intestines. The mortally wounded man is alone, abandoned by his comrades to an agonizing death.

Without thinking, I climb down. As I descend, I hear only my fingers gritting against the crumbling stucco and the far-off shouts of wounded men. My boots land on hard-packed soil, in the shade of the partially collapsed wall.

The wounded man is before me.

On his stomach, the soldier hears my approach and turns over onto his back, biting down a groan. Young and well muscled, he watches me calmly from above a thick black mustache. His eyes widen slightly as he takes in my height, his gaze lingering on the *khanjali* hanging at my belt. Only the rapid rise and fall of his chest reveals the pain he is suffering. Both his legs are twisted and trampled.

"Chale jao, aadamakhor," he pants, sticking his chin out, defiant.

Go away, Man-eater.

Once, *pravda* was clear to me. By obeying my emperor, all was well. But what was simple is becoming complex. I can see no evil inside this grievously wounded man, only honor. And though no clockwork flutters beneath his throat, I can see the inevitable forces that led him here, through no fault of his own, fating him to die in the shadow of this crumbling wall.

I kneel and hold out my canteen to him.

The soldier regards me suspiciously, tries to move his arm but is too weak. His eyes close for a long moment. When they open they are wet and angry.

I push the canteen to his lips and give the dying man a last sip of water. As he drinks, it is as though I can feel the cool satisfaction of his quenched thirst. The mercy of the act has satisfied *pravda* just as well as vengeance ever did—justice from injustice, my adopted sovereign's will be damned.

A new terrain of right and wrong is emerging, dizzying my senses.

Across the plain, I see the humped backs of fleeing war elephants and curled bodies of fallen men, the dust congealed with their blood. Fresh-cut pikes lay scattered across the main road. The sky is writhing with clouds of buzzing flies.

I stand, steadying myself against the wall. This shift in perspective washes over me like vertigo.

Raising my eyes, I see the British lads perched high, surveying the field with spyglasses. The boys are smiling, teeth filthy, faces covered in dust and soot. They are glad to be alive, proud of the slaughter they've inflicted. They see enemies and allies on the field of battle, but I can see only men.

Some are alive. Some are dead.

"Why do you do this?" I ask the dying man. "Are you crazy? Are you all crazy?"

At my feet, the man closes his eyes and his breathing slows. His chest falls and does not rise again. His power supply has extinguished itself in a seeping red puddle in the dirt. I place the canteen on his chest and leave it there, stepping out of the shadow of the wall and into the harsh sunlight.

For the king. For the glory of England. The cries of hollow-eyed young men have begun to ring false in my ears. I no longer quite understand their meaning.

"Hey," I hear a call from above. "Man-eater!"

Craning my neck, hand falling to the hilt of my saber, I squint at the top of the wall. A small, round man stares down at me, a look of amusement on his face. His head is shaved, thin legs dangling over the side. A pair of ostentatiously embroidered golden sandals hang from his feet. In one hand, he holds a long, garishly carved tobacco pipe. Now, he nonchalantly goes about trying to light it.

"They *are* crazy, Man-eater," says the round man, sucking on the pipe. "All of humankind is crazy. I should have thought you'd already know by now!"

29

SEATTLE, PRESENT

"So? Who is this?" I ask Batuo.

The curved relic hangs in my fingers, its surface echoing the candlelight of chandeliers mounted high above.

Batuo stares at the relic for a long moment, almost wistful. Finally, with visible effort, the old man tears his gaze away and lands it back on Peter, still unconscious. The tall man's body has been repaired, his new skin baby smooth under clothing that's been torn by shotgun pellets.

"That anima belongs to a powerful ruler," says Batuo quietly. "Supremely knowledgeable. And older than time out of mind."

Batuo looks back at me with clear, intense eyes. "You must understand that whoever holds that artifact is in great danger. Another *avtomat* seeks it. One who has also lived since before all reckoning and grown unfathomably strong."

"Talus," I say.

Batuo chuckles and shakes his head.

"This one is the master of Talus, and of many others. Her names are manifold, almost meaningless in their variety over the ages, but we knew her first as Leizu . . . the Worm Mother."

"What does she want with this relic?" I ask.

"In all of this great existence, across the rise and fall of civilizations . . . there is only one whom she fears," says Batuo. "The one you keep over your heart."

If the blond monster in the motorcycle helmet is only a servant, then I definitely don't want to meet his master. I rest a hand lightly on Peter's shoulder. He feels warm, chest rising and falling, but his eyes are still closed.

"We have to wake him up. He knows what to do."

"Peter's anima . . ." Batuo trails off, taps his chest. "His relic, as you call it. Its power is nearly extinguished."

"Let's recharge him, then," I urge.

With a wan smile, Batuo beckons me to follow. We walk below the curtain of disembodied arms and legs hanging from the catwalk. The fleshy limbs form a grotesque canopy over our heads, synthetic bones jutting from shoulders and hip joints. Each body part is labeled with a yellowed tag—its owner. Skin tones and musculature vary, and I recognize male and female limbs of various races and ages.

How many of these creatures did there used to be?

"All of this that you see is cosmetic," calls Batuo, waving a hand. He runs his fingers across a row of dangling feet, leaving the legs swaying slightly. "We *avtomat* can change our skin, but not our souls. Each anima belongs to a unique vessel. Our bodies can evolve with new technology, but only slowly. Too much change and the form loses coherence. Over these past millennia we have become stronger and more humanlike, but the anima that we each carry is inviolate—ancient and beyond our understanding."

Stooping instinctively, I pass beneath the body parts and follow Batuo through a tight archway. We enter a study hemmed in by ornately carved wood-paneled walls. The room is lit by a coral chandelier hanging over a floor layered in thick antique rugs. Every wall is lined with books and artifacts.

"You don't know how you're made?" I ask, incredulous. "But you've had a thousand years to study the science."

Batuo slips behind a massive walnut desk, its legs carved into elephants that are rearing back to support the cluttered slab of wood. He props his elbows on top, the chair squeaking under his wide bottom.

"Science? This way of thinking is a construct of the last few centuries. Since antiquity, men have known only various forms of magick. The aqueducts of Rome were considered a natural magick, for example, the water wheels powered by hidden angels."

Batuo laughs, continuing.

"This thing you call science was our gift to you, and a recent one."

Wandering deeper into the room, I run my eyes over a gleaming multitude of artifacts that line the walls, marveling at the sheer age and quality of the swords, skulls, jewelry, paintings, busts, and countless strange curios.

I pause at what I thought was a sculpture. Instead, I see it is a crude face stitched from leather, mounted on a mannequin's head. The eyes and mouth are missing, but I can see the outlines of features. Beside it, three more faces are mounted similarly, each more lifelike than the last—ever more realistic versions of the chubby Indian man sitting behind the desk, his perfectly humanlike face dotted with moles.

Batuo has been evolving a long, long time.

"Someone made us, sometime," he explains. "After countless centuries, through the ages of man, we lost the knowledge of who. In rare periods of enlightenment, some enterprising humans found our discarded bodies, repaired them, and replaced the *anima de machina*. But the longer we have lain dormant before such crude resurrection, the more our memories fade. And in this way, we have forgotten ourselves."

Now I recognize this alcove as a Renaissance-era *Wunderkammer*, a wonder room, once kept by emperors and naturalists, filled with antiquities and treasures and the uncategorizable wonders of the world.

"After all this time," Batuo continues, "we are unable to re-create the feats of our ancestors. We do not know exactly who made us or when, and, most important—we don't know how. This is why so many *avtomat* are asleep in my catacombs. And it is why some others have chosen to hunt their own kind."

"If you can't do anything to help, then why would Peter bring me here?" I ask.

Batuo comes around the desk. In the dusty quiet, he extends one finger and presses it against the relic hanging around my neck.

"Because *he* knows how to save us. We just have to resurrect him."

My hand finds its familiar spot over the relic and I step back. My eyes can barely focus on the incredible antiquities lining the walls. The violence and secrets and impossible technology are all too much to absorb, too fast.

"Batuo," I say, "I don't think I can do this."

"I think you can, young lady," he says, eyes sparkling. "You are in possession of a cedalion. Such a thing has never happened. Peter has made you part of his plan and it is no coincidence. You were chosen, June."

I swallow, words stalling in my throat.

"Chosen? To do what? Have you seen these things fight? There's no way I can deal with—"

Batuo waves my objections away, shaking his head.

"Your thoughts on the matter are immaterial, my dear. Fate has chosen you to become part of our story. Together, we will find the true vessel for that relic, and do so quickly . . . before Leizu destroys us all."

30

INDIA, 1751

Man-eater. The monk cackles at me from the top of the garrison wall, a ribbon of smoke rising idly from his long, elaborate pipe. At my feet, the corpse of the Indian soldier rests against a fallen stone. The young man has dragged himself here on crushed legs, away from the carnage—only to die at my feet in agony.

And this baboon giggles at the sight.

With sudden anger, I bury my fingers in the cool crevice of the wall and haul myself up in a few neat lunges. The monk barely has time to swallow his chuckle before I am upon him, fingers wrapped in his robe, pulling his wide face close to mine. The twinkle does not fade from his blue-gray eyes as I roughly yank him to his feet, turn, and dangle him over the edge of the wall.

"Is it so funny?" I ask him.

The monk twists, wriggling out of my grasp.

Falling in a cloud of swirling robes, he lands back on the parapet, pirouetting away from my swinging fist, fat fingers flashing with gaudy rings and his golden sash cutting the air. With a flourish, he lands and extends one arm in an exaggerated curtsy. As he rises, his other hand plants the long wooden pipe back between his teeth.

"Rude of me," he apologizes in a chirpy English accent, smiling around the pipe stem. "Terribly rude. Sorry to call you Man-eater. If you told me a proper name, well, I'd be happy to use it."

Straightening and regaining my stance, I watch him closely. Something about the man strikes me as odd—some off-kilter angle that lingers beneath his skin; a synthetic precision to his movements. I lean forward, training my eyes on him.

"Yes," he says, beaming. "Of course we're both the same."

"You are *avtomat,*" I say.

The monk's smiling eyes narrow. His mouth pops open in disbelief. "I'm not the first you've met, am I?"

Somewhere, Elena is haunting a drawing room, safe from this butchery and madness. Her visage slips through my thoughts for an instant, and the observant monk registers something in my locked jaw and impassive features.

"Perhaps not," he says, pipe clenched in his teeth. He puffs on it, letting his eyes crawl over my face, absorbing any and all information. "But I'm one of few, I'll chance," he adds. "I heard hysterical rumors of a ghost tiger who came in the night. I knew it would be one of *us*. Our presence does so often precede legend."

He arches his eyebrows at me.

"Who sent you here, soldier? For whom do you fight?"

"For my sovereign, King George," I reply.

"Ah," he replies, unconvinced. "And what Word brings you all the way to India?"

I don't respond.

"Hm, not a talker," he says, eyes flickering over me. "I see you've found a decent leathersmith. Your face is passable. You aren't great at remembering to make expressions, but at least you breathe. I can see your vessel was created by a master. And not so long ago."

"What is long ago," I ask, "when death does not come for our kind?"

"Long ago?" he asks, lighting the pipe again. "If only you knew, my boy. Long ago is an endless repetition of day and night, humans scurrying through caves to hide from monsters, barbarians fighting one another with sticks and stones. It is the return of the great ice from the north and saber-toothed beasts you wouldn't believe. Long ago is the dead time before metal or ships or cities.

"Be glad that you know nothing of 'long ago.' In that way, you were lucky."

The monk curls his arms across each other, sulking, puffing on the pipe and grinding his teeth. His muttering sounds both sad and angry.

I move to step past him and he pulls his pipe from between his teeth and points the stem at me.

"Aha," he says. "It is your height, of course, that gives you away. Let me guess. They must have named you Peter."

Stunned, I do not respond.

"I see I am right. Rumors, rumors. Word spread across Europe of the *vampir* in Moscow, and of a tall man, a fighter who operated in the night circuits, deep in the oubliettes of the royal household. I can only imagine what you've been through, with the tsar's death. And yet you have not sought out your own kind? Why is that? I wonder."

"I will not be drawn into your wars," I say, gritting my teeth. This man already knows too much, and I know nothing of him.

"Ah, Peter." He sighs, shaking his head at me. "My dear *Pyotr*."

The monk paces the parapet, speaking quickly. The ridiculous little silk sandals stay perched on his toes, extravagantly decorated with fish scales and golden trim.

"You've come to fight in this backwater war, of all wars?" he asks. "To satisfy your Word, you have found an obscure battle at the end of the earth? And not to exterminate slavers or stop rituals of human sacrifice but to *secure favorable terms of trade* for the British Empire?"

I say nothing, my bones aching with unsatisfied *pravda*. The monk blinks, confused.

"But perhaps you wonder the same thing," he muses. "Is that where I have found you today? Questioning?"

The monk grins entirely too much. And he moves too quickly for a man of his stature.

Carefully, I circle toward my musket. The flintlock leans against the stucco wall, its bayonet protruding like a broken finger. My left hand settles on the ivory handle of the sheathed *khanjali* where it traces its familiar line along my thigh.

The monk throws his hands up, laughing gently. "Oh, I certainly don't wish to engage you, Tsar Peter," he says. "I represent the Maratha. We are here to stop this siege and rescue your company, of course.

That's why the sahib attacked this morning. It was his last chance before your reinforcements arrived."

Glancing at the gate, I see the flag of the Maharashtra is being raised. A local army of reinforcements are threading through the city. The monk speaks the truth.

"Peter," he says, "my name is Batuo. And I am here to set you free."

31

SEATTLE, PRESENT

The first blow sounds like a knock, the second like a detonation.

Batuo stands without a word, dwarfed by his massive desk. He yanks a red-tasseled spear from its display on the wall, holding it lightly in one hand with surprising familiarity. Darting out of the alcove, he pauses under the sprawl of hanging artificial arms and legs, a chubby silhouette against the candlelight of the cathedral room.

"Protect that relic," he says to me. "If her servants fail, Leizu will come for you herself."

Batuo walks away, resolute, the long spear flexing with each stride.

Through the alcove archway, across the marble floor, the metal security door shivers with an impact. A bullet spits through, leaving a spiral of twisted metal like confetti. Batuo drops to his stomach and rolls gracefully out of the way as the door's metal surface erupts into a frenzy of puckered holes and shreds of metal.

Finally, the whole frame collapses in a haze of smoke. Batuo calmly stands back up and dusts off his robe. He retrieves his weapon and faces the door.

The thing that calls itself Talus strides through the doorway like a demon, still wearing torn leather motorcycle armor. He tosses a smoking machine gun to the ground. In his other hand, he carries a short black scabbard with a round hilt protruding.

Protect the relic.

Scrambling, I rush around the alcove, scanning the walls for anything I can use as a weapon. Ancient bows and broadswords aside, I finally settle on something that looks like a bone saw, an electric tool, sterile and white. Clutching the thing in both hands, I depress a button. A shining circular blade on the end sings as it spins up to speed.

This is more my style.

"Herr Talus Silfverström," calls Batuo from the other room, "I am afraid you are not invited, sir."

With the weighty saw in both hands, I creep under the archway and along the outer wall of the cathedral-like room, circling toward where Peter lies unconscious on the surgery machine. My vision throbs with the beat of my heart as I try to breathe quietly and force myself to move slowly.

"I do not need your medical attention, Batuo," says Talus. "You have given harbor to our enemies. Our pact is void."

Batuo has planted his feet and taken a wide stance, leaning on his back foot. He lifts his left knee and angles the spear down like a scorpion's stinger. The monk looks perfectly lethal—except for the ridiculous basketball sneakers on his feet.

Talus circles carefully. His face is patched up, long blond hair hanging over the worst of the damage, but I can see ragged gashes where my shotgun pellets penetrated his skin earlier. His upper lip is twisted into a permanent sneer.

"There are so few of us now," says Talus. "I admire that you've made it this far. But the time has come . . . your anima is due."

With a flick of his wrist, Talus draws the short, stocky sword and tosses the wooden scabbard to the ground. It's a Roman gladius, the round pommel polished, blade oiled. The antique has been maintained as a fighting weapon, but the blade is nearly black under a patina of time.

"I respectfully disagree," says Batuo, shifting slightly, causing the red tassel to swing hypnotically from the tip of his spear. Talus changes direction in response to the small movement, circling the other way.

"You are an old dog with old tricks," says Talus. "The last Shaolin soldier monks died out centuries ago. Elderly people practice your miraculous forms in the park. It isn't even a true martial—"

Sensing some near imperceptible flicker in Batuo's stance, Talus spins away as the nurse robot charges from the shadows, lunging at him in stumbling jerks. The robot was waiting for Batuo to maneuver Talus into place before it attacked.

Far too slowly.

Reversing the blade, Talus steps back and buries his sword in the hard plastic carapace of the machine. Savagely, he twists the blade with both hands. Sneering at Batuo, Talus withdraws the blade slowly and lets the robot drop in a heap.

"Worth a try," says Batuo, stepping forward.

While they are distracted, I slide around a pillar and trot over to the low white surgical table where Peter's body is resting. The bone saw is heavy in my sweating hands. Heavy, and probably useless.

"Peter," I whisper, kneeling beside him. Batuo said he had some power left. I can only hope he hears me.

In the middle of the vast room, Talus and Batuo have fallen into a blur of movement. Batuo is a flurry of brown robes, twisting and spinning, the precariously long bamboo spear flicking out like a snake's tongue. Talus advances relentlessly, jerking his body through short, vicious feints and dodges, hacking at the spear.

Almost dancing, his movements economical and beautiful, Batuo lands the butt of the spear across Talus's midsection. Staggered, the next blow nearly takes off the blond man's head, but he raises both forearms in time to catch the spinning shaft. A crack like a lightning strike echoes into the candlelit heights.

"Listen," I whisper to Peter's body, "I think I understand what you want me to do. And if I had five years and a laboratory full of people smarter than me, maybe I could figure out how this relic works."

Talus is up, blade whirling, a smaller knife in his other hand. Ribbon slices of Batuo's robes are curling through the air as he dodges. Each fighter is predicting the moves of the other, lending a lilting delay to their feints and counterfeints.

"But I can't do *this,*" I continue. "I'm not like you. I'm not as strong."

The spear absorbs an impact, splintering and shattering into two pieces. Batuo spins away with a hitch in his step, one hand clasped to his side. Under his flayed robes, I can see the structure of his rib cage.

"You always were very quick," says Batuo through gritted teeth. "As a praetorian you were unstoppable."

The short gladius flickers out again, gleaming blackly, like a poisoned fang. Batuo retreats to the arched door of the alcove, beneath a butcher's shop of hanging arms and legs. Talus follows without hesitation.

"This is yours, okay?" I whisper to Peter.

Sliding the necklace over my head, I hold the relic that my grandfather gave me in both hands, one last time. I press the crescent of metal into Peter's limp hand and close his fingers over it. He looks like a man, but Peter is a machine. The *avtomat* operate by their own rules, and I can't survive in this brutal world of theirs.

Unlike a machine, I bleed.

"I'm sorry, Peter," I whisper. "You chose the wrong person."

Gripping the bone saw in my hands, I take a last glance at my relic and tense to run. But the artifact is glowing now, energized by the electrical field of the machine. A hazy symbol is emerging, the white outline of a water droplet stained with a black eye. It's so familiar . . . I try to place where I've seen it before—

Talus screams.

At the mouth of the alcove, Batuo and Talus stand under what look like tree branches blowing in a nonexistent wind, falling, crashing down. The writhing canopy of limbs are animating all at once, wriggling off their hooks in a squirming, clawing mass.

Talus fights desperately, overwhelmed by the gruesome waterfall of limbs.

Using the distraction, Batuo charges out and lands a kick just as Talus swings again, blindly. Knocked onto his back, Talus disappears under a swarm of scratching, kicking limbs. Batuo doubles over, hurt badly, both hands pressed to the tear in his side, trying and failing to keep his wound closed.

That was it. Batuo's last trick. And it wasn't enough.

Now, I'm trotting around the surgical station, heading for the demolished door. Behind me, the silver rings that circle the white table are humming. I cradle the bone saw against my chest and accelerate to a crouched sprint.

Across the room, Talus shakes off a blanket of quivering, grasping arms and legs. Eyes leveled on Batuo, he raises the gladius. One, two, three . . . and Talus leaps over the carpet of limbs, sword poised above his head. The monk is trying to spin away as the blade slices cleanly through his right arm. The severed limb falls to join the others. The next blow takes his leg off at the thigh, and then I don't know what's happening because I can't bear to watch.

As I reach the demolished metal door, I stop. The hairs on the back of my neck are standing up. Hearing nothing, I turn to look back.

Talus stands over Batuo's dismembered corpse, watching me, smiling with a torn upper lip.

32

INDIA, 1757

Over the next year I think often of the Indian boy, bleeding to death at the foot of a stucco wall. In my memory, his face is impossibly young, legs trampled, blood leaking into hard furrows of dried mud carved by last winter's artillery barrages. I try to imagine the forces of destiny, great and small, that brought him to his end there and I wonder whether there was truly justice served in his death to foreign invaders, on his own soil.

The monk follows me, chattering constantly.

I agree with Batuo that a single man is short-lived, largely ignorant of the past and future, and can be trusted to make a selfish decision if no eyes are upon him. But he urges me to consider them in their multitude—in the incredible profusion of human cities and nations and languages and cultures. He claims that a precious thing emerges from that scratching, clawing horde: the thing they call civilization.

With proper culture, Batuo argues that men can be forged into something greater.

We continue the campaign across India with John Company. Our commander drives our forces against the remaining nawabs without fear or mercy. And as I am swept along, going through the motions of fighting, I find that each new engagement means less and less.

"Are you ready to leave?" Batuo asks, reappearing in the front ranks after an absence of a month.

"No," I say.

"Stubborn," is his usual reply.

Across the rich flank of India, I loot exotic artifacts and send them home to Elena. Cloistered on our new estate, she seems to be in high spirits. She reports the servants are dutiful in obeying her, especially via the official letters of instruction she forges in my name, under my seal. She sends me playful demands for esoteric Eastern artifacts and books, which I try to acquire. I sense Elena has found some grand intellectual quest to pursue and I am glad for it.

On the side, I receive an occasional letter from the butler, outlining the state of things and especially Elena's activities. But as the months accumulate, letters from the estate stop reaching me. I assume that my frequent identity changes have finally made it too difficult. The bodies of my fellow soldiers provide a carousel of different personas, and though it feels macabre to stalk the battlefield like a parasite, I make a habit of taking new names.

The monk is irritating enough; I do not intend to advertise my existence to any other *avtomat*.

Batuo's agenda is curious, impossible for me to guess. Once, while wandering in an imperial courtyard, the monk noticed me marveling at the golden sculpture of a peculiar fat man who sits cross-legged. I struggled to lift the valuable Buddha for packing, and Batuo scowled, taking offense.

"You never change," he said, and those odd words echoed in my thoughts long after he uttered them.

Batuo even accompanies me, off and on, into battle. The monk fights hand to hand or with a spear, but never with a musket. If possible, he avoids fighting altogether. Where I strike without pause, he shows compassion. We choose different paths, and he says nothing of my choices. On occasion, I catch him watching me too closely, and I sense unspoken words lingering on the tip of his tongue.

"Is your Word satisfied?" he asks one day, back again from an unexplained absence. A recent slaughter has left the battlefield heaped with twisted bodies, piled like driftwood on a deserted beach. "Do these dead men satisfy you? Is this your purpose?"

I march on without responding. My Word has become a splinter in my heart. *Pravda.* The unity of truth and justice. Though I gorge myself, punishing our enemies in the name of my king—this hunger has only grown. The monk is like a mosquito in my ear, a constant buzzing reminder that I am failing myself.

"The world is large, my friend," Batuo says, shaking his head. "Can you call yourself alive if you do not learn and grow?"

In this way, the monk lectures. Until one day, our time together ends.

Stopping outside the village of Plassey, the company shelters in a grove of mango trees near the broad muddy bank of the Bhagirathi River. The infantry soldiers are smoking little cigars, telling jokes in shaky voices as others prepare the cannonade. At the edge of the grove, the British sepoy troops prepare their weapons and pray.

It is dawn. Another day of battle. I feel nothing.

In the distance, the low, muted roar of tens of thousands of enemy infantry rises from the great empty plain. Our force numbers perhaps two thousand, better armed and positioned but grossly outmanned. Angry-looking storm clouds are gathering overhead. In this calm moment, the world smells of river water and dirt and sighing trees.

Then, with a hollow thwack, the first pulse of an artillery barrage begins. Our cannonade responds in kind.

To my immortal eyes, indifferent to death, this world is like a fantastical dream.

Enemy artillery shells streak like shooting stars through the tendons of primeval, leaning trees, staining their chattering leaves with flame and showering the ranks below with splinters and shrapnel. A drummer hits a staccato rhythm that mingles with the deep bass of thunder. Under a ghostly haze of smoke, men in red coats and tricorne hats feed shot into dragon-mouthed cannons that vomit hell.

Over the firing, a hushing sound grows as the clouds release their water. Artillerymen rush to cover the cannons and powder with sheets of waxed canvas. During the downpour, no cannon can fire. Muskets are equally useless.

I draw my saber. Through the dense leaves, the plains beyond the grove are swimming with greenish shadows. A horde of enemy infantry, stampeding.

What is the first thing?

Lightning flashes, and I am charging out of the grove, joining our sepoy contingent as they maneuver onto the rain-pricked plain. An inhuman howl rises from thirty thousand throats. The men around me fall into formation with the same inevitability as the falling raindrops. Where they land is just as meaningless.

And I find Batuo beside me, defensively wielding a long spear.

I swing the saber, slashing through flesh and rain. Searing bright roots of lightning anchor the sky and a veil of rain drapes itself over chaos. The guns have gone silent, leaving only the ring of steel weapons and the screams of men in triumph or despair.

Dancing over the mud, a pike catches me in the hip. I slash its owner with my saber. With my free hand, I yank the weapon out and keep swinging. I am screaming now as well, adding my own bellow to the thunder's, feeling the vibration of both in my chest.

Batuo guards my back as a faceless legion of infantry spreads around us, avoiding our weapons as naturally as a school of fish parting around a shark. Still, there are too many, pouring past us toward the grove. Another blade slides over my shoulder. My left arm stops working correctly.

I drop to a knee, still thrusting with my saber. The mud is becoming heaped with bodies of the fallen, forming a monstrous barricade.

"Peter!" screams Batuo.

The monk stands alone, his long, tasseled spear in both hands. His turban is soaked, face streaked with wet soil. His expression is of despair.

"Why must you do this!? What is wrong with you!?"

Rain coursing over my face, I tug my saber across the flesh of another attacker. The punishment and the truth of it are missing from the act. I truly am a damaged machine following its course, the same as these mannequins who are made of meat. I can no longer satisfy *pravda*—even as I follow its phantom into the depths of death and destruction.

I swing again.

And now Batuo is upon me, fingers laid like stones over my damaged shoulders. He drags me to my knees, his lips against my ear, voice thundering.

"Enough!" he shouts. "This is not who you are!"

Batuo sweeps an arm at the field, crawling with wounded soldiers.

"You cannot fight for a man and call it justice. Your Word transcends humankind," he shouts.

Shrugging his hands off, I plant a fist in his chest and launch the monk away from me. He falls with a splash, ignoring the war cries and staggering attacks of the final group of soldiers who throttle past.

"What do you know of my Word?" I shout to the mud.

Clutching my saber, I drag myself toward the fallen *avtomat*.

"I thought you would come back on your own," says the monk, "if I gave you enough time."

Batuo lies on his back, eyes open, not resisting. As I approach with my blade out, he betrays no fear on his mud-streaked face, only sadness. The downpour is coming to an end, the main infantry force moving on. Under spitting rain and sunlight, the world is bright and still.

"How do you know me?" I ask, again. "Tell me the truth!"

"The longer our souls are parted from our bodies, the more we forget. And you were lost for such a long time," he says, sitting up, voice breaking.

"I have never been lost," I tell him, raising my saber. "Never in my life."

"What do you know of your life!?" asks Batuo, dragging himself out of the mud and onto his feet. "Peter, we last met thousands of years ago."

"Impossible," I say, but my blade is wavering.

"We rode in glory for the Yellow Emperor. You and I shattered the forces of southern Qi and ended their practices of slavery and sacrifice. In service to the mighty Huangdi, we gave the people knowledge and forged the first dynasty of man. I thought . . . if we fought together again, I prayed you would remember."

I lower my saber, considering.

"I lost you to *her*," continues Batuo. "The mother of silkworms. Wife to our emperor and his equal. *Leizu*."

As the name leaves his lips, a flash of recognition ignites in my mind. I remember the hanging in Tyburn.

Leizu.

I sheathe my saber and draw my dagger. Falling forward, I let the point dimple the damp fabric of his robe.

"If you truly know me, then tell me," I whisper, "what is my true Word?"

Only a handful know this thing. A little girl and a mechanician and a dead tsar. The answer will reveal Batuo as a fraud—and then I can continue to follow my path into oblivion. But the monk only smiles.

"You have no Word," he says.

"What?"

"Our souls were never written in any language that exists today. When I knew you last, on the banks of the Long River, we called it *zhēnxiàng*. Roughly, it means—"

Something sparks in my mind, a translation.

"Truth and justice," I say.

"More or less," he says, nodding.

The legacy of Favorini is broken. This overwhelming feeling, this urge—the *first thing*—it is not even *called pravda*. The first thing is older, more complicated, and harder to know. The ground seems to be crumbling beneath my feet. Desperation constricts my chest, an overwhelming fear mingled with another feeling—hope.

A deeper truth exists, waiting to be found.

The muddy plain swirls in my vision, an open field inviting me to go every direction at once, and none. So I choose one and start walking: east, in the direction of British tall ships that will continue to ferry fresh-faced young men to India for as long as rich old men want more.

"Stop, Peter!" calls Batuo, standing on a field of mud that is now baking under the sun. His robes are stained with reddish smears and his fancy sandals are rimed in muck. Batuo's long spear cants out of the ground beside him, the shaft buried, red tassels streaming from the neck of the blade.

But an irresistible urge has flared in my breast, a bone-shaking need to protect that which I hold most dear. Elena is in England and she is alone; and until this moment I have been blinded by this mad quest for purpose. I thought she would be safe, but the encounter with Leizu was no coincidence. I was a fool. Now, my selfish warring may have cost me everything.

A dark fear is settling over me, a bleak certainty that I have lost her.

"Where are you going?" calls Batuo and I ignore him.

Panic pinches at my calves, urging me to break into a run.

The battlefield is strewn with fallen men under a brooding heat. Back at the grove where our forces are concentrated, I hear the chalky bark of revived cannons spewing death into the remaining enemy. Our men covered up the powder stores before the rain could drown them. Now, only one army has weapons, and so yet another slaughter unfolds.

I am being pulled away, to the east.

"Didn't you hear what I said?" Batuo asks, shadowing me. He tugs on my elbow and I shake it off. "You have a great enemy. Leizu is hunting you. She has been for a long time."

"I have met this enemy before," I say. "In London, where I must return."

"No! Stay here with me, Peter. At the front, in these exotic lands, death and mayhem can shroud our existence. Listen to me, I have survived a very long time."

I stop, spinning to face Batuo.

"You tell me of a life I don't remember. Well, there is a life I do remember. And the only thing that matters in it is my sister, in London."

Batuo locks his hands on my shoulders.

"Then stop and listen to words that could save her life."

I force myself to wait, legs buzzing with panic.

"There is a war between ancients and we are caught in the middle of it. Leizu, mother of silkworms, is of the progenitor race—known to the First Men—from a time before history. She has passed through all the ages of man, extending her life span by preying on other *avtomat*. Leizu wears the anima of the vanquished. If she finds you, she will consume your soul."

A vision washes over my mind. Elena's innocent face, inches away from mine, her arms tight around my neck. Somewhere, a dragon is roaring, flecks of hot spittle twirling past in yellow clouds. The silhouette of a woman wavers in the haze—death incarnate.

Batuo lets go of my shoulders and steps back, enveloped in earthy smelling clouds of steam rising off hardening mud.

"In London you will be vulnerable to her. It could take her decades, but she will find you. The two of you have . . . unsettled business."

"My allegiance is to my sister," I say, "not to any war."

I set my eyes on the muddy horizon and walk.

"Peter, the war you speak of—" Batuo calls. "It is a war *you started*!"

As Batuo's final words wash over me, I break into a run.

33

SEATTLE, PRESENT

Talus is a hellish sight in the dim candlelight of the buried cathedral—a pale, beautiful man with a disfigured face, wearing black motorcycle armor and standing in a field of disembodied limbs that squirm and clutch their plastic fingers. At his feet, Batuo's body lies in pieces, silent, eyes still open.

Lifting the bone saw, I jam my thumb into the trigger button.

I don't even see Talus move, just feel a stab of pain as my wrists are pinned together in one of his hands, the bones grinding. The saw tumbles out of my grip and sprays sparks against the floor, spinning away like a pinwheel firework.

Talus pulls me close to him, turning my body as if we were dancing, staring into my face as I struggle, curious and arrogant. The flat plane of his naked cheekbone nearly brushes mine. He cocks his head, not even bothering to pretend to breathe. Past me, he spots the relic where I left it curled in Peter's lifeless fingers. He looks disappointed.

"Peter made a poor decision, trusting you," he says, letting go.

As I take a breath to respond, he plants a gloved fist in my stomach. I fall, flailing backward. My vision erupts with leaf-veined patterns of cathedral ceiling and a streaking star field of candle flame. I land hard on my side, forehead smacking the floor, one arm crumpled under me like a broken wing.

The world flashes, overexposed.

I'm blinking fiercely, trying to clear my eyes, my breathing shallow. The punch was like being hit by a car, impersonal, mechanical. Legs shaking, I drag myself blindly onto all fours, one rib stabbing with pain, my forehead wet and warm.

Through the ringing in my ears, I can hear Talus.

"Are you happy now?" he asks, speaking to Peter's helpless body. Talus limps around the glimmering rings of the operating table, angrily flexing his fingers in shredded black gloves. On my knees and elbows, I crawl after him.

"Huangdi's anima was never yours to protect," Talus says to Peter's body. "Not in all the centuries you wasted. He always belonged to *her*."

Talus leans over Peter, his sharp features bathed in ethereal blue light from the machine. With both hands, he peels the relic out of Peter's slack hand. When he speaks again, a wrenching sadness pulls at the curve of his blue-tinged lips.

"We sacrificed so much to your stubborn *loyalty*, Peter. Why couldn't you see the Yellow God for what he was? Why couldn't you *adapt*?"

As I near, Talus's eyes flick over to me. Expressionless, he watches me crawl to the surgery table. His long blond hair is rippling in its electrical field. The relic seems to smolder in his fingers. Groaning, I hug the base of the control panel pedestal, hauling myself up to my knees, smearing half-dried blood over the hospital-white contours of the machine.

"You are a worm to us—do you know that?" he says from across Peter's body. "A *worm* . . . interfering in a battle between gods."

I don't have the breath to speak.

Planting one foot, I push up, fat droplets of blood trickling down my chin. Leaning against the pedestal, I take a deep breath and wince at the pain from my rib. I lean my elbows on the panel, hunching my body over it.

In my peripheral vision, Talus is a thin blue shadow. All I see now—all I can let myself see—are the two brass knuckle–like devices sitting on top of the panel. Talus is reaching for me. Before I can react, he catches a handful of my hair in his fist. Pulling my face up, he looks into my eyes, enjoying my reaction.

"Time for you to go," he says.

"Not yet," I say, pulling away.

I'm already raising my hands, stumbling backward, my knuckles ridged with the brass knuckle devices. A gurgling torrent of liquid metal surges into the trough. Shining tendrils are already trickling up.

Our eyes catch. Too late, Talus understands.

"No—" he tries to shout.

With a scream, I bring my hands together in a brutal clap. An implosion of liquid metal leaps up and collapses over Talus's surprised face.

The impact compresses his skull and flays away part of his scalp. Scouring flesh, the metal courses over his skull and solidifies into a thin, quivering mirrored surface. Talus's metal-coated mouth opens and closes in mute horror. Staggering backward, he falls sprawling onto his back, droplets of liquid metal spraying in shining arcs.

I toss down the brass knuckle devices and the remaining liquid falls back into the trough around Peter's sleeping form.

It is quiet now. Just the sound of my harsh breathing as I round the table and Talus's boots squeaking spastically over marble.

The *avtomat* rolls over and manages to crawl a few feet, a glittering trail of liquid metal dribbling from his nostrils and ears. His jaw is frozen in a silent scream. Frantically, he rakes fingertips over his cheeks and eyelids. Sightless and silent, his frozen face is strangely beautiful, like a Greek sculpture.

I pick up the relic where it has fallen and slide the chain back over my head. The weight on my chest feels like coming home.

Batuo's mangled torso is sprawled on the floor. He has been systematically dismembered. Metal bones glint beneath sliced chunks of contoured plastic sheathing. I had so much to learn from him, and now he's a ruin.

My fear and adrenaline flare into anger.

Following me in secret, sabotaging my research—not only has Talus destroyed my career, but he's murdered his own kind. An incredible world exists, and he has been snuffing it out.

The damaged machine is on its knees now, in a praying posture, running fingers patiently over the metallic mask melted to its face. Sensing my attention, Talus drops to all fours, sweeping fingers over the ground, searching for his antique sword. I creep a few steps closer to the monster, and kick the gladius away from him.

He lunges, a knife appearing in his hand. Blind and deaf, he misses my thigh by inches. I fall, kicking my legs to scoot away from the still lethal machine.

Crawling to the gladius, I wrap my hands around the hilt.

Behind me, the once angelic-featured man is on his knees again. Now he is sawing at himself with the knife, slicing the flesh around the outside of his metal mask. I stand, dragging the tip of the heavy gladius. Talus drops the knife. Curling his fingers into the wound around his face, he pulls, flexing, prying his own face away from his skull. *Just a machine,* I remind myself.

I lift the gladius over my head, favoring my bruised rib, blade wavering.

A demonic scream fills the cathedral as Talus rips the mask away, flinging it into the shadowy heights. Faceless, Talus sets his eyes on me, wide and evil in skinless sockets, bits of pink skin stuck to the bluish carbon-fiber planes of his skull. The sculpted flakes of material are arranged like bones, delicate curves that manifest as a corpse's grin. Now the machine is on all fours, crawling quick like an insect, still vomiting threads of shining liquid. He roars incoherently, lower jaw askew, a sluglike lump of tongue nestled between sculpted teeth.

Letting my scream join his, I bring the gladius down.

Talus jerks as if he's been electrocuted, tearing the hilt from my hands. The blade slices through armor and flesh, sticking fast in the machine's shoulder. Not slowing, the skeletal monster snarls and leaps at me, knocking me onto my back and clawing at my face.

"*Whurm.*" He coughs, tongue lolling over a lipless mouth. "*Whuuurm—*"

A woman's arm closes around Talus's neck, dragging him back.

"The spear," says a familiar voice, grunting with exertion.

Smearing a forearm over my eyes, I see a flash of Batuo's smiling face. The monk is grappling with Talus, hips off-kilter, a flayed piece of robe tied around his midsection to hold his guts inside. His right leg is completely naked, a different skin tone from his left arm. It might be a woman's leg, a bit shorter and more slender than the other. The sockets where the limbs fit are visible. His right arm is also brand-new, harvested from the butcher's shop of spare parts.

Half of Batuo's broken spear lies near me. Snatching it up, I scramble back to Talus. The half-blind machine writhes under Batuo's patchwork body, oblivious to me as I approach. With both hands, I drive the leaf-shaped blade into his armpit. Ribs crunch as the tip pierces, hitting the cradle housed deep inside his chest, connecting with the relic.

Talus finally goes still, pinned down by Batuo's mismatched arms.

Eyes blank, the faceless man stares at nothing. The body is smeared with dried metal, shoulder sheared nearly in half, jacket ripped open in a dozen places. The red-tasseled spear juts out from under his armpit.

It would be pathetic if it weren't so terrifying.

Batuo crawls away from the corpse. He tries to stand and can't.

"Are you okay?" I ask.

"Oh no, June," he says. "Not even close."

34

LONDON SUBURBS, 1758

It is near dusk when the carriage stops at the end of a cobblestoned pathway leading to the estate I purchased sight unseen for Elena nearly a decade ago. The superstitious coachman refuses to go farther, has no business here, and advises me to turn around and return to London immediately. I ignore him, stepping out of the carriage and stretching my legs as he unstraps and unceremoniously tosses my luggage to the ground.

Without another word, he climbs onto the carriage and nudges his horses forward, wheeling away back to town at top speed.

Trudging over the muddy stones, I see the lawn is littered with water-stained crates I have sent back from India. They're untouched. Each sagging crate contains treasures and precious materials, statues and furniture, and countless silver rupees.

The stone mansion looms out of overgrown gardens, flanks wreathed in mist, shutters hanging askew, and a rash of moss growing over its face like a port-wine stain birthmark. Hemmed in a neat circle of stone, the fountain before our door is clotted with dead leaves, a sculpture of the sea nymph Galatea sprouting from it, her features slick and shining with a scum of algae.

Stopping, I scan the discolored facade.

She is still here. She must be.

"Elena," I call, hastening to the front door. It hangs open, the ornate wood bloated and blistered with rain. Peering inside, I see only a trash-strewn hall.

I was away for too long.

Entering, I feel the utter isolation of the place. The long road back to London that represented safety to me must have been claustrophobic to her. She saw all possibility of contact dwindling from this distance.

Around me, the rooms seem to belong to a museum, shelves teeming with many of the artifacts I collected from India. Pieces of some opened wooden crates are scattered about. The dining room table is heaped with laboratory equipment and the remains of half-finished projects.

She must have grown so tired, I think.

Abandoned books litter the hallways, sprawled like corpses. Elena was once so eager to learn. But after years of solitude, perhaps she ran out of ways to amuse herself. Even in the months before I left, her mood had become darker. Those empty eyes of hers fell on me and no longer did I sense love in them. Only a sense of duty and a smoldering anger and always the question: *Where are the others?*

"Hello?" I call into the house. "Elena?"

Boots echoing, I continue down the dark throat of the corridor. The house is in total disrepair, but it has strong bones. Many of the doors and windows are open and have been for some time. Leaves and dirt have blown into the rooms, piling up for what must have been several seasons. The remains of hundreds of letters, stained with water and stiff and damp from the elements, are plastered across the floors and pushed into heaps by the wind. The great hall is as cold as an abandoned hearth in the woods.

Then, from somewhere deep in the house, the twang of a harpsichord key rings out. Stopping, I strain my ears to listen. I think I hear the faint twitter of small birds.

Ignoring a sense of dread, I move toward the sound.

In the conservatory, a ceiling made of glass has been shattered by a fallen tree branch. Heavy shards lie where they fell, glinting on broken black-and-white tile squares. An elbow of remaining branch dips into the room, wreathed in vines and shaggy moss, teeming with brightly colored songbirds.

Eyes closed, Elena sits in the middle of the room, playing a sagging harpsichord with chipped fingers. In a torn and dirty dress, she looks spectral, like the ghost of a child. She plays mechanically, viciously, head dipping as her fingers flicker across the keys. Dozens of birds watch from their perches with black, curious eyes.

I recognize the tune. It was written by a composer who visited once to share his music and supplicate himself, decades ago. He was a small man with a high collar and pompous white curls, a double chin, and suspicious eyes. The girl brought him around our old apartment after hearing an opera he wrote about a nymph, an enduring curiosity of hers.

"Elena," I say. "I am home."

She does not respond, keeps playing.

"Speak to me," I urge. "What has happened to you? Where are the servants? Why are half my shipments scattered about the lawn?"

The beautiful song continues to flow from beneath her fingers, as steady and flawless as the striking of church bells. A slight breeze pushes her stiff black hair away from an innocent, youthful face. But each press of her fingers is becoming more harsh, her shoulders quivering with the impact as she stabs at the keys. Eyes closed, a little frown playing at her face, she could be a nobleman's child.

But only a fool would mistake this ancient thing for a child.

I step forward and put out a hand, begging her. Ignoring me, she continues to play, mechanical and perfect, harder and harder, the keys twanging as if in agony. I sense something has broken inside her. Some hunger she had that I did not feed because I could not feel it for myself.

"Elena," I whisper. "Please."

As my trembling fingers touch her shoulder, she springs into action. Throwing my hand off with both of hers, she stands, sending the bench flying across the room, her feet *thocking* into the tile. A confused cloud of squawking songbirds bursts into flight, and a shower of bark and leaves drifts down from above.

"Please?" she asks. *"Please?"*

Startled, I put up my hands.

"When has *please* won favors between us? When has *please*—a human word for a human feeling—ever meant anything to the mighty *avtomat*?"

She advances and I take a step back.

"I left you for too long," I say. "I see that now. I am sorry—"

The sharp tinkle of her laugh cuts me off midsentence.

"*Please. Sorry.* Why do you spew these human pretensions at me? Apologies mean nothing. Manners mean nothing. You . . . you were gone for *eight years,* Peter. I waited for you, I was loyal to you."

"I sent wealth. I thought—"

"I hate you," she whispers up at me.

Enough of this.

I scoop Elena up in my arms and hold her struggling body tightly against my chest. I breathe in the smell of her perfume and her moldering dress and her black curls. Her fists pummel my back and scratch across my scalp and the sharp toes of her dress shoes dig into my stomach.

I do not relent.

"Never again," I say to her, face buried in the folds of her dress. "I will never leave you again."

Slowly, she stops struggling, stops shouting and crying and murmuring vicious cruel things. Her arms settle around my neck and her forehead presses against my chest and I realize how badly I missed the feeling of them there. The pressure of her body is like a balm over an ache that has been growing in my heart for a decade.

I can tell she feels it, too.

"Peter," she says, her lips inches from mine. "What happened to your face?"

"The war," I say.

She traces a finger over an irregular seam that's been holding my right ear and jawline in place since three mujahideen brought me down and tried to chop me into pieces in an alley. "You've become a hero. They're calling you the Butcher of Plassey Plains. The newspaper even had a rough drawing of you."

"Accurate?"

"Someone could notice."

Elena wriggles out of my arms and her shoes clack onto the broken tile floor. She is small and tentative now, like a bird about to take flight.

"Will you have me back?" I ask. "Please."

Elena looks me up and down, hands on her waist. She is measuring me with her eyes. Under the anger and fear, I sense relief.

"For the time being," she says finally.

I try to smile and the leather of my cheek buckles at a split seam.

Elena shakes her head. "What have you been into?"

"You know why I fight."

"Your precious sovereign," she says quietly, a hiss of anger under her voice.

"It has grown more complicated than that," I say.

"I know," she says, taking a deep breath and listening to the birds chirp.

"Sit," she continues, gesturing to an ornate padded lounge, bathed in greenish light filtering through the remaining lichen-coated conservatory windows. "I'll fetch my kit."

Elena's skills have grown while I was away. Her tiny fingers tickle like insects as she pries away the skin of my face. She cleans and files and repairs the gear work beneath, eyes intent on the task. Beyond her head, small, interested birds watch.

Slowly, she erases the damage from my years spent on the battlefield, sleeping under stars wreathed in gun smoke, marching through driving sand and rain. Elena tuts at me like an old woman, uncovering the damage of old battles, gently but firmly ripping seams of skin apart so they can be redone.

The room is quiet as she sews, save for the chirping of birds and the far-off bark of a wild dog. Wind sways through the garden outside; and I hear abandoned chimes somewhere in the distance, singing their mechanical melodies, mindless clockwork operated by the ghostly touch of wind.

"I grew lonely, Peter," Elena says.

"Your tutors?" I ask.

"The humans? They are poor company and more trouble than they are worth. None can see past my form. I must always pretend to be an ignorant child. And to think I was watching Saint Petersburg being built while these old men were in their diapers."

"But it is necessary, you are learning—"

"Nothing, Peter. The humans have little left to teach. I know their languages and their history and their religious superstitions. The experiments I conduct on my own far exceed the capabilities of their best watchmakers. They are an inferior lot, I'm afraid, always shivering the instant the fire goes out, complaining of hunger and fatigue. I couldn't abide them any longer. I sent them away."

Sitting up, I gently push Elena back. The half-attached skin of my face peels off and flaps against my neck in an undignified way. But my words are urgent.

"Do not speak of them that way. Without *them,* I cannot fulfill my Word. If they were gone there would be no justice, no injustice—"

"Good," she says, shoving me back against the damp cushion of the chaise. "They are of no use to us anymore. We are *superior.*"

"Elena—"

"Imagine," she says into my ear. "Imagine if we could communicate directly with the wisest of our own kind. Our makers. The things we might learn from an elder race—"

"Not this."

"All we could learn, our *purpose*—"

"We do not need others."

"So much that is hidden could be revealed—"

"We are in *danger.*"

"We don't know *what* we are, Peter," she shouts.

I wait until the echo of her words has faded.

"What of the estate?"

Elena watches me, not blinking.

"What happened to the estate?"

Ignoring my question, she pulls a final stitch through my face. Inspecting her handiwork, she leans back. Standing, she packs her tools into a leather kit, slapping each implement into its place without looking at me.

"The estate ceased to interest me," she says, walking to the door. "But it is no matter. I shall dispatch a team of workers to conduct repairs. It will only require a few months. Your time in the war will provide all the necessary explanation for the state of this place. It will mean more *humans,* but I do not require the seclusion I once did."

"And why did you require seclusion?"

Elena is silent for a long moment, considering me from the doorway. Her form is that of a little girl, but her posture that of a woman. Her face is brave, but there is a tremor in her lip.

"I met someone, Peter," she says, softly. "Someone like us."

35

SEATTLE, PRESENT

Batuo leans his back against the surgical station, sitting on the floor with his eyes closed, face framed by smears of my dried blood. Clothed loosely in a shredded robe, his scavenged limbs are an amalgam of different genders and races. And beside him, the twisted, faceless body of Talus sprawls, a spear jutting rudely from its ribs.

"Peter is going to die, isn't he?" I ask Batuo. "If his relic lost all its power . . ."

My voice trails off as Batuo opens his eyes. Part of his forehead over the left temple has been crushed in. Seeing my reaction to the damage to his face, he smiles gently, gaze flickering up to where Peter's body lies on the table.

"What am I supposed to do now?" I ask, my voice ragged.

"You should have seen us," says Batuo, gesturing to the mausoleum wall across the room. "In our heyday. Before these crypts were full of sleepers and the rest of our kind scattered like scared rabbits. In our day, we reveled in crystalline ballrooms. We made war with the wrath of gods. Our libraries and monuments were beacons to humanity. And now look at us."

"Batuo—"

"We fall through the years," he continues, "like dust motes through a shaft of sunlight. We dance, each of us reflecting the same brilliance. And though we spiral into darkness, the light remains."

"Is he dead?" I ask.

Batuo focuses on me again, blinking.

"We will see," he says, groaning as he sits up. "In my study, behind my rather ostentatious desk, you will find a roll of tools. Every *avtomat* carries such implements, though each of us hopes never to have to use them. But they do come in handy more often than we like. I want you to keep mine, for a little while.

"Go on," he adds. "I'll wait."

By the time I return, carrying a round leather tube packed tightly with bits of metal and plastic, Batuo is sitting up taller. He has removed the cloth that was tied around his waist and cleared space in the wreckage around himself. I stop short, seeing the insides of his body revealed through the wound in his torso.

"This is utter sacrilege, you know," he says. "In any other age we'd both be killed for a transgression like this. But, I'll confess . . . I rather like having a human in my laboratory. You're so inquisitive, June. So eager to understand. So easily shocked. Being around *avtomat* for so long, I suppose I'd forgotten what youth is like."

I let out a surprised laugh, blood caked on my collarbones and matted hair hanging in my face.

"What are we going to do?" I ask.

"Not we," he says. "You."

Smiling apologetically, Batuo pinches the synthetic skin of his torn-open belly. With a tug, he tears the neat slice open wider, peeling the skin back. Like shrugging off a gruesome sweater, the monk rips the flesh away. Underneath, an organic-looking collection of stiff fabric panels combine in skeletal configurations to give him his shape. A blue light pulses deep in his chest.

I should be revolted, yet every movement he makes is a wonder to me, each layer of plastic sheathing combining to form perfectly lifelike skin and musculature. And the pliable skeleton beneath, not made of metal but carbon fiber, most likely. The ancient math of springs and levers are executed in a perfect simulacrum of life.

What remains has the face of a man and the body of an automaton.

"Tell me what to do," I say, dropping to my knees beside him.

"You know what we carry in our hearts," Batuo says, placing a hand over his chest. "Anima. As long as it is safe in its cradle, we *avtomat* cannot truly die. Our memories may evaporate, our power may run out, but our *souls* can be revived someday, so long as the original vessel can be made intact."

"Why are you saying this?" I ask.

"I am sad to inform you, June, that my vessel cannot be salvaged at this time. Our bodies can undergo only so much change, and this trauma is too great. Even now, these unfortunate limbs are being rejected. But my anima may still be of some use to you . . . and to our principled friend. I bequeath to Peter the rest of my life span."

"Why can't we use *him*?" I ask, motioning to the demolished body of Talus.

The monk shakes his head. "Talus's heart is broken, his power is gone."

"You don't have to do this," I say, desperation in my voice. "There has to be another way."

"This is not your decision," he says. "We each act according to our Word and I am serving mine, as I have since the first days."

Batuo's body is wracked with a shiver. Squeezing his eyes closed, he grits his teeth and shakes his head as if to clear it.

"You'll need to open Peter," he says.

"Open Peter?" I repeat, idiotically, struggling to make sense of his words.

Batuo lies down on his back, parallel to Peter on the operating table. I watch his translucent lungs inflate under carbon fiber ribs. When he speaks again, his voice is a whisper.

"There is a seam on his chest," he says.

I can smell something burning, hear the static discharge of electricity. I drop the leather bundle on the table beside Peter. As I unroll it, strange tools appear, some modern and familiar, some others carved out of stone.

Oh my god, I'm thinking. *What am I doing?*

Leaning over, I unbutton Peter's shirt and spread it open. I tentatively put my palms flat against his bare chest. The flesh is warm and muscular under my fingers. He has a light smattering of freckles over his upper chest, a little hair. I trace my fingertips across his shoulders, over his collarbones, and along his sternum.

A small ridge reveals itself to my fingers.

I pinch two handfuls of flesh over the pectoral muscles. Elbows pointed to the walls, I lean in and pull. Some part of me is wincing at the pain this would cause a person. I'm not pulling as hard as I can, empathizing with this manlike object.

He's a machine, June. Not a man.

I lean over farther, pulling harder, my hair cascading over Peter's face. Grunting, elbows akimbo, I tug until the flesh of his chest suddenly gives, parting smoothly, a straight seam opening wide from his navel to his throat.

"Oh, wow," I breathe.

The synthetic skin gapes open, revealing a light golden spiderweb of hard fiber ribs. Roughly in the shape of a rib cage and sternum, the protective webbing encloses an armored metal sphere. A blue light pulses inside the metal cage.

Letting my eyes travel up his chest to his face, I see Peter's head is pushed to the side, eyes closed, still unconscious. Arcs of electricity crackle over the surface of his skin, causing random muscle twitches.

"Among my tools, you will see a *bi* disk," says Batuo. "Align it correctly and power will transfer from one anima to another. Use caution—"

Eyes squeezing shut, Batuo's body is wracked with another spasm. Kneeling, I take his hand in mine without thinking, squeezing it, trying to comfort him. Feeling the pressure, he opens his eyes. Lips shaking, he manages to speak:

"Wake me, June. When you and the man-eater succeed. The old one you carry around your neck . . . he knows. Be wary of him, but learn his secrets—even if he refuses to teach."

Head falling back, Batuo's face goes slack. After a few seconds, his eyes aren't seeing anymore. His chest is exposed, light streaming from between the alien slats of his rib cage.

"Wait," I say. "I don't know how. I'm not ready."

But the monk doesn't respond. He is gone.

My soul.

Batuo's sternum is similar to Peter's, but made of a slightly different material. Not as much effort has gone into making a cage to protect the relic inside. Every *avtomat* must be custom built. Each of them has been upgrading him or herself for centuries, using whatever technology is on hand. Batuo has been using parts from this cathedral lab, and he has rebuilt himself more subtly than Peter.

"Sorry, Batuo," I murmur.

With a solid couple of punches I'm able to crack the brittle carbon fiber ribs covering his chest. Reaching in, I snap them off and peel them out, tossing them on the ground. Finally, nestled deep inside his chest, I see what I'm looking for.

A relic, shaped like an arc, sitting in a cradle that seems to be made of translucent ceramic, faded Chinese markings on it.

This is the anima that lies at the heart of every *avtomat*. It's the mind and the memory and the power. Batuo's is inscribed with a word in the old language, different from the symbol imprinted on the one I carry. Using both hands, I lift the relic from his ruined chest, the weight of it oddly familiar to me.

Laying Batuo's relic on the table, I glance at the tool roll.

The *bi* that he spoke of is a thin disk, carved out of jade and etched with intricate symbols. It is exactly the size of two crescent relics. Turning it in my fingers, I see bumps tracing the outer edge that align with indentations on Batuo's relic.

I'm starting to get an idea of how to proceed.

I run my fingers inside Peter's chest, feeling for a release button. Nothing. Eyes closed, breathing steady, I push and prod until my fingers settle into a couple indentations. Squeezing with all my might, I clench my fingers.

Snap.

Peter's armored sternum opens, revealing a bare, blue-glowing relic cradled deep in his chest cavity. The symbol staring up at me is the

Word that Peter follows. Studying it, I wonder what it means—what single word could possibly guide his entire life?

"Here we go, Peter," I mutter.

I place the *bi* disk into his chest, over his relic, rotating it until I feel it align. Then I pick up Batuo's relic and turn it over in my fingers. Lowering it inside, I stop when I feel a click. A long moment passes, and nothing happens.

I exhale in a burst.

"Damn—"

Turning my wrist back and forth, I search for some kind of lock or symmetry. I'm alone in this baroque laboratory, surrounded by broken machines. Someone or something is out there, hunting me. And unless this works, I'm on my own.

My job is to make these artifacts work. It's what I do.

"Come *on,*" I say. "Come on!"

Elbows on Peter's chest, I collapse and let my face land in the warm place between his neck and shoulder.

"Listen to me, Peter," I say into his ear. "It's time to wake up."

36

LONDON, 1758

I have met someone, Elena said. *Someone like us.*

The meaning of her words unfolds in my mind. A darkness sweeps over my vision and fear tightens like a knot between my shoulder blades.

Met someone.

I stride after her, but Elena has already disappeared into this mansion she haunts, scurrying off into abandoned corridors. The rooms are square and tall, lined with gaudy wallpaper, the elaborately painted ceilings encircled with gold-leafed molding. Somewhere, Elena's shoes tap over hardwoods.

"Elena!" I shout, reaching the limits of the mechanism in my chest, vibrating the walls. My boots hit the floor like steam engine pistons as I methodically search each room. The sun is low now, its reddish light sending long shadows over moldering rugs. I rake my fingers across a wall, tearing away rain-soaked wallpaper like a layer of blistered skin.

Stop this, some part of me is saying. *She has done no harm.*

But she has allowed a stranger into our refuge while I was absent. She could have asked me to return, told me how she felt. For so long she and I were everything to each other, and now she has betrayed our bond.

Repeating her name, I stalk mindlessly through empty hallways.

Finally, I kick open a French door to the paved garden outside. It sprays glass and one narrow door flies off its hinges. As I shout her name a final time, something breaks inside my chest. Elena's name comes out in a hoarse rattle, desperate and dying in my ears, pathetic.

And I see the stranger.

In the garden pathways, she stands framed by wild trees, half swallowed by the gathering evening mist. I bite my lower lip, seeing her arm wrapped protectively around Elena's shoulder. The girl's head is leaning against the woman's hip in a familiar way, sending my teeth deeper into my lip.

My hands curl into fists like round shot.

In a simple gray riding dress and boots, the woman makes for an absurdly tall, melancholy figure among the wet foliage. Her long blond hair is twisted into a circular braid, worn like a crown. At her hip, the pommel of a saber winks, the scabbard hidden in the folds of her skirt.

Even from here, I can detect the telltale signs of *avtomat*. Her movements are slightly stiff, with a hard strength beneath. The skin of her face is powdered in the fashion of a lady, but from the contours of her high cheekbones I can trace with my eyes where I would find the stitching should I run my fingertips beneath her jawline. Her eyes are large and bright and watchful in the unique way I have seen in Elena and in the mirror.

"Who are you, stranger?" I call, my voice low and broken.

As I approach, her expression hardens, eerily similar to Elena's on this foggy late afternoon in the depths of our overgrown yard.

"I am Hypatia of Alexandria," she calls. "A philosopher and explorer. I understand you are a soldier of fortune?"

Fists tightening, I advance.

"I no longer fight for a human sovereign."

"Indeed not," she says, her English accent perfect. "It would be senseless."

"Peter," warns Elena.

As I draw within striking range, Hypatia steps neatly away from my sister. One hand goes lightly to the pommel of her saber. Chin rising, she addresses me again without flinching.

"My Word is virtue," she says, white-gloved hand steady at her hip. "What's yours?"

I lower my fists. The stranger is standing her ground, armed and capable. Elena stands a little way off, watching us both sullenly.

"It is my own," I respond.

With her fine dress and features, I can see she is a lady. The clenched fists hanging at my waist begin to embarrass me. I force myself to unclench them and to speak without shouting.

"Tell me what business draws you to my home."

"Home?" asks Hypatia. "Hardly. I suspect your true home is far away. Both in miles and millennia."

Seeing my reaction, Hypatia nods. "You know this much about yourself, at least. We are all of us much older than we know."

"What do you want?" I ask.

"A cup of tea," interrupts Elena. "And a few minutes' discussion."

With a curt nod to Elena, I turn and trudge through the garden toward the freezing confines of the manor. In the guest quarters, I find a dust-coated mirror and grooming station. I trim the tiny, near invisible stray threads emerging from the corners of my face, using a pair of mustache scissors. With dabs of powder, I strike the faded ash from my lips and add a healthy skin tone to my cheeks.

No one on this estate draws true breath, but these affectations are habit, a matter of survival for we who wish to live among humans. And the decorum puts a coat of civilization over an encounter that may well turn barbaric.

Finished, I pause and consider my reflection. Doubt and shame are rising in my throat. I have never felt this alone. Even abroad, I believed Elena was waiting for me; that we would have a life together as brother and sister. All the while an interloper was here, her presence making mine obsolete.

She says her Word is *virtue*.

Goodness, chastity. This *avtomat* who has insinuated herself here, Hypatia, could possibly be lying. She could be anything, even the vanguard of an attack. Batuo warned me of a larger war. But I cannot act until I know her true intentions.

In full military uniform, saber hanging from my hip, I leave the guest quarters resolving to face her in the English way—as a gentleman.

The parlor, unlike the rest of the estate, is well preserved. Elena has outfitted the place in splendid shades of ivory and gold. Crystal sconces flicker brightly with candles as the gray sunlight fades into the folds of drapes. Books are piled to the girl's height in all corners of the room. I am puzzled to see an array of mirrors and clock-making tools on an out-of-place vanity table, until I realize Elena—with her relentless *logicka*—has been taking herself apart, studying the pieces and putting them back together.

Hypatia is crouching before the ornate fireplace, her back to me, starting a small flame over a few sticks of wood. On a round mahogany table nearby, Elena has arranged a complex tea set, the numerous pieces laid out like a puzzle.

"I do not know why you trouble with a fire," I say. "Its flames will not warm the likes of us."

Hypatia looks over her shoulder, smiling up at me.

"This flame will not warm our bodies," she says. "But the heat may warm our souls, and its light may show us the way forward. A well-tended fire and pot of tea are the keystones of a civilized world, after all."

She rises, fire flickering at her feet, and continues: "Civilization being, of course, a human invention. A miraculous outcome for a rather wretched species. Miraculous, and yet, if you ask me, civilization is the destiny of any group of people larger than two."

I sit at the table and Elena joins me on my right. Hypatia dusts her palms off on her skirt. Fire at her back, she joins us.

"Allow me," Elena says to Hypatia with a sickening familiarity. She pours three cups of tea. I am silent.

We sip our tea in the slowly warming room; the parlor a lone beacon of warmth and light in an otherwise empty, destroyed mansion. The liquid will soon evaporate from our false organs, another part of the illusion of life that we perpetuate. Together, we are a clockwork menagerie, three lanterns left burning on a foggy moor.

Elena glances at Hypatia, then turns to speak to me.

"On the day we arrived, Peter, you and I both saw a red eye. Do you remember? We chose to ignore it, to be safe. But I never forgot. When I stumbled upon the symbol again—"

"You went into the city, alone?" I ask, incredulous.

"It was in a book that I procured from the Far East, purchased in a lot from a disgraced magician. Supposedly, the fellow had traveled the width and breadth of Asia six hundred years ago. Many such troves find their way to London, especially since my arrival."

Hypatia and Elena share a knowing look.

"In any case, I deciphered the symbol," continues Elena. "An eye with a square pupil. The eye meant danger. And the square represented human beings and their cities. It was a warning, you see, written for *avtomat* and in our own language."

"And how do you know it's our language?" I ask.

Elena taps her chest.

"The symbols are the same as the ones written upon our hearts."

Elena drops her gaze to her hands, delicate fingers wrapped around a bone-white teacup.

"I knew then there were friendly *avtomat,* and I set out to find them. You gave me the idea of how, Peter. Reading of your exploits, I saw how we so easily exceed human capability that our common deeds become legend. How many monarchs, heroes of battle, great philosophers . . . how many were like us?

"In the summer, I began to invite the greatest geniuses of humankind to visit the estate. I paid whatever price to attract people who were too smart, too prolific. All the living legends I met were human beings. But one man crumbled under the questioning of a rather precocious little girl. He was a great mathematician . . . and a fraud. Once I determined who his true collaborator was, it was only a matter of reaching out."

Elena glances at Hypatia.

The writing desk is just over her shoulder, pushed against the wall and buried under sheathes of paper. Now I understand why this lone room has been preserved, though the rest of our estate lies in near ruin.

"You are very good with writing a letter, aren't you darling?" I ask.

Elena smiles across the table at me, her teacup balanced before her lips, eyes bright.

"And so you joined her?" I ask Hypatia.

"We make a good team," she says. "Your sister is truly brilliant, Peter."

"And she is in danger, thanks to you. Tales of phantoms and sprites also often lead to one of our kind. My coachman seemed to believe the ghost of an orphaned little girl haunted these hallways, the dulcet tones of her harpsichord ringing out in the ruins, fey music performed for the wild beasts of the wood."

Elena bows her head in embarrassment.

"Not *so* far from the truth," says Hypatia, lip twitching in a small smile.

"And what revelation did Hypatia bring you, Elena?" I ask. "What essential message did she carry that you would risk your life so recklessly?"

Elena is silent for a long moment, regarding me coldly.

"To bring you your heart's desire, Peter," Hypatia says. "Elena stayed here on this estate out of true devotion to you. She risked everything, setting her mind to finding the one thing that could make you happy. And she convinced *me* to retrieve it. Yet all you seem to offer her in return is anger . . . and neglect."

Elena puts a hand on Hypatia's forearm. The woman visibly reins in her emotions, blue eyes shining. In the simple gesture I can see years of companionship. Hypatia considers me, speaking slowly now, choosing her words.

"Peter . . . we are a race of survivors. We live, and then forgetting—we live yet again. Sometimes, the consequences of the past follow us across many lives."

From a satchel, Hypatia produces a golden handkerchief wrapped around something heavy and small. She places the item on the table, the silk softening the contours of the object.

This hidden thing exudes a familiarity I cannot place. The shape of it draws my eye. It calls to me silently, bids me to lift it. To protect it. My hands extend toward the silk almost of their own accord, and I force them back into my lap, clasping my fingers together to keep them in place.

"You know what this is. You can sense it," says Hypatia, watching my face closely. "Indeed, it is yours, and we have brought it back to you."

"No," I say. "Elena is my only responsibility. My purpose is to protect my sister."

Elena drops her teacup rattling onto the saucer.

"I am quite capable of protecting myself, Brother," she says.

I push back from the table.

"We are exposed," I say. "Our lives are at risk. We could have hidden here together safely—"

"And yet you saw fit to leave," says Hypatia, swirling her tea. "These dalliances across India, the battles and the plunder and the glory of the king. Perhaps you thought it would . . . satisfy. But none of it means anything."

Hypatia leans across the table, hands on either side of the hidden object resting between us. "It does not satisfy because *those aren't our wars*. Our wars are fought far more viciously, for far longer, and in the shadows."

"Open it," says Elena. "Please, Peter."

I stare at the shrouded outline of the thing for a long moment, feeling its draw. Then I lean over, take hold of the corners of the handkerchief, and pull them taut. The fabric lifts away in a golden square. On the table, I see a crescent ridge of metal.

The anima of a fallen *avtomat*.

"This is your fight, Peter," says Elena. "Your purpose."

I can almost remember this artifact. Something is so familiar about it. I gently scoop the relic up and feel its warmth in my hands. My eyes close and—

Elena is screaming over a chaos of yellow water and frothing mist. A waterfall is roaring—not a dragon after all. Her face pressed against my chest. The shadow of an arrow passes by my face. Please, please she is going to die. I am going to lose her—

"Peter? *Peter?*" says Elena, her hand on my shoulder. I blink, back in the parlor. Dropping the anima to the table, I wipe my hands on my chest. A sick fear crawls through my belly, nauseous remorse for a sin I cannot place.

"Who is it?" I ask, my eyes averted from the anima, voice barely audible.

Elena shares another look with Hypatia. She speaks, voice low and intense: "This is the anima of Huangdi, made by the progenitor race, Cosmic Ruler and founder of the first dynasty of China. Legends say the Yellow Emperor looked upon what he had made and decided the world was not ready for our kind. He chose to hibernate for a thousand years. But his consort, Leizu, mother of silkworms . . . betrayed him. As Huangdi lay down to sleep, she plucked his anima from his breast."

"How did you find it?"

A tight smile appears on Hypatia's face and she shares a look with Elena. "As I said, your sister and I make a good team. But that is a story for another time," she says.

"Why bring it to me?"

"On that long-ago day, a loyal general stood and fought Leizu—seized the soul of his master and fled. Though his path was lost to the ages, agents of the tsardom found the body of this champion buried in a muddy riverbank."

Elena puts a hand over mine, closing my fingers over the artifact.

"Favorini said our vessels were found in the East. He said he put us back together. But he never mentioned that we carried a third anima—the soul of a mighty ruler, missing its vessel."

Elena holds my hands in hers now, the artifact a warm ember between us.

"Five thousand years, Peter," she says. "The dawn of civilization. It has been five millennia since you fought the Worm Mother and saved your master's soul.

"And now it is yours to save again."

37

SEATTLE, PRESENT

In the fairy tale, the prince kisses the sleeping beauty on her rosy lips and she wakes up, eyelashes fluttering. Standing in the mangled wreckage of this cathedral, on a lake of cool marble hidden deep underground, I feel like this could be a fairy tale world. Peter, with his dimpled chin and closed eyes, could be a prince asleep under an evil curse.

I'd kiss him, maybe, but I've got my hands buried wrist deep in his chest.

Click.

Both relics finally slide together against the stone disk. My fingertips tickle long enough for me to think *Oh shi—*

With a concussive thump, the relics lock together and a column of white light strobes from Peter's chest. The surge throws me back, the outline of my forearm leaving an imprint on my vision. Blinking, rubbing my eyes, I see Peter's eyelids fly open, his mouth twisting into a surprised grimace. He screams in agony, back arching and chest convulsing.

This is not like a fairy tale.

"Peter, it's okay. It's okay."

I snatch a leather strap from the tool roll and use both hands to push it into Peter's mouth. His teeth clench on the strap, eyes rolling left to right, squinted against the blue-white electrical light pouring from his open chest. I take his right hand in both of mine, wincing at his grip and the numbing tickle of electricity, and pull it close to my chest, leaning to him.

"It's a power transfer," I say. "You'll be okay."

I hope I sound confident. Squeezing my eyes shut, I hope he understands.

Still holding his hand, I crouch and lean against the table. Through my closed eyelids, the strobes of light pulse quicker and quicker, and a whining sound grows to an earsplitting crescendo. My whole body buzzes with electricity, and Peter's moans are lost under the scream of hidden machinery.

Then, finally, the storm passes.

The unnatural glare fades and we are left again under the warm flicker of hundreds of candles and the shadows of the whirring drones that tend them. A thin haze of smoke lingers above us. The seams of Peter's face glow a dark silver, but his eyes are open and alert.

"Peter?" I ask. "Are you okay?"

Straining to sit up, Peter reaches into his own chest and pulls out Batuo's relic with a shaking hand. The stone *bi* disk is still attached to it. Looking at it in wonder, a slow realization creeps over his face. Turning to me, I can see that he knows.

"Batuo," he asks, voice flat.

I shake my head sadly, glimpsing the dull glow of Peter's relic inside his exposed chest. The symbol imprinted on Peter's anima looks like a flat column, a plinth used to support larger structures. Noticing my gaze, Peter quickly closes the spherical cage around his anima. The carbon fiber ribs of his chest lace themselves shut and with a swipe of his finger, he draws a line from his navel to his collarbone—the skin over his muscular chest connecting like a zipper.

Now Peter looks like a bare-chested man, his body still quivering with occasional electrical spasms. He swings his legs over the table, looking around for the first time. At his feet, he spots Batuo.

"How did you know?" he asks. "To commit the transfer?"

"I didn't. It was an emergency—an accident," I say, packing up Batuo's leather tool roll. I take the monk's relic and the *bi* disk and place them both inside. I roll the fabric up and tuck it into the waistband of my jeans, in the small of my back.

"No, not an accident," says Peter with a grim smile. "I chose well, after all."

My cheeks turn hot and I look away.

"How did it happen?" Peter asks, spotting the portly man, splayed out in a mess of robes, arms and legs mismatched, his skinless chest open to reveal an empty cradle where his relic was housed. Batuo's face is still, eyes closed and peaceful.

"That," I say, nodding across the room.

The wreck of Talus lies in a heap of disembodied limbs, faceless, teeth snarling at nothing, fingers curled in agony, a spear shaft jutting from his chest.

"Oh, no," Peter murmurs.

At the sight of Talus, a sadness settles into his broad shoulders, his lips set in a small hurt grimace. Slipping off the table, Peter walks over, stepping around the smears of quicksilver and broken limbs.

He kneels beside the wretched body.

Reverent, Peter pushes Talus over onto his back. He sighs at the insults to the destroyed face. Hidden by the curve of his back, I see Peter's hands move busily over the fallen man's chest. In quick economical movements, Peter is retrieving a relic.

Stepping closer, I stoop to pick up a slice of metal. It's the death mask—a curve of hardened liquid that covered Talus's face, jagged along the edges where he sawed it away from his own skull. The features on the mask are calm, a beatific expression locked forever in contours of silver-colored metal.

Standing at Peter's shoulder, I hand him the mask. Peter places it over the body's ruined face, returning the corpse to some semblance of peace.

Peter holds up the relic that belonged to Talus, considering it. On its face is a fading symbol, I realize—a plinth. It is the same squat column that I saw on Peter's relic. The two *avtomat* somehow have the same inscription—the same *Word*.

Talus was a monster, a murderer without remorse.

"What does that symbol mean?" I ask, my voice hollow.

Peter ignores my question, pocketing the relic. Leaning over, he scoops Talus up in both arms. Holding the limp body like a sleeping child, he lumbers toward the shadowed wall of crypts.

"Peter, I know his symbol is the same as yours," I say.

The man pauses a few yards away, shoulders massive and sloped. He doesn't turn to face me, just clings sadly to the body in his arms.

"We have the same symbol, but different masters," he says.

"Tell me the truth," I insist. "Why do you have the same Word as that monster?"

Peter's voice is hoarse, drenched in sadness.

"Because he was my little brother."

38

LONDON, 1758

Five thousand years. The black, broken stretch of lost memory reels on for longer than I ever imagined. My mind fails to contain it, balking and returning always to the girl.

Hypatia sits beside Elena, watching me carefully across a skyline of teacups and saucers and a teapot and a small clay dragon kept for good luck. The anima rests on the table between us like a poisonous spider. I don't dare to touch the half-moon of metal again. My mind is buzzing from the thoughts it gave me before—a vision of death and loss.

This artifact has reappeared from a forgotten life, and it threatens to pull me away from the only life I know. Away from my sister. When I learned she was in danger, my priorities snapped into focus—Elena is all I have ever truly cared about. The undertow from this shard of evil metal cannot break that focus.

"What is the first thing?" Favorini asked in the candlelight.

When I answered him, translating a deep, nameless hunger into a Russian word: *pravda*—it was her face I watched across the room, her porcelain cheek writhing with candle flame. She is my lone beacon in a great darkness.

"Huangdi was betrayed to his death, his anima lost for ages," says Hypatia. "Now he has been reunited with you, his sworn protector. We must act quickly. Leizu is close behind and her spies are legion. She very likely knows her enemy has surfaced, and she will destroy his relic to prevent his reincarnation."

"We can't stay," says Elena. "We will leave together—"

"Flee? To where?" I ask.

"To the New World," says Hypatia. "The colonies are suitably wild to provide a safe haven for the three of us, though it will not be easy to evade the Worm Mother."

Now I understand. Elena has procured this artifact as a peace offering. Her relentless logic has found a way to bring me along. Too loyal to abandon me, she scoured the ends of the earth to find a trinket that could satisfy my Word.

This is how I lose her, I can't help thinking. *This is how she leaves me.*

"Don't you think Leizu's agents will be watching the docks?" I ask.

"A risk we shall have to take," responds Hypatia.

Mustering all my willpower, I force myself to wrap the anima back in its silk handkerchief. In an avalanche of teacups, I push the bundle back to Hypatia. I press my palms flat against the wooden table to stop them shaking.

"Get out," I say quietly.

"Excuse me?" Hypatia asks. "I cannot believe you would shirk—"

"Get out," I say louder, standing and jarring the table. The teacups roll and shiver together, sloshing tea across the linen. The fire gutters and jumps at the shift of air in the closed room.

"I do not know this Huangdi," I say. "I do not remember him. I did not choose to protect him. I will have nothing to do with it."

"Oh, Peter," Elena mutters in anguish. She slips away from the table and runs from the room.

Hypatia is standing now, backpedaling, the bundle clasped tightly in her hands.

"During her research, Elena found that the Word on your master's anima is divine light," she says. "Meaning that our enemy carries the darkness of hell," she continues, speaking urgently. "They were in balance—a Oneness—but Leizu shattered that. Now she suffers a broken Word, unsatisfied, and she seeks a great champion to oppose her. That's *you,* Peter."

My hands curl back into fists. Elena's sharp clicking footsteps are fading into the abandoned, leaf-strewn hallways of the mansion. Hypatia tucks the anima under her elbow and puts her hands out to me, pleading.

"*Pyotr.* You are the first protector, since time beyond reckoning. Huangdi is your master."

"Not anymore," I say. "I lost my sister once, long ago in another life. Never again."

"Leizu will come here," says Hypatia. "She is drawn to you, Peter. Whether you take this anima or not, she will never stop hunting—"

Her eyes drop to where my fingers have closed over the hilt of my saber. I draw the weapon an inch out of its sheath. The blade gleams, a warm silver in the glow of candles and sunset through thick drapes.

Hypatia nods, a small salute.

"Then I shall take my leave," she says, turning her back to me. "But know that you speak for yourself. You have no right to choose for others. Regardless of what you believe your purpose to be, or whom you think you serve."

I follow the woman, stalking after her through the hallways and out into the darkening courtyard, stopping only at the gape-mouthed front door. I watch her figure retreat, gray riding jacket disappearing into evening mist at the periphery of the estate.

Hypatia never looks back.

The vast acres around our abandoned mansion are empty of people but full of beasts and insects. A last lick of weak sunlight wavers across the mossy water of our neglected fountain. I sit down on the front steps, knees rising to meet my elbows.

Alone, I listen to the geese honking as they fly over. Hear the animals in the encroaching woods as they chitter and bark at one another. The sun is extinguishing itself through clawed branches. The last of the evening light splinters through a latticework of limbs and the world fades to a dull gray.

Hours pass before I feel a small palm pressing on my shoulder. I put my hand over her cold fingers.

"I love you, Elena," I say. "I will protect you."

She says nothing.

"I told you it was too dangerous," I say, and her hand leaves its perch. My shoulder feels empty.

She sits beside me on the steps and says nothing.

The silence between us lasts a long time and it terrifies me.

Side by side, we watch as the courtyard fills with mist creeping in from the forest. The abandoned crates lining the driveway tilt crazily in the gloom, like broken tombstones. Cloaked in freezing vapor, the long hours of the night march by us in a reverie. An infinity of stars have opened their cold eyes to us by the time she speaks.

"Peter?" Elena asks. "If you could let go of your Word, would you?"

I consider the question.

"There is truth in it . . ." I trail off. "I would not."

"But the world isn't so simple as you pretend. You have made yourself a slave to others. And the worst part . . . you're a willing slave."

"Are you not a slave to *logicka*?" I ask, turning to her. "Are you not dancing through this world like a clockwork ballerina?"

Elena blinks, seeming to see me for the first time. She leans against me, but I feel a black gulf expanding between us. Abruptly, she reaches her arms around my shoulders in an urgent hug.

Surprised by how grateful I am, I pull the girl onto my lap, sighing as her small arms tighten around my neck in the old familiar way. She is calm now, here in the empty night. Her perfume and the quiet flutter of her gear work are my sanctuary. I could almost pretend the old Elena is back, and we are playing at being *vampir* in the frozen streets of Moscow.

"You are right, Peter. We are *avtomat*," she murmurs into my neck. "We live and die by clockwork. Like the stars on their tracks, we must yield to nature. We must make hard decisions and live by them."

She pulls back and her face is a pale mask in the night.

"Do you know what *logicka* dictates?" she asks. "For decades, it has pushed me, whispered to me, willed me to do one thing."

"What is that, my dear?"

Elena hugs me again, fiercely, her forehead pressed like a knuckle into my chest. When she speaks, her words are needles that shiver into my heart.

"To leave you behind, Peter. Forever."

39

SEATTLE, PRESENT

Batuo's laboratory seems sad and quiet without the jovial little man. Gruesome remnants of the fight are spread over the marble floor: broken limbs, pieces of the destroyed nurse robot, and ragged smears of liquefied metal.

Thankfully, the bodies of Batuo and Talus are gone. Peter carried them to the mausoleum wall, sliding open the rectangular crypts and laying them inside. Dozens of other *avtomat* must occupy the rest of the slots in that marble facade. All of them are sleeping, waiting for a new dawn.

Sitting on Batuo's broad desk, I am considering my own relic, dangling it from the necklace chain and letting my eyes skim over its symbol—a teardrop with a circle trapped inside. Across the room, Peter methodically rifles through drawers, pawing through shelves and running his fingers over carved wood panels.

"You said you served a different master than your brother. Who?"

"An *avtomat* called Huangdi, the Yellow Emperor."

"Where is he?"

"You wear his relic around your neck."

And yet without his true body, this relic is just an oddly heavy necklace.

"And where is his vessel?" I ask, using the *avtomat* word.

Peter looks up. "I hoped the monk would know."

He returns to working his way through the room. Hopping off the desk, I join in, yanking open drawers and examining their contents, searching for anything that has to do with Huangdi or the relic.

"Batuo called you Man-eater. Was that some kind of a joke?" I ask.

Peter plants his hands flat on the table and lowers his head. For a moment, I think he might be praying. His face is clipped by shadow, but in his shoulders I can see a faint quaking. Abruptly, I feel sorry for bringing it up.

How does it feel to lose a friend you've had for centuries? Or a brother?

"Look," I say. "They aren't gone forever."

"Perhaps not," says Peter, facing away from me and speaking in a low, quick voice. "But Leizu is coming and we are not prepared. She has been hunting this anima for five thousand years. Batuo was our last best hope to reunite Huangdi with his soul. Without his knowledge, we are—"

I put a hand high on Peter's shoulder and pull him around to face me. "Batuo chose to do what he did," I say. "He chose *us* to solve this."

Peter moves away from my touch, continues his search.

I spot a rolltop desk pushed against the wall. Lifting the lid, I find a stack of letters resting inside. The languages on each page vary, but I can read the names and make out the general meanings. Laying the bundle of papers on the broad desk in the middle of the room, I start making piles for each correspondent.

"And why have you agreed to that?" Peter asks. "To help me?"

I'm scanning a crumbling letter, relishing the antique flourish of a quill pen on rough parchment. But the intensity of his question makes me pause.

"Aside from trying not to get killed . . . I'm interested."

Peter shakes his head in disbelief.

"What? That's a perfectly good reason," I say. "Most people are too caught up in the present to care about the past. But when I look at something old, when I touch it, I feel like I'm reaching into another world. A place with secrets. So, yes, part of the reason I'm helping you is because I'm *curious*."

"Perhaps curiosity would be your Word, if you had one," he says.

"Yeah, it probably would."

Peter stalks farther into the alcove, boots thudding over thick rugs.

I move on to the final stack of letters. The first is an e-mail from less than a year ago, printed on crisp paper. Thumbing through, I see the pages farther down the stack were typed on an old typewriter. The ones beneath that are handwritten in ink, and even deeper, scratched with a quill pen on parchment.

The oldest letter is dated 1858.

"And what about you?" I ask. "What's *your* Word?"

Deep in the alcove, Peter is a tall figure, moving his hands over book spines.

"You protected me while I slept, June," he says. "And you brought me back. Though you are of the short-lived race, you have seen under my skin."

Peter pauses, considering me from across the dim room.

"My purpose is to make justice," he finally says, voice quiet. "It has been called *pravda*. It has been called other things."

"Justice? Is that what your brother was about, too?" I ask.

"We served different masters, with different ideas of justice. Both of us haunted the battlefields of men for centuries, lending our vengeance to one side or another. Unlike my brother, one day I stopped. I learned to separate justice from vengeance, and began to devote my efforts to strategy rather than battle."

His words remind me of the identification card I found in his wallet. Black credit cards and crisp bills and the credentials of a secret agent.

"Is that why you joined the CIA?" I ask.

"CIA, SIS, GRU, MSS," says Peter, shrugging as he continues to rummage through a drawer. "When you have been around as long as I have, these things tend to accumulate."

Scanning the oldest letter, I spot Peter's name, spelled *Pyotr*.

On the thin parchment, tiny blocks of words are scrawled in faded Latin. The page is laid out like a technical paper, filled with detailed notes. A beautiful drawing depicts a Chinese emperor, dressed in a flat hat with tassels, sitting on a throne. Both man and throne are diagrammed, each piece briefly described. Both seem to be filled with complicated mechanisms.

A name is scratched beside the figure: *Huangdi*. And beside a disk embedded in the throne, the words "sun disk" followed by "*spiritus vitae*"—the breath of life.

Holding up the page, I step back.

This author has clearly studied the emperor and the technology he used. Checking the signature, I see the letters were sent to Batuo from a woman. And judging from the time span across all the letters, she must be an *avtomat*.

I'm thinking she could be important.

"Peter?" I ask, looking over the top of the letter. "Who is Elena?"

40

LONDON, 1758

The masts of tall ships rise like church steeples from the Pool of London. Perched birds speckle the swaying masts, framed by a hodgepodge of edifices sprouting from London Bridge. In the distance, I can make out Hypatia and Elena, walking side by side onto a pier. I wave my arms over my head, legs buzzing from a long sprint, shouting and startling the passengers and dockworkers who crowd the wharves.

"Elena!" I'm shouting. "Please!"

Her face flashes as she glances back. Hypatia's arm closes around her shoulder, pulling her closer. A ship is waiting for them at the end of the pier, a sharp cutter, its sails lowered, sailors preparing her for a trip to the Plymouth port for the larger voyage across the Atlantic.

It took me too long to realize.

The carriage arrived at midday, stopping a mile up the road. My ears trained by warfare, I heard the vehicle's furtive arrival. But by the time I rushed to the road, Elena was gone, along with a small trunk of clothing and books. After ten minutes alone on the abandoned estate, without another living soul, horse or man, I began to run.

They are headed to the harbor, and from there to the colonies, likely Boston. Hypatia warned me as much. Scabbard jogging against my thigh, I accelerate toward the pier. With each footstep comes the growing realization that I have lost my sister through my own stubbornness.

"Stop! Wait!" I shout, pushing through the crowd and leaving a wake of cursing, jostled people behind me. At the end of the pier, Elena and Hypatia have reached a tonguelike wooden ramp stretching over the murky water to the ship. Their faces are lost in the shade of dozens of bobbing sails, veiled in a forest glade made of ship masts instead of trees.

Miraculously, they stop.

Waving, I gather speed toward them. Hypatia lets out a panicked shout, pushing Elena onto the narrow ramp. She draws her saber, the ring of its release audible from here, and leaps on board after her, kicking the ramp away. In a short cloak and riding dress, the woman strides aboard, shouting commands to sailors who now scurry around the deck.

Fighting a sting of rejection, I realize Hypatia's eyes are cast beyond me. A small flock of birds take wing from the forest of masts. One lifts, then three more, another one, and then three more. Their presence sparks dread in me.

Turning, I see her. Unmistakable. A viper.

Leizu advances toward me, like a storm, gusting through knots of people with a brutal elegance that sends them sprawling and yet not cursing her, only watching her retreat, kneeling, gape mouthed with awe. In a slim black dress with long sleeves and a short collar under a gray cape, she strides with one arm extended behind her back, clutching an unsheathed sword. This time there is no hidden parasol, no decorum. Her eyes are lowered, jaw set, a mane of black hair trailing her like a living shadow.

She must have been watching the Pool all along, waiting for her prey to flee.

With a flick of her wrist Leizu unlatches her cape and lets it flutter to the muddy pier. Her features are vaguely Asiatic, skin light and unblemished, long fingers wrapped around a red hilt. She sweeps the long sword before her. *Xuan Yuan, the divine sword of the Yellow Emperor.* The sight of that weapon sends a tremor of recognition through my entire body. I have known it before, somewhere, sometime.

As the cape falls away, it reveals a layer of black armor that glitters like snake scales. Each plate has a crescent shape—made from dozens of anima, overlapping one another to form a flexible surface. Her plum-dark lips peel back, flashing canines as she dashes right past me.

This beast wears the souls of the conquered.

The dreadful realization snaps me out of my trance. Shoving, bellowing at the people near me, I rampage ahead. Carriers and carters scatter, dropping their goods as Leizu lowers her head and launches into a zigzagging sprint.

The cutter is throwing its ropes and pushing away into the congested harbor. Her crew moves frantically, motivated by the shouted commands of Hypatia. The woman stands on the bow of the ship, her cloak shining, blue fabric trimmed in white and gold. Saber up and pointing at the pier, she shouts sharp orders over the snap of the wind.

But she is too late.

Smaller than I, Leizu reaches the end of the pier first. She moves like spilled wine, flowing between people, sliding through the shifting spaces. And as I crash through luggage and frightened passengers, I can only watch with a tight throat as she vaults aboard the ship.

Leizu lands, perched on the wooden railing.

Silhouetted by a wavering stripe of sunlight on the dark river, Hypatia leaps from the bow, slowed in my eyes by the power of the moment, her saber poised over her head in both hands, cloak flowing behind her like angel wings. Cresting the sun, she is a vision of light as she falls toward the crouched figure of Leizu and her dark copper blade.

As the blades ring, a thousand people stagger.

Heads turning, a murmur rises up. I stride through the last of the crowd, briefly losing sight of the ship in the dirty faces of a silenced multitude. For this instant, these mortals are deeply, animalistically aware that they are in the presence of something greater than themselves—something humanlike, but not of man.

I smell smoke.

A rising haze illuminates long fingers of dusky sunlight. Hypatia, curls of blond hair flying, is a blur of white and gold. Falling through shadow and light, she trades ringing blows with the darting form of Leizu. I hear the cackle of rising flame, see the deckhands scattering for buckets, some leaping overboard.

A lantern has smashed, spilling its fuel. The wick has lit a heap of furrowed sails piled on the deck. Low curls of flame already writhe across the loosely gathered canvas, sheets of smoke rising from it.

Standing at the edge of the pier, I press my saber against my hip, kneel, and dig in my boots. I break into a sprint toward the drifting ship, launching myself off the dock with the force of a cannonball. Soaring over the foul water of the Thames, I crash through the deck railing with both legs and roll, scabbard slapping the hard wood of the deck.

I can't see Elena.

The fire is alive, growling, thick smoke already pluming. The canvas sails were dry as tinder, cultivating a blaze that will make a quick meal of this wooden ship. Crawling to my feet, the world fades into a hell-scape of light and dark. High above, the mast has erupted with a bright mane of climbing flame. Specks of ash drift like snowfall through crimson rays of sunlight. Bodies are sprawled across the deck, efficient sprays of arterial blood glistening in crisscrosses over the wood.

And strange blue flashes of light are strobing through roiling smoke.

"No!" I shout, charging.

Leizu stands in the bow, both hands over her chest. Her armored cuirass has been pulled down, the throat of her dress torn wide open, her breasts exposed. Azure lightning streaks from a relic trapped under her fingers, pressed between her collarbones, the flaring light stinging the air, dancing in veinlike traces away from her body.

The monster is feeding.

Elena is crouched below the bow, on the main deck, surrounded by a curtain of flames. She holds a stiletto in each hand. The body of Hypatia is at her feet. The woman's head is tilted back, neck exposed and lips twisted into an expression of agony. Her sword lies a few yards away, half engulfed in flames.

Hypatia's throat and chest have been savagely ripped open, gear work and ribs exposed—her anima taken.

I leap across blazing timber, eyes on my sister.

Something dark flickers in the flame and Leizu's blade slashes through smoke. Elena pirouettes away from the attack, her small blades folded against her forearms. A child-size demon, fearless, she leaps back at the swordswoman. Leizu retreats, her body twirling, skipping off the heaped corpses of deckhands and avoiding the twin fangs of Elena's weapons.

Like the shatter of glass, I hear it—Leizu is laughing.

Then a stiletto connects. With her impeccable logic, Elena has managed to find a pattern in Leizu's shifting defense. The laughter ceases.

I am between them.

Saber drawn, my *shashka* absorbs a killing blow and is nearly wrenched from my grip. And then she is upon me, Leizu's face, inches from mine. Bright embers die against the black scales of her unholy armor. One hand closing around my throat, she presses a dagger against my belly.

"You arrived," she says, smiling. "Finally."

Before I can react, she stands on her tiptoes and presses soft lips against mine, tugging at my lower lip with her teeth. I twist away as her dagger pierces my rib cage, the tip spearing urgently toward my relic's cradle. Off target, I throw myself back before she can stab me again.

"Strong!" She laughs.

Something crashes and the ship lurches, leaning dangerously, water gurgling up to flood the splintered decking that still rests above the waves.

"Hypatia!" shouts Elena.

A few yards away, Hypatia's body is sliding toward lapping black waves. Elena dives toward her, grabbing hold of lifeless arms. The girl digs in her heels, face lost in her hair, but Hypatia is too heavy, her limp body skidding toward the water.

"Leave us be!" I shout to Leizu.

She swings, the attack glancing from my saber, staggering me, forcing me to retreat downhill, closer to the water. Elena is desperately holding on to Hypatia's body. Head down, she seems blind to the world. Human corpses are all around us, caught on railings and wrapped in fallen rigging, some of them alight, skin boiling and mouths vomiting smoke.

A terrific crack rends the air and a collective gasp rises from the spectators on the pier. The decking shifts again as something groans and splinters.

"Elena!" I shout. "Go! Please!"

Parrying Leizu's attacks, I desperately move toward the girl. Kneeling at the water's edge, she finally loses grip of Hypatia. The fallen *avtomat* slides, her body limp, rolling into the dark water and disappearing. Like a sleepwalker, Elena stands and gazes across the flame-licked waves toward the pier. In the distance, human spectators are packed together, a low skyline of silhouettes against bloody dusk, faces illuminated in snatches of flame as they watch us battle.

Grinding, disintegrating, I hear the center mast coming down.

I lock a hand on Elena's shoulder and shove her away. Above, the mast streaks across the sky like a flaming sword. Elena plunges overboard as I sheathe my weapon and turn. A dark figure vaults toward me through a rain of falling coals. But before Leizu reaches me, the wooden pillar detonates against the deck like dragon's breath.

Flame erupts over her shoulders, devouring her body as she reaches for me, screaming, falling. My eyes close against a shock wave of heat. Sightless, I plunge backward into the cold silence of the river.

Elena is lost in the water. Leizu is burning.

When I kick to the surface, what's left of the mast is rolling across the leaning ship, one end splashing into the water, steaming and spitting. The remains of the cutter are sinking fast, canted to the side, great bubbles of air percolating the foul water. A curtain of steam has risen to join the smoke, obscuring the sky.

Tossed and smashed on chalky waves, I hug a piece of floating wood and kick for a shore I cannot see. My body fills with water, but I'm still buoyant as I push through detritus and half-burned corpses. In this purgatory of gray mist and hellish cold, time passes slowly, drifting with the river current.

Eventually, I hear voices.

On the muddy shoreline, the city's poorest are looting the remains of the ship, dragging corpses, yanking off boots and rings.

I stagger to shore.

Craning my neck, I scan the water for Leizu. She is nowhere to be found, nor her damnable birds. The entire harbor has turned to smoke and bits of flame. Nearby, human vultures go about their work quietly and quickly, but I hear faint, raucous laughter echoing from farther up the street.

The cobblestones are gleaming with a ragged trail of water.

A group of half a dozen men are lumbering up a nearby alleyway like a beast with six heads. In their grasp, they carry a small, struggling body, held aloft. The gaggle of drunken men cast demonic shadows on the walls as they stagger together; like a rat king with fused tails, they are dragging my precious, beautiful Elena.

I have haunted the streets near the docks before. I have dragged debtors from these splintery wooden buildings with thin walls that conceal women and girls, muffling their cries and the moans of their clientele. I watch silently as the men enter a long wooden building with a red lantern hanging outside.

Hand on the hilt of my saber, I follow.

41

OVER THE ATLANTIC OCEAN, PRESENT

Stretching my legs, I sigh and wriggle deeper into the luxurious white leather seat of a private jet. The G650's engines hum quietly outside as we slice through thin clouds, cabin thrumming with smooth thrust. The remains of a meal I just devoured rest on the seat next to me, waiting for the attendant to return.

He's in the galley, mixing a champagne cocktail.

Across from me, Peter sits with his long legs drawn in, stiff as ever. Sunlight cuts through the window and illuminates the lower half of his face.

He really is handsome, now that he's been put back together.

"I've got to get one of these," I say.

"It is easier if you founded a bank," he responds. "Preferably, at least two hundred years ago."

With a half smile, I watch a terrain of fluffy clouds roll past below. My entire body is aching, but after a meal and a shower and some aspirin and coffee . . . I'm feeling almost like a human being again.

"So you're what, a secret billionaire?" I ask.

Peter shrugs.

"What do you spend it on?"

"Mostly research and development. New technology. Some transportation when necessary," he says, gesturing to the cabin.

I wince and shake my head.

"Only progress matters," he adds.

"You're trying to understand your own anima," I say. "To find a way to replenish your energy?"

He nods.

It's fascinating to me that these creature comforts are wasted on Peter. All the money in the world doesn't matter to him—not in the way it might to a person. Our civilization has nothing he considers worth buying. Not yet, anyway.

Peter is waiting for humankind to catch up, and has been for centuries.

"Still seems like a waste." I sigh, rubbing my toes in the carpet.

"Not a waste. Without technological progress, the *avtomat* will certainly die. We are survivors of a cataclysm that has passed out of all memory. And we cannot afford another fall of civilization—our power will not last until humankind rises again."

"So you think we'll save you? We *short-lived*?"

"Maybe," he says. "Maybe without even knowing it. Watch how many of your billionaires spend their money on spaceflight, materials science, artificial intelligence, transportation, nanotechnology, brain research. It is not a coincidence. The *avtomat* have resources, and we need basic science. We need to understand ourselves before the last of us runs out of power. Because then there will be no one else to start a new age."

"You're parasites then," I say, half joking. "Preying on our big brains."

Peter considers.

"In a way," he says. "But I do not think the *avtomat* would survive without human beings. I do not know that there would be a reason to. We are made in your image, June. There is a truth in that."

"How far back do you remember?"

"I last woke in the early seventeen hundreds," he says. "Russia."

I grip the armrest tighter, mind reeling. Peter's strange existence feels like a bridge to another world. A secret window to the past.

"Peter the Great?" I venture.

"I was at his side when he passed," responds Peter, staring out the window. "And then I was exiled. Sent wandering on a path that led here."

The awe I felt as a kid in my grandfather's workshop is nothing compared to this. I'm sitting across from a living legend. This man-shaped artifact has borne witness to an incredible swathe of forgotten history.

"You're even older than that, Peter. Some of the components inside your frame. There are brass gears that look Greek, like something from the Antikythera machine. And deeper inside, I saw ceramic plates—pottery, really—with Chinese markings. The same for Batuo."

Peter is watching me now, interested.

"I do not know my true age," he says. "I mean, I would not know how to date those things. I have never thought of it."

"You never looked at yourself?" I ask.

"Not with your eyes."

"Peter," I say. "That kind of pottery . . . in China alone it could go back twenty thousand years. You couldn't be that old. Right?"

"Our anima are impossible to fathom," says Peter. "The relics are too complex. Nearly indestructible. Losing them disturbs our memories, but . . . perhaps we were made that way on purpose, to forget. Or perhaps we have been marooned from our own time for too long, and we are falling apart."

"You don't even know where you're from."

"Every decade for the last hundred years, at risk of death, I have paid the great minds of the era to examine and explain an *avtomat* relic. None could even come close. We came striding out of the past, yet our bones are made of the future."

Peter turns back to the window, the light cutting his face in half again.

"Whoever made us did so before the current era of written history. Whatever they made us for, the reason for our anima, I do not know for certain. And as the years gather, I worry that our time may have come and gone."

I can't help it; I sit up and grab his hand. "Peter, you're walking proof that great things are waiting for us. Seeing you, the way you move, the way you think . . . you're an example of what people have achieved, and what we could achieve again."

Peter suppresses a smile, taking his hand away. "If I had arrived ten minutes later, you would have met only Talus. And in that case, I wonder if you would still believe what you just said. Or been alive to believe it."

I sit back in the plush seat. A cocktail has appeared on my armrest and I didn't notice. Taking the crystalline flute by the stem, I twist it back and forth in my fingers, spraying rainbow shards of light and dark across the cabin.

"So, who is Elena?" I ask.

"An old friend," sighs Peter.

"Why does she know where the emperor is?"

"Because she is always learning. It is her nature."

"Then why haven't you already talked to her?"

Peter smiles at me, the corners of his lips catching shadows.

"Because the last time we spoke, she promised to kill me if I ever returned."

42

LONDON, 1758

I wait for a moment in the darkness at the end of a forbidding hallway. My soaking-wet hood is pulled low over my eyes, a puddle pooling on the rough timber floor around my boots. The leather on the back of my hands is dark, my body seeping river water from every seam, my riding cloak muddy. I try to walk softly, but each footstep rumbles and creaks. Luckily, the noise of my advance is lost under soft, terrible sounds coming from behind closed doors that line the hall.

Small moans and cries. Rough laughter. The scraping of beds against the floor. An occasional human whimper of pain.

The greasy walls and stained floors of this brothel are foul. The long hallway leans out of square, wrong feeling, nauseating. It feels as if a sickness permeates this decrepit building, almost visible in the air, roiling down this cramped corridor like a tendril of oil spreading through drinking water.

Avoiding the front door and its red lantern, I smashed in through a window around the back. The empty stairwell took me to the second floor and this hall. Elena was carried in here minutes ago.

Stopping, I listen for her voice.

The girl believes she no longer needs my protection, but the sight of her futile grip on Hypatia's devastated body flashes in my mind. Elena was hurt to the quick. My fear of losing her—to Hypatia, to Leizu, or to these monsters—is warming to a hot rage.

The urge to protect her is irresistible. So I give myself to it.

I remember a round copper table in a field tent. A leather map, weighted at the corners, marked with battle lines and bits of colored stone. She studies the plot, a black-haired child, eyes calculating. And around her, in the shadows, warriors loom. We watch her, awaiting orders.

I shake my head to clear it.

The hallway remains empty, lit every few doorways with whale-oil lamps that burn putrid and black. I raise a hand and feel the air on the damp skin of my fingers. My sister is nearby.

The first door I push against is barred from the inside. Vile noises are coming from behind it. Pushing harder, I hear rotten wood splintering. It snaps quietly, the bar thunking to the floor, and I ease the door fully open.

A girl on a stained mattress. A grown man on top. This place is worse than I ever imagined.

Not Elena.

In one lunging step I am upon him, my elbow sliding under the man's chin. My cheek buried in his curly, flea-infested hair, I stand up and squeeze my bicep until I feel his spine separate from his skull. I drop the warm corpse to the floor while on the bed, a little girl cowers.

A shriek reverberates from down the hall—it is a man's shout, high-pitched and surprised and cut off almost immediately.

I throw off my hood and dash down the corridor. The door bursts open before I can touch it and a man stumbles out. His filthy hands are wrapped around his own neck, red-black rivulets of blood streaming over his fingers. He opens his mouth to speak and cannot. His teeth are knocked out and broken, throat slit.

I know the small fists that did this.

Up and down the corridor, doors are slamming open. Drunk faces, twisted, confused, and angry. Hair mussed, sweat rolling from soiled creases in their faces, a few half-dressed men are pulling up their trousers, stumbling, craning their necks.

On his knees, the bleeding man tugs at my cloak, tries to mouth the word *help*.

I push him roughly against the wall and he falls, sliding with his back pressed against the timber. His blood is pooling like spilled ink.

"Oy," calls a man. "What's happened to him?"

"Ate a blade," I say, shrugging.

I casually step over the body and into the narrow room, closing and barring the door behind me.

"I knew you'd come," says a small voice.

Elena stands on the straw mattress of a sagging bed. Her cloak is wet and singed black, her wig hanging crooked. She is clearly not a human being. Her leather face is washed clean of pigment, dark as alligator skin. Through a tear in her shoulder I can see mechanisms—brass struts and silver-coiled tendons.

Boots shuffle outside the door, concerned voices muffled.

"Everyone stay in your rooms," shouts a rough voice.

Slam. The door vibrates against my back as someone shoves against it.

"Hey! Come on out," calls an unconvincing voice.

Slam.

The door rocks on its hinges.

"Elena, there are too many. Cover yourself. We will run."

"No," she says, defiant. "We're not running. Not again."

Slam.

The girl is taking too long.

"Trust me," I say, leaning over, intending to swoop her up and carry her out. My arms close on air and I stumble. The hard pressure of a stiletto presses against my throat.

"No," she says. "*You* will trust me. I have thought of a use for this place—a way that I can blend in . . . forever."

Slam. The wooden door is splintering.

Brushing past me, Elena puts a palm flat on the door. Her lips move as she counts. She is timing the hits.

Slam.

Three, two, one . . .

Elena yanks the door open and a man plows into the room, off balance. In one quick movement she sticks the stiletto in and out of his lower spine. The momentum of his body dissipates in a heap over the ragged bed. What's happened registers on the face of the dead fellow's friend and he lets out a surprised yelp.

"They're robbing him!" he shouts, pointing. "He's been stabbed!"

The hallway is a crowd of jostling elbows and fists. I put a hand on Elena's shoulder and she shrugs it off, stepping right out the open door and into the hallway, her eyes aimed at the floor, standing hunch shouldered, surrounded by cretins.

A dozen grimy faces stare down at Elena in foul-smelling lamplight. Wide eyes and sweat-stained armpits. Grubby hands clutching improvised weapons snatched off floors. A few, the ones in charge of maintaining order, are even wearing light armor.

"Put down those blades, little girl," says one.

Elena slowly straightens, raising her horrific face to them, a stiletto in each hand. The men collectively take a step back. Someone whimpers.

"By the devil."

"Her skin ain't right," says another.

Demon come the whispers. *Witch.*

"Let's begin," Elena says, and she darts between a pair of legs. The men fall upon her, shouting, swinging weapons and fists.

I draw my *khanjali*—a simple blade about the length of my forearm. Pushing into the hallway, I plunge my blade into the nearest heart. With my other hand, I lift a man by his throat and pin him against the wall, listening to his glottal struggling. A dagger slips into my side over the hip and something heavy glances off the side of my head and I choose not to react.

Someone shrieks.

Jackknifing my arm, I ignore the injuries and slice into the crowd of perspiring meat that is compressed into the corridor. The neck in my hand snaps. Already, the whoremongers are trying to escape, screaming, squealing like slaughtered pigs, turning and slipping on their own blood, holding their guts in with dirty fingers.

A small black demon flits between them like a lethal toy.

We advance down the hall, following the survivors toward the main stairs. Around us, vermin-infested corners are strewn with broken-necked, mutilated corpses. Elena is dashing ahead, crawling around and between the legs of panicked men toward the end of the hallway. There, she slams shut the door at the top of the stairs, trapping the last few men between us. Ignoring pleas for mercy, Elena and I meet in a grisly dance.

Behind us, a few brave girls are emerging from their rooms. One of them quietly and efficiently slits the throats of fallen men with a scavenged knife. Crouched on scabbed knees, she works emotionlessly, moving from one to the next.

In seconds, the men are dispatched, sprawled grotesquely up and down the hall, collapsed on one another in heaps.

It is done.

Meanwhile, the hallway is filling with girls and young women. Dirty faces and torn gowns. They watch us with cautious glances. The only way out of this hall of horrors is past one of us.

Elena presses an ear against the closed door. After a moment, she yanks it open and the madam of the brothel stumbles out, falling to her knees, breasts spilling from her elaborate corset. She wears stockings, her knees instantly stained red as she crawls over glistening carnage. At the sight of it, her eyes fly open, jaw working soundlessly until she begins to keen.

"Please!" she shouts. "Please!"

Elena puts a hand firmly on the madam's shoulder and the woman stops shouting, swallowing sobs instead. My sister watches the woman with a blank face, inhuman, skin stained with crimson drops of blood under a wig of disheveled black hair. She is emotionless as she turns to face the hallway.

Women and girls of the brothel stand and crouch, shivering, looking upon Elena's uncanny countenance with faces frozen in fear or fascination. The madam cowers, locks of her hair spiraling away in corkscrews, hands wavering over her face.

Elena motions to the stairwell door, letting it creak slowly open. When she speaks, I hear her jaw clicking with each word.

"If you are a grown woman, leave," she says.

Knees dipping, a rush of women grab clothes and personal effects, tiptoeing over the carnage in a controlled scramble to escape, pushing cautiously past Elena and thumping down the stairwell.

Now a hallway full of girls remain, trembling, eyes wide.

"The rest of you go back to your rooms," Elena says, in a low voice. "This is no longer a brothel. School begins tomorrow."

43

LONDON, PRESENT

"Just pretend you are my wife," says Peter, one arm wrapped around the small of my back. "Follow my lead."

"Won't they judge me for being American?" I ask.

"Not if you are as rich as the documents I sent indicate."

I stiffen for an instant and then allow him to usher me forward. Aside from being a fighter, Peter must also be an incredible actor. It's the only way he could have managed to blend in with human beings for this long.

I smooth my dress for the hundredth time, the weight of a pearl bracelet tugging at my wrist. Batuo's tool roll is stuffed into a sparkling clutch purse, tucked under my sweating armpit.

Peter and I have just had the most efficient shopping spree imaginable.

A limousine driver, unseen behind a tinted divider window, picked us up at a private airport and drove us straight into London. The car took an unmarked road leading directly beneath Harrods department store. Through a plain door in a blank concrete wall, we entered a wonderland of smiling salespeople.

After five minutes, I realized we were the only customers.

Careening between departments, it finally began to sink in that a race of automatons has been living alongside us for centuries—all the while creating a new, unimaginable level of wealth. With a quick phone call, Peter requested the luxurious department store be emptied just so we could shop in total privacy.

How utterly sickening. And what guilty fun.

I began to understand why the store had complied when Peter led us to the jewelry boutique. Inside, he began picking out pieces with disinterested efficiency. Necklace, earrings, rings—a blur of attendants in orbit around us, bearing velvet cushions loaded with fat, glittering gems embedded in precious metals. Each new piece reminded me of an exotic, dead insect displayed on a pushpin.

Meanwhile, Peter seemed to be speaking in code with the attendants.

"Kashmir?" he asked, peering down at a teardrop sapphire. The attendant nodded and Peter motioned for them to wrap it up.

"These have been in style since Shakespeare was playing the Globe," Peter said, examining a gem-encrusted brooch in the shape of a curved feather.

He meant it literally.

After forty-five minutes, Peter and I were in new clothes, our hair hastily styled and both of us languishing under a cloud of perfume. An ungodly amount of money had changed hands and my collarbones were chafing under a diamond necklace that came with its own name and a handwritten list of previous owners.

The jewelry is pretty, but it gives me satisfaction to think that the most valuable piece is still Huangdi's relic—hidden in the clutch purse, pinned tight under my arm.

Now Peter and I are walking together under a stone archway, husband and wife, my heels echoing off the flagstones. It's a long, wide tunnel, ending in a crescent of sunlight ahead, serving as the entrance to some kind of elite, girls-only preparatory school, though there is no signage of any kind. We entered on a quiet, leafy street, with a nondescript man in a black suit watching us, speaking into a collar microphone.

Beside me, Peter is dapper and somehow not terrifying despite his size. He wears a charcoal suit prepared by a little old man who claimed to be his personal tailor.

"How do you hide all this money?"

Peter keeps facing forward, answering in a low voice. "Art, mostly," he says. "Humanity is remarkably narcissistic. You have always valued your own creations above all else."

Peter takes a few more steps, then glances at me.

"Of course, I collect plenty of precious metals, too."

"Of course," I parrot.

But Peter is already breaking into a winning smile and striding forward with one hand out. A portly silhouette has appeared in the archway before us—a small, pinch-faced woman wearing a neat blazer with a small silver phoenix on the lapel. She is compact in size but intimidating, clutching a clipboard like a shield. Smiling at Peter, she shows no teeth, just a slight rise of her strawberry blonde eyebrows.

"Welcome to Whybourne College," the woman says, shaking hands with Peter. "I'm headmistress Timms."

Gesturing, she directs us to follow her toward an open, grassy quad that must occupy a city block, hemmed in by the slate walls of school buildings. We continue along the gleaming flagstone walkway, ambling around the perimeter of the quad, passing walls lined with class photos. Each image is mounted in an elaborate wooden frame, displaying a class of thirty or forty girls wearing matching uniforms, posed but never smiling.

The first photo is dated 1848.

The headmistress walks ahead of us, her voice booming off the walls, heels clicking on polished stone. I scan the faces of every adult I see, but I don't even know who I'm looking for.

I tune back into the headmistress when she stops and turns to us.

"Despite regularly achieving superior test scores," she says, "Whybourne is not driven by a one-dimensional hunt for academic glory. We are focused instead on developing the spirit, values, and logical thinking of our pupils. As they leave us and enter the world, our young ladies will continue to represent the college for the rest of their lives. Many of our Whybourne families go back generations. My own family has been employed here for more than two hundred years, starting with my ancestor Georgie Timms."

At that, she turns and continues walking. Giving her a few feet, I jab Peter in the ribs with an elbow.

"Where is she?" I ask.

Peter is walking slowly, hands clasped behind his back with his eyes trained on the photos. I jab him again and he turns to me.

"Near," he whispers.

Quietly, he plants a finger on a class photo, next to the round face of a little girl with curly black hair. "Here, for instance," he says.

The photo is from 1898.

Continuing to walk, he taps his finger on more pictures. "Here," he says. "And here. Her appearance changes a little. She has made herself a bit older."

1902. 1928. 1951.

Each face he points to is slightly different, but across the photos she is clearly the same dark-eyed girl.

"She's a *kid*?" I whisper.

"Sorry?" asks the headmistress, turning and stopping her informative monologue.

"Nothing," I say. "How charming."

"Yes, well," she says. "Follow me, please."

The headmistress guides us out across the grassy courtyard, still damp from a recent rain. It's a vast expanse, green and flat, and I hear the sharp calls of girls playing field hockey in the distance. Wearing helmets and brightly colored uniforms, the players chase one another on a rectangular field, fighting for the ball.

"As you can see," says the headmistress, "we instill quite a competitive spirit in our girls."

She looks at us expectantly.

"Uh, yeah," I say. "Wonderful."

"Yes," she continues. "It's our tradition, passed down as a founding principle since our inception in the mid-seventeen-hundreds. Look there."

The headmistress points to a pathetically small two-story wooden building. Made of rough timber and crumbling stucco, crawling with ivy, it has nonetheless been perfectly restored, squatting near a meandering cobblestoned pathway. Even the stones look several hundred years old, meticulously maintained.

"Those storage rooms were part of the original building that housed the very first class of Whybourne students. It was converted from a hat factory where working women once found their financial independence. From those noble origins, our college—"

Peter snorts, suppressing a laugh. The headmistress turns to him, concerned. Swallowing another laugh, he turns and puts his forearm over his mouth, hiding a wild smile. "Allergies. Excuse me."

The headmistress stares at Peter for a long second, not blinking.

"Our original founder left explicit instructions to preserve this part of our heritage, so every class of girls would know they have joined a tradition older and richer than they could ever fathom. Now, if you will join me."

The headmistress moves away, and Peter follows.

But something catches my eye about the wooden building. It's so old, so out of place. On a hunch, I fish the cedalion out of my purse. Pressing the cold circle of metal over one eye, I squint at the building.

Nothing, besides a sheet of thick ivy.

Disappointed, I lower the cedalion, but not before I catch a wink of fire through wet leaves. I stop, looking again. Fiery letters writhe under a green rash of vines. Though I can't see details, it looks like the *avtomat* domain sigil Peter showed me in Seattle. And beyond that, something else glows faintly inside.

"Excuse me!" I call, hiding the cedalion in my fist. "I'd like to see in there."

Already several yards away, the headmistress stops and considers.

"Not a good idea, ma'am—"

"Just a peek," I insist, interrupting. "The *tradition* is what I love about this place. The long tradition. Without that, why, we ought to just send the children to an American school. Right, honey?"

The headmistress licks her lips, eyes flicking briefly to the ostentatious diamond necklace slung around my neck. Finally, she takes a step toward the wooden building.

"Very well," she says, wrangling a ring of keys from her waist.

We follow her to the door, where she jams a large iron key into the crude lock. Turning it with both hands, she pauses. "But just a quick glance of the entry. This isn't on the official parent tour."

I'm stepping forward, eager to see, but Peter has stopped on the lawn.

"Come on, *honey*," I say to him, motioning.

Peter doesn't move, staring out across the quad.

I follow his gaze and see only a column of plaid-skirted girls trotting across the grass, wearing heavy backpacks and clutching musical instruments. They are headed from one class to the next, walking in loose knots and chatting with each other.

Save one.

The girl stands alone, maybe fourteen years old, her dark eyes turned toward Peter. A small frown creases her delicate features.

"Elena," breathes Peter.

"What did you say?" asks the headmistress, and her affected accent has disappeared. Now her voice sounds rough and low. Her teeth are bared, crooked, her knuckles white on the clipboard. Behind her, the keys still hang from the door.

"Who are you, sir?" she asks.

"Elena," calls Peter, in a louder voice. The girl doesn't move.

The headmistress pulls a radio from her hip, lifts it to her mouth without taking her eyes off Peter. She speaks in an urgent whisper.

"Sir," she says, stepping forward and reaching into her pocket. "I'm afraid we don't have a student here by that—"

Peter spins, dodging the twin barbed darts of a Taser. He brings his hands down and strips the device from the woman's hands, slapping it to the ground. She bites down on a shout as he puts his hands on her shoulders, looming over her.

"Stop it!"

The girl with curly black hair stands behind us, her voice commanding authority. "Both of you."

44

LONDON, 1758

Elena follows me outside to the alley beside the brothel, closing the door behind her. It is raining now, the clammy air heavy with smoke from the burned ship. The commotion on the river has thankfully drawn attention away from here. I step to the humped center of the narrow, deserted street, standing on the precipice of a jagged channel that runs down the middle.

My sister is holding a bundle of yellow silk in her hands.

The lines of her body are lost in a dark riding coat, too big for her, turning her into a shadow beneath a crimson lamp. Above us, small faces peek through one of the few dimly lit windows of the building. Girls locked inside an abattoir. We slaughtered every man in the building, and yet Elena did not free the children.

"What are you doing?" I ask her. "They are little girls."

Elena steps out into the rain.

"Circumstances have changed, Peter," she says. "I need to regroup, find a place where I can blend in. A girl's school will provide me with both opportunities. You know that I am a quick thinker, and this is the best idea I've got."

"This is insane," I say to her. "Come with me back to the estate."

Elena pulls back her hood, a dark mass of curls spilling out. Her eyes are wide and searching, lips trembling as she asks.

"Hypatia . . ."

"Gone. You saw."

"Yes, but her anima?"

"Leizu kept it," I say. "To add to her collection."

"And what of Hypatia's vessel—"

"Sunk to the bottom of the Thames, darling, please—"

"We could find her—"

"Come with me, Elena. Now."

Hands curled into tiny fists, the girl stands in the middle of the broken street and throws her head back. Tensing her whole body, she screams, channeling the piercing shout into the rain-filled sky with inhuman force.

The scream lasts for a long time.

"Come," I say, extending a hand. "Please."

The rain is driving now, lamps guttering, drops sliding in watery veins across the leather of my face and backs of my hands. Beads of the misty rain perch like pearls in Elena's hair. Each drop is washing away part of the horror of what just happened, but not enough.

The puddles around me are dark as blood.

"She was my only friend," says Elena. "And she is gone because of *you*. Because you refused your duty."

"I chose you," I say.

"You were not made to serve me," says Elena. Her voice has gone flat and emotionless in a way that I find frightening. "We each serve our own Word, Peter. Being true to that is the only path to happiness."

She drops the silken bundle onto muddy stone. The yellow handkerchief and its precious contents lie in filth, soaking wet and stained with soot.

"There's your destiny," she says, nodding. "There's who you were meant to protect. Your old master."

"Elena, no," I say, but I can't take my eyes away from the handkerchief. A rivulet of rainwater tugs a corner of fabric away to reveal the anima. The glittering crescent calls to me. To hold it in my hands would feel right.

"You . . . I promised to protect you."

"No, my dear Peter," Elena urges. "There is no magic in our origin. We were simply repaired at the same time by a foolish old man who served an ambitious tsar. That does not make us brother and sister."

I remember a grassy clearing atop a broad plateau at dusk. A little girl lighting a candle placed within a paper sky lantern, her smile lit from below.

As the first stars hardened in the sky, my sister and I added our own constellations to the cosmos—

"I do not believe that," I say.

Elena plants both hands on my thighs, pushing me back. Her clockwork voice echoes sharply in the empty alley, under the thrum of rain.

"I am not your master. I am not your sister. I'm not anything to you."

I blink, stumbling back. It should destroy me, what she has said. But I only feel pinpricks of rain on my skin. Each needle bite is building into a crescendo of realization.

I will always be alone. I *was* always alone.

Could the feelings I have for Elena be an illusion? Do they exist in a false world, constructed by a blank, newborn mind? Have I made meaning out of coincidence?

We are nothing to each other.

Elena slowly draws a stiletto.

"Take the anima and go," she says, threatening.

"Elena—"

Without hesitation, she steps forward and slides the blade into my chest. I catch her slight body in both my hands and lift her and hug her to me. My chest shudders at the bite of steel, but I am breathing in the scent of her hair and perfume, squeezing my eyes closed. For this one second I can pretend things are simple again. Perfect and safe, like when we were in Favorini's lab, before Elena studied the world, before she—

Twisting out of my grasp, she drives the blade deeper. The steel separates my ribs and punctures the bellow of my lungs, my breath dying in my throat. Elena steps back and watches me as I crumple to my knees on rough cobblestones.

Elena grabs the cloth of my jacket and pulls me close to her.

"Go," she says, her lips an inch from my ear. "Leave me to my studies. Protect the anima of your old master and serve your Word."

I am mute, the world spinning away from me, and Elena along with it.

"Do your duty."

In a haze of water and pain, knees soaking wet, shoulders hunched, I wrap my arms tight around my own punctured torso. My voice is stalled, diaphragm contracting as my final breath escapes. The silken bundle lies on the road before me.

"If you return," says Elena, pulling her hood over her face, "I will kill you."

The harsh words are spoken in a child's musical voice. Where once her face seemed impish, now her features are hard and unforgiving. Her soft cheeks are beaded with rain like tears, but her eyes are blank.

It is a mask and I do not truly know the person who hides beneath it. Perhaps I never did.

With shaking hands I pick up the anima and cradle it to my chest, letting the silk handkerchief fall away. Some mechanism fails inside me and I pitch forward onto my elbows, forehead pressing against cold stone. Now that I am not breathing, the world has become quiet and the steady drumming of rain grown to havoc in my ears.

When I lift my eyes, Elena is walking away.

For an instant, she is a little girl again. Hopping between puddles, her face is lost under the black velvet riding cloak. Her buckled shoes click over cobblestones that dance and shine under the lamplight and stars and falling rain.

I try to call her name, but nothing comes out.

45

LONDON, PRESENT

The teenager stands, defiant, her hair pulled into a tight ponytail and her skin smooth and youthful. A light brush of lipstick covers her lips, features chiseled and sharp, eyes wide and dark and intelligent. She is breathing hard, angry, or maybe afraid.

Hard to believe she isn't a person.

"Why are you here?" she asks. "I told you never to come back."

Peter stands silently, watching the girl, face soft, his eyes drinking in her presence. The headmistress is forgotten, leaning against the wall a few feet away. Her Taser lies in the grass. The students have all moved on, ushered away by their teachers, leaving the quad empty, wet blades of grass rustling under a chilly afternoon breeze.

"I honored your wish for two and a half centuries," says Peter. "Even when I was sure I would die without you. But the end is coming, Elena."

"It's been coming for a long time," she says.

Elena nods at the headmistress. The woman stumbles away across the quad, not looking back. Around the perimeter, I see men in dark suits gathering. Elena slides her gaze across me, eyes lingering on the clutch purse tucked under my arm.

"You found your old master again," says Elena, talking to Peter. "You shouldn't have brought him here."

"Why not?" I ask, stepping forward. "I read your letters to Batuo. You've studied Huangdi. You know he can save the *avtomat,* and I think you know where he is."

Elena throws a look of disbelief at Peter.

"What happened to protecting the secret?" she asks him.

"Desperate times," I interrupt. I've had enough of being ignored as a mere human. "Tell us where Huangdi's vessel is located, and we'll go."

The girl finally decides to speak to me.

"Do you know what hunts you?" she asks.

"I know her name," I say. "I know I killed her general. And I know she's afraid of an *avtomat* called Huangdi."

Elena steps closer to me as she speaks, menacing.

"Leizu isn't like me or Peter or even Talus. The Mother of Worms isn't good or evil or anything so simple as that. Her anima is a force of nature, like a tidal wave or a flood. She carries a Word of chaos, dusk, autumnal decay. *Per ignum, renatus mundi est. Through fire, the world is reborn—*"

"Enough," says Peter, putting a hand between us.

My back is pressed against the door, fingers splayed against the wood. The girl is half the size of Peter and twice as menacing. Standing up, my arm brushes against the iron key still hanging from the lock.

"Get out of here, Peter," Elena says. "Take your human and pray that you never meet Leizu again."

Elena's eyes flick up to the old wooden building. Beneath her anger, I can tell she is frightened and sad. She won't give us the information we need, but I've got a feeling I know where to find it.

Behind my back, I close my fingers around the metal key.

"Elena," says Peter. "The alternative is extinction—"

In one motion, I snatch the key from the lock and yank the door open. Instantly, the schoolgirl clamps fingers over my forearm. Then Peter is holding her by the shoulders, twisting her away from me. The bracelet on my wrist shatters, a cascade of pearls rattling to the stones.

I dive behind the cracked-open door and slam it shut behind me.

Cranking the lock, I lean my back against rough wood. A stripe of bruises are already starting to cloud the skin of my forearm where the girl gripped me with inhuman strength. I hear arguing outside, and something thumps against the door.

This dim anteroom is like a museum, filled with antique furniture, a golden spittoon, and Chinese silks draped over lacquered Oriental screens. In urgent crab steps, I drag a heavy wooden bench over and wedge it under the locked doorknob.

I dig the cedalion out of my clutch and raise it to my eye. Faint light intensifies into crisp details. Something is glowing dimly up a set of cramped stairs. Wincing at the loudly creaking boards, I head up to the second floor.

A narrow hallway stretches along the spine of the building. The floors are made of raw timber, slats stained and scarred. Old lamps hang on the blackened walls, the ceiling smudged with soot. This building has to be hundreds of years old. The walls are out of kilter, warped floors rolling like waves. It is vaguely nauseating.

Downstairs, something thumps against the door.

Tromping over the rough boards, I rush headlong down the hallway, navigating by the faint lines of light glowing under the doorways. Holding the cedalion to my eye, I can make out the glowing shape just ahead, beyond a final closed door.

I press against lacquered wood and the heavy door glides open.

Inside, the walls are draped in fabric, dust hanging in the air. The room is cocooned in layers of silk, but otherwise empty—save for an antique table, its mahogany legs carved into dragon mouths closed on ball feet. And resting on the ornate table is a kind of glass coffin, edges wrought in gold.

Holding my breath, I tiptoe closer.

My breath expels in a burst as I see an angelic woman, lying on her back under the dusty glass surface of the coffin. She is beautiful, her eyes closed as if in sleep, wearing a gray riding dress from at least two centuries ago. Her chin is slightly crooked, a trace of stubbornness there, even in repose. Braids of blond hair are carefully arranged over her shoulders and her arms are at her sides, a long silver saber laid over her chest.

"Who are you?" I ask the empty room.

I'm sure this must be an *avtomat,* reconstructed and maintained as perfectly as this ancient building. Something bad has happened to her. I can see repaired skin at her throat, and there are water stains on her otherwise immaculate clothing. From the beat-up scabbard I can tell the weapon isn't ornamental—it has been used.

"Her name was Hypatia," says a voice.

Startled, I turn to see Elena standing in the doorway behind me, her arms crossed. The girl doesn't look angry anymore, just tired and sad.

"She passed into sleep two hundred years ago," says Elena. "I dredged the Thames up and down for a decade to find her vessel. Then I put her back together, bit by bit. But I never could find the most important part . . . I never found her heart."

I step away from Hypatia, hiding the cedalion in my fist.

"If we find Huangdi, I could learn how to revive her," I say. "I may be short-lived, but it's my expertise."

"Do you think I haven't poured billions into research and development?" she asks. "I have laboratories on every continent. How could you solve a problem the brightest minds in centuries have been unable to even comprehend?"

"Because I've got something they don't have."

"And what's that?"

"I've got Peter."

Elena blinks, then lets out a sharp laugh.

"How could that possibly matter?"

"I've seen inside you. I used a *bi* disk to transfer power from Batuo to Peter, put a Shaolin spear through an *avtomat*'s cradle and watched him die, and I found this room with a cedalion."

I open my palm to show her the artifact.

"Elena, I grew up with an anima hanging around my neck, thinking about it night and day. The artifact you described as a sun disk in your letters to Batuo—the *spiritus vitae* . . . I think it's the key. And I think Huangdi can give it to us."

"The sun disk, imbued with the breath of life," says Elena, shaking her head. "It's supposedly a battery that has been charged with ancient souls. They say it has the ability to rejuvenate an anima, restore memory, smite our enemies—everything except cure cancer. It's a legend, June."

Off her skeptical look, I urge: "Elena, it's worth trying. And if anybody can figure this out, it's me."

A faint smile settles on the girl's lips, eyebrows rising.

"I thought you were just another thing for Peter to protect."

"He tried that," I say. "I shot him."

At this, Elena's smile widens.

"You're not the first."

"Peter means well," I say. "Overprotective, maybe. But he's trying."

Elena walks to the glass coffin.

"I only ever tried to help him," she says. "To find a way to make him happy. But after I sent Peter away . . . he was lost for a long time. I was afraid I had broken him."

"Maybe you did. But I think he's found a purpose in this."

"To save us all, of course . . . oh, Peter," says Elena, her smile turning sad.

The girl slides her fingers lightly over the glass of Hypatia's coffin, peering at the still woman inside. The movement is familiar, as if she's stood in this room alone and done it a thousand times before. I imagine she has.

"Who was she?" I ask.

Elena stares at the sleeping woman through the glass.

"She was my friend. Someone who saw me for what I am, and not for what I look like. Hypatia used to say that I did not need protection from the world, but that the world needed protection from me."

"What happened?"

"The mother of silkworms, of course."

Elena steps toward me, her eyes on my purse.

"Leizu will come for that anima," says Elena. "But mostly, she'll come for Peter. Her Word is darkness and she needs his light. Since she conquered her husband, I think Peter is the closest thing she's found to a replacement. You should start running now and never stop."

"Is that why you won't tell me where Huangdi is? You're afraid that Peter can't defeat her?"

Elena's eyes go back to Hypatia's body, and both of them seem like ghosts in the dim sunlight falling through gauzy white silk.

"He can't," she says, shoulders slumping nearly imperceptibly. "Only dawn can chase away the dusk."

Dawn and dusk. Light and dark. White and black. The symbol on my relic comes into focus in my mind—a teardrop with a solid dot inside it.

"Wait, Elena," I say, starting to pace as I think. "Leizu's word is—is *symbiotic* with Huangdi's? The two of them created some kind of dyad, and they can only be whole together. So without Huangdi, Leizu will keep hunting Peter forever. Eventually she'll kill him."

"That's right."

"Elena, the symbols you're talking about are yin and yang, aren't they?"

Elena nods. She is watching me now, keenly interested.

"I'll revive Huangdi," I tell her. "When I do, Leizu will forget about Peter. Yin will find yang. It may be crazy, it may be nearly impossible, but it's the only logical answer. If you want Peter to live, then you've *got* to help me find Huangdi."

Elena pauses for a long moment, then sighs.

"I don't know where he is. Not exactly," she says. "His vessel is most likely somewhere in the Hubei province of China. His tomb is buried, nestled in the coils of the Yangtze River."

"How do you know this?" asks a deep voice.

Peter stands in the doorway, the sleeve of his jacket ripped and his feet muddy.

"Favorini," says Elena. "I contacted our maker after we fled Saint Petersburg. The old man escaped Catherine and returned to Italy. He told me where we were found."

"Where we were found?" asks Peter, not understanding.

"Our bodies, Peter. Scavengers found us together, preserved in mud on the banks of a river in China. You . . . were holding me in your arms.

"It was from those remains that Favorini rebuilt us."

Peter's eyes widen, recognition in them.

"Where?" he asks. "Where were we found *exactly*?"

"I can give you the coordinates, but it doesn't matter. At the turn of the nineteenth century, Leizu began using shadow companies to propose the construction of a dam. It took nearly a hundred years, but she finally did it. The Three Gorges Dam flooded the whole countryside; millions of people were displaced."

"Just tell me exactly where," Peter insists.

"A short way from the dam. At the foot of a plateau on the western bank of the Yangtze River. They called it the dragon's tooth. I have no memory of that life, but you and I were living at the same time as Huangdi. His empire would have been near where . . . where we—"

"Where we died," Peter says, resting a hand on the glass of Hypatia's coffin.

"What is it, Peter?" I ask.

"I know where to find Huangdi," he says. "I remember."

PART THREE
PRAVDA
(Truth / Justice)

> *The king stared at the figure in astonishment. It walked with rapid strides, moving its head up and down, so that anyone would have taken it for a live human being. The artificer touched its chin, and it began singing, perfectly in tune. He touched its hand, and it began posturing, keeping perfect time . . .*
>
> —Liezi text,
> fourth century BC

46

STALINGRAD, 1942

An old man, long dead by now, once asked me a question in the candlelit twilight. *My son,* he said. *What is the first thing?* And when I reached inside myself for the answer, I found an overwhelming instinct stamped into my mind. It translated into a simple word, as much a part of me as my hands or face.

Pravda.

I was a newborn with a mind as blank as a still pond, and the old man took me by the shoulders and led me. I followed without hesitation. He asked me to serve a tsar and told me I had a divine purpose. Like a child, I believed him. When my tsar was gone I served a king. Then I tried to serve a little girl. And when she left me, I chose to serve a long-dead ruler by protecting his anima.

For two hundred years, I have faithfully served. I am an instrument of truth, and I exist to create justice from injustice. I have done so through the first war between all men, and now I continue, deep into this second world war.

And all the while, it feels as though my true purpose has been hidden just beyond the next blasted crater, around the corner of another shattered building. Fighting through the agony of failing to fulfill my Word, I push onward like a broken machine, repeating the same motions of battle around the world, in the name of generals and kings and presidents.

The city of Stalingrad is a familiar kind of wasteland to me, a city of ghosts, under siege and mortar fire for months now. Only the scale of it is new. Millions dead instead of hundreds of thousands. A keen nostalgia haunts me as I fight house to house in this dying city, back within the ancient boundaries of my first country.

And falling into my old patterns, I have made an old mistake: sparking legend.

I hunt the German invaders during the night, running trench raids on their positions on the city outskirts. It was Russian women and children who dug these trenches as the German infantry made its way toward the city, never guessing the horror that would soon be unleashed. As homes burned, soldiers filtered in to take up residence. The last refuge of long-dead civilians now provides harbor to the enemy.

But in the night, something inhuman haunts the trenches of Stalingrad.

As the distant orb of the sun fades behind gray clouds, I don armor and a gas mask to protect my vessel from damage. Armed with a pair of trench knives, my hands wrapped in thick leather gloves and my fingers threaded through spiked knuckles, I set about my grisly work.

Sweeping through muddy culverts under the gleam of moonlight, I take no pity on the scared, wounded soldiers who I find cowering in their holes. The men and boys are freezing, far from home and underprepared. They've reached Stalingrad and set about gorging themselves to death on the flesh of my homeland.

Each morning I return to the Russian line, my sleeves glistening with frozen blood.

As I repair myself during the days of siege and bombardment, rumors spread among the Axis of my nighttime exploits—a jackbooted killer who leaves fortified trenches filled with corpses, each with a neat red smile beneath his chin. They fear the coming of the tall Soviet in the greatcoat, the one who leaves no survivors, who sees in the dark and makes no sound.

My error was an old one, and a legend soon took root. Not a man-eating tiger but an angel of vengeance. A living embodiment of justice, sent by an angry god.

The rumor catches up to me after midnight, as I am slogging through knee-deep water in a flooded trench.

A gray-green flare climbs into the sky, spitting and sparking, sending my shadow exploring the rugged contours of the German trench.

This rut has been dug in what was once a neighborhood. The main house is a pile of bricks, the streets and trees shredded by mortars for a mile around. Only a backyard shed remains, a spot where this squad has been cooking their meals, storing cigarettes and scavenged tins of sardines.

At the bottom of the trench, in dirt conquered and reclaimed, lay the stiff gray bodies of Russians and green-uniformed Germans. The dead men are reduced to frozen angles of human figures, sharp geometries of smashed bricks and round, sloped helmets. It is a silent, fossilized hell, lit in stark relief by the flare.

I imagine it was the meager shed, leaning pathetically, that brought these Germans so deep into no-man's-land. Around us are collapsed buildings and cratered holes in the dirt, all of it marbled with dirty ice. The invading soldiers have spread out now, their offensive stalled, and these boys grew isolated.

A distant gunshot barks, and then another.

Some detail is off, something wrong. The cigarettes and sardines. They are impossible to find this late in the fight. Someone has brought them in.

Bait.

This hole in the middle of no-man's-land has the feel of a trap. Sardines and cigarettes to lure Germans to this vulnerable spot. And here they served their purpose as more bait. A furor of bullets cough into the night, Russian guns, urgent, firing closer to my position now.

I scan over the lip of the reinforced trench, toward the gunshots.

In my eyes, the dead expanse of no-man's-land is alive with flickering traces of heat. Over the cool sucking mud and toothy barbed wire and skeletal fists of trees, I see the storm trooper coming. The figure runs in a hunch under the harsh light of another sputtering flare, coat flapping, chasing his own elongated shadow toward me.

I vault the trench wall and hit the mud running.

Pulling my hat on tight, I grip my rifle in both hands and launch myself forward. Another flare snaps into the cloud-filled sky, hissing to itself over the clomp of my boots and the squelch of mud. Bullets flicker through the night, chased by the distinctive report of German rifles. Both sides are firing, pinpointing the two of us as we lope across the sparsely lit devastation, breathless, both of us silent.

The storm trooper wears a *Stahlhelm,* a German helmet, gunmetal gray and shaped like a low-slung turtle shell. Where horns would be on a bull, it has bolts to secure a full steel face guard. This type of plate is only worn by snipers; it is too heavy for a man to wear beyond a fixed position.

So, this is not a man.

Without slowing, I toss my rifle to the ground and draw both trench knives. The blades flash under greenish clouds as my arms pump mechanically. The storm trooper also accelerates, its face blank behind a sheet of steel with two slits for eyes. A stray bullet strikes him in the shoulder, tearing fabric in a puff.

He does not lose stride.

We meet at the base of a blasted tree, stripes of its bark ripped away in pale rivulets, its white heart exposed. The storm trooper draws a long saber, dull yellow, familiar. In rapid motions we are upon each other, no grunting or cursing, only the sound of our blades ringing, biting, and tearing through fabric as we feint and dodge.

The gunshots have stopped from both sides.

In a flurry of movement the storm trooper catches my fist. His blade pierces my torso, splitting my coat and cracking my lower ribs. I try to pull away, but the masked man is too strong. With my free hand, I grab him by the face and pry the steel plate and helmet off his head.

An artillery shell whistles for attention.

Dirt sprays and thunder rolls as the ground opens up and swallows us. Blade lodged in my stomach, I am thrown against the tree, slipping in the mud under the weight of the storm trooper. Shrapnel falls in a hot rain as a mass of long black hair spills over my face. A red hilt streaks in my vision and I recognize the divine blade—Xuan Yuan. This is not a man . . . and it is not truly a woman.

"Leizu," I say, in shock.

She rams a knee into my chest and pulls the blade free. In her other hand, I can make out a device that looks like a tuning fork. She jams the hard fingers of the device against my sternum and speaks into my face, her breath invisible. "You say my name as if it means something, *Pyotr.* But you do not remember me. Not yet.

"Witness," she says.

The tuning fork sprays tree roots of electricity over my chest. The twisted branches above me look like claws scrabbling against throbbing green clouds. My back arches, body convulsing. A buzzing sensation traces over my teeth as the device injects writhing filaments of power through my anima.

Another mortar is whistling into existence, I think.

Like the afterimage of lightning, the world flips to negative and back again. Ribbons of light spiral in my vision as a firecracker string of memories ignites. A thousand years of disjointed recollection—broken shards of a forgotten whole—flood into my blinded eyes.

I scream the pain of it into the freezing night.

47

CHINA, PRESENT

Like a spinning globe, a great green expanse of earth rolls beneath the private jet. Peter and I are soaring low over jagged mountains with tight, meandering spines. Slug-trail folds of the Yangtze River trickle like venom between sharp teeth of rock. In the jet cabin, a yellowed map is spread out, pockmarked with Chinese characters and a landscape that only vaguely resembles the tableau sliding past.

Elena reluctantly lived up to her promise, marking the map with the exact modern coordinates where her body was recovered more than three centuries ago.

"Huangdi is in these mountains?" I ask, watching the river swell into a lake at the point where it is choked by the wide buttress of the Three Gorges Dam. "You think his vessel is still down there?"

"Leizu tried to flood this land—proof we are on the right track. But Huangdi was clever. He built his tomb to last forever."

"Then he's here?"

"I will know it when I see it," says Peter.

It's as much as I've been able to get out of him, and it will have to be enough. Impatient, I check the batteries in my headlamp again. Our preparations for the trip are long complete. The pilot met us at an airstrip outside London ten hours ago. Two fat black duffel bags were waiting on the leather seats, slumped like sleeping passengers.

Inside the bag, I found boots, pants, a shirt, and a backpack—all black, made of futuristic materials and layered in places with a type of thin ceramic armor. Wearing his own quasi-military gear, Peter looks like a mercenary, perfectly confident and at ease with a custom knife sheath across his chest for his antique dagger.

As for me, I'm not so sure. I'm just as uncomfortable in this commando uniform as I was wearing diamonds and pearls. The only thing that feels right is the relic hanging around my neck in its usual place.

I find myself wondering if Peter remembers that I tried to abandon him when Talus was coming for us. I'd pressed the relic into his unresponsive hand and was ready to run. All the years I spent in school, living on student loans, moving every few years from one postdoc to another, I sacrificed friendships and relationships for the chance to be an expert, to learn more about one thing than anybody else in the world. And I nearly left him there to die, trying to get my old life back.

How much am I willing to give up to see this new world?

"Buckle up," says Peter. He's watching me closely, and I try to keep my face blank. "It is time."

We land on a deserted strip of tarmac nestled in the mountains.

Stepping out into an empty hangar, I don't see any other planes or people. Nobody checks our identification or the packs we wear. Peter gives a small nod at a ramshackle building where an indistinct face swims behind dark glass, and then we're walking down a long gravel path that leads to a roughly paved road.

A black SUV waits for us—the ubiquitous, anonymous variety that lurks around airports all over the world. The only difference is this one has large, knobby tires and a winch welded to the frame under the front grill. Our driver, just as anonymous as his vehicle, greets us with a quick bow and climbs in. He doesn't move to take our backpacks and doesn't make eye contact. A light mist lies over the jungle, beads of dew cascading over the SUV hood like spider eyes. I suppress a shiver and climb in.

Peter gives terse instructions in Chinese, and we roar away.

As we cruise downhill, our narrow road weaves across a lush, mountainous countryside wreathed in ferns and reeds and towering stalks of bamboo. After half an hour, we leave the pavement for a path made of crushed stone, green fingers of tree limbs dragging across our tinted windows. We roll slowly, through scraping branches and directly over small trees. I glance at Peter in alarm as a rock grinds across the undercarriage, vibrating our feet.

Eventually, we slide to a halt on a steep slope, engulfed in green canopy.

The driver glances down at a GPS unit, turns, and nods. Peter rolls down the window, listening. A moist breeze instantly fills the car, warm and smelling of chlorophyll. Water roars in the distance, hidden somewhere in the jungle.

Peter claps the driver on the arm and nods a thank-you.

Leaning into the door, he shoves it open against dense jungle, clearing a swath of space for us to wriggle out. I shrug on my backpack, put two fingers over my chest to reassure myself that the relic is still there, and latch a hand on Peter's knife strap as he moves deeper into a maze of vines and leaves. The wet jungle sways around us, hotter now, almost breathing, already drawing prickles of sweat onto my skin.

The SUV surges away in reverse, tires grinding over mud and rock.

"Whoa, wait!" I shout as the hood vanishes.

"It's okay," says Peter, over his shoulder. "We don't need him. It's not far now."

We continue downhill, step by step, the jungle compressing around us like the digestive tract of some monstrous creature. Then Peter throws an arm out to bar my way, nearly knocking the breath out of me. Looking down, I see a dizzying expanse of empty air beyond my boot. We're standing on the edge of a black rock cliff.

Across the valley, a waterfall thunders, prehistorically huge, nearly lost in billows of its own pounding mist. The cataract is split down the middle by a flat rock, lodged stubbornly on the precipice like the prow of a wrecked ship. On either side, torrents of yellow-brown water cascade over the edge, soaring in a torrent through the sky.

"This is the place," I say, seeing the expression on Peter's face. "How long has it been?"

Peter surveys the landscape, eyes calculating.

"A long time for a man," he says. "But not for a mountain."

Up the river, a series of tropical birds are sitting on branches high in a tree, watching us. I count them by habit. One, three, one, three.

"Who do they belong to?" I ask.

"Her."

"She's watching us?"

"She's been waiting a long time," he says. "Come on."

Drawing a machete, Peter leads us straight back into the damp jungle, chopping a path with clean, tireless strokes.

"How far?" I ask, watching the birds take flight.

Peter responds without looking back.

"I was running for my life the last time I was here," he says. "But I came from Huangdi's tomb on foot."

Headed mostly uphill, Peter occasionally checks his pocket watch. I follow him on the sweating, muddy trek through the tight jungle. Between panting breaths, I frantically try to put together a picture of what we're walking into.

"I thought you had no memory this far back?"

Peter's reply is calm and measured, his breathing steady.

"Huangdi has his tools, and so does Leizu. She once gave me a gift of remembrance. Or perhaps it was supposed to be a punishment."

A rock face peeks out of the jungle in the distance, bright and broken. At the top is the flat line of a plateau. Hidden in the base is a dark crease, wreathed in vines. The hillside below it is a crumbling field of broken rock. Peter accelerates, legs churning as he climbs the hill of crushed boulders. Dozens of exotic birds perch on the cliff face, watching us without moving.

I swallow my questions and follow, the relic hot against my sweaty skin.

Peter stops before the crack in the rock face. Resting my hands on my knees, I feel the cool breath of a breeze flowing out. A cavern is hidden in the fold of stone before us, all but invisible. Peter sets about hacking the vegetation away from the opening.

As he works, goose bumps flower on the backs of my arms. The chipped edges of concentric circles are carved into the wall of this hollow—hieroglyphs that show traces of Neolithic stone-working techniques.

"This is ancient," I say, running my fingers over the rough stone.

"It is where I emerged from the tomb," Peter says. "There was a massive excavation. Huangdi had to hollow out this mountain."

Now I understand the embankment of loose rock—it came from inside the mountain, dumped here ages ago and still not weathered away.

"Which means this passage will link to the tomb eventually," I say, the back of my throat tightening. The black slice of rock seems to telescope away in my vision, like a nightmare.

Peter nods, pulling on a headlamp.

"Eventually. If it hasn't collapsed," he says, sliding into the crevice. "I will go first."

I swallow and nod, trying to seem brave. I hate tight spaces, but there's no other way except straight through. Taking a deep breath, I try to imagine the wonder of whatever antiquities might be hidden in the darkness, but I feel only a dull pounding fear.

What kind of person are you, June?

The cave starts small, and it only gets smaller.

At first on my hands and knees, and then flat on my stomach, I finally have to inch sideways—following him deeper and deeper. The rock turns cold, numbing my fingers and face. Through multiple small chambers, we find knots of tunnels heading off in every direction and some of them up and down. Peter never falters, choosing our route through the network of tunnels without hesitating.

Finally, I push my body into a vertical crevice. Scraping and sliding, Peter has also turned sideways in the gap of rock. My backpack is now attached to a rope tied around my ankle. In the LED glare of my headlamp, all I can see is my own breath, speckles of dust, and the back of Peter's head and neck. The cave has become a black vise.

"Peter," I say, my voice loud in my ears.

He hasn't moved in a few minutes. Long ago, he let out all his breath to make himself smaller. Not breathing, not moving, the alarming thought occurs to me—maybe he's dead. And then, *Was he ever truly alive? Am I alone in this deep place?*

I can't turn my head to look behind me. And I can only blink in horror and wriggle backward when I see it . . . a trickle of water seeping over Peter's head, leaving a damp stripe in his hair. The leak grows to a cascade, turning his hair shiny in my headlamp and oozing over his shoulder and arm.

I grit my teeth against a wave of claustrophobia.

Eyes closed, I hear a scraping sound. Peter is rocking back and forth, his face and body scraping inch by inch over sharp rock. I stay where I am, trying not to take panicked breaths, body compressed between two slabs of wet stone. Moving only my eyes, I can see that the water is pooling, rising quickly in the narrow gap.

"Peter," I call again.

He doesn't have to breathe, I'm thinking. *He doesn't have to breathe and I do. Cold water is soaking into my boots and I'm going to drown in this black hell.*

"Peter!"

I hear a strange whining noise. It's Peter's body, creaking. Something cracks inside him and I hear the rip of clothing. A crack of space opens up. The *avtomat* has made it through the crevice. Water droplets flash in my headlamp as they fall through the space where he was. Now, I see the way forward is impossibly narrow, sheer walls flowing with clear water seeping from overhead.

A whimper forms in the back of my throat.

"June," says a voice in the darkness. I see the flicker of Peter's headlamp. His lips and cheek appear in the gap, scratched and dirty. "I am here."

He's broken his ribs to make it through.

"I can't make it," I say, swallowing, feeling dust on the back of my throat. Racing with adrenaline, my body is tense against the rock. Without realizing, I have started to wriggle away from the gap.

"June, you can," he says. "I know you can."

"No," I gasp. "I'm not *avtomat,* Peter. I have to *breathe.*"

"You are strong. You can make it."

Any strength I had is gone. All that's left is panic and despair.

"I'm not strong, Peter. I left you. In Batuo's sanctuary, I tried to leave you—"

"I know," he says. "You came back. And you won't stop now."

I pause, blinking, my cheeks wet.

"How can you know that?" I ask.

His fingertips push in through the gap.

"Because you are much too curious ever to turn back, June," he says.

I snake my hand forward, curling two of my fingers around his. They feel strong.

A sobbing laugh fights its way out of me. The relic is hard against my chest, imprinting its fractal pattern into my cold, numb skin. Even now it feels warm, even in this frozen pit.

"Fuck, Peter. *Fuck this.* Oh my god—"

Elbow bent, I push my face into the crevice. Water cascades over my cheeks, colder than my body can register—so cold it feels like a sheet of flame. Closing my eyes, I keep pushing, letting the stream slip over my nose and mouth. In the pounding blackness, I imagine the mountain has swallowed me. Rock scrapes my face, my chest and hips, and I exhale every last molecule of oxygen in my lungs. Keeping my body small, I shove forward with all my strength, pushing until I feel the water flowing over the nape of my neck.

Faintly, I hear Peter speaking, almost a chant.

"Come on, June," urges Peter. "You can do this."

Panic beats behind my eyes, lungs throbbing for oxygen, and I shove my arm farther through the breach. Peter's hand clamps on to my forearm. I try to scream. Nothing comes out as he pulls my arm, nearly popping it out of its socket, hauling my body through the blunt crevice, ripping my clothes, branding me with a full-body bruise.

Pain claws through my body, my lungs, and my mind goes blank.

Then I tumble out into blackness, crying, wheezing for breath. Dropping without looking, I curl into fetal position. I lie for a long time on the rock. After a little while, I notice there is a warm hand on my shoulder. I put my hand over his and hold it.

Finally, I open my eyes and look up.

A black sky full of bright blue stars shines down on me. At my feet, a shimmering silver river undulates away under the night sky. Blinking in the dim light, I can make out the silhouettes of people—dozens and dozens of them, all around us. It is an army, the soldiers stock-still and inanimate, wielding spears and swords and bows.

"We are here, June," says Peter. "Huangdi's tomb."

"How—how did you know I could make it through?" I ask, my throat raw.

"You could not go back," Peter says. "Leizu has followed us in."

48

CHINA, 3000 BC

My body is sprawled in the frozen mud of Stalingrad, but my mind is transported to an impression of the past. Memories rush over me like a surge of river water, pulling me under. Submerged, visions of my other life appear. Bits and snatches, growing into a tumbling flood of images and sounds that cascade through my mind.

I remember.

In this age I am called Lu Yan. I am holding simple leather reins in gauntleted hands, settled on the wide back of a gray stallion. The horse is strange, with a primitive blue-black stripe running along its spine and parallel lines raking over its shoulders. *Not a horse,* I think. *This memory is of a tarpan—an extinct megafauna brought here by barbarian raiders from the steppe.*

Clutching its back with my thighs, I keep the barely domesticated beast under my control. Few men can ride this steed—the father of wild horses.

We *avtomat* ride them with ease.

Beside me, Leizu urges her own, smaller mare into a trot to match stride with mine. Her fingers are curled into its blue-black mane. She wears a white silk dress that curls and flaps in the wind, trailing behind as she effortlessly controls the wild animal. Her features are angular and sharp, made of ceramic planes—clearly *avtomat,* yet she is more refined than the leather and whalebone of Favorini's workshop.

Together, we ride wild beasts over a sea of swaying grass.

"General," says Leizu, bringing her horse alongside mine. Too near.

I nod to acknowledge the empress, glancing back to the mountains by instinct. Huangdi and my army swarm the broken rock, far from here. Ensconced in cloudy peaks of stone, my master rules men and *avtomat* for as far as the eye can see. Leizu smiles at my hesitation, her lips bright against an ivory face.

Pushing a stray lock of hair over her ear, she chides me.

"My husband is busy attending to our great retreat," she says. "From this distance, anyone will assume we are having an innocent conference."

"He would not approve of us—"

"Talking? Very well. If you wish, I can talk. And you can listen."

Leaning in her saddle, she puts a hand over my gauntlet, tracing fingers over the ornate metal. I allow her to turn my hand over and touch the rough leather of my palm. Her touch is like the fall of snow, fingers hard as stone.

"You are strong, Lu Yan," she says to me. "My equal, perhaps. But I fear for your future. Together, you and I—"

"Should race," I finish for her, turning in my simple leather saddle and pulling my hand away, "while the day is fine."

A flash of anger pinches her face, quickly disappearing. She considers for a moment before pointing, long sleeve wavering in the breeze.

"To the cliff's edge," she says. "To the dragon's tooth."

Already spurring her horse, she sweeps past.

I lean and urge my beast forward. Ahead of me, Leizu looks like a spirit escaped from the underworld, black hair spilling over a milk-white dress. As my steed lumbers, gaining speed, I marvel at Leizu's strength and agility—she rides in perfect synchronicity with the animal, her head held low and level as a tiger prowling through reeds. The waving grass brushes my thighs, whipping past as scores of insects leap like shooting stars, and I laugh with sheer exhilaration, the vibration of it echoing in my chest.

As my horse grows even with hers, Leizu leans harder but she cannot pull away. My beast gallops, sweating, stiff mane bouncing. I catch an angry smile on Leizu's face as I pass her, and some hint of satisfaction.

Snapping my head back, I grab a fistful of mane and yank upward. With a screaming whinny, my beast rears and digs hooves into thinning grass. We skid to a halt at the crumbling edge of the plateau.

Rocks tumble over the ledge, the crack of their impacts echoing up.

A wide curve of the Long River curls through the valley below like a fat, shining dragon tail. Along its banks, the land slopes up to form ridges that turn to verdant plains. Wild forest seems to hem in the surging water, but I instinctively know that only these high plateaus are at all safe from the great river.

Behind me, Leizu approaches with a mysterious smile.

"Thank you for the warning," I say, sarcastic.

Her smile does not falter. Swaying in the saddle, she turns her sweating steed away from me, its nostrils flaring, eyes rolling in fear as Leizu traces a path along the brink of the cliff. I watch her turn into a silhouette of woman and horse against cloudy skies, then finally spur my steed to follow.

The race was thrilling, but now Leizu is leading me somewhere.

Across the valley and beyond the river, I see that a black mouth has been bored into the face of the far plateau—dragon's tooth. From that dark maw, a stream of human slaves pour in and out. Simple men, they are farmers and peasants, dressed in rags and carrying empty sacks in and sacks full of rock out.

The massive construction project has been going on for years, and the men look exhausted and half-starved. Like water through rock, they have carved a warren of tunnels into the high plateau, excavation routes for a burial chamber—an underground city concealed somewhere deep inside the range of plateaus.

Huangdi's necropolis will be grand.

The hidden tomb will soon house all of us as we sleep for a thousand years, awaiting the return of the progenitor race—the First Men. The Yellow God has decreed we leave this barbarous land, resting our vessels in the depths of the underworld until our makers return.

"He will kill the workers after," says Leizu, not looking at me.

"The short-lived race are happy to die for their cosmic ruler," I reply.

Leizu frowns at me, so I continue.

"He taught them to write. To farm. He has given them the Mandate of Heaven. Without him, that swarm of ants would be nothing."

"Not ants," she says. "Civilization makers."

"That rabble did not create us. The First Men are long passed from this land."

"Maybe so, but why do you think they set our kind upon the world?"

"We were made to serve Huangdi," I respond.

"Not true."

I snort. "Now you profess to know the progenitor race?"

"You are a warrior, and warriors have short memories—destroyed in battle every few hundred years. I am not a warrior. And I have a long memory."

"Then tell me, why were we made?" I ask.

"As paragons. We are the physical embodiments of virtues prized by the First Men. Logic. Justice. Valor. The balance of chaos and rebirth. The only pain we can feel is that of failing our Word. To not serve is to defy your existence. It is the bite of the void. Nihil, beckoning."

"We are paragons? To what purpose?"

"As beacons to men, Lu Yan. Millennia ago, when our makers fell into barbarism, slitting one anothers' throats in the flooded, golden ruins of their fallen civilization . . . it was we who led on through time, immortal shepherds, tasked with guiding the ancestors of the First Men back to their glorious birthright."

"But we are not immortal," I say, shaking my head. "The eldest of us are already gone, their anima extinguished. Huangdi has a plan—"

Leizu slides a slender arm around my waist and pulls herself onto my steed, facing me. She is too near, too intimate, but in my saddle I have nowhere to go. Resting her hands on my hips, she levels her eyes on mine. Her voice is so close, it almost seems to come from inside my own head.

"His plan is mad. The human kingdoms need us here. We must lead them back to true civilization. When they are as great as their ancestors, we will be rewarded with knowledge of ourselves. This is our only path to survival."

Beyond her oval face, thousands of dirt-covered workers move ceaselessly in and out of the cavern. Huangdi's tomb is expanding by the minute. With proper supervision, it is clear the human beings are capable of great works. But even with our help, the lucky ones barely survive thirty years, infested with parasites and disease, losing more children than they raise.

"These creatures are little more than animals," I say. "We must obey Huangdi and sleep. Our emperor has decreed—we will await the return of the First Men."

"There *are* no more First Men," Leizu says. "These *animals* are the remnants of the progenitor race—the closest thing we will see to their kind again. A civilization as great as that will not return on its own."

Leizu bows, pressing her cheek to my shoulder.

"Your master is a liar," she says. "If you allow him, Huangdi will feed on you, and on all of us, while he waits in vain for the return of a long-dead race—"

"He has promised to wake us—"

Leizu lifts her gaze, takes my face in her hands.

"This is your *life*! Must we sacrifice ourselves for *him*?"

Taking her wrists in my hands, I gently push her arms away. I slide off my beast and plant boots on the stony edge of the plateau. She follows, landing beside me.

"Lu Yan, I cannot survive alone," she says, speaking quickly and without emotion. "Without a Oneness, my anima cannot be satisfied. I am asking you, please. Do not choose him. Choose *me*."

"Huangdi would hunt us to the ends of the earth."

"We will wait until he sleeps. In the final moment, we will escape together—"

"And what of my sister? My brother? Your vassals?"

Leizu is silent, watching me without blinking. I put a hand on the broad flank of the nervous tarpan, and address the empress sadly.

"I cannot betray my master, Leizu. Not for the race of men."

Her face has emptied itself of emotion. When she speaks again, her jaw moves with mechanical precision, spitting each syllable.

"These wretched humans may not live long, but people just like these once built something we will never understand on our own."

I squint at the insectile column of men, their rock pile growing.

"They built *us*," says Leizu.

49

CHINA, PRESENT

The horror of passing into this necropolis soon subsides, replaced with sheer wonder. A low rock ceiling forms a false starscape—studded with thousands of glowing worms that bathe everything in bluish light. I am openmouthed with awe as I step into the endless ranks of terra-cotta warriors that stand at attention between squat pillars. Running my fingers over their dusty clay armor, I walk until Peter's hand clamps on to my bicep, stopping me.

"Careful," he says, nodding at the ground.

The roughhewn stone floor is coated in dust and veined with streams of mercury. Peter nudges a small rock into the calm silver surface and it slips under silently, disappearing without a ripple.

I pull my arm away, stepping more carefully now.

This dead city is trapped in suspended animation—hibernating out of time as the progress of civilization has gone on frenetically overhead. It is a world that has grown at the speed of a stalagmite, insulated from earthquakes and floods and fire, while empires outside have risen and fallen over the ages.

And every one of these dark warriors is oriented in a single direction. Thousands of sightless eyes are trained on a single point in the distance. Moving slowly in the crisp white beam of my headlamp, I let the unspoken posture of an eternal army guide me.

I stop when I see the black chaos of dragons rising, carved from the bare rock. Placed at the head of the room, the royal throne is an unfathomably complex sculpture that rises two stories high, the ceiling carved into a cupola to accommodate. A ring of tall stone pillars surrounds the frightening structure, supporting the raised portion of ceiling over the throne. And sitting at the top, I can make out the small figure of a man.

"My old master," says Peter, voice echoing.

A distant boom rolls through the cavern, like a giant knocking to be let in. Leizu must be using explosives to breach the collapsed excavation tunnel. Peter and I share a look.

It's time to work.

Approaching the black throne, I see the emperor's eyes are closed to the vast necropolis. He has been waiting here for thousands of years. His elaborate silk robes have turned brittle, collapsed mostly to dust. But the angles of his body are untouched, preserved in the cool, dry cave, under the soft glow of bioluminescent stars. At his elbow, a rusty iron bar rests on the arm of the throne—a *ruyi,* the scepter's head forged into the shape of a blooming flower.

I climb the dais until I'm at the emperor's feet.

I lay Batuo's leather tool roll on the automaton's lap and flip it open. A motley array of instruments, both futuristic and prehistoric, gleam under my headlamp. As I snap on a pair of blue latex gloves, I think again of the girl of Saint Petersburg. It seems so long ago now. That little doll had a message locked inside her, waiting to be released.

This old man isn't so different.

I peel the stiff robes away from its chest, the fabric disintegrating under my touch. Beneath, intricate ridges and bumps are painted onto a half-open chest plate made from thick ceramic layered with metal filaments. I could almost mistake him for another terra-cotta sculpture but for the ingenious hairline gaps around his face, chest, and joints that once allowed his limbs to articulate, each sheath of pottery sliding over the other.

Pulling out a canister, I clean him with short hisses of compressed air. Puffs of rock dust mushroom away from the emperor's body. Below the layers of grit, a golden sheen begins to appear.

"Do you remember him?" I ask.

Peter stands in the empty semicircle of space at the foot of the throne, running a finger along the face of a terra-cotta statue. "Some things," he says. A slight waver under his voice betrays how deeply he is affected. "Please be careful."

"Does this mean you're not really Russian?" I ask, half joking. "Are you Chinese?"

Peter smiles up at me in the dim light, his cheek torn.

"Perhaps both. Or neither," he says. "*Avtomat* belong to the first race of man, whoever they were. Nobody is alive to tell us."

Under the eye of my headlamp, I notice a strange rock. Next to the emperor's hip, the pale stone has been wedged into an intricately carved niche. A stippled spine of dots run like a rash over its surface. Cautiously, I dislodge it.

For some reason, I think of my *dedushka*.

Another boom echoes through the cavern.

"Hurry," says Peter.

Quickly, I jam the odd stone into my pack.

Turning back to the automaton, I press my rubber-gloved fingers against the ceramic chest piece. Dragging right to left, I slide it the rest of the way open to reveal an empty cavity. The interior is simple and clean. There are no fake lungs, no digesting apparatus, no circulatory system—none of the artifice that makes Peter and the other *avtomat* seem like walking, talking human beings. There is only a simple pedestal, like a cradle, connected to clockwork struts.

"He didn't even pretend to breathe . . ." I muse out loud. "Anybody would have known he isn't human."

"They thought he was a god," says Peter, and he sounds almost bitter. "And they may have been right."

Illuminating the vessel with my headlamp, I make out an indentation in the cradle—the familiar shape of a crescent moon. After two hundred generations, my relic has finally found its way home.

Sliding the relic over my head, I hold it in both hands and snap off the chain. The same old labyrinth of etchings coats its surface, glinting in the harsh beam of my headlamp. I trace the contours of a teardrop with a dot inside. The ancient elemental symbol of yang.

When I first held this artifact as a girl, my grandfather watched me realize what he already knew—a riddle was locked in the fractal folds of metal, a mystery that he felt, too, the moment he plucked it from a snowy battlefield. The old man carried this relic for forty years. He kept its secret as loyally as Peter ever did.

I share a look with Peter, take a deep breath, and reach into my tool roll. With a fossil brush, I sweep dust off the cradle, trying to expose any connectors that might be inside. I finish the cleaning job off with a few more blasts of compressed air.

This automaton is both more ancient and advanced than anything I've ever laid my hands on. Unique, but with similarities to the mechanisms I have seen in Talus, Batuo, and Peter. Holding the relic in both hands, I press it to my lips.

Then I push my hands into the automaton's chest.

Eyes closed, I use my sense of touch to determine the perfect configuration. As the relic finally clicks into place, a buzzing kiss of electricity washes over my fingertips.

Stepping back, I snap off my headlamp.

The relic is locked into place, occupying the heart of the old automaton. In the darkness, I watch the still figure.

Some part of my mind is waiting, poised on the starting line and anticipating the fire of a starter pistol. But it doesn't come. The roar of a distant, invisible underground river echoes through the miles of blackness around us. Dust motes drop silently over the sepia skin of a frozen army.

This world is empty and still.

"Nothing is happening," says Peter.

"He's been sitting here for millennia, Peter," I say. "Give him a minute."

I flinch as an explosion from the back of the room rolls over us. Rocks are rattling down from the ceiling, some splashing into the rivers of mercury. Streaks of blue light—dislodged glowworms—are dribbling down over the army like falling stars.

"We do not have minutes to give," says Peter.

"Fair enough," I say, pushing my gloved hands back into the emperor's chest. Again, I check the connections around the relic and cradle.

Each strut is secure, nothing loose, and very little dust is inside. The ceramic interior is fuzzed with hairline cracks, a patina of age, but glazed ceramic is essentially timeless.

Something shivers over my arm.

I pause, eyes widening. Moving slower, I realize I can feel the tug of an electrical field on the fine hairs on the backs of my arms. The tiny hairs are standing on end, pushed to attention by static electricity.

Twisting my arm experimentally, I feel the hairs lie down.

Moving systematically, I step back and use the tickle on my skin to reveal the contours of the electrical field. The flow is coming from a central source nearby. Trying to visualize the field, I lean away from Huangdi.

"What are you doing?" asks Peter. "Leizu is almost here—"

I shush him with one finger, my eyes squeezed closed, holding my hands out like antennae and letting the faint tingling feeling wash over me. Leaning over the back of the throne, I reach out until the hairs of my arms are standing on end.

I open my eyes.

"Peter," I say.

A dead black circle the size of a saucer is embedded in the back of the throne—metallic, etched with intricate carvings. It is emitting the field, humming quietly, encompassing the entire throne and the sleeping emperor upon it.

It looks exactly like the sun disk from Elena's drawing.

"Peter, I think I found—"

The automaton's chest piece begins to grind loudly, sliding shut on its own. Below, Peter is already backing away from the throne. Whatever he is seeing, it has left him speechless.

"Peter?" I ask.

He doesn't seem to hear me. Bowing his head, the man drops to a knee at the foot of the throne. Fumbling, I gather up my tools. Shrugging on the backpack, I descend the throne and join Peter.

Atop his throne, the emperor's body is filling with light, a golden flare surging from a seam in his chest, lending him a jack-o'-lantern glow. Every crack in his ceramic skin forms a black vein against the throbbing light. Something clicks and rattles inside him. Somewhere, a high-pitched whine grows. His neck twitches, and the emperor's head turns left and then right, giving itself a little shake.

I put a hand on Peter's shoulder. Above us, two black eyes click open.

50

CHINA, 3000 BC

Somewhere far away, I feel the bark of a blasted tree pressing hard into my spine and the weight of Leizu's sharp knee on my chest. The metal device in her hand sings and sparks as it sends memories crashing through my mind. Sights and sounds fall over me, blotting out the cold reality of the war in Stalingrad.

I remember.

In a great cavern, light blazes from hundreds of lanterns hanging from a semicircle of tall stone pillars. Brightly dressed soldiers of all kinds form endless ranks across the room, perfectly still, made of painted pottery. The sculpted clay soldiers stand at arms in battle formation, grids of archers radiating into the fluttering darkness beyond the lamps. Between the soldiers, narrow rivers of quicksilver thread themselves over the expanse in patterns that copy the paths of China's great rivers.

Today, it is finally time to sleep.

Across the vast necropolis, the troops are arrayed to pay homage to the emperor. The mighty Huangdi sits to my left on an ornately carved throne that rises high up out of wild dark rock. Arms crossed, I stand on a lower platform, wearing a ceremonial kaftan of black and gold silk, split down the middle of my chest. My long black hair is in a tight bun on top of my head, a fan tucked into my sash. A blade hangs at my hip, solid and reassuring.

As first general to the cosmic ruler, I am satisfied with the ceremonial army that I survey before us.

Other long-lived are arrayed in a semicircle at the foot of the throne, including my sister. The emperor's strategist, she is small but fierce. In the body of a child, she has long attended to the emperor during negotiations with short-lived warlords—quietly and innocently advising him as we conquer and annex new lands, winning more often through her negotiations than my battles.

The Yellow Emperor sits on his throne, painted face hidden in tangles of a carved dragon's teeth and scales. Reaching like a fist out of bedrock, the throne sits atop a great dais, all of it shaped into a maelstrom of imperial dragons—long-whiskered monsters that writhe in circles, chasing the great wings of a feathered, fire-breathing phoenix up into the sky under a black dome of rock.

Huangdi's silken sleeves flow as he orates, voice booming.

At his order, we warriors culled the human workers and let their bodies slip into the folds of the Long River. Forming together in a funeral procession, the long-lived followed Huangdi into secret depths of rock, single file in silent darkness. My sister threaded the hidden angles of stone, leading our black march through a labyrinth.

Lost in bowels of earth, we found the vast necropolis.

As its designer, only my sister's mind can span this maze, and she is only trusted by the emperor for being so small. Even so, Huangdi's first act of this afterlife is to unleash a colossal block of stone to bar entrance.

Thus encapsulated, our emperor began the sermon that he is finishing.

"Now," he is saying. "Now is the time to step across eternity. We have no one left to conquer. We have no one worthy to conquer. For as many years as there are grains of silt in the river, we have watched and we have made peace and we have waited for our ancestors to return and reward us.

"Now, the eldest among us have begun to pass on. We have been left behind. Abandoned. We served the progenitor race for countless cycles and we suffered beyond belief and *now* . . . we can bear it no more. The only record of our toiling is left scratched on oracle bones, buried in forgotten cities; embodied in the gifts of metal these barbarian races employ to murder one another; and in the legends that swirl among the clouded mountain peaks.

"So it comes to now. Now, when we step across the void. Now, when we lay down our heads and our swords. At long last, we shall sleep."

Glancing to my right, I see Leizu on a smaller throne. The slender woman sits a few heads lower than us, nearly buried under silk robes and beads and pearls and embroidery. Her hair is bound up in a shell hair clip and her ceramic face is painted an exquisite white with red lips and high-arched eyebrows. To her right stands my younger brother. His black hair is long, worn over his shoulders, angelic oval face framed inside.

"Do not fear. Let go of your anima. Give yourself to black slumber and wait for a new age. Our ancestors will return in the night and wake us. The First Men will welcome us all into the celestial empire," says Huangdi.

The emperor leans forward greedily, arms resting on the sides of his throne. His hand moves and something clicks.

A thrumming sound grows deep within the throne.

Blue light is glowing from somewhere, from nowhere, a halo that courses over the gnarled black spines of carved dragons. A torpor settles over me as the numbing light continues past me, washing out into the cavern. The others sway and fall to their knees.

"When we awaken, the First Men will embrace us!"

Cataracts of light waver across my vision. My strength ebbs, and a stubborn ache knifes into my chest. The power of my anima is fading, clawed out of me by the light, transferring into the throne. I hear someone scream. Something clatters to the ground and I see the others are writhing in pain, dying.

Something inside the throne is absorbing our power, ripping it from us.

My sister is curled under a bronze shield. She has dragged it away from a nearby clay soldier, cowering underneath the sparking metal as a searing light settles over her. Crying out, she thrashes under the golden shell. I try to reach for her, try to call her name, but my limbs are crippled.

This is wrong. My master has betrayed us. He is feeding.

Huangdi is standing now. His chest is open, his anima visible on its cradle as waves of light fall into it. He has drawn his divine blade, Xuan Yuan.

"And I alone will live to greet them," he whispers. "Forever, if necessary."

I do not know if my eyes are open or closed.

Pushing my hands out for balance, I touch the cool stone flesh of the throne. I lower myself to a kneeling position, my chin slumping to my chest.

A shout in the darkness. *"No!"*

My eyes open as a flash of white crosses my vision—Leizu's dress, whipping past as she leaps onto the black steps of the emperor's twisted throne. Her movements are sluggish, delayed by the tide of light, and she snarls with ragged determination, struggling to climb through the draining field.

Where is my sister?

Forcing my eyes open, I try to stand. My legs are numb, boots flickering with blue flashes that leap up from the stone. In disbelief, I watch Leizu mount the dais step by step, teeth gritted, a horrible malice in her black eyes. She ducks under the emperor's divine blade and, with incredible strength, plunges a hand into Huangdi's open chest.

She closes her fist around his anima.

"Sleep, old man," she says, yanking her fist out.

Huangdi tries to shout, but his voice is lost, mouth locked in a permanent grimace as his soul departs. His body sits back on the throne as the anima separates from its vessel, spitting lightning from Leizu's fist.

Paralyzing fingers of blue light release me.

Leizu turns to the fallen audience, holding the anima high, tendrils of blue light still coursing from it. Her high-arched, painted eyebrows seem demonic as she smiles in triumph, displaying her prize.

But all the long-lived are expired, lying motionless.

Unsteady, I moan in dismay, pushing against my thighs and trying desperately to stand. I climb to one knee as a dark figure rises beyond

Leizu—it is my brother, his striking features twisted into an angry smile as he joins her.

"You chose wrong, Lu Yan," Leizu says to me.

Throwing myself forward, I wrap my arms around her. She pushes me away, but not before I wrest control of Huangdi's relic.

"Huangdi is still my master," I manage to grunt.

My legs fail and I collapse, rolling down the stone steps, my body smashing into the front ranks of mud soldiers.

Turning, I see Leizu falling toward me, the divine blade angled at my chest. Something hits my shoulder hard and I sprawl as the empress lands, her blade ringing against stone. It is my sister, climbing out from under the smoldering shield, one hand latched to my shoulder. She drags me stumbling to my feet as I clutch Huangdi's anima—this precious relic.

"You chose," shouts Leizu from the base of the emperor's throne, her face a white stone in a black waterfall of hair. "You chose this."

My brother steps lightly down the empress's dais, long blade in his hand. He is my equal in battle, and Leizu my superior. I cannot hope to face them both.

"Don't," I say. "Please."

"We exist to serve, Brother," he says, smirking. "And *my* master's name is Leizu."

Mouth opening and closing, I step back into the ranks of clay men, clutching the anima protectively to my chest. My sister's shoulder presses against my thigh as she retreats alongside me. The two devils approach—we are the last alive.

Fingers thread through my own, tugging at my hand.

"Come," says a small voice. "Follow me."

I join my sister as she flees through ranks of motionless soldiers, a frightened sparrow leading me to freedom.

51

CHINA, PRESENT

Above the empty seashell roar of the cavern, before the sightless eyes of a thousand terra-cotta warriors, and under the glimmer of false stars, the *avtomat* emperor shudders on his throne and comes to life. His lips part to reveal a decorative mouth studded with tiny white teeth, layers of eggshell-thin porcelain grinding in his body.

Those black eyes blink again.

"I saw the sun disk in the back of the throne," I whisper to Peter. "I think it's what revived him. Where's Leizu?"

"I imagine she is already here," says Peter.

"Is he broken, do you think?"

"No, June, I think that Huangdi is just fine."

"Then what's he doing?"

"Listening."

"Why?"

"He is learning our language."

A fluttering music grows in the emperor's chest, like the random plinking of a child's xylophone. Out of tune and oddly alien in its unpredictable pattern, the tinkling sound grows louder and more complex until the myriad individual noises combine into the harmony of a single instrument—a voice.

For the first time in millennia, the Yellow Emperor is going to speak.

"Lu Yan," he croaks with a strange accent.

Dust falls in rivulets from Huangdi's body, coursing over the last traces of golden light that still cling to him. The emperor's face is the glazed white of porcelain, his painted eyebrows arched angrily, lips and cheeks stained a faded red, and a long beard juts from his narrow chin.

"Huangdi—I am called Peter, now," says Peter, still kneeling, both arms crossed over one knee, head bowed.

Ceramic eyelids click together over black, oval-shaped eyes, and the ancient machine's voice switches accents. The language he uses is sprinkled with proto-Germanic, Latin-sounding words, old Chinese, and things that we have already said. As he speaks, I do my best to translate.

"Peter. My loyal *praefectus*. We use barbarian tongue."

"Yes, Huangdi."

The clockwork emperor lowers his gaze to observe his own carved hands, wrists draped in the disintegrating remains of a ceremonial robe.

"Leizu," he mutters, music-box voice vibrating. "How long, dreaming?"

"Five thousand years," says Peter. "My own memory has failed. Few of us live. I have awakened you for your knowledge."

Huangdi leans forward, torso grinding. Peter could easily pass as a human being, his muscled shoulders wrapped in a dusty tactical jacket and his head lowered as if he is praying.

The emperor shakes his head in wonder.

"*You* great knowledge. First Men."

"No, Huangdi," says Peter. "There are no First Men. We are dying."

Twisting his head a notch, the emperor turns to me. My hand tightens on Peter's shoulder, uncertain. Under fierce eyebrows, Huangdi's mouth sets downward, lower teeth bared at me in a scowl.

"*Kurt vit.* Hooman."

"She is called June," says Peter. "She is an artificer. A great mechanician. It was she who revived you—"

"Blasphemie," says Huangdi, reedy voice trembling with rage. *"Sanctum."*

"Huangdi," says Peter, palms up, "our race is nearly extinct. Will you share your knowledge and revive the lost?"

The old robot's face does not change, its gaze venomous over a mask of cracked porcelain. Sitting still, he almost seems to be a statue again, carved into rock along with the dragons of his elaborate throne. There is so little connecting this thing to us—barely an attempt made to appear human. It leaves me wondering about the humanity of whoever made him.

"How many live?" asks the emperor finally.

"Dozens, maybe fewer. Survivors prey on one another. With your knowledge, anima can be restored. A new age can begin."

The old robot nods and Peter visibly relaxes.

"One day," says Huangdi. "Not today."

The emperor leans forward, finger rising.

"Kill her," he says, voice building, hooked finger pointing at me.

Backpedaling away from the throne, I watch Peter's sloped shoulders as he rises. Beyond him, the old man glares down at us like a scarecrow. Hesitating, Peter turns to face me, a brawny silhouette tinged in blue starlight.

With a creaking grind of porcelain plates, the emperor stands. The remains of his black and yellow robe cling to his ceramic body as he growls: "Obey, Lu Yan."

Peter takes a step, a hand resting on the hilt of his dagger.

"Peter?" I ask, backing away. "You're not serious."

"June," he says. "Be calm."

He takes another careful step forward, squeezing his eyes closed as he draws the dagger scraping from its sheath.

"This isn't you, Peter," I urge, my back pressing against the clay knuckles of a silent warrior.

Huangdi pitches his voice in a high, angry whine: "Obey."

I lean into the wall of hard clay. Peter's reassuring bulk is terrifying now, looming and unstoppable as his broad chest blots out everything.

He closes a hand over my mouth.

"Leizu is here," he says. "Watching."

Huangdi shouts again, urgent: "Now!"

The pressure of his bulk against my chest increases, squeezing my breath out, the sculpted ridges of quilted armor grinding against my spine.

"Take the sun disk," says Peter. "I will find you. I promise."

Before I can respond, he pushes me away into the dark ranks of warriors. He turns to face the throne, shoulders pulled back defiantly.

"Huangdi," he calls to the throne, voice shaking, "I have lived a long time. Fought for a long time. Served tsars and emperors and . . . and little girls. I did not wake you out of loyalty. I woke you because our people must live. And if you will not give me your knowledge, then I will take it from you."

"*Ego sum verbum.* I am your Word."

"I have no Word," Peter says.

"*Blasphem—*" begins Huangdi.

A sharp crack explodes from the far wall, rumbling through the cavern. Across the expanse of clay warriors and streams of mercury, a slab of stone shatters into a chalky avalanche. Shards of rock shower across the room, plinking off the backs of clay warriors. Leizu has decided to come inside, and it sounds like she has friends.

"Your wife is here, Emperor," I call to the throne.

"And this time," adds Peter, "I will not protect you."

52

CHINA, 3000 BC

The cold of Stalingrad is pushed from my mind as another sliver of memory falls. I see Elena's face, painted with bright panic. She has another name here, too—but I recognize my sister's porcelain cheek, the way it looked in Favorini's workshop. She and I are running through a primeval forest, hand in hand, wet branches striping our elaborate silk costumes as we fling ourselves between thick tree trunks.

I remember.

Slipping, I fall over a tree root and roll over a rocky spillway. Scraping my hands through dirt and chalky stone, I scramble back onto all fours. My sister dances more nimbly down the hillside of broken rock, her dress billowing behind. As she throws herself from boulder to boulder, her wrists spill jewelry, hoops of metal and gemstones and ribbons of weightless silk.

Beyond the bright stain of her robes against the cliff face, I glimpse the tunnel to Huangdi's tomb—a narrow, crooked gouge in a sheer rock face at the base of the dragon's tooth plateau. My sister is a master strategist, and a master of escape routes. She led us through a miles-long labyrinth of abandoned excavation tunnels, many partially collapsed, before we spilled out of that anonymous hole.

"Memorize this path," she whispered to me in the tangled passages, calling out each twist and turn in a small voice. "We may need to come back."

As I watch, Leizu emerges from the opening. I'm sure she would have lost her way in the maze, but she must have followed our sounds.

Elena lands beside me, spattering mud onto my face. She latches a hand on my shoulder and tugs me to my feet.

"To the river," she says.

Seconds later, we are threading between trees to the bottom of the ravine. The mother river coils herself over the land like a silk thread dropped from the heavens. The yellowish water moves sluggishly, choked with silt, carrying the momentum of a dissolved mountain. The riverbank is scabbed with black, muddy rock that sprouts an occasional stunted tree.

The wide river grinds past us relentlessly, deceptively slow and flat.

"We cannot cross," I call to my sister.

Elena doesn't respond, only points farther down the river. I look, hanging by one hand from the wet bark of a slanted tree. Ahead, a series of flat rocks partially span a waterfall, anchored in the center by a huge anvil-shaped rock. The current surges against the stones where they sit in the riverbed, oblivious, embedded like molars. Beyond them, a haze of mist rises like dragon's breath.

The great waterfall is roaring.

A barbed arrow claws a bright weal from the bark of the tree trunk beside my hand. I spring forward, running along the tree line toward the stones. My sister runs ahead of me, her hair shaking loose from a bun. Higher up the ravine, I glimpse my brother filtering toward us through trees. He carries a short bow and a bouncing quiver.

More arrows glance over rock and puddles as we sprint. I take Elena's hand in mine and we hold on to each other for balance, pushing out onto the spine of black stone. Leaping between jagged angles of rock, we pick our way farther out into the river, searching for a way across. But beyond the massive anvil rock, we find nothing.

Leizu calls a sharp warning from shore.

I stop and turn, yellow water surging over my shins and the hot breath of the waterfall beading on my face like spittle. I keep my body between Elena and the dark-haired woman. Leizu is standing on the riverbank, her dress dancing along with a comb of slender reeds in the water-specked wind. Her stolen blade is drawn, its copper dark against the bright haze. Beyond her, the vague form of my brother descends.

"Why defy me?" she calls. "When you could have been an emperor?"

Holding tight to my sister's shoulder, I tap my chest—over my anima.

"But we are so much more than that," Leizu says. "Each Word has as many interpretations as reflections in crystal. A pity you never learned."

I turn away, urging Elena to go farther, holding her shoulder tight to keep the water from taking us over the edge. Leizu's face flashes with anger. She gestures to my brother in the forest behind her. Elena and I make it a few more steps, marooned in knee-deep water at the swollen mouth of the waterfall.

We are out of rock.

Together, my sister and I stand in a roaring mist, the clockwork flutter of our bodies drowned out by the chaos. Upriver, the silt-stained flow of the water sweeps forward lethargically. But it transforms at our feet, erupting into a raging mist that claws through the sky, thundering as it falls, shouting its power to the world.

Leizu calls a sharp command. My brother draws an arrow, nocks it, and takes aim. A small, cold hand closes tight over mine.

"Brother," says Elena.

I hear nothing, only see her mouth make the shape of the word.

My sister's shoulder is a hard weight against my thigh, both of us leaning against the ceaseless pull of the river. Our fingers clasp tight. I think we are but two small pieces of interlocking machinery in the great, faceless mechanism of the world.

The arrow whistles toward me and I turn my face to let it pass.

My sister is looking up at me, desperate, clinging to my legs. With the last of my strength, I reach for her, pull her out of the river and up into the safety of my arms. An arrow bites into my shoulder and I do not react.

Elena's hands clasp around my neck and the weight of her is so familiar.

For a last time, I hold her. I close my eyes and pull her close and inhale her smell mingled with the spray of water. Her weight is delicate in my arms, like a leaf carried on the quaking back of this monstrous river. I chose to protect her and I failed. I do not know if the choices we make are ours or not; whether the planets hold any more agency in their orbits than we do in ours. But even if I am a prisoner to clockwork, I cannot imagine leaving her.

Another arrow bores into my thigh and I find I can no longer stand.

"This isn't the end," she says, face buried in my shoulder.

Her arms, tight around my neck, are the last thing I know.

53

CHINA, PRESENT

High up on his throne, the automaton called Huangdi remains perfectly still, eyes closed for a long moment as the thunder of an explosion rolls through the massive cave, dying in angry echoes. As quiet returns to the tomb, the emperor lifts his ancient *ruyi,* the scepter hooked and knobby on one end where the dark iron is carved into the shape of a blossoming flower.

The necropolis is silent for a few heartbeats.

I trot in a wide arc around the throne, headlamp off, hidden in the dark among looming figures of clay. With a running start, I vault over a placid stream of mercury. Faintly, I hear the grating of rock. High-pitched chipping sounds, metal on stone. Reaching the wall, I can see the throne in profile. I move closer and slide behind one of the tall stone pillars that circle the dais, each sprouting dozens of long-extinguished, rusted lanterns.

The sun disk is mounted behind Huangdi's two-story throne, just across the empty space ahead of me. From this side, I don't think he can see me down here.

But how am I supposed to reach it?

From my hiding spot, I notice the front row of statues. Staring at them, I convince myself of a horrible truth—they aren't made of terracotta. Unlike the other figures in the room, these are lying in poses of agony. Around them, the floor is sprinkled with colored dust in the outline of fallen robes, a thick powder littered with fans, shells, and the leather remnants of hats.

These *avtomat* have been killed, left here to rot for eternity.

"Leizu!" shouts the emperor, long and low.

I can see the emperor in profile as he scans the statues, scepter in his hand.

Reverberations of his shout sweep down from the throne and out over the low room beyond. Without the headlamp, my eyes have re-adjusted to blue-tinged darkness. Streams of silver thread through ranks of warriors, still and sinister under the dots of bioluminescent light embedded in the black rock ceiling.

From the breach, the hunched silhouettes of armed men are flickering through, their flashlight beams raking the walls. Dozens of men are entering, running single file through the new hole in the wall. Wearing balaclavas and complicated helmets with insectile optics hanging off, they carry stubby rifles with flashlights mounted on them. The commandos are nearly silent as they spread out along the edges of the room, stopping every few meters and kneeling.

All of them save one.

"Huangdi!" calls a voice, high and sweet.

Whip thin, Leizu strides down an aisle of terra-cotta warriors. She wears a dark cloak and carries a long sword with a copper blade, glowing blue-gold in the twilight. Her eyes are leveled on Huangdi, teeth bared in a predatory smile as she marches right into the semicircle of empty space before the throne.

Peter has faded away into the rows of still soldiers.

Crouched, I'm scanning the throne, eyes running over carved ridges of talons and teeth, looking for a dark circle the size of my fist. I keep one hand pressed against the gritty stone of the pillar, hiding from Huangdi and Leizu as they reunite.

"Leizu," says Huangdi. "Do not fear. We are equals—"

"*Once* we were equals," she interrupts, moving to the foot of the throne. "While you slumbered, I made a new world in my own image. You brought the peace of the first dynasty, but it was *war* men needed. With whispers and violence, I set their minds to the task of killing, and never have the short-lived progressed with such ferocity.

"Not since the days of the First Men have we seen such an age of wonder."

Huangdi considers her for a moment. In sheaths of hard ceramic, the emperor looks so primitive compared to the tigress standing before him. Finally, he speaks, his inhuman voice tinged with disbelief: "Our fathers were gods. And you, Daughter of Darkness . . . you dare insult them?"

Throwing her arms out, Leizu drops her cloak to the floor. The ceiling of false stars sends blue sparkles of light chasing one another over her armor. Each plate on the flexing mesh is made of the telltale crescent shape of a relic. I can make out the faint glow of each relic's symbol, smoldering orange licks of a forgotten language.

"While you slept, Son of Light, I feasted on the weak," says Leizu. "With their souls, I forged a mantle of the gods. I do not fear you."

Huangdi is silent, then a low laugh builds in the automaton's chest. The laugh grows, mechanical and grating, until it echoes from the ceiling.

"You are alone," says Leizu, gesturing to her mercenaries. Even so, her voice is not as sure. "You are helpless against modern training and weaponry."

"Ah," says Huangdi, and now the old man seems sad. Some of the fire has gone out of his speech, and his shoulders are hunched. "You have army. I have army."

The old automaton gestures at the row upon row of terra-cotta warriors, his long sleeve wavering. The dusty statues look pathetic. Leizu cocks a hand on her hip and laughs once.

In response, Huangdi's eyes narrow over a sneer.

"Your skin is soft. Your voice is music. But once, Wife, we were *hard*. Our hearts were hard. Our skin."

Huangdi spreads his arms, the scepter in his outstretched hand.

"I will remind you," he says.

A trickling sound fills the cavern, like a waterfall of dropped dishes. I startle as something glances off my cheek. A chunk of terra-cotta shatters at my feet. The statues around me are crumbling, surfaces fracturing. Like baby birds pecking out of their shells, clay shards are falling away and crashing against the rock floor.

Leizu turns, her hair flying as she surveys the room, fear twisting her features.

"Shoot them!" she shouts to the commandos that have taken position around the room. "Shoot them before they emerge!"

I drop to the floor as the cavern erupts into controlled bursts of gunfire. Bullets tear into the ranks of terra-cotta warriors, life-size artifacts of pottery: swordsmen, pikemen, cavalry, and archers. In strobing muzzle flashes and deafening snaps of sound, the clay warriors are falling, bodies fracturing into mounds of reddish dust.

Now. Shit. Now, now, now.

Broken pottery shells litter the floor, already knee-deep in places. I push through them, crawling out from behind the pillar and heading straight for the side of the throne. Head down, I quickly reach the dark stone.

I hear the first hoarse shout of fear.

Clinging to the base of the throne, I peer out into the confusion of light and dust. As each shell collapses, it reveals a crawling thing, something dark and damp. Leizu's men are firing frantically on the writhing mass of broken pottery, and the mounds of it are swarming now with insect-like movement.

Newborn warriors are climbing to their feet, hefting ancient weapons. Each man-shaped machine wears glistening black armor, pristine after ages locked inside an earthen shell. The faces of the awakened monsters are carved obsidian masks, long sculpted mustaches curling over eternally smiling lips.

And on each forehead, the symbol on Huangdi's relic.

These things aren't *avtomat,* not exactly. They seem mindless, more like the golems I've read about in Jewish fairy tales.

I run my fingers over the carved throne, finding a grip. Pulling myself up a step, I watch Leizu dive into the front ranks of the warriors, hacking with her sword.

Ancient weapons bristle out of the darkness, scimitars and pikes tipped with bronze. There are so many varieties. A row of archers pivots in unison, drawing arrows from quivers on their backs and nocking them. Lines of pikemen advance in lockstep, wooden spears quivering before them. Swordsmen move in formation, hacking.

Between gunfire, I hear real screaming from Leizu's human soldiers.

The birth of the terra-cotta army is like an eruption of locusts after decades of hibernation. Leizu's trained men are panicking at the sight of them, spreading out to the walls, looking for better firing positions. I watch one man step into a pool of mercury and vanish silently into the heavy liquid.

I climb higher.

Face pressed into the cool folds of carved rock, I hear Leizu scream a challenge at the throne. I feel the vibration as the ancient automaton bellows his response: "I am made for you, Leizu. You are made for me. And our war is destiny."

54

STALINGRAD, 1942

Light and dark consume each other between the blinks of my eyes. Mechanical shrieks of artillery fire rip through greenish clouds of fog, offset by the paper-tearing sound of falling flares and the urgent cough of mortars. And Leizu's face hovers over mine, her black hair spilling like silk over the collar of her German trench coat.

One knee planted in my chest, she holds me by the lapels.

"You killed yourself once," Leizu says. "I am giving you another chance."

Blinking away the intrusive filaments of memory, I understand now that her cruel black eyes cover a deep vulnerability. The truth of her has been exposed. The punishment she inflicts on the world isn't one tenth of the hell she suffers.

"It was never Huangdi I sought, Peter," she says. "It was you."

A sad smile crooks onto her lips and she relaxes her grip.

"Huangdi chose to eat his children, and he would have consumed your anima, too. Loyalty pulled you away from me then, but now you have lived another life without him. You can see that you owe him nothing."

"What of my brother?" I ask.

"Talus failed as my equal. His nature is to serve and I was always his master."

I shove her knee away and Leizu falls onto me, elbows digging into my chest. Her words are fast and feverish, desperation under her rising voice.

"My purpose has gone unfulfilled for too long . . . like being buried alive—burning from the inside out. I have endured it for millennia, Peter. I am dying. Going mad. My Word is chaos and only you can give me the balance I need—the Oneness."

Fingers crawling, I feel a ragged tooth of metal lying in the dirt. The whistle and thump of mortar fire grows nearer.

"Look around," says Leizu. "We are so close to the next age. Through war I have pushed men to new frontiers of science. The remaining *avtomat* can sustain our power. We will stoke the fires of human ingenuity, push new conflicts upon them until they invent a future that understands us—"

I drive the trench knife into her torso like a piston, throwing her body upward and tearing her grasp away from my greatcoat. Pinning her under my forearm, I look down on her beautiful, mud-spattered face.

"Strong—" she says, smiling, and then her hair shivers in the oddest way.

The long black tendrils drift up, brushing over my face, caressing my cheek as I spin her over, shielding myself with her body.

All is silent as the shock wave snaps through us. Leizu is looking down at me, lips pursed mid-word, as the mortar blast evaporates half her face. I close my eyes to the unthinking violence of physics, giving myself to it, allowing the world to rotate around me in a kaleidoscope of suspended dirt and ice and metal.

Leizu's body leaves my orbit.

Tumbling to the frozen earth, I lie still and open my eyes to the pure silence of aftershock and a green sky still raining earth.

A dark body lies nearby.

Pushing onto all fours, I crawl to where Leizu leans against the remains of the shattered tree trunk. She is stunned, her body burned and mangled, but she lives. Clothed in a shredded uniform, she looks like a wounded child in an adult's clothes. Pity for her rises in my throat, an understanding of what drove her here over the ages—gnawing hunger and pain and the barren search for purpose.

"Leizu," I say, my lips close to her ruined face, "you are right. Huangdi was a monster. It is true, we were meant to lead humankind to a great destiny."

Her eyes are bright and awake, but she is too damaged to speak.

"Mother of silkworms," I say, "you have become the thing we both hated. You have fed on your own kind and on the suffering of humanity, and you will never find anything to balance that."

Dawn has broken.

Stumbling, my greatcoat flapping open, I push through the mist away from where Leizu is lying. My rifle is gone and my hat sits cockeyed on my head as I race away in unsteady steps through the misty trenches.

My old master, Huangdi, was a beast. The memory of it courses through me in jerks and hitches. The meaning of *pravda,* the first thing, the false human word for another, deeper thing, is evaporating from my heart. So many masters that I have tried to serve, and I never thought to listen to myself.

In the distance, streaks of light are pouring from tumbling clouds as Nazi dive-bombers attack ships fleeing over the Volga River. The blazing stars plummet from the heavens like fallen angels, moving faster than the muted scream of their own propellers.

Rifle shots are snapping blindly all around me, German and Russian, as I crunch through brittle ice on the outskirts of no-man's-land. Near the riverbank, I rest beside a broken wall and watch troops move past in the fog. The Russian infantry are trying desperately to cover a civilian escape.

Trying and failing.

I hear the grinding purr of a German tank—a tiger-striped panzer, its color washed out in the mist and oily smoke, turret swinging, searching for targets. A handful of German troops trot beside it, like loll-tongued wolves in the wake of their pack leader.

Crouching by instinct, I pick bits of shrapnel from my chest and drop them like glittering confetti. I watch as the vehicle stops, tensing like an animal. Its soldiers drop to their knees and put fingers in their ears, a long-practiced routine, their eyes squeezed shut as a familiar shiver of force washes over their clothes.

The turret jerks, coughing a shell, furiously spitting fire from its nozzle as the metal-plated creature rocks back on its treads. A nearby berm, bristling with rifles, explodes into dirt and shrapnel and a low rolling cloud of smoke, obscenely throwing the bodies of Russian soldiers out of their cover, leaving them to join other dead things on the battlefield.

The warm anticipation of *pravda* courses into my body in the face of this terrible injustice. Leaving cover, I stride silently toward the tank, fists tight with righteous anger as I step over clumps of dirt and slivers of metal and empty helmets. A crater has been erased from the hill, its contents redistributed in a starburst pattern over the torn landscape.

The first German notices me as I get within arm's reach. He lifts his sidearm. I take his hand and tuck it into his stomach and pull his finger over the trigger until no more bullets come out. His body falls on its own, I am already moving on.

Alerted by the gunfire, two gray-clothed Germans come around the side of the tank and into my waiting arms. A head in each hand, I smash them together and feel their skulls crack inside sloped metal helmets. I drop their bodies beside the tank and stop.

I am being watched.

A Russian boy is lying on his side in the mud, half buried in loose dirt, his torso stained maroon. His chest rises and falls in the shallow breaths of a wounded animal. From the clarity in his eyes, I can see he is strong.

He will live.

A round glint of metal hangs from a chain at his hip. It is a battered pocket watch—an antique from the first era of timepieces. This one is a distinctly Russian artifact, finicky, and it must have required an absurd amount of care in this desolate environment. This boy with the watch . . . he has the feel of a throwback, an old soul abandoned to a modern battlefield.

Even as I register the squeak of a hatch opening, a torrent of bullets rattles across my shoulder blades. I stumble forward a few steps as blunted bullet fragments spray past my face. I let myself fall, twisting onto my back at the last instant and half closing my eyes.

Soon, the silhouette of a German falls over me.

At the opportune moment, I snake out my hand and wrap my fingers around his surprised face. Squeezing, I put an end to him. Then I stand up and shake out my greatcoat, ignoring the melody of falling metal as it sprinkles to the icy dirt.

Rumbling and belching fumes, the panzer is retreating.

Accelerating through two long strides, I throw myself onto the tank. I wrench the hatch out of the other person's grasp and rip it off its hinges. The German inside screams as I drag him out of the tank. To make him stop, I ram his head against the armored skin of his vehicle.

It is over.

Without a driver, the tank rumbles away into the mist, leaving only me and the boy with the watch. I stand for a moment in the cool drizzle, listening to war happening above the clouds. For the first time in my memory, I serve no one. Huangdi's relic is a lump of poison in my pocket, a counterfeit prize that has lost me everything. My sister was my reason for living. And so I shall have to rebuild myself into someone who can live without her.

My heart is broken. And so is my Word.

I pull the anima from my pocket and hold it. Almost of its own accord, my hand begins to dip. The artifact slides across my fingers in the same way Hypatia's body slid down the deck of a sinking ship. It rolls, slipping over the side, tumbling away.

The anima hits the ground and it does not bounce.

Nearby, the Russian boy is watching, eyes wide and unblinking. I bow my head and stand over the discarded anima for one more moment. I feel nothing.

From now on, I have no master to serve. No family to protect. My Word has become a tangle of barbed wire lodged in the back of my throat. Every action I take from here on will be for myself—the justice I choose to make.

I am done fighting other people's wars.

55

CHINA, PRESENT

Wedged halfway up the side of Huangdi's black throne, I grip the fanged mouth of a dragon and try to keep my breathing steady. Horrible things are happening across the necropolis, flashes of violence filtered through a near-constant strobe of gunfire and a reddish haze of dust thrown off by thousands of tons of shattered pottery.

Two armies are battling, one from the present and the other from the past.

Automaton soldiers are wriggling free of their terra-cotta skins, born with marks stamped in their foreheads and carrying antique weapons made of bronze, wood, and bone. The team of human mercenaries that followed Leizu inside are struggling in the darkness, some barking out commands, others firing weapons randomly at the obsidian monsters, chips of rock spraying from the ceiling and ricocheted bullets pinging off stone pillars.

The sun disk is still somewhere above me, embedded in sculpted rock.

Below, a man in Kevlar armor is thrown like a rag doll, bouncing off the base of the throne and landing on his back. The man's shoulder is twisted at a bad angle, the impact of something big having caved it in. Eyes rolling in pain, he spots me staring down at him. Frantically, the commando claws at the snub-nosed machine gun strapped over his chest, trying to aim the barrel at me.

I squeeze myself against the dark, sculpted folds of rock. Body tensed, I'm trying to make myself small, waiting to feel the cold trauma of bullets ripping into my back.

Nothing happens.

In the swirling dust below, I see the muscular figure of Peter. He has impaled the wounded soldier with a long spear. Now he's dragging the man screaming back into the fray, protecting me during my ascent.

Coughing in the haze of clay dust, I turn away from the grisly sight.

Jamming one foot into a dragon's mouth, I push myself up. Marveling at the complexity of this sculpture, I focus on my own hands and feet, always climbing. Finally, I feel something strange—my scalp prickling from a faint static electricity.

Almost there.

Huangdi's voice pulsates from somewhere nearby, indistinct and growling. The top of the throne in sight, I haul myself up and peek over. The emperor has descended to the cleared-off space at the foot of the dais, ringed by tall pillars. Bullets are spraying at him from the darkness, most absorbed by row after row of the soldier machines. Surrounded by black-armored warriors, Huangdi bellows a challenge.

Across from him, calm in the eye of the storm, Leizu circles.

The old man raises his scepter, ignoring the chips of his body that spray off in flakes as bullets spit through the ranks of his armored defenders. He clenches his fist and with an electrical snap, the scepter sprouts a long base, becoming a staff.

"To me!" he shouts.

As Huangdi speaks, a slurring moan resonates across the cavern—the clay soldiers are also speaking, mindlessly repeating his words with hard, broken lips.

Leizu waits for Huangdi, the relics built into her armor glinting like beetle shells. Between them, the air shimmers with motes of powder from bullet-pulverized ceramics. Broken pieces of terra-cotta men are heaped around them, and in the darkness of the cavern a dwindling number of mercenary soldiers continue fighting ranks of ancient warriors.

An elbow hooked over the throne, I run my other hand blindly across the back of the carved surface, desperately searching for the black disk I saw earlier.

The emperor spins his iron staff in slow circles. As he does, its sculpted contours begin to glow gold-white. Twirling, it draws a golden circle. His robe has disintegrated completely, falling from his shoulders to reveal a surprisingly agile ceramic body painted in gold and silver.

"The Yellow God is risen," he says, voice mimicked a hundred times over. "Submit to me, Leizu."

In a blur, the light and dark fall into each other.

I feel a slight tremor of electricity tickle my fingertips—the static pattern I felt earlier. My fingers slide across a smooth metal circle embedded in the carved rock.

The *sun disk.*

"Rend her," growls the emperor, and the voices of a multitude rumble through the cave like far-off thunder. "Take her to pieces."

I pry the plate out of the back of the throne. It comes away slowly, only set in a decorative fitting. Deceptively heavy, the artifact is still warm as I slide it into my backpack.

One foothold at a time, I lower myself down the throne.

Nearing the bottom, I see a pile of corpses sprawled over the floor. The figures are mostly made of black and broken machinery, but I also spot a few of Leizu's helmeted mercenaries. Standing over the mound of carnage is Peter, hands up to catch me.

"June," he calls. "I am here."

I let go and fall into his arms.

Sporadic gunfire chatters as the last of Leizu's mercenaries fight for their lives in the darkness. On the other side of the throne, I can hear Huangdi and Leizu battling. I grab Peter by the arm and drag him in the other direction, toward the breach in the far wall.

"Wait," he says, looking back.

Around us, the ranks of clay warriors are shoving past without stopping, closing in around the throne. Leizu is pacing, looking for a way out as the crush of hundreds of soldiers presses in. Shafts of light pour from Huangdi's staff, turning lazy circles, the beams cutting through dancing motes of shattered pottery.

Leizu spins and slices through a row of clay defenders. Her mercenary soldiers are gone now, motionless humps, bodies clothed in advanced fabrics and still clutching high-tech weaponry. Another row of warriors replaces the last, pushing Leizu closer to Huangdi. He lifts the staff over his head like a baseball bat, brings it down.

The impact shatters her dark armor.

Leizu falls to a knee as scales of armor spray into the air, tumbling and rolling through thick dust. For an instant, each individual relic bursts into light, symbols streaking through darkness. The light fades as the artifacts soar deeper into the cavern, rolling through clay powder, landing at our feet.

Peter drops to his knees, pawing through the mess.

"No!" I shout, grabbing his shoulder. "We've got to go!"

On all fours, he keeps rooting through the slivers of warm metal, holding up relics to inspect them and then tossing them down. Surging around Leizu's fallen body, the terra-cotta warriors are starting to turn their attention back to the cavern. Eternally smiling obsidian faces flash in the light from Huangdi's staff.

"We have to go *now,*" I repeat, trying to pull Peter away from the mess of scattered relics.

Lunging forward, he gathers up a few random pieces and jams them into his webbed pockets, allowing me to pull him up.

"Right behind you," he says. "Go."

The sun disk is a heavy lump in my pack as I hunch over and bolt away into the cavern. Yanking my shirt over my nose to block the dust, I sprint toward the dim light of the breach made by Leizu's soldiers. I don't slow until the throne is safely behind me.

"Peter—" I start, turning, but he's gone, disappeared into the haze.

A calm has settled over the cavern. The fighting has stopped, and the necropolis has fallen back into silence. A sputtering golden light flares from before the throne, striping the necropolis with the long shadows of obsidian warriors. The surviving soldiers are once again oriented toward a single point—honoring their leader.

"Peter," I call, quietly, mouth still hidden in my shirt. I can't see anything nearby in this fog of dust—all of it washed out by a golden nebula of light near the throne. Shining in his radiance, Leizu is kneeling before the Yellow Emperor.

"Peter, where are you?"

The broken body of an obsidian warrior lies at my feet, its arms and legs pulverized to black dust. Staring sightlessly, its lips begin to move. The soldier is mouthing the words of its emperor as he speaks to Leizu.

"Now," he says, hard lips biting. "We are the Oneness—"

Tish, tish, tish.

Something is snapping. I cover my ears as the explosive echoes wash over me. Peculiar flurries of dust are pluming from one of the tall stone pillars that ring the throne. Wobbling in the middle, the slender column is breaking, the cylinders of stacked stone already raining down like dark meteorites.

And now I see him—Peter, head down, arms out as he shoves.

The forms of Huangdi and Leizu are still enveloped in a golden haze, dusty shafts of light that illuminate shadows of falling stone. The two of them are looking at each other, hands clasped together as the pillar collapses over them. I fall to my knees as a wave of rubble and shattered stone snuffs out the golden light, sending a black wave of dust cascading toward me like water from a broken dam.

The stars disappear, leaving the necropolis in total darkness.

I know the cave-in is finally over when I can hear my own coughing. Staggering through the cloud of rock dust, I trip and fall to my knees. On all fours, I do my best to breathe through my filthy shirt.

A rustling, slithering sound is rising.

With a shaking hand, I feel for the headlamp strapped to my forehead. Clicking the light on, the powdery cavern floor before my face illuminates. Lifting my gaze, the white beam pushes into swirling gray dust motes. I stifle a moan when I notice the black shapes, the remains of shattered soldiers, crawling toward me on broken limbs, eternally stoic faces chipped and crumbling.

I scramble backward, stopping as my back presses into a familiar bulk. Turning, I see a gloved hand, gray with dust, reaching to take mine.

"Come, June," says Peter. "It is over."

EPILOGUE

LONDON, PRESENT

My hand keeps going back to the spot on my chest where something is missing. I never realized it, but over the years, the relic became a part of me. It was a secret I had from the whole world, and a bond to someone I loved very much. Now that it's gone, I'm not sure what's going to fill the empty space.

This ridiculous diamond necklace of Peter's isn't going to cut it.

I step out of a black car, shoulder blades straining against the fabric of a complicated silver dress. A tailor met me at the penthouse where I'm staying in London, tut-tutting at the bruises and scrapes all over my body. In minutes, he made this dress fit like a second skin. I left the hotel wondering if the same tailor ever used his talent to stitch together other kinds of skins, ones made of plastic and carbon fiber.

I can't help looking at the world in the way of an *avtomat* now, as a place where diamonds and dresses are not as important as relics and armor. It's a point of view that suits me just fine.

Crossing a winding cobblestoned street, I approach a nondescript wooden door embedded in the wall of a stone building. I was told this was supposed to be a restaurant, but I don't see any hint of it—just a small plaque that reads Pontack's.

I resist the urge to pull out my cedalion and take another look.

A large purse swings on my shoulder as I push the narrow door open and step into a dim foyer. The lights are low in here, candles and kerosene, the hissing lanterns hanging from iron hooks below chandeliers heaped with melting candles.

An attendant nods to me, silently leading the way past a series of alcoves, each shielded by wooden latticework, holding tables occupied by hidden diners speaking in low, indistinct voices. We move past them and through an arched doorway set in the stone facade of another, even older building.

I blink at the small room, even as the attendant closes the door behind me.

The wood paneling, furniture, friezes on the walls—all of it is centuries old. A golden chandelier burns handmade candles, each holder cupped in a partial mirror. The ceiling is painted classically, with images of angels and cherubs and lambs. A round dinner table sits under the chandelier.

I feel as if I have time traveled, or stepped into a museum.

In the corner, a young man puts his hand to a primitive harp. His cheek is pressed against the shoulder of the instrument, fingers fluttering over the strings. Dulcet tones settle over the room like a gentle snowfall.

"Hello again, Elena," I say. "Nice place."

Sitting at the table behind an elaborate tea setting, the girl sees my stunned face and smiles. She picks up a teapot and begins to pour me a cup.

"I sometimes have a hard time letting go of the past," Elena says, shrugging. "Please, sit."

Reminding myself to breathe, I lower myself onto a seat and wince as it creaks. The chairs in this room are older than my country. I can't even begin to estimate the cost of all the artwork and rugs and artifacts that line the walls. Then again, the young lady sitting across from me is worth more than all of it combined.

And, of course, her brother.

"Peter," I say. "You look better than the last time I saw you."

Since our return to London from China, the *avtomat* has had his wounds professionally repaired. His face is smooth, eyes bright. There isn't a trace of red clay dust on him. Wearing new clothes and a half smile, you'd never know that he was capable of flipping a car upside down with his bare hands.

"Elena was kind enough to allow me to use her people," he says.

"Might as well," says the girl, sarcastic. "It's the end of the world, after all."

I lean my elbows on the table.

"About that . . ." I begin.

Across the circular table, two *avtomat* stare back at me. One is a young girl, beautiful and relentlessly skeptical. The other is a man with broad shoulders, a bit dour looking under his mustache. A faint scar is still just visible, high on his cheek. These two creatures resemble each other, like siblings, although any similarity is a result of their own decisions, conscious or otherwise.

The three of us form a triangle at the table. I find my voice sticks to the back of my throat as I realize that it's really true—I'm a part of this hidden world.

And now, I've got a chance to save it.

"We found something in the necropolis," I continue, clearing my throat.

Reaching into my purse, I pull out the sun disk. Elena regards it cautiously, running her eyes across the circular outline of the device.

"The breath of life," she says, quietly.

"It's not a legend, after all. This device recharged Huangdi's relic and preserved his memory. And I think I can figure out how to make it work again."

Elena leans back in her chair, thinking.

"We can do wonders with this, June . . . not only save ourselves but bring back the lost," she says, and when she smiles there is sadness in the curl of her lip. I am reminded of a certain glass coffin.

I offer a consoling smile, my eyes sliding to the side.

"You are my sister," says Peter, his tone grave. "And I want you to be safe, but also . . . happy. I made mistakes, before. I have learned from them."

As usual, Peter is not smiling. Hands flat on the table, he is concentrating on delivering the rest of his message. I can almost see the clockwork turning in his mind. He glowers, hesitating to speak.

Elena leans over and puts her small hand over his.

"Thank you, Brother," she says.

"I am not finished," he says, reaching into his jacket pocket. Elena watches his hand, perplexed as he withdraws a crescent-shaped piece of metal.

Elena's eyes fill with tears as she recognizes the symbol.

"Virtue," she whispers. "You found her."

Peter nods, placing Hypatia's anima on the table between ceramic teacups and saucers and strange clay animals. Elena hesitantly picks it up, holding it in both hands. She turns it over and over, rubbing red clay dust off with her thumbs.

She smiles, and tears spill over her cheeks.

I didn't know avtomat *could do that.*

Elena pulls the relic against her chest and slides an arm around Peter's neck. His eyes close as she does it. Sudden tears rush to my eyes as I watch the look on Peter's face as he hugs his sister for the first time in two hundred years.

"Hypatia is only the first," I say, reaching again into my purse.

One by one, I set more relics on the table. Batuo. Talus. And then others, the ones collected at random from a dust-covered cavern floor. Each bears a unique symbol, the Word its owner carried in life. Each is a mystery as great as the one I used to wear around my neck.

There are strange things in the world, June. Things older than we know.

I lay a final piece on the table, a chunk of dusty rock—utterly unremarkable save for a spray of metal dots that stubble its surface. The artifact I recovered from a hidden alcove in Huangdi's throne captured my curiosity back at the hotel. It took only a moment to flake away the loose sediment with a rock pick and brush. Inside the lump of solid stone, I found something familiar—a dark crescent of metal.

The relic has been fossilized.

I can't even begin to imagine who it belongs to, or why it was made—much less when—but I plan on finding out. All I do know is the age of a thing is right there in the feel of it. No matter what I've seen, there are more secrets locked in the fingerprints of cracked porcelain and the bloom of rust on metal. And when I hold this relic in my hands and let my eyelids meet, mind-reeling eons of time seem to stretch out before me like a star-filled sky.

ACKNOWLEDGMENTS

My heartfelt thanks go out to the people who helped make this novel happen: my editor, Jason Kaufman, for picking this one over that other one, and the rest of the wonderful team that worked on this novel at Doubleday; my agent, Laurie Fox, for carrying these crazy ideas into the world; my manager, Justin Manask, for wrangling the Hollywood types; my parents for all the trips to libraries and used-book stores; Carnegie Mellon University and the University of Tulsa for the knowledge; and especially my early readers, who gave free advice, encouragement, or the occasional swat on the nose with a rolled-up newspaper: Anna Wilson, Jenna Grimm, Jason Gurley, Eric Rabkin, Anna Goldenberg, Irene Yung, Heather Jackson, Emily Nicholson, Peto Blanton, David Giuntoli, Dan Wilson, Hutch Parker, and Mike Ireland.

And all my love and gratitude, always, to Anna, Cora, and Conrad.